# Clearly Charmed

After stints working in entertainment and advertising, Amy True turned to chasing her one dream: writing romance. She can often be found in her local writing spot sipping her favorite iced tea (with a touch of lemonade) and putting together playlists for her next books. When she's not daydreaming about her next cinnamon roll hero, Amy is traveling with her family, reading good books, and plotting her next small-town romance. While she grew up only ten minutes from Disneyland, which inspired her love for storytelling, she now calls Arizona home.

## Also by Amy True

### Ivy Falls

*Meet Me in Ivy Falls*
*Finding Love in Ivy Falls*
*Welcome Home to Ivy Falls*

### Sisters of Harvest Moon

*Clearly Charmed*

AMY TRUE

# CLEARLY Charmed

canelo
HERA

DK | Penguin Random House

First published in the United Kingdom in 2026 by

Hera Books, an imprint of
Canelo Digital Publishing Limited,
20 Vauxhall Bridge Road,
London SW1V 2SA
United Kingdom

A Penguin Random House Company
The authorised representative in the EEA is Dorling Kindersley Verlag GmbH.
Arnulfstr. 124, 80636 Munich, Germany



A CIP catalogue record for this book is available from the British Library.

ISBN 978 1 83598 466 6



Printed and bound in Great Britain by Clays Ltd, Elcograf S.p.A.

Look for more great books at
www.herabooks.com | www.dk.com

1

FSC www.fsc.org MIX Paper FSC™ C018179

*For all the eldest daughters…*

*May your labor, light, and love never go unnoticed.*

*'Suddenly, quietly, you realize that – from this moment forth – you will no longer walk this life alone.'*

Robert Frost

# Chapter One

## *Tasty Afternoon Snack*

There's a special place in hell for people who let their dogs go off leash in the woods.

Flora, my Mastiff Doberman mix, loped alongside me as we hiked up the trail leading to the top of Elderberry Ridge. Birdsong echoed through the trees. The lemon-drop sun descended, stretching shadows into shapes that resembled storybook monsters. Goosebumps skidded over my skin as the clouds rolled in and the temperature dipped.

Late August was my favorite time of year in Colorado. Warmer days turned into cooler nights. At dusk, the symphonic chirp of crickets slipped in through open windows. The damp scent of the woods, sometimes falling rain, often lulled my chaotic mind into a dreamless sleep.

Some people took vacations to exotic places with white sand beaches. Turquoise water for as far as the eye could see. When I wanted to escape, I came to these woods and let the precious silence fold over me like a warm blanket.

I gripped Flora's leash as she pulled me forward. Just as we reached a small rise, a chocolate Labrador retriever with a massive block head shot out of a dense set of trees.

Panting hard, the dog circled us twice before he sprawled in front of my feet.

'Where'd you come from?'

His thick neck was void of a collar. A low simmering heat rose in my veins.

Off leash *and* no tags. Dammit.

'Hello,' I called out, hoping the owner would emerge from the woods. The dog continued to pant at my feet. His pink tongue flopped out of the side of his mouth. Brick-red mud clung to his wet fur and paws.

I yanked off my backpack, shoving aside the collapsible water bowl and the few treats I'd packed for Flora. At the bottom, I found a small length of cord and made a leash. I slid it over the Lab's head and coaxed him to the side of the trail. As he walked, I clocked his movements. Sturdy body. Normal gait. No visible injuries.

Flora and the Lab sniffed each other while I leaned against a nearby boulder to wait for the owner. Rabbits hopped out of low-lying bushes. Prairie dogs skittered across the tops of jagged rocks. The Lab strained against the leash, eager to chase after the small animals. Flora gave him an annoyed look and settled down onto her belly like she expected a long wait.

She wasn't wrong.

Ten, fifteen, twenty minutes slid by without a sign of another human.

'All right, boy,' I said tugging on the leash. 'Let's head down and figure this out.' Flora jumped up and stayed beside me as we made our way down the trail.

With each and every step, the weight of the day knotted in my shoulders. Pounded inside my temples. I'd been up since four, tending to Mrs Werlin's pregnant pug, Lola, whose distressed and tiny body required I take her puppies by C-section. Three girls and a boy. Bringing new pups into the world was one of the best parts of being a veterinarian, but by the end of the day I was ready to crash.

Thursdays were my busiest at the clinic, but today was my little sister Aster's birthday, and she insisted we all meet for dinner at Grandmother Clo's. That gave me just enough time to watch the sunset from the top of the ridge before I had to head to the party. Now that idea was shot to hell, thanks to some idiot.

When we reached the service road at the edge of the trail, I pulled my phone out of the pocket of my joggers. A thud of heavy footsteps sounded through the woods, followed by a deep voice calling out, 'Indy! Indy! Here, boy.'

The lab whined and yanked on the leash like he was a bottle rocket ready to ignite. Cracking sticks and breaking branches cut through the air. A man crashed out of the woods, tripped once and hit the hard-packed earth, turning a full somersault before landing with a thud. The dogs both barked, rushing up the trail beside me.

Starfished across the dirt was a guy with long athletic legs and at least two days of reddish-blond scruff covering his chiseled jaw. His eyes were closed, his chest rising and falling with heavy breaths. An odd flutter filled the space below my breastbone like a feather caught on the wind.

'Hey, are you all right?' I bent down next to him, quickly scanning him for injuries.

'Give me a minute.' He shifted his legs and curled his hands open and closed.

It wasn't hard to figure out why he'd taken a header onto the ground. I'd seen it too many times on the trails. Weekend warriors who wanted to play in nature for a while without understanding the terrain. Bought boots at some fancy outdoor store, not realizing they'd be stiff to walk in, not to mention causing painful blisters.

The Lab was quickly at the guy's side, giving his face a slobbery lick. 'It's all right, Indy.'

'Are you hurt?' I said.

He opened his eyes, which were a shade of deep periwinkle you only saw painted in a late twilight sky. The sense that I knew him somehow washed over me like a gentle rain. I searched his face, examining the sharp curve of his cheekbones and the sturdy set of his jaw, trying to recall if we'd ever met, because I knew every local in Harvest Moon.

'I'm… fine,' he stuttered, sitting up slowly, his gaze never leaving my face.

A raw scratch slashed across his cheek. A swatch of what looked like black ink colored the side of his left index finger. 'Nothing really hurts, except maybe my pride.' His rough laugh boomeranged through the trees.

Indy kept nuzzling him and he rubbed the scruff on the dog's neck. 'Glad I found you, boy.'

The whoosh of his relieved breath made the fire in my veins settle to a low simmer. At least he gave a damn about his dog, even if he'd let him run around unsupervised.

He rose to his feet and that lightness in my chest returned. I was five eight and this guy towered over me. He took a step closer, and Flora let out a guttural growl, placing her body between me and him. I gave her head a loving pat. 'It's okay. I've got this.'

'Thank you for finding my dog.' He tugged off his blue baseball hat, swiping at the pieces of reddish-gold hair plastered to his forehead. 'We were playing catch in that small stream farther up the trail. Indy's ears went up all of a sudden, and he took off like a shot. That's weird for him. He usually sticks to my side like glue.'

He leaned over and pressed his hands to his knees, sucking in large breaths. Hiking in the high altitude was no joke. At this point on the trail, we were hovering right near 8,000 feet.

'It wouldn't have happened if he'd been on a leash. There are black bears, elk and other dangerous wildlife around here. It's not safe for dogs to be running loose.'

He sucked in another thick breath, the vein in his throat beating wildly like I made him nervous. I was used to that reaction from folks in town but not from a stranger.

'Indy doesn't do well with leashes,' he said.

'Well, *Indy*, I'd guess, would prefer not to be a tasty afternoon snack for a black bear, either. He should have tags too.'

'Yeah, collars are also not his thing.' He gave me one of those grins I'm sure made women all hot and bothered. All it did was set my blood back to a high boil. 'I'm Bryce O'Dell, by the way,' he said, holding out his hand.

I shook the leash in his direction without answering, because I wasn't in the habit of offering my name to strangers. Indy whined, took a step back, and landed on top of my feet. The touch set off a chain reaction I'd come to know well. My breathing slowed like I was being powered down. Pressure built in the back of my eyes, forcing them to close. A sharp metallic taste flooded my mouth and coated my tongue. A flash of muted red and yellow color lit up behind my eyes, followed by a sharp swell of light-headedness. Several emotions hit me at once. Elation followed by hunger, melting into a nauseous ache that seeped straight through my skin. All warnings this dog was ill in some way.

I wobbled on my feet, the sound of Bryce's voice echoing in my ears.

'Uh, miss? Can you hear me?'

I settled into the swirl of color swallowing me, my brain racing as I did a mental scan of this dog from nose to tail. No broken bones, but something in his system was definitely off.

Flora barked once and nudged my knees with her head. The tingling in my feet and legs floated away like smoke from an extinguished candle.

'Hey, are you all right?' He cupped my elbow, and match met kindling as a molten fire raced through my veins. Holy crap. Who was this guy?

Slowly the color faded behind my eyes, and once I pried them open I found him staring at me in a horrid kind of confusion. It was a look I'd spent a lifetime ignoring. Usually, I could brush it off, but I found myself stricken by his reaction.

'Are you sick? Do you need help?' His warm hand stayed firm on my arm.

'It's all right,' I said, taking a step away from his touch. 'I have a small condition that forces me to take a break every once in a while. Not a big deal.'

'Condition?' His gaze moved to where Flora kept her wide body pressed against my leg. 'Oh, I've read about this. Dogs can sense sickness, right? They can smell when a diabetic's blood sugar is high and alert them. Make them get help. Is that what happened?'

'It's something like that,' I said, running a hand along Flora's back to reassure her.

'Should I make a call? Give you a ride to get help?' He scrubbed his hand over his tense jaw, his gaze wandering over my eyes and nose, stuttering on my lips, until he figured out he was staring a beat too long. 'Do you live around here? I could take you and your dog home. It'd be no problem.'

The cautious look I shot him had him raising his hands. 'I swear I am *not* a serial killer.'

'That's exactly what a serial killer would say.' Flora whined again, and he pressed his lips thin in concern. 'I'm fine, and, yes, I grew up here, which is how I know what is *in* these woods,' I said, trying to steer the conversation back to the matter at hand.

A cloud inched over the setting sun, and he tilted his head to the purpling sky. 'You're lucky. This place is beautiful. I sort of feel guilty that it's my first time here. My uncle has a cabin on the other side of the ridge. Well, *had*. He passed recently and left it to me.'

'Sorry to hear that. What was his name?'

'Richard Morrison. He was my mom's brother.'

An image of a man about his height with a full white beard filled my head. 'Didn't he used to manage the ski hill?'

'Yeah, but he got sick last year. My mom offered to come and help him, but he refused. I'm here to figure out what to do with the place now.' He leaned back on his heels and tried to hide his grimace.

'You should get boots that go up higher to protect your ankles. Take smaller walks to break them in.'

'Is it that obvious I'm a newcomer out here?' He glanced at the impression his body left in the dirt. 'Don't answer that. My stumbling out of the woods ass over teakettle like a total idiot probably gave me away.'

'Ass over teakettle?' I bit back a smirk. 'That's an interesting turn of phrase.'

He rubbed the back of his neck uncomfortably. 'I like words. How a well-written sentence can turn your entire way of thinking upside down.'

Wow. I was not expecting that kind of response from some dude who stumbled out of the woods looking like he couldn't figure out his location without some kind of complicated GPS toy.

'You said "city". Where are you from?'

'Los Angeles.'

My gaze darted back to his boots. 'Are you staying or selling?'

Once people spent time in Harvest Moon and realized it didn't have a major coffee chain, or one of those big warehouse stores, they raced back to civilization as quick as they could.

'Don't know yet.' He hesitated before saying, 'I've only been around a few days.' A breeze blew across the trail, rustling the bright green leaves in the trees. 'It's nice and quiet here, though, especially in these woods.' Indy let out a small bark, and he bent down to give his dog's head another pat.

'There are some beginner trails. At the bottom of the hill there's a map. I suggest you look at it before you hike again.'

He crossed his arms over his broad chest. 'Any chance you'd want to meet out here some time? Show this *beginner* those trails?'

I huffed out a laugh. The last thing I had time for was a date with some stranger. There was no point to it anyway.

'If you can read, you can figure it out.'

Flora nudged me again, my muscles still aching and pulsing.

'You're sure you're okay? That I shouldn't call someone for you? Maybe a boyfriend? Husband?'

'What you *can* do for me is take care of your dog from now on,' I said, ignoring his probing of my relationship status. I patted Flora's head and she let out a low bark, reminding me of what I had to say, even though it was going to be all kinds of awkward. 'You should also take Indy to the vet. Get him a full physical.'

'A physical? Nah. That's not necessary. I took him in a few months ago. He got all his shots, and the vet said he was in great shape.'

The dog panted happily at Bryce's side, but that nagging itch in the back of my brain kept repeating his dog was ill. Telling him I was a vet was on the tip of my tongue until his phone rang. He glanced at the screen, the lines around his mouth tightening before he silenced the call.

'I need to go. Thanks again for grabbing him.' He tugged on Indy's leash and sped in the direction of a small black SUV parked further down the service road.

Flora nuzzled into my side just as my own phone buzzed in my pocket, reminding me of the time. I hustled to my truck and pushed all of Flora's ninety pounds up into the cab. I drove away, not bothering to give Bryce a second glance. A part of me wondered if I should have pushed more. Insisted he get Indy checked out. But years of experience told me he still wouldn't believe me. Strangers never did.

# *Chapter Two*

## *I Can Smell the Woods on You*

'You're late, Dandelion!'

Grandmother Clo didn't bother to look at me as she stirred the red sauce simmering in the big pot on the stove. The turquoise and silver rings covering her fingers danced in the low kitchen light.

'Hello to you, too,' I said, letting Flora off her leash. She sniffed at the familiar surroundings before nosing her way out through the screen door to the deck.

The cabin where I'd grown up had most of the living space on the second story. The front door was on the first floor along with a bedroom that once belonged to my younger sister Lia. A wide set of oak stairs led to the second floor. As soon as you were on the landing, the space opened into a massive chef's kitchen that spilled into a family room. The entire back wall was nothing but windows, allowing a clear view of Meadow Lake.

Grandmother Clo kept her focus on the pot. Her shoulders scrunched up around her ears.

'Rabbits stealing from your garden again? You only call me by my given name when you're irritated.'

'They took a bunch of tomatoes and a cucumber this time!' Her stirring grew more agitated. 'How can those little buggers possibly carry a cucumber?'

It was hard, but I bit back a smile because Clo was serious about her summer garden. 'You could always put up a fence.'

She pushed out her lower lip. 'No. It's not natural.'

I laid a hand on her too-bony shoulder. For all intents and purposes, she and my late grandfather, Beau, had raised me and my two younger sisters while our mother was off 'finding herself' at some weird commune or artists' retreat. It was hard to watch her age, but while her stature may have shrunk over the years, her bossy attitude only swelled.

'Where have you been?' She tugged at the light strands of hair that had escaped my ponytail. 'And don't feed me nonsense about work either. I can smell the woods on you from a mile away.'

'And they accuse us girls of having magic.'

She threw me a sour look because she hated any mention of magic.

I reached out and patted her hand. Her rigid posture eased as she sank into my touch. When people started whispering about me, they often wondered, usually out loud, if my 'special touch' worked on people as well as animals. Thank goodness it didn't or I would have had to move into the forest like some hedge witch.

'I tried to go for a hike, but it was interrupted.'

Her stirring stopped. 'Bears again?'

I'd had one close call a year ago, and I'd made the mistake of telling Clo about it. Now she worried every time I hiked, because all sorts of creatures liked to trail me through the woods. Having a connection to animals was fine as long as they were domesticated, but wild animals were a whole other ballgame, which is why I often carried bear spray.

'No. An idiot on the trail lost his dog. Had to reunite them. Not a big deal.' I didn't mention that I sensed his dog was sick or that the idiot had the most beautiful blue eyes I'd ever seen.

'Now that you're here, make yourself useful and set the table. Lia is finishing up some search and rescue training, and Aster called to say she's helping one last customer.'

'What? Then why did you give me grief about being late?'

'Because I expect you to be on time. Five minutes early, in fact. Your sisters,' she grumbled, blowing a curly gray hair off her forehead, 'they're a whole other matter.'

As Clo continued to stir the sauce, I walked out of the kitchen toward the rectangular dining table my grandfather had fashioned out of an alder tree as a wedding gift for her. With care, I set out the cutlery and glasses. My gaze stuttered on the chair where my grandfather once sat.

The table was the centerpiece of our family's life. Scrapes, spills, gouges in the aging wood marked past holidays, birthdays and, sadly, funerals. Aster was even born on the rug next to it when she showed up a week before her due date. Her early arrival pleased our mother, because she'd sworn from the beginning that her third baby girl was going to have all the attributes of a Virgo. Sensitive. Loyal. Most of all creative. She was, of course, right about everything. My youngest sister was all of those things, especially creative, owning our town's only floral business, The Bloomin' Blossom.

Once the table was set, I walked past the wooden hutch that was covered in generations of family photos dating back to my five-time great-grandmother, Sylvia, and her daughter, Ambrosia Perkins. Two of Harvest Moon's first settlers after it was incorporated in 1874. I always loved the sepia-toned photo of mother and daughter. The two of them smiling ear to ear as they leaned against the doorway of the apothecary they'd owned until Ambrosia's death in 1934.

Flora greeted me with a soft bark when I stepped onto the porch. In the low evening light, the lake was a deep shade of sapphire. The water level settled well below its dirt-hardened shore. It wouldn't rise again until this winter's snowpack melted in late spring.

A cool breeze slid through the swath of ponderosa trees, nudging the hanging baskets dripping with ruby-red geraniums. The plants were my grandmother's pride and joy and probably why Aster was so obsessed with flowers too.

Clo often claimed gardening had become her passion because she'd never planned on being a mother. That all she'd ever wanted was a quiet life where she could live in the mountains, enjoy the fresh air and get her hands good and dirty in the dark soil surrounding the house. It's why she'd named her only daughter Belladonna. Her arrival both beautiful and mysterious, because all her doctors insisted Grandmother Clo could never get pregnant.

Flora popped her head up and gave another whine. I bent down and placed a kiss on the top of her warm brown head. 'You did good today. Although, you didn't need to growl at the guy. I had it under control.'

A vision of Bryce stumbling out of the woods made my blood heat again. There was something strange about his presence I couldn't put my finger on. I was usually pretty good about hiding my intuition about animals, but the episode today hit me like a baseball bat to the chest, and I'd had no other option but to stay planted and accept the rush of feelings.

The first time the sensation happened was a few days after my tenth birthday. My mother showed up without warning and whisked me and my sisters off in an old car painted a muted shade of avocado green, the inside reeking of cigarettes and stale pizza crust. We drove at least an hour until we pulled up beside a roadside petting zoo with goats, chickens and roosters. I walked among the animals, loving how the goats scampered around the small fenced-in pen. That was until one nuzzled under my hand, and the strange feeling descended. I sensed the blood as it beat in the animal's veins. The cracking and popping of its joints rang in my ears. A flood of pain, suddenly making my own bones ache. There were the flashes of red and yellow behind my eyes, before a wash of understanding hit my brain. I sank down onto the dirt and lifted the goat's back right leg. Sure enough, a woman's earring was embedded into its cloven hoof. I pulled it out, and the small creature bleated a thank-you before scampering off.

Belladonna witnessed the entire event. She came up beside me, dusted away the straw and mud clinging to my sparkly pink skirt. Those violet-colored eyes we shared were wracked with fear. She cupped my cheek and asked what was wrong. Through tears, I explained the bursts of light, the weakness that had flooded my body, the agonizing crush of the animal's pain.

I expected her to be distraught. Worried that her oldest child was obviously having some kind of breakdown. Instead, she pulled me close. Whispered that I'd imagined it all. That I needed to forget about it.

Back then I craved any kind of attention from her, so I quickly agreed. Now, the memory sent a chill down my back. I snuggled closer to Flora, the sound of Clo's humming floating out the door toward us.

Canyon wrens chattered in the trees. The rabbits Clo was constantly battling hopped across the grass. A fawn and her doe inched out of the woods. Their silvery eyes veered in my direction before they walked to the lake's edge for a drink.

I let myself relax, until the quiet night air was interrupted by the tinny grind of gears. Lia insisted her old Jeepster Commando was a workhorse that would never die, but the moaning of its ancient engine, which had been rebuilt at least four times, said otherwise.

I heard the spin of tires against gravel and a minute later, she accelerated up the steep driveway that was tucked back a half-mile from the main road. I moved out to the edge of the deck and waved to her as she got out of the car. She gave me her regular grunt before disappearing inside the front door.

Like she'd done with me, Grandmother Clo called her by her given name, Camellia, raked her over the coals about being late, and then promised we'd eat once Aster arrived.

Lia stopped at the fridge, popped open a beer and strode out to join me on the deck. 'What's up her caboose? Squirrels burglarizing the garden again?'

'It's rabbits this time.'

'Gotta give them credit for their bravery. I wouldn't want to go up against Grandmother Clo.'

She scrubbed a hand over her short brown curls. A rare smile lifted her lips, causing the dirt smudged on her cheeks to crack. There were moments when I thought none of us girls looked alike, considering we had different fathers. But then Lia would grin, showing me that dimple we shared, or Aster would give a weird little snort of a laugh like Lia's, and there was no mistaking we were blood.

I pointed to the mud clinging to her boots. 'Outdoor training today?'

'Yep. Teaching the new volunteers about rappelling and tracking.'

While I leisurely enjoyed the local trails, I preferred the comforts of TV and a real bed. Lia, on the other hand, was born to live her life outside.

When we were kids, Grandmother Clo had to tie neon-orange ribbons to the trees, limiting how far Lia could explore. In our grandmother's words, if she hadn't made boundaries, Lia would have hiked all the way to the county line.

She worked as a firefighter/EMT at the one and only fire station in town but spent most of her free time exploring the local forests and volunteering for the county search and rescue.

Lia took a long pull on her beer. Tugged the red bandana away from her neck and let out a weary breath.

'New SAR volunteers pretty green?' I said.

'That's an understatement. I caught one of them about to touch poison hemlock today. Another one practically passed out when I told him we had to keep an eye out for bears.' She took another drink. Shook her head. 'One of them is staying in those rental apartments above Mo's Tavern. I shit you not, the first thing out of his mouth after I introduced myself was would I show him my magic?'

I curled my fingers along the railing. 'What did you say?'

'I told him I only showed my magic on the fourth date.' She winked, and a laugh burst from my lips. Lia could be gruff, but she also had a wicked sense of humor.

'You have to talk to Mo again,' she said, quickly sobering. 'Spreading stories about us at the tavern has got to stop. Every time it comes up, it's like I take two steps backward with the new volunteers or the people on shift with me. We were on a call last week searching for a missing teenager who wandered away from his campsite. I stood on Razor Edge Bluff, doing what I usually do. Listening. Trying to sense the direction of the wind. How quickly it would pick up and mask the scent I was tracking. Everyone stopped what they were doing to watch me. Study me like I was some kind of fucking bug under a microscope.'

She snapped her mouth shut like she couldn't say what she wanted. Since we were kids, she'd been closed off. Guarded. But in the last year, she'd gone from being quiet in crowded rooms to full-on anti-social, and it was beginning to worry me.

'That can't keep happening, Dani.' She kept her focus on the beer label, rubbing at the bottom edge with a ragged fingernail. 'It messes with morale and makes things damn weird.' She took another drink, draining the bottle. 'Maybe I should've taken that job in Leadville. If the three of us weren't here, the gossip, the crap they say about us, would stop.'

'First of all, you can't leave. Aster and I need you here. Second, the town just plays up the magic nonsense to bring in tourists. We have to ignore it. The more ruffled we get, the more Mo and the others will play it up.'

'Don't you get tired of the whispers and strange looks? I've watched people at the clinic. It's like they're readying themselves for some kind of show every time they have an appointment, even if that means your reaction might confirm their animal is sick.'

'It's not that bad.'

She gave me that usual dead-eyed stare.

Was it annoying that people drove from four counties away to come to my clinic because they'd heard a ridiculous story about me from a neighbor? Yes. Was I tired of people, like the guy on the trail today, looking at me like I had three eyes when I told them something was wrong with their animal? Of course. What I didn't mind was the fact that those rumors kept me busy enough to hire a vet tech and a receptionist. That my clinic was usually booked out weeks in advance. If that meant dealing with a few whispers, some odd people and their curiosities, I'd take it, because I was still treating their animals and catching illnesses before it was too late.

My phone buzzed with a text from Aster. I went inside and showed it to Grandmother Clo.

'Well, if she's stuck making a late order for tomorrow, we may as well eat,' she huffed.

We assembled around the table. Lia and I sat across from each other, our spots since we were toddlers. Grandmother Clo set down the spaghetti and meatballs while Lia passed around the salad. It felt weird to eat a birthday dinner without the guest of honor, but when Aster got wrapped up with an arrangement it could take a while.

As we ate, Grandmother Clo prompted the always tight-lipped Lia to tell us about her week. Reluctantly, she recounted a story about how her SAR team rescued a pair of out-of-towners stranded high up on a bluff.

'Why do they always go on a hike with exactly one small bottle of water to share?' She slapped her napkin down beside her plate. 'There are signs all over the trail entrances about proper shoes, and carrying enough water, but these people watch influencers living the "outdoor life", and suddenly they think they're ready to climb Everest.'

Lia continued to gripe about unprepared hikers, forcing my thoughts to the guy, Bryce, on the trail today. The way he seemed at ease in his own body, even after he took a header onto the ground. How Indy's low whine still rang in my ears.

Dammit. I should have pushed more. All I could hope was that he cared enough about his dog to get him checked out.

Once the dinner dishes were cleared, Lia filled the sink with soapy water. We fell into our roles, her washing and me drying.

'I heard a bit of news from Larry Eggers. You know him, he's one of the older guys at the station. Big belly. White beard.' She scrubbed the soapy dish with a bit too much force. 'There's a rumor going around that some big-time reporter is coming here to check out the town.'

I held my breath for what I knew was coming next.

'Apparently, part of that story is supposed to be about the town's complicated history with magic, which will, of course, include us.' Her deep brown gaze cut to me. 'Has anyone contacted you?'

'No,' I said roughly. 'You?'

She shook her head and handed me a dish, which promptly slid through my trembling fingers. The jarring sound of it shattering against the floor made Clo scurry into the kitchen.

'Well, dang it.' She sighed. 'That was one of my favorites.'

'I'm sorry, Clo.'

She must have heard the hitch in my voice, because she patted my arm. 'No worries, my girl. Accidents happen.'

I shot Lia a dark look, warning her not to say a word to Clo, who would lose it if she learned anyone was coming to town to mess with the McGuire girls.

Lia ran to the pantry and returned with a broom and dustpan. I picked up the larger pieces of porcelain with the hand-painted strawberries along the rim. It was part of a set gifted to Clo from Grandpa Beau. My stomach soured as I gathered them in a pile. Lia began to sweep up the shards until her back stiffened, her head snapping in the direction of the porch.

'Is there a problem, Lee Lee?' Clo said.

'Car racing up the driveway.' Her eyes pinched at the corners as she concentrated on what only she could hear. 'Two-point-five-liter engine. Four cylinders. Probably small SUV.'

We all rushed to the deck. A minute later a black SUV moved up and over the rise. The car came to an abrupt halt, and a familiar-looking pair of boots hit the gravel. Fear was etched into the lines around deep blue eyes. That odd flutter filled my chest again.

I bolted down the stairs and flew out the front door. Bryce's eyes bulged as I raced toward him.

'You?' He cocked his head. 'I'm here… looking for a Dr McGuire?'

'That's me,' I said, ignoring the shock on his face.

'Why didn't you…?'

I shook my head at him. 'I'm guessing you're here about your dog?'

Instead of answering, he walked to the back of his SUV and lifted the tailgate. Indy was splayed across an old orange-and-yellow beach towel. When Bryce touched him, the poor dog could barely raise his head.

'He's been vomiting for an hour. Refuses to eat or drink anything. And, even though he's house-trained, he's had numerous accidents like he can't control his bladder. Please.' His voice bordered on panic. 'Can you tell me what's wrong with my dog?'

# Chapter Three

## *Member of the Family*

The county road was darker than the blackest ink. Only a few people used this side artery that led out of town and onto the main highway. I drove past rows of ponderosa trees lining the old lane. Bryce stayed right on my bumper, his headlights seeping through the back window of my truck like dwindling candlelight.

From the cursory exam I'd done at Clo's, it was clear Indy was in bad shape. Once I explained the situation to my grandmother and Lia, asked them to apologize to Aster for me, I told Bryce to follow me to my clinic.

Ten minutes later we sped past a large sign on the side of the road. Carved into the wood were the words Harvest Moon Animal Clinic, Dani McGuire, DVM. I turned at a small lane you'd miss if you didn't know where you were going. Fifty yards ahead sat what used to be the county firehouse. My sisters thought I was losing it when I bought one of the oldest buildings in town, but the A-frame structure built from wood milled from our local trees had been one of my favorites since childhood. The minute I heard it was on the market, I raced to the realty office to put in a bid. Luckily, no one had as much as glanced at the building in two years, and it became mine without too much trouble.

The scent of wet animal and disinfectant hit me as I walked through the solid oak door with Flora trotting beside me. It'd been seven years since I took ownership of the space, and although it was a lot of work to turn it into my clinic, it was worth it. The warm wood interior and twenty-five-foot pitched roof were breathtaking, but the real reason I loved the place was the square footage, which allowed me to build out three full exam rooms, a single surgery space and a closed-off area to house my X-ray machine. The firefighters' sleeping quarters on the upper floor became my private apartment.

Bryce rushed up behind me with Indy limp in his arms. We walked past the semi-circle reception desk, and the small waiting area with a half dozen plastic chairs. I pushed through the door separating the clinic from the public space and headed down a short hall, turning into one of the exam rooms.

Bryce placed Indy on the rectangular steel table. Flora lay on a dog bed in the corner, her worried gaze glued to her new friend.

That stinging electrical zap shot through my body as I ran my hands from Indy's neck down the length of his body. My senses could tell me this dog was sick, but it could never replace the important steps used to figure out a full diagnosis.

My fingers glided through his fur, not detecting any odd lumps or bumps. Bryce stood frozen, his gaze tracking my movements. I gripped Indy's muzzle, prying open his mouth to discover his gums were close to white. When I pressed my stethoscope to his chest, his elevated heart rate warned I needed to figure out what was happening quickly.

I ran the symptoms through my head. My first thought was some kind of poisoning, especially with the vomiting and incontinence.

Bryce laid his hands on top of his head. His shoulders quaked as Indy stayed still.

'Has he had these symptoms before?' I said.

'Never. Besides being neutered, he's only had to go to the vet for his shots.'

Indy stayed still on the table, drool pooling around his mouth.

'Did you feed him anything out of the ordinary today?'

'No, but I was searching those woods for him for over thirty minutes until I found you. He could have eaten anything.'

I bit back another lecture about Indy being in the woods without a leash because the terror in Bryce's eyes was too much.

'We need to start with fluids. Can you hold him?'

He replied with a weak 'Yes.'

I moved around the room, pulling out a syringe, electric clippers and an IV bag.

'Keep your arms around him. I'm going to shave down the hair on his left paw and insert a line for fluids. In his state I don't think he'll move, but it's better to be safe than sorry.'

Bryce circled Indy in his arms while I went to work. Once the fluids were on board, I said, 'My instincts say this is a reaction to something he's ingested, but let's rule out that he does not have any kind of obstruction.'

'What does that mean?' he blurted out.

'I need to do X-rays on his abdomen.'

What little color he had in his cheeks faded.

'It's only to be on the safe side.'

He carried Indy into a room farther down the hall while I held on to the IV bag. After shooing him and Flora out the door, I slid on my lead apron and positioned Indy on the table to get a good view of his stomach. I took a couple of pictures, finding no problems in his stomach, bladder or intestines.

What the hell was wrong with this dog, and why did I feel consumed with figuring it out for this poor animal and a man I'd only known for a few hours?

Bryce carried Indy back toward the exam room. We weren't ten feet from the door when the poor dog vomited. Panic creased every line in Bryce's face.

'It's okay,' I said, trying to reassure him. 'Set him back on the table inside.'

As I passed Indy's mess, the pungent scent filled the air and it quickly solved our mystery.

Bryce's pacing grew more frantic in the exam room. 'On the trail earlier, you knew Indy was sick. You told me to get him checked out. And Mo at the tavern said you had some kind of magic, but I didn't listen, and now my dog can't even move.'

I hated the way he stared at me – an odd combination of wonder mixed with uneasy trepidation. Like he was grateful for my help, but all the rational parts of his brain were telling him none of this should be possible.

'That's not what we need to discuss right now.'

'What's next? How do we help him? I'll do *anything* to make sure he's all right.'

'Your dog is going to be fine. I know exactly what's wrong with him.'

His reddish brows jumped to his hairline. 'You do?'

'It's marijuana poisoning.'

'Marijuana?' he yelped.

'Yes. When dogs ingest it, they can become very sick. Could Indy have gotten into something at your cabin?'

'No, I don't do that,' he said through clenched teeth. 'Are you sure that's what this is? It doesn't make any sense.'

I hitched my thumb back toward the mess in the hallway. He disappeared and a few seconds later the low sound of 'fuck' filled the air.

Once he was back through the doorway, he said, 'I swear he didn't get sick because of me. This won't kill him, right?' He took a wobbly step closer, and white-knuckled the edge of the exam table.

I grabbed his hand. 'Bryce, *do not* pass out. I don't need two patients right now.'

'Okay, Dr McGuire. I just need a second.' He took a thick gulp. Focused on our linked fingers. 'How do you make him better?'

'The IV will help flush the toxins out of his system. Get him rehydrated. I'm also going to give him anti-nausea meds to help with the vomiting. And you can call me Dani.'

'What else, Dani? Please, put me to work.'

The desperation in his voice, the fear in his eyes, shook me. I'd usually insist the owner go out to the waiting area, but in this case I knew Indy would do better if Bryce was close.

'In the cabinet above the sink are extra towels. Grab a few and put them around Indy so we can keep him warm.'

While I got my materials ready, he grabbed the towels and made sure Indy was covered.

'What can I do next?'

'Come to the other side of the table and hold Indy still.'

Over the years, I'd dealt with a lot of owners. Most of them treated their pet like a member of the family. A small few were not as dedicated, often balking at the cost for their animal's care. Then there were owners like Bryce, who clearly made their pet their whole world. That kind of dedication made me want to do everything in my power to give their animals the best treatment possible.

'Teenagers love certain secluded spots on the ridge, because they can go there and party. My guess is Indy found something they left behind. By the color and smell of what's in the hall, I'd guess pot brownies. Which is like a one-two punch because of course the weed is bad, but so is the chocolate.'

He murmured another low 'fuck' before he said, 'Sorry about the language, but this really scared me.'

'Don't apologize. An animal getting sick can be frightening.'

I went to the small supply closet at the back of the room and returned with a handful of items. Bryce's gaze narrowed on a long white tube I'd set on the table. 'That looks like what you use to apply caulk around the bathtub.'

'It's activated charcoal. The nozzle helps me get it down his throat. It'll bind the toxins in the stomach and limit absorption.'

Luckily, Indy was alert enough to swallow. I kept his head at a level position and placed the tube with a syringe-like end into his mouth. Bryce's intense stare never left me. I squeezed out small amounts to ensure Indy could swallow without choking. After I was finished, I asked Bryce to set Indy on a nest of clean blankets I had waiting on the floor. Flora moved from her spot in the corner and lay beside him, taking her clinic mascot role seriously.

'I'll keep Indy here tonight. Do some blood work and monitor his electrolytes. You can come back in the morning to get him.'

His hands stilled in the dog's deep brown fur. 'May I… stay a little while longer? I can't leave him right now.'

I had strict rules about emergency cases and sending owners home so their animals could rest and recover, but for some reason I could not say no to him. It was an odd and reoccurring feeling that was beginning to make me wonder who this guy was, and why he felt so important to my life.

# Chapter Four

## *Present in My Dreams*

I moved around the room, putting away supplies and throwing out bits of trash. Bryce studied my every step, his jaw working like he had multiple questions but couldn't quite figure out how to ask them. It was the same way my ex, Max, behaved when we first met at vet school. It wasn't so much fear as a sense of confusion, wonder and awe.

I walked to the closet and pulled out a bucket and some rags to clean up the vomit Indy left in the hall.

'What are you doing?' he said.

'Can't leave that mess out there. My staff would not be happy if they came in tomorrow and found it.'

Before I could object, he pulled the bucket and rags out of my hands. 'He's my dog. I'll do it.'

When he returned a few minutes later, I showed him where to toss the garbage and wash his hands.

Once he was done, he slid down onto his belly and focused on measuring the rise and fall of Indy's chest.

'He really is going to be fine,' I said.

'I get it, but this reassures me.'

The room went silent again as I tidied up the floor and counters.

'Nice diplomas,' he said, tipping his chin to the black frames that hung on the wall. 'Undergrad and vet school at Colorado State. Did you like it there?'

'Fort Collins is a wonderful town. Lots of locally owned shops. Good food and people. I guess it reminded me of this place. Why it felt a little like home.'

He worked his teeth over his bottom lip. 'Have anyone special there?'

His attempts to probe my relationship status were getting more pitiful by the second.

'I was with someone for four years, but we wanted different things and broke up.'

He did a poor job of hiding the spark in his eyes. 'Did you always know you'd come back to Harvest Moon?'

'Yes. My sisters are here. My grandmother, who you just met, practically raised us. She's getting older, and I wanted to be close.'

'Was that one of your sisters at the house tonight?'

'That's Lia. She's a firefighter/EMT and also volunteers with the county SAR team.'

'SAR?'

'It's short for "search and rescue". She's been with the team for ten years.'

I never spoke about my personal life with owners, but I found myself at ease with Bryce in a way I hadn't with any man in a while.

'And does she… Well, Mo said she has gifts too.' He shook his head like he couldn't believe his own words.

His questions reminded me why I didn't share personal information with owners. Lia was right. I did need to have another talk with Mo.

'I don't discuss my sisters with strangers.'

Hearing the sharpness in my voice, Bryce turned his attention back to his dog. 'Thank you for helping Indy,' he said softly. 'He's gotten me through a lot of difficult times lately.'

He went back to stroking his dog's head. 'It's just my mom and me. She was close to her brother. Spent a lot of time here after I went to college. She was always encouraging me to visit. To spend more time with her and my uncle Rich. I always had an excuse. A better opportunity.' Hard lines pinched around his mouth. 'Sounds shitty, right? A mother who does everything for her only child, and a son who can't spare a single minute for her, because he's too caught up in his own life.'

I wanted to say he was lucky to have a mother who was present. Who wanted to spend time with him, but I stayed quiet, not wanting to think about Belladonna and all the ways she'd failed me and my sisters. How I would have given anything for her to be the kind of mother who wanted to be around us.

An unsteady breath slid past his lips. 'Sorry. Didn't mean to unload on you. It's only that for a moment tonight I thought I might lose Indy, and it scared the crap out of me.'

He gave his dog another loving look, and it made my heart tug. Since I was a child, I'd been drawn to animals. I'd had the incident with the goat, but long before that I'd felt a strange pull toward all kinds of creatures. They were always present in my dreams. Hopping across my path on the trails. Appearing like strange and gentle guardians when I walked by the lake.

When I was young, Grandpa Beau regularly took me to see the horses at George Spellner's farm. As soon as we arrived, the animals crowded against the walls of their corral like they wanted my attention. For hours I was entranced by the way the horses pranced around the paddock. Stayed still as statues as I offered them apples from the palm of my hand.

That love of animals is what also drew me to Max at vet school. He was a tall, stocky guy who looked like he could lift an entire refrigerator, but when he worked with a bird, lizard or any kind of small animal that he could set in the center of his giant palm, his voice went gentle. His eyes softened as he examined the creature. He used to give me that same kind of serene gaze when we lay together in bed, until at some point he decided I wasn't what he wanted anymore.

'It's interesting how animals weave their way into our world. Give us comfort when we least expect it.' I sat next to Flora on the floor. 'Your fear is totally understandable.'

Bryce leaned back against the wall, and Indy had enough energy to inch forward on his paws and lay his head across his lap.

'Indy. The name suits him,' I said.

'That wasn't me. He was abandoned behind an American Legion Post in Pasadena. The veterans took him in. Fed him. Called him Independence. Indy for short. They were all too old to keep him, so they took him to a no-kill shelter. I found him there a few weeks later.'

I moved my hand down to Indy's mouth to check his gums again, which were finally pinking up.

'Flora?' he said. 'That's an unusual name too.'

'Flower names run in my family,' was all I gave him.

'Have you had her since she was a pup?'

'No. I'd been in practice for about a year when we had a two-day white-out snowstorm that shut down the mountain passes. I went outside after it was over to clear off the steps outside, and there she was asleep on the porch. Poor thing was curled up like she was doing everything she could to stay warm. She didn't have any tags.' I gave him that same stern look from the trail. 'I called around town, but nobody knew where she belonged. My guess is someone wanted to get rid of her, saw a vet's office, and decided it was as good a place as any to dump her. Bastards.'

I ran my hand over Flora's head, and she let out a contented huff. 'My plan was to find her a good home, but once I started clinic that day, the animals gravitated toward her. Dogs, no matter their size. Cats too. Even had a rabbit hop right up and nuzzle one of her giant paws. Flora stayed calm through it all. After that, I decided the clinic needed a mascot. She's been by my side ever since.'

'And she helps you, too.' His knowing look said we were back to the magic. 'On the trail, why didn't you tell me you were a vet?' He paused like he was going to say more but then snapped his mouth shut.

'I'm not in the habit of giving out personal information to strangers. And even if I'd told you, would you have listened?'

He glanced at the frames on the wall again. 'I'd like to think I would have, but you didn't give me a chance.'

There was that flash of familiarity again. Like I'd known him my entire life, and it was beginning to freak me out.

I jumped up and moved to the door. 'Leave me your number. I'll have my receptionist call you when Indy's ready to go tomorrow morning.'

He stood, wincing as he straightened up. Those stupid boots.

'Clean your blisters when you get home or they'll get infected. Wash the skin with soap and water, then slather them in Vaseline. Use a few Band-Aids to cover them overnight.'

He scrubbed at his jaw again. 'Band-Aids? Vaseline? Not sure my uncle Rich has that stuff at the cabin.'

I rolled my eyes and pointed to a plastic chair. We didn't have human patients, but my vet tech, Bree, insisted we keep a small first aid kit in every room.

'Sit and let me take a look.'

His wide, grateful smile sent that flutter through me again. Once he was in the chair, he tugged off his boots. He winced at the blood stains on the heels of his socks, gingerly peeling them off his feet.

'Yep, you're a mess.'

He let out a low chuckle like he knew I meant more than his feet.

I slid on some gloves and bent to check the damage. Quarter-sized blisters covered his skin. The affected areas around them were an angry shade of red.

A low hiss escaped Bryce's mouth when I cleaned the wounds with soap and water.

'First human patient?' he joked.

'No, a few years ago I was driving down from Fort Collins and came upon a car accident. A tourist hit a patch of black ice and spun out. Smashed his head pretty good on the windshield.'

He gave another wince.

'I made sure the guy stayed stable. Applied pressure to the wound until the sheriff and ambulance arrived.'

'I've watched you in action twice now, and all I can say is that the animals in this community are damn lucky. If I was staying, you'd definitely be Indy's vet.'

That awestruck stare was back, and I found myself focusing on the dusty blue rings that surrounded his pupils.

He leaned in, his warm breath close. Too close. He reached out and tucked a loose hair behind my ear. His gaze searched mine, that narrowed, questioning look returning. This time it wasn't about the rumors. It was about a raw need that wasn't hard to miss. A need I shockingly felt too.

Indy made another small whine, and I was reminded that this guy was a stranger. A stranger I had zero intention of kissing.

'You can put your boots back on.' I pulled off my gloves and busied myself with putting a sample tube of Vaseline and a handful of Band-Aids into a plastic bag. 'Here.' I shoved them at his chest. 'Use these for the next few days.'

Indy gave another low whine from his pile of blankets, and I scurried away to check his heart and lungs. 'Looks like the marijuana is working its way out of his system. He'll be better soon.'

'I don't know how to repay you for jumping in to take care of him so quickly.'

'Oh, you'll get a bill,' I joked as I headed toward the waiting area.

'I'm being serious. Let me at least buy you dinner.'

'That's not necessary.' I stopped at the reception desk and plucked a business card off the counter.

'Are you sure?' His gaze lingered too long on my lips, and that spark of heat licked through me again.

'Yes, I'm sure,' I said roughly. 'You can do one thing for me, though.'

He inched in closer. 'What's that?'

'Get Indy a collar. Use a leash on the trail. By your reaction tonight, I know you're a good owner. Prove it by getting him tags, just in case he gets away again.'

He let out a huff of a laugh. 'Okay. We'll follow doctor's orders, I promise.'

'Write your number on the back.' I pushed the card across the mahogany counter toward him, not wanting to touch him and risk another spark of whatever the hell that was in the exam room. 'My assistant will call you in the morning. You can pay for my services then.'

He grabbed a pen out of a coffee cup sitting on the desk and scribbled out his number. 'I wouldn't leave Indy with anyone else, but you're...' He chewed on the corner of his lip. 'Like I said, I think you're something special.' He handed me the card, and I slid it into the pocket of my joggers.

'I'll see you tomorrow,' I said.

He walked to the door and paused. His shoulders hitched up as he took two solid breaths. Quick as a flash, he spun on his heel and walked straight for me. Before I could react, he tugged me in by the waist and circled me in a tight hug.

'Thank you, Dani.' His words were a soft sweep over the cuff of my ear.

The 'you're welcome' stayed lodged in the base of my throat, because the weight of his arms around me, the press of his body against mine, felt too right. Felt too much like coming home.

When I didn't move, he pressed a warm kiss against my cheek. That flutter in my stomach became a rush of warm gold flooding my veins. Everything was Bryce. The soft sweep of his hair against my cheek. A scent of ink and cedar on his skin.

Just as I relaxed into his touch, he pulled back and gently pressed his hands to my cheeks. There was a flicker of hesitation, like he was wondering if this was too much. If he should let me go. I should have told him yes, stepped away, but that feeling that somehow we were tied together cemented me to the floor.

Without thinking, I leaned forward and pressed a firm kiss to his lips. I started to pull away, thinking this was such a bad idea, until he dug his hands into my waist, deepening the kiss. I ran my tongue over the seam of his lips, and the rumble in his chest vibrated through me. His hands curled behind my neck, lining up our bodies like two puzzle pieces locking into place.

This was more than a kiss. It was a sunrise on the morning of a first snow. Warm syrup on pancakes. The first taste of cotton candy at the county fair. Like he felt it too, he spun me around and pressed my back to the desk. His kiss became more insistent and greedier.

What was happening right now? I was kissing a stranger. A man who looked at me like I was a mystery he desperately needed to solve, but still, I leaned deeper into him, unable to shake the feeling that I was meant to be in his arms. That my body was made to ease perfectly into the lines of his tight, warm form.

His fingers moved up my sides, inching beneath my T-shirt. It'd been too long since a man touched me, because the scorch of his hands made me whimper. He nudged me tighter against the curve of the reception desk, his mouth making small bites against my lower lip.

I settled my hands on his shoulders, and he used his tongue to paint a sensuous line down my neck and across my collarbone. He let out his own growl when I tugged the shirt out of his jeans and slid my hands over his hot skin. I sucked in a quick breath when his thumb traced the peak of my nipple.

'Should I stop?' The warmth of his breath against my tender skin sent a shiver down my spine. 'Dani,' he said with gravel in his voice. 'What do you want?'

There was no way this guy was staying around. He'd enjoy a few days in the woods, and then when he got sick of the quiet, the rural isolation, the fact that he could never get a strong Wi-Fi signal, he'd head back to Los Angeles. But, I had to admit there was a powerful chemistry between us. Some sort of odd tether that drew me to him, which made absolutely no sense.

His arms tightened around my waist, and he tugged me closer. The heat of him pressed against my core. We were eye to eye, breath to breath, heartbeat to heartbeat and there was no place to hide from his intense gaze.

'Say the word and I'll let you go.'

My brain went back to all the reasons this was a bad idea. He was a stranger. A client. I knew nothing about him apart from the fact that he had a single family tie here that no longer existed. I should have stepped out of his touch. Ignored the way his scent was intoxicating. But then that flutter returned to my chest, and the heat between my legs grew until I listened to my body and thought, *Fuck it*.

I pressed my mouth to the hollow at the base of his throat. He moaned as I nipped and bit my way across his skin. The pulse of blood in his veins hummed beneath my tongue. I tried to tug off his shirt, needing to feel more of his skin, but his hands shot out and stopped me. Like he'd been zapped by some invisible force, he quickly disentangled himself from my touch and stumbled out of reach.

'Holy shit. That was unexpected. I'm sorry if that was too much,' he said roughly.

Like I'd forgotten the English language, I stayed quiet. That brilliant light in his gaze went out, and the ache of not touching him shook something loose I'd kept buried for years.

'Uh, what time tomorrow should I be here to get Indy?' His voice was robotic. Too much like Max was in those final days.

'I'll call you once I've assessed his status, made sure he can hold down some food and water,' I replied just as woodenly.

'All right. I'll talk to you tomorrow.'

He raced for the front door like he wanted to be anywhere but near me. I stayed planted in place, unsure if what had just happened was real or a very hot hallucination.

I pressed a hand to my lips, the feel of his mouth a lingering phantom's touch. On shaky legs, I sank down onto a nearby chair, my head a jumble of shock, panic and a dizzying kind of euphoria I could not explain.

Flora trotted toward me and nuzzled my knees, instinctively knowing I needed comfort. A pall of dread seeped into my bones as I gazed at the closed door. My one shot at love had walked away from me. Any chance I ever had at a happily-ever-after disappeared the moment Max decided I was no longer part of his narrative or his future.

I was always going to be alone, and no matter how much I wanted to fight it, the truth was clear in the sound of spinning tires as Bryce's SUV screeched away into the night.

# *Chapter Five*

### *Suspicious of Outsiders*

Nobody believed the online reviews about Drip! Drip! Hooray!

Like most of the colorful Victorian-style shops lining downtown Harvest Moon, the building that housed the apothecary was hard to miss. The outside was painted in a shade of deep blue with muted orange trim. Inside it was, in fact, a pharmacy that also housed one of the best coffee shops for a hundred square miles, according to its 527 five-star ratings.

I pushed through the creaky glass door and headed past the shelves crammed with ibuprofen, allergy medications and various drugstore shampoos. Fred Ellery, our longtime pharmacist, and winner of the town's pie-eating contest for five years straight, talked to a tourist at the register. As I passed, he smiled and gave me a casual wave.

At the back of the store sat a horseshoe-style counter with gleaming steel-curved edges. My best friend, Elena, scurried around, balancing two small plates and a carafe of freshly brewed coffee, a warm nutty scent filling the air.

Lia sat at the white Formica counter reading the newspaper. Her dark curly hair drooped over her forehead in a big poof.

I slid onto the red vinyl stool beside her. 'Aster's not here yet?'

Lia glanced at the oversized watch on her wrist that had belonged to Grandpa Beau. When we'd lost him seventeen years ago, there was no doubt it would be hers. She'd always admired the way the old timepiece sat against his brown, weathered skin. How it made its own clicks and whirs that fascinated her.

She'd been the closest to our grandfather, who could coax a smile out of her when no one else could. Even though Lia kept her emotions tightly in check, there were moments when I'd watched her solid walls tremble. Like she was still grieving his death, and other things she would never speak about.

'When is our little sister ever on time?' She kept her eyes on the paper but added, 'How's the dog from last night?'

'Doing well. I released him to his owner early this morning.'

I'd forgotten we'd decided not to open the clinic until one o'clock today, so my receptionist and vet tech were getting a well-deserved morning off. When Bryce appeared at the door first thing, eager to see his dog, I abruptly shoved his bill at him, advised that Indy should be on a bland diet for the next few days and ushered him straight out of the clinic.

'You're usually firm about not taking on emergency cases unless it's someone local. What was different about last night?'

There was a small, irritated twitch in her jaw you'd never notice unless you knew her well. Out of the three of us, she was the most suspicious of outsiders, especially when they'd been influenced by the tales around town about our supposed 'powers'.

'I'd actually seen the dog earlier in the day on the trail. Met the owner.' I tugged on my ponytail and lowered my voice. 'I'd sensed there was something wrong with the dog, so it wasn't like I could turn the guy away.'

She gave me a hesitant look. 'I get it, but still…'

'Don't worry, Lee Lee. He's from LA. He'll tire of this place and go back to where he belongs soon enough.' I hoped I was right because any future interaction with him was going to be all kinds of awkward, especially since my brain kept flashing back to that hot kiss, and the jarring way he'd pulled away.

'You sure about that? Even though he was freaked out about his dog, he still looked at you like you were Vega, Lyra's bright star, appearing right after sunset.'

I tried not to roll my eyes at Lia's dramatics, but I had to admit I'd seen that look too as he pressed his hands against my cheeks. Searched my eyes for permission to brush his mouth over mine.

'Who's the brightest star?' Elena set down a perfect London Fog in front of me, the sweet scent of vanilla syrup filling my nose.

Lia cocked her head in my direction.

'Oh, okay, now I need details.' Elena brushed back her curtain of long, shiny black hair, and set her elbows on the counter.

'It's no big deal. I met a guy out on one of the trails yesterday. Told him his dog was sick. Of course, he ignored me. A few hours later, he showed up at Clo's while we were waiting to celebrate Aster's birthday. He was freaked out because his dog was not eating and very lethargic.'

'He showed up thanks to Mo's big mouth,' Lia added.

The warm brown lines around Elena's mouth pinched. Like Lia, she was fiercely protective of me. We'd met on the first day of seventh grade when she'd marched straight up to me, her pigtails swinging across her shoulders, and announced she was new to the school and wanted to be my friend.

I loved that she was brave and outspoken. When one of the local boys started chanting 'witch' at me, she kicked a soccer ball straight at his gut, sending him tumbling to the ground. Ever since that day, she'd protected me like a lioness, even though she knew after twenty years of friendship I could fight my own battles.

'And this guy's a stranger?' Elena said.

'Yeah, his uncle owned a place over near Greer's Bluff, but he died recently and left it to him,' I said.

Elena propped a hand on her hip. 'So he does have ties here?'

'Yes, but I don't think that matters. By the non-existent tread on his hiking boots, and the way he stumbled through the woods, there's no way he'll stay long.'

She grabbed a rag from under the counter and casually said, 'I don't suppose either one of you has heard about some reporter from Metropolitan Lifestyle Network that's in town?'

Lia gripped the edges of her paper. 'Who told you about that?'

Elena stuffed the rag into the front pocket of her red-and-white-checked apron. 'Judge Greene and Mo were chatting about it at the tavern last night. They said he's already sent emails to half the town. A lot of the questions were about the town's history.' Her gaze darted to the ground. 'And the founding families, specifically yours.'

'Well, shit,' Lia hissed. 'That's not good.'

'It's okay. Nothing says we have to talk to him,' I said, trying to reassure her.

'Doesn't matter. I've read enough about some of our wildfires to know that writers can play fast and loose with the facts. If this guy wants to build up some crazy story about this town, he'll do it. Hell, Mo and the other shop owners will help him, because it'll be good for business.'

'We can't jump to any conclusions. Maybe he'll figure out how boring we are and leave,' I said.

Lia quirked a thick, dark brow at me. 'Right, and a bear doesn't shit in the woods.'

'What do bears do in the woods?'

Aster was at my elbow and I jumped. 'Where the heck did you come from?'

'Through the front door, silly.'

Maybe it was her slight frame, or just her tiny feet, but Aster had a knack for making zero noise when she entered a room. When we were kids, Lia and I tried to talk secretly about the whereabouts of Belladonna, because any mention of our mother always made Aster weepy. But just when we thought we were alone, Aster would appear like she'd sensed our fears. Knew we were hiding our emotions. Looking back at it now, it was the first signs she was showing of her connection to people, we just didn't know it yet.

She set her big leather bag on the counter and took the stool next to me. I tried not to smile at this month's choice of hair color – a vibrant shade of lavender.

'What were you all talking about?'

Lia and I loved to tease her so we both gave her an empty stare.

'Fine. Be that way.' She snatched her purse off the counter. 'Guess I'll go open the shop, considering no one has said, "Sorry your birthday dinner got messed up last night."'

Before she could get more than a few steps, I called for her to come back. Lia quickly echoed the same sentiment.

Aster stilled and mumbled, 'Give me one reason why I should?'

'You'll be leaving your present behind,' I teased.

That'd definitely do the trick, because Aster loved surprises just as much as she loved using her gift to find people their perfect love match.

Aster's shoulders continued to droop like a well-loved rag doll until Lia sang out the first line of a song, and I followed. In terrible harmony, we belted out Blink 182's 'What's My Age Again?' It had become our tradition since Belladonna ruined the birthday song for us years ago by stating it was 'too commercial' and made us 'conform like robots'.

Yeah, our mother was a real ray of sunshine.

Not really. But Aster, she was a burst of golden light after forty days of cloud cover and deserved to be serenaded in a loud and very off-key way.

While we sang, Aster did a little dance. When we came to the final line of the song, she did an extra shimmy before throwing herself into our arms. We held on to the hug for a few extra beats like we always did before Lia broke away. Five seconds was her limit for human touch.

Elena gave us all a clap and then winked at Aster. 'Saved a chocolate croissant for you. Should I put a candle in it?'

'Yes, please.' Aster beamed.

Once Elena left, Aster focused on me. 'I forgive you for leaving last night before I got there, but I do need the details on what happened. Grandmother Clo said something about a handsome guy and an injured dog?'

Lia snickered at the 'handsome guy' comment.

As I told Aster about the pot brownie incident, she tapped her long nails, painted a shade of eggplant, against the counter. Tilted her head at me if she was seeing something none of the rest of us could. She huffed out a breath, swapped a hesitant look with Lia I did not like.

God, I hope she didn't sense the stench of regret from my encounter with Bryce this morning. Or even worse, the heat I'd felt when he'd kissed me last night, or the ache that stirred in my chest when he'd pulled away.

'Dani, you do need to talk to Mo again,' Aster started, and I sagged in relief. 'Sending a stranger to our grandmother's house without any warning is all kinds of wrong.'

I gave Lia the side-eye.

'What? It came up last night after you took off. We both agree Mo is getting out of hand.' She blew a wayward curl off her forehead. 'Whenever business gets slow in the tavern, all these tales about the "magic in Harvest Moon" and the witchy McGuire sisters come out.' Her laugh was caustic. 'It needs to stop because it messes with all of our lives.'

She and Aster swapped another weighted look.

'Okay,' I said, swinging a finger between the two of them. 'What else are you keeping from me?'

'Tell her, Ast,' Lia urged.

'A few people have come into the Blossom lately under the guise that they want flowers, but then they get all weird. Ask what color I see in them. Demand I find their exact match so they can be with the love of their lives.'

'And the last weirdo?' Lia pressed.

Aster nervously twirled a lock of hair around her finger. 'He mentioned, well, asked sort of forcefully, if I could be his match. Which is both creepy and ridiculous, because most people know I can see everyone's color except my own. A flaw in the design, so to speak,' she said bitterly.

I grabbed the edge of the counter to stay steady. Tourists had always been weird around us, but I drew the line at people who invaded our space and acted like complete weirdos.

'What did you do?' I said.

'Dalton was in the shop keeping me company. He chased the guy out, and the loser never came back.'

'Aster,' I said on an unsteady breath. 'Your best friend also has a business to run. He can't always be there to protect you.'

She waved away my worry. 'Dalton has enough staff to sling pizzas. And you know so much more good than bad comes from what happens when I help people.'

When Aster was four, she started drawing vivid pictures of family and friends. Their outlines were always in very specific colors. Orange for me. Dark green for Lia. Belladonna a deep, nearly blackish purple. Grandmother Clo, a complete counter to her daughter, was a shade of honey yellow. When it came to drawing herself, Aster only used a white crayon, because for some odd reason her gift didn't pertain to herself, which, even though she brushed it off, bothered her.

Belladonna noticed her artistic gifts and quizzed her about it. Grew uptight when she questioned Aster about what she saw, felt, when she met new people. Our pediatrician had a name for it – synesthesia. Belladonna argued he was wrong. That Aster was only highly sensitive and creative. An empath who sensed people's worries and fears. Connected with their vulnerability.

'This is the reason why that reporter coming here is bad, Dani. We've already got issues in our own lives just from the whispers,' Lia said. 'Imagine what a hellscape this place will become if Harvest Moon gets put in the spotlight again!'

'Again?' Aster said with a questioning look.

Lia ignored her, snatching her paper off the counter and pretending to read. When she got in a mood like this, it was hard to reason with her.

'Sterling roses are supposed to be delivered today for Mayvis Turner and Jacob Orlow's wedding this weekend,' Aster squeaked out. She always got uncomfortable when Lia went sullen.

'That sounds pretty. Are they having a lot of guests?' I said.

'Only close family and friends.' She waited for Lia to add something, but she remained concrete stiff on her stool.

Elena returned with a vanilla latte for Aster. A bright pink candle sat in a decadent chocolate croissant made by the bakery next door.

Aster closed her eyes and blew out the flame. Even though I clapped along with Lia and Elena, a knot lodged into the center of my chest. I hated that none of us could be normal in this town. That the rumors of magic still tainted things.

It wasn't always this way. For over a hundred years, Harvest Moon had been like any other quiet mountain town. Sure, there'd been whispers off and on about the founding families, specifically the Perkins line on Clo's side. They'd all been silly tales told over beers, or around campfires, until Clo began dating Beau McGuire. People loved to talk nonsense about the couple who could make anything grow in the harsh clay soil, and whose families were rumored to have a special intuition, a gift, for mining silver in the local mountains.

Over the years, the stories ebbed and flowed until our mother, Belladonna, was born on a dark night with thunder and lightning battling in the midnight air. With her thick, black hair and violet eyes, our mother became a legend, a whispered fear, among the locals. It didn't help to quell the rumors when at eighteen she started disappearing for long periods of time, only to return eight months pregnant, never telling a soul who any of our fathers were.

Aster let out a moan as she took a big bite of croissant, a wide smile lighting up her face. This was what she deserved – pure joy, not menacing assholes, or rumors about who, or what, she was.

'I still can't believe it's been a year since Mayvis came into the shop looking for a bouquet for her mama,' Aster said, wiping her mouth with a napkin. 'That day when she spoke, her essence, a sharp, bright mint green, floated around her body. Not a week later, Jake came in to buy flowers for a co-worker's birthday. His color matched Mayvis's perfectly. I introduced them a few days later, and now they're getting married,' she said proudly. 'That's what I want to focus on, not the other stuff.'

Lia grumbled on about Mo, and I took a sip of my drink. Elena moved around the counter, collecting old dishes and mugs. The sound of footsteps headed our way. As soon as I saw the blue hat, the threads of reddish-blond hair poking out the sides, I slid down in my seat.

Bryce studied the chalkboard menu hung on the wall.

'You've got to be fucking kidding me.' Lia tipped her chin, narrowing her stare on his hat. I hadn't noticed it yesterday with him tripping across the ground, but the small yellow stitching at the back of his hat said Metropolitan Lifestyle Network.

Aster gave me a confused look as I sucked in a sharp breath.

No. It wasn't possible. Bryce was the reporter?

My mind spun back to what he'd said about the importance of words. The smudge of ink on his finger. The phrase *ass over teakettle*.

Dammit. I'd missed all the signs.

His gaze flicked in our direction and he did a double take. 'Oh, hello,' he said too hesitantly. He moved toward our end of the counter. 'You must be Aster. I've heard good things about you.' He reached his hand out to her. 'I think I messed up your birthday celebration yesterday. I'm sorry.'

The veins in Aster's neck started to throb. Her pupils blew wide as her breaths went thready. Instead of greeting him, she pressed a hand over her mouth, all the color draining from her cheeks.

The coffee in my stomach threatened to make a reappearance.

This could not be happening.

I knew that wide-eyed stare and exactly what it meant.

# Chapter Six

## *Forever Cursed to Be Alone*

'Orange,' Aster said on a choked exhale like there was something stuck in her windpipe.

I stayed pinned to the stool. Behind me the sound of Lia grinding her jaw set my own teeth on edge.

Aster had to be wrong. Max had been my soulmate, until he decided to leave me. Bryce was a stranger. The reporter we all dreaded meeting.

Elena had been my friend long enough to understand what was happening. Her brow arched as if to say, *Oh, shit* and *Is this the guy from the clinic?*

I gave a small nod, and she spun on her heel.

'Hey,' she said a little too loudly. 'What can I get for you? Coffee? The pastries from next door are still warm too.'

Bryce took in my blazing stare and made an uncomfortable swallow. 'I'll take a coffee. One sugar.' He backed away and found his own seat at the opposite end of the counter.

Elena rushed toward the kitchen, and Aster squeezed my hand. 'I'm sorry, Dan.'

That tug in the center of my chest on the trail. The drive I felt to help him last night. Was that all linked to this revelation?

'I don't understand, Ast. How can there be two matches?' I asked.

'There can't be.' The way she bit into her lip, frantically tapped her nails on the counter, warned this was going to be bad. 'Your color… it's unique. It's like persimmon with a gold outline. I've never seen that color except for with you.' Her gaze darted to Bryce. 'And, well, now *him*.'

'But you swore Max was her match,' Lia insisted.

I hated thinking about Max, but flickers of him kept creeping back into my life. We'd met the second day of veterinary school. When Aster came to visit a month later, she revealed that he and I shared a color. That small nudge made me brave enough to ask him out on a study date. For the next four years, we were hardly ever apart.

When I decided I wanted to return to Harvest Moon to set up my own clinic after we graduated, Max had other ideas. One minute we were sharing our lives, and a little bungalow in Fort Collins, the next he was making a dozen excuses about why we wouldn't work. Two days later, he was on a plane to Cheyenne to join an established vet practice. Heartbroken does not begin to describe the crushing weight of what I felt in the following months and even years.

I spun Aster's stool until we were knee to knee. 'More of an explanation. Now!'

'Max was the same orange shade as you… but… well, but he just did not have the golden outline,' she said meekly. 'I was younger back then. My skills weren't as honed, and…' She broke off and dipped her quivering chin.

'Finish what you were going to say,' I urged.

'You've always looked out for me and Lia. Never had a life of your own thanks to Mother. I didn't want you to be alone, and I thought Max's color was close enough.'

*Close enough.*

This was worse than a punch to the gut. It was a penetrating cleaver to the heart. All this time I'd thought Max had been my one true love and that against every part of fate in the universe, he'd walked away from me. This news should have made the ache in my bones lessen, but it didn't.

I pulled Aster's birthday gift wrapped in sparkly purple paper out of my messenger bag and shoved it across the counter toward her. 'I have to go.'

'Dani, wait!'

I couldn't listen to her for a minute more. The walls were closing in, and the air – there wasn't enough of it.

I raced past Bryce and headed for the door. Once I was outside, I bent over and pulled in as much oxygen as I could.

What was I supposed to do with this information?

For over seven years, I'd believed that the man who was supposed to be my one true love had chosen to walk away from me. That I was forever cursed to be alone. Now, this guy I barely knew, the one who kissed me like it was his sworn mission, was here to report on my town? My family? He out of all people was supposed to be 'The One'?

Another thought walloped me in the chest. Last night he knew who I was, and he didn't say a word. Didn't confess the real reason he was in Harvest Moon.

Now I was sure I was going to be sick.

I had to move. Shake off the feeling of ants crawling beneath my skin.

Tourists crowded the narrow sidewalks, darting into the outdoor gear and Western-wear shops that lined the main path through downtown. The scent of charred burgers and green chile cornbread floated out of the Black Cat Brewhouse. Next door, two children raced out of Charm's Candy Shoppe, each holding one of their signature caramel apples. Families carried bright yellow bags from Magic and Mischief, the T-shirt and souvenir shop. I tried not to wince at the logo – a wand with sparks flying out of the end.

I headed for the corner where the familiar white spire and neon lights marked Spirits and Spells Tavern. An older man to my left stumbled as his pit bull tugged on his leash, dragging him straight in my direction. Further down the street, a mini schnauzer let out a frenzied bark when I walked past.

A simple walk downtown could be chaotic for me when people were out and about with their animals during the final days of summer. The chatter around me rose as people questioned what had gotten into their animals.

I kept my head down, passing by Mara, the deputy mayor's daughter, who sat on a bench outside Ghoulishly Good ice cream. She let out a startled cry when her beagle yanked free from his leash.

'Come back, Banjo!' she cried.

The dog cantered toward me and flung his compact body into my arms. Sweet and slobbery kisses covered my cheeks.

'Hello, Banjo.' I laughed, despite my foul mood.

'Gosh, Dr McGuire, I don't know what's gotten into him.' Mara gave me an embarrassed smile. 'I haven't seen him run like that in a long time. He's almost thirteen, and my dad says age is slowing him down.'

I held out the dog to get a look at him. Nice wet snout. Clear eyes. I was happy that not a single shock raced through my body. Banjo had helped Darren, the deputy mayor, and his pre-teen daughter through some rough days over the last few years, and I was thrilled he was in such good shape.

'You obviously take great care of him.'

'Thanks. He's my best pal.'

'Keep up the good work! We'll see you two at his next checkup.'

She smiled, tugging Banjo back to the bench while I ducked inside the tavern.

Dark wood and low lighting made the space feel like a cave. A lingering scent of stale beer and day-old French fries coated the air. An old George Jones song warbled out of the ancient Wurlitzer in a back corner.

The town's ex-mayor, and local farmer, Randall Pelgrew, was in his regular spot at the bar. A half-empty mug of the local dark stout sat in front of him. His long-time friend George Spellner sat next to him nursing an iced tea.

Randall's thick gray brows bunched together as soon as he saw me. 'Oof. Who put a bee under your bonnet?'

'I've got a guess,' George said, tilting his pointed chin to the end of the bar where Mo stood.

Sensing a storm brewing, they quickly vacated their stools. As George walked past, he said in his deep gravel-laced voice, 'Got a pregnant cow that had a real hard time giving birth last year. Could you come out and take a look at her when you get a chance? I promise to corral the other cows in a different pen.'

The last time I was at his farm, a dozen of his cows trotted toward me. They were beautiful Jerseys with a dark fawn coloring. I moved around the corral, greeting each of them by the head, but the more I interacted with them, the tighter they circled me until I had to climb over the fence. George apologized profusely, but I waved him off knowing they meant me no harm.

He waited for my answer. Gave me that typical knowing look I got from most of the locals. I bit my tongue. There was no use in telling him I did not have magic, only great training, and perhaps a sense of calm that attracted animals. I'd learned long ago that my protests fell on deaf ears, though. People in town had been telling themselves stories about the McGuires for so long that no one cared about the truth anymore. There was also the fact that the mythical tales added cachet to our little town, which was always competing with other places like Salida and Leadville for precious tourist dollars.

'Yes, I'll stop by next week.'

'Thanks, Dani,' he said before heading out the door.

I pulled in a solid breath and walked to the end of the bar. Mo stood behind the long maple-hued counter having a friendly conversation with a man who, by the looks of it, had just purchased a ridiculously oversized cowboy hat from one of the local stores.

'Excuse me. I need to have a word with the owner.'

The man heard the steel in my voice and inched away from the bar.

Mo gave me that customer-friendly, all-teeth smile. 'Dani, can I get you a drink?'

'Let's not play games, Maureen. You know why I'm here.'

The tense set of my voice stopped more than one conversation in the room.

She tucked her chin. Good. Maybe she felt a little guilt. 'I have some work to do in the office. Care to join me?'

Without waiting for an answer, she walked in the direction of the area behind the bar and past a small square kitchen. Her low-heeled boots clacked across the old pine floor. Tight silver ringlets hung down the back of her faded black T-shirt.

When we reached the door to her small, cramped office, she waved a hand as if inviting me in.

'This is as far as I go.'

'Suit yourself. Probably better that you don't stay. It'll start all kinds of rumors, and you know how the locals love to gossip.'

It was hard not to roll my eyes. She was the reigning queen of spreading tales in Harvest Moon. They may as well give her a crown and a damn scepter, because word from her spread faster than any Wi-Fi signal around here.

'I'm tired of repeating myself, but I'll say it for like the fiftieth time. Stop telling any tourist who will listen that my sisters and I have magic. It's not true, and it screws with our lives.' She started to protest, but I held up a finger. 'And don't you ever send a stranger to Clo's house again.'

She hitched one boot over the other and leaned into the doorway, attempting to act casual, but she couldn't hide the uncomfortable tic in her cheek. 'I admit the thing with Clo was wrong. But in my defense, that reporter was freaking out over his dog and it was scaring my customers.'

'That's no excuse for what you did.'

She raised her hands in surrender. 'Fine, but I have to ask why you get more ornery than a black bear right after hibernation if what we all say is untrue?'

'Because those stories you spew make people act weird. They come into my clinic expecting me to recite some damn incantation before I treat their animals. Every time a new person joins Lia's SAR team, they stare as if her head's going to spin around before she predicts where they'll make their next search.'

'But Aster…'

I held up a hand to stop her. 'My little sister has synesthesia. There's no magic to it.'

'You can't deny her ability with matchmaking, Dani. Hell, most of the marriages that have happened around here in the last four years are thanks to her.'

'She has a kind and empathetic heart. Sure, seeing color helps, but she's also very good at reading people.'

Her mouth twitched with a smirk. 'Like you can read animals?'

'I'm not doing this with you,' I spat out. 'It's not my problem that you and a bunch of other people in town keep telling lies about my family. Peddling the word "magic" like it's some kind of commodity to sell burgers and beers. If you keep telling people nonsense, at some point they're going to expect proof. My sisters and I *are not* witches, supernatural beings or whatever else you feed the gullible tourists. Stop taking away what we have in these mountains.'

She crossed her arms over her chest. 'And what exactly am I taking away?'

'Our peace.'

Her gaze suspiciously darted around her office, and a sickening truth hit me.

'Did you have something to do with the reporter coming here?'

She headed back to the bar, ignoring my question.

'Are you freaking kidding me, Mo!'

She grabbed a glass from the drying rack under the bar and filled it with water from a nearby tap. Like she needed to buy time to figure out a story, she took a long sip.

'You know as well as I do that Harvest Moon is constantly vying for tourist dollars,' she finally said. 'If you and Aster want to keep your businesses going, it only makes sense to play into the lore. Get some good press out of it. A piece in a magazine like *Metropolitan Travel and Leisure* could be a game-changer around here.' She clucked her tongue. 'And that Bryce guy isn't too bad to look at either.' She leaned in too close. 'Word around here is that you helped save his dog. That's an excellent way to earn some goodwill from him.'

'Goodwill? I didn't know he was a journalist until ten minutes ago.'

'Oh.' She shrugged. 'Well, I'm sure you made a good impression.'

Calling him an idiot on the trail. Yelling at him about his dog being off leash. Kissing him like needing air was optional. I'm sure all of it made one hell of an impression.

'Stop the bullshit, Mo. You know what happened the last time a journalist came here.' The memory of it made me shiver. 'It was chaos.'

She gave a resigned sigh. 'All right, that time wasn't great, but this will be different.'

'He's not going to make your burnt-hockey-puck hamburgers edible. Or help you sell any more cardboard-tasting pizzas straight from the microwave.'

She had the gall to look indignant. 'My food… is passable.'

'We can keep going round and round, but maybe it'd be better if I sent Clo down to talk to you. That would be an even bigger spectacle than the show we're putting on right now.'

That steely façade of hers crumbled. Most of the town, except for maybe Judge Greene, was terrified of my five-foot-one grandmother. From the outside she may have looked as kind as one of the Golden Girls, but she had a sharp tongue that could shred you to pieces in mere seconds.

'Fine. I will stop playing it up for business.' She pointed a finger at me. 'That doesn't mean I can stop others from talking about your family. Your line is deeply embedded into this town, and so is its rather interesting history. My not talking about you and your sisters won't make the stories go away.'

'It's a start.'

I began to walk away until she called out, 'My Betsy is moving slower these days. Okay if I bring her by the clinic and have her checked out? I'm worried about arthritis.'

Feral cats had become a town issue over the last few years. One of their favorite spots to roam was in the alley behind the tavern. Mo had taken to one ginger in particular, and now Betsy was her constant companion in the small clapboard house she owned near the edge of town.

She gave me a hopeful look, because she knew I could not turn down an animal in need.

'Call Jessa and set up an appointment.'

Her tight shoulders gave an inch. Dealing with my sweet receptionist was easier than getting the stink-eye from me. 'Thanks, Dani.'

'Keep your word this time, Mo.'

I moved out from behind the bar. A few locals lined the counter waiting for top-offs on their beers. More than a few gave me that curious gaze I hated.

I'd never seriously considered leaving Harvest Moon. It was my home. But on days like this, when the shroud of gossip and the burden of stories spun about my family were almost too much, I wondered what it'd be like to take off and never look back. Have a life where no one had any preconceived notions about me. Where I could just be a normal person, run my practice and have what I'd demanded of Mo.

Peace.

Only a few steps outside the tavern, I came to a stumbling stop. Bryce leaned against the crumbling white paint on the building. His toned arms hung loosely at his sides. Red-hued stubble covered his chin.

*Persimmon with a gold outline*, Aster had said. I narrowed my gaze like I thought I could envision it. Instead, all I saw was the pinch at the corners of his crystal-blue eyes. Eyes that screamed he was a damn liar.

# Chapter Seven

## *Weird and Uncomfortable*

'How did you know I was here?' The edge to my voice was sharper than a blade.

'I didn't at first. Came by to say thanks to Mo for telling me where your grandmother lived so I could get Indy to you last night.'

My blood pressure skyrocketed again. 'You can go in and talk to her now, because I'm done in every sense of the word.'

He tugged his hat down. Blew out a rough breath. 'I know this is wild for me to ask, and, of course, you don't have to answer, but are you all right?'

*Was I all right?*

'Are you screwing with me right now?' My roar made him take a step back. 'Was this a game to you? Figure out a way to intercept me at the trail? Play nice. Maybe even make your dog sick, all in the hopes you might get some information for your story?'

His eyes went wide. 'Not telling you who I was at the clinic was a dick move, but purposely making my dog sick? Not even you believe I'd be that craven.'

'Don't act like you know me,' I flung back.

'I swear on the trail I had no idea who you were, Dani.'

'It's Dr McGuire.' It was a petty comeback, but I wasn't feeling kind at the moment.

'I swear to you that it wasn't until I asked Mo for help with a local vet that she gave me a name and an address.' He scrubbed a hand behind his neck. 'If you recall, you didn't introduce yourself on the trail. Not until you walked out of your grandmother's house did I realize who you were. At that point, I kept my mouth shut because I was desperate for you to help my dog.'

'And after? When you knew he'd recover, but you still kept quiet. Kissed me,' I said with an indignant huff. 'What kind of man does that?'

He let out a heavy breath. 'It's why I pulled away from our kiss. It wasn't fair to you. I should have come clean as soon as I knew Indy was out of danger.'

'What stopped you?'

'The minute I told you why I was in Harvest Moon, the easy rapport between us would've disappeared. I meant what I said at the clinic. You're very good at what you do. I wanted to be in that space with you without it getting weird and uncomfortable.'

'Well, guess what? It's worse than weird and uncomfortable now.'

'Yeah, I know that, especially after you shoved me out of the clinic this morning.'

The streets filled up around us with tourists darting in and out of the shops. More animals tugged their owners in my direction, and panic filled my chest. The last thing I wanted Bryce to see was the way the dogs in this town reacted to me. He'd already gotten too much of that with Indy.

I took off in the direction of the pharmacy, and like a bad rash, Bryce was hard to get rid of.

'You seem like a quiet, reserved sort of person, but you were giving Mo an earful in there.'

Now he was eavesdropping?

I came to an abrupt halt, and he had to put out his hands so he wouldn't crash into me. His warm fingers skimmed over my shoulders and, damn, did his grip make the blood hum in my veins. Flashes of the way he cupped my head, slid his lips over my mouth, made heat rise on my cheeks.

'Not that it's any of your business.' I forced myself to take a step away. 'But I was ordering her to stop telling people like *you* that my sisters and I have magic. It's all a bunch of bullshit to make tourists visit the town.'

'Magic? Yeah, I don't believe that, but those kinds of stories start somewhere. I'd be interested to know their origins.'

I did not want to have this conversation with him, but maybe if I gave him a small portion of the truth, it'd satisfy him enough to let the whole thing go.

'My grandmother's side of the family settled in Harvest Moon right when it was incorporated in the late 1800s. There was a big cache of silver here, and it drew people to the town. Legends whispered over the years said my ancestor Sylvia Perkins had a knack for finding pockets of silver in the mountains. That made her family rich. Because she and her husband were good prospectors, stories were spun about her' – I made air quotes – '"gifts" for finding the motherlode. Somehow over the decades those *gifts* became magic. It didn't help that my grandfather Beau had a way with the mountains too, being able to turn the roughest terrain into farming land, and that my grandmother Clo could grow anything in the soil.' I gave a sad sigh. 'You give a spark of a story like that some oxygen, and it blazes into a wildfire.'

'Clo? Was that the older woman I met last night?'

'Yes, her daughter, my mother, Belladonna, has quite the reputation around here. My sisters and I have spent years battling all this magic nonsense and it's exhausting.'

He was about to ask me another question when Julius, a seven-year-old Great Dane, buzzed toward me, tugging along his owner, Judge Greene.

'Hello, Dani,' the judge said in a no-nonsense voice before turning his attention to Bryce. 'Who's your friend?'

'He's *not* my friend.'

Bryce flinched again and the judge took a protective step toward me.

'This is Bryce O'Dell,' I finally said. 'He's Richard Morrison's nephew.'

'Oh.' The judge pulled the cream Stetson off his head and placed it over his heart. 'Your uncle was a good man. Played more than one game of poker with him. Sorry for your loss.'

'Thank you, sir.'

He scanned Bryce for a minute, rubbing at his trimmed white beard. 'You taking over his cabin on the bluff?'

'Thinking about it.' Bryce's steady gaze flicked in my direction. 'This place is starting to grow on me.'

Julius stepped in and nuzzled my leg. No shock or pain. Good. I loved this big oaf of a dog. I patted his massive head, and Bryce shot me a smile. Did he think he was off the hook? Because he wasn't.

The judge gave me a questioning look until a few more dogs began to race in my direction, and Julius tugged on his leash, eager to greet them. The dogs did a weird kind of circle dance around me, and I held my breath as Bryce's gaze morphed into confusion.

The judge cleared his throat, urging Julius back to his side. 'Be sure to familiarize yourself with the laws around here, son. Don't want to see you in my courtroom.'

'Uh, yes. Of course, sir.'

The judge pulled Julius away, but the dogs stayed in a tight formation around me, happily panting and waiting for head pats. Bryce crossed his arms over his chest, amusement tilting up the corners of his lips.

Refusing to give him any kind of reaction, I spun around and broke away from the pack. With long determined strides, I headed toward the pharmacy again, praying the dogs would not follow. This had turned into a miserable day, and all I wanted was to go back to the clinic and forget about the last few hours.

Bryce caught up to me but stayed quiet. We shouldered past more tourists carrying bags from the Spell Book Spice Shop and Abracadabra Antiques.

'The dogs around here like you. That happen a lot? Them coming to greet you like that?'

'I'm the local vet. They know me,' I said with a casual shrug.

I picked up my pace, not wanting to see that look of curiosity on his face for a second more.

'Answer one question for me and I'll leave you alone,' he said, keeping up with me. 'You barely touched Indy yesterday on the trail, and still you knew he was sick. How?'

His curious stare, the tilt to his head, was nothing new for me. Since I'd returned to town, more than a few people had questioned how I could diagnose their animals so quickly.

'I noticed his pupils were larger. That his balance was slightly off. It's what vets do. Assess animals. Notice symptoms.'

My car was only a few steps away. I had to get there and stop this interrogation before he made me so mad I said something dumb.

'And the way you hit the ground on the trail? You looked out of it. That didn't have anything to do with his diagnosis? Why you told me he should see a vet?'

I pulled in a full breath while internally cursing my inability to hide my instincts or my physical reaction.

'It'd been a long day at my clinic. I was tired. There's no mystery to it.'

'As a journalist, I have to admit the stories Mo spins are interesting.'

'Let me guess. She told you my mother suspiciously wound up pregnant three times. No fathers in sight. That she floated in the lake in front of my grandmother's house surrounded by flowers, did some incantations, and poof, her babies were gifted magic.'

He scrubbed at his chin. 'Yeah, it was something like that.'

I huffed out a bitter laugh. 'Well, if you believe that, I'll sell you some magic beans that'll grow into a giant green stalk. Take you to a magical place with a golden singing harp.'

His full lips quirked up into a wide smile. 'I know better than anyone you need a good lead if you're going to sell a story. What Mo is spinning does feel pretty contrived…'

'But…'

He took two steps closer. That scent of ink and cedar heavy in the air.

'None of what she told me matters. The truth is that I'm here to do a puff piece. Take some gorgeous shots of the scenery. Sell the small-town charm.'

'If that's the truth, the people here will be more than happy to talk to you.'

'Everyone but you, I take it.'

'Oh, you *do not* want to talk to me.' I crossed the street to get to my truck and barely had the door open, when he jogged after me.

'Wait. What about the…?' His heavy gaze darted to my lips.

'Don't worry about the kiss, Bryce,' I said, that awful ache crowding my chest again. 'It was nothing. An emotional reaction to what happened to Indy.'

'I disagree.' He stepped closer as I slid behind the wheel. 'I may have been wrong about not telling you who I was, but you know as well as I do that our kiss was…' He gave me a rueful smile like he was replaying it in his head.

'A mistake,' I said emphatically.

He sighed. 'What about the other thing?'

'For a serious writer, you sure talk in circles.'

'Why did you take off from the coffee shop like your ass was on fire?'

Ice shot through my veins at the reminder of what Aster had revealed. That Max was not my soulmate. That this stranger in front of me with hair that was the shade of the valley at dusk, and eyes so brilliantly blue it was hard not to stare, was supposed to be my perfect match.

No. Aster had been wrong once. She was wrong this time too.

'It was just a small sisterly disagreement.'

His mouth thinned like he didn't buy my answer.

'Make sure Indy stays hydrated. Eats small bits of food over the day.' I turned on the engine, hoping he'd get the hint.

'I noticed the signs around town about your vaccination clinic tomorrow. When is it over?'

'Three o'clock.'

'If Indy is up for it, I was considering taking one of those beginner trails you mentioned yesterday. I'll be there at four. I think Indy would like to see Flora.' His gaze locked with mine. 'It's been a long time since I've connected with someone the way I did with you last night. Don't shut me out, Dani. We can put rules in place about my job. What is on and off the record.'

A flicker of vulnerability flashed across his eyes, and for a moment I let myself believe it was real, until I remembered that his job was to get close. Squeeze as much information out of me as possible so he could get his story.

'It's clear where we stand now, and I can tell you for a fact that neither I, nor my sisters, will be speaking to you for your article.'

He gave a nod like he was expecting that answer. 'Figured as much but let me counter with this. Everyone in this town is eager to speak with me. Would you rather I get stories about your family second-hand from a person like Mo, or get the real story from you?'

'What I'd rather is that you leave town and never come back.'

'There are several reasons why that can't happen,' he said with a heavy sigh.

Yeah, this was going to be way more than a 'puff' piece.

'Dani, I'm going to be here a while. The article is for the summer issue so it won't be due until the end of December.'

I gripped the steering wheel. Heaved in a full breath at the thought of having to avoid him for several months.

'Please give me a chance. Google me. Read my work. You'll see that I'm fair.' He trained that deep blue gaze on me. 'Meet me tomorrow. You can ask me any question about my writing. How I'm planning to approach the article.' His pleading look was meant to soften me up, but I wasn't buying it.

All that time in the clinic, he'd had every opportunity to confess who he was. To tell me the real reason he was in town, but he'd stayed quiet. Then there was that soul-melting kiss, which I thought was spontaneous, born out of a complicated mixture of fear and relief, but now it felt contrived. Another way to get me to let my guard down. The deceit and manipulation reminded me too much of Belladonna, and I refused to have one more person like her in my life.

'Goodbye, Bryce.'

I shooed him away before yanking the door shut. His determined look warned he wasn't giving up, but neither was I.

I'd spent a lifetime protecting my sisters from people who stared. Spoke in whispers about us. Bryce was just one more person to add to that list.

# Chapter Eight

## Tender Heart

As usual, Normie Jewel was at my door five minutes before the vaccination clinic was due to begin. His pitch-black cocker spaniel, Odie, chased his tail in a circle, and Normie struggled to hold tightly to his leash.

An electric zing slid over my skin as Odie clipped me with his back end.

'What can I do for you this morning, Normie?'

He gave me that impish look like *you tell me*. 'Need you to give Odie the once-over. He's been scratching everywhere.'

This was Normie's way of getting out of making an appointment or, you know, actually paying. He'd show up at the door only minutes before a clinic, claim I was working anyway, and beg that I take a few minutes to check out Odie. I'd let it go on for a while until Jessamine, my receptionist, told me that if I kept it up, every old timer with an aging dog would show up expecting treatment for free.

Bree, my vet tech, stepped out of an exam room with her arms full of puppy pads and boxes of sterile gloves. When she caught sight of Normie, she gave me a withering look, shook her head, her long dark-brown ponytail swinging like a pendulum behind her. She and Jessa were definitely in agreement about the situation.

I should have turned Normie away. Ordered him to make an appointment for another day, but poor Odie kept scratching his right ear.

'Bring him into Exam Room Two.'

When we walked past Bree, she quietly griped about my tender heart.

It was true. I hated to see an animal in pain.

The thought sent me back to my argument with Mo yesterday. I could explain it over and over until all the air was gone from my lungs, and still no one in Harvest Moon would get it through their thick skulls that what I had was *not* magic. It was exactly what Bree was mumbling about. A tender heart. A certain intuition and connection to animals. A quick eye for spotting and sensing symptoms. It was part skill, but also years of education and training.

Normie settled Odie on the steel table, and I spent the next twenty minutes cleaning out a month's worth of infected, crusty yellowish-brown gunk from the dog's ears.

Bree paced outside the exam room. Flora bounced happily beside her like it was some sort of game. More than once, Bree gave Normie less than kind looks as the waiting area filled up for the clinic. When I was done, I set Odie down and let Normie clip on his leash.

'I have your info in the system, Normie. You'll be getting a bill for today.'

He started to sputter on about the special clinic, how we were open anyways, until Jessa appeared and escorted him to the front desk.

For the next five hours, Bree assisted me as I gave shots for everything from kennel cough to parvo, distemper and feline calicivirus. We chatted with both locals and people who came from as far away as Silverton. Because most of the animals were young, there wasn't much of a chance for that zap of dizziness to crawl up my spine.

When our final puppy, a French bulldog, aptly named Pierre, was carried off by his owner, I collapsed into the small gray loveseat next to the front desk. Jessa rushed past me and locked the door. Flora melted onto her favorite fluffy dog bed in the corner of the waiting area. Being an emotional support dog was rough work too.

'What was our count today?' I said through an exhausted yawn.

'Thirty-nine dogs and twenty-three cats,' Bree answered, taking the seat beside me. 'And before you ask, we are up ten animals from last month. That email to shelters across the counties, advertising the clinic, is working,' she said, way too pleased with herself, considering the email was her suggestion.

'Nice work. What about the other thing?' I prompted, knowing she and Jessa would never tell me if I didn't ask. They both gave me what looked like an orchestrated shrug.

'Ladies,' I pushed.

'Fine,' Bree grumbled. 'That couple from Silverton, and the older woman from Longmont, might have been whispering about looking for pentagrams and spell books on the shelves in the waiting area.'

I groaned and dropped my head in my hands.

'Everyone else was nice and normal,' Jessa offered way too brightly.

'See, not everyone thinks you're going to hex them. Although maybe you should consider that option with

Normie.' Bree gave me a grin that fell somewhere between amused and serious.

Jessa tucked a loose blond hair behind her ear and glanced at Bree. If I didn't know them so well, I would have missed the slight hint of tension.

'And what else? May as well spill it all.'

'I noticed some supplies were moved around, and that blanket you like to use after anesthesia was on the floor in Exam Room One,' Bree said.

'I was going to tell you about that.'

Bree set her chin, waiting for an explanation.

I glanced at the reception desk, remembering my body pressed against it. Bryce's mouth hot against my neck. A zip of heat raced through me. Crap. I hoped that didn't happen every time I looked at the damn desk.

Bree cleared her throat. Crossed her arms over her chest. She got all kinds of squirrely when I brought in emergency cases on my own without any kind of backup. Thanks to town gossip, she and Jessa knew about my special touch with animals. How people often reacted to me, which made them overly protective.

'On the Elderberry Ridge trail two days ago I met a guy.'

A pleased smile bloomed across Jessa's lips.

'No, not like that.'

Well, okay, he was hot. Clear blue eyes that reminded me of the lake in the peak of summer. Toned arms that were more than a little distracting. He was a good kisser, too. Had an instinctual way of putting his hands in all the right places. Too bad he was also a damn liar.

'His dog was off leash.'

Bree cursed under her breath. More than a few times, we'd had to stitch up dogs who'd gotten an angry slash from a bear, because they were roaming the woods without supervision.

'The dog sat on my feet, and I knew something was wrong. The owner came barreling out of the woods a little while later, and I told him to keep an eye on his dog, that he could be ill, which, of course, he took as all kinds of weird.'

'That doesn't explain the emergency,' Bree pressed.

'The dog grew sicker. The man, Bryce, he found out I was at Clo's and brought the dog to me there. I checked him over. He was in bad shape, so I told the owner to follow me here.'

Jessa shifted in her chair, her eyes clouding with worry. 'How did he know about Clo's? Better yet, how did he know you'd be there?'

'Fucking Mo,' Bree spat out.

I wasn't the only one who wasn't thrilled with Mo's need to push the magical lore around town.

'What was wrong with the dog?' Jessa asked.

'Marijuana poisoning.'

'He let his dog ingest that shit? What an idiot,' Bree said.

'It wasn't his fault. The dog must have found it somewhere on the trail. You know how the high school kids love to hike up to the ridge at night and get high.'

Jessa's lower lip quivered. 'Is the dog okay?'

This was why I'd hired her the second she came in to interview two years ago. She was barely out of high school then, but she was organized, good with the owners and had an even gentler heart than me, which was evident by the four dogs and three rescue cats that lived with her in the small house she shared on the outskirts of town with her boyfriend, Stewey.

'Indy got activated charcoal and a lot of IV fluids. I watched him for several hours into the night. He was doing better yesterday morning, and I released him to Bryce.'

Bree arched a dark-brown brow. 'I've worked for you for nearly three years, Dani. You've never let an owner stay here during an emergency. You always say it's a firm and fast rule that owners distract their animals. That they need to be apart to rest.'

It was my rote reply anytime an owner begged to stay. But there was something in the way Bryce's voice trembled, how he looked like he was losing his best friend, that made me let him hang around and help. It was a decision I was still regretting.

'Indy,' Jessa blurted out. 'I like that name.'

'He's a good dog. Bryce told me yesterday afternoon that he's recovering nicely.'

'Wait, you saw this Bryce guy twice in one day?' Jessa asked.

'Yeah, he came into Drip! Drip! Hooray! when I was there with Aster and Lia.'

'It didn't take him long to find the best coffee spot in town.' A hint of respect crept into Bree's voice.

'It's my fault I didn't pick up the blankets. Didn't mean to worry you, Bree.'

'Just glad it wasn't some kind of break-in,' she said.

'In Harvest Moon? Hardly.' I jumped up from the chair, stretching out my arms and legs. If I was quick, I could get in a hike before sunset.

'You sure you don't need anything else?' Bree asked, giving a quick glance at Jessa and then at the door.

'Is there something going on tonight I should know about?'

Jessa tucked her chin, and Bree shifted on her heels. 'Uh, we had plans to see a concert in Vail.'

'Why didn't you say anything? Get out of here. I can clean up what's left.'

'Are you sure?' Jessa asked softly.

'It'll take at least an hour to get there. Go. I've got this.'

Jessa dashed behind the desk and grabbed a mound of papers and envelopes. 'Here's the mail, and a few lab reports that came in late yesterday.'

I grabbed the stack from her and cocked my head to the door. 'Out, both of you. Have fun and get some rest before Monday. Poco is on the books to be neutered.'

'About time,' Bree muttered.

Poco was a local stray who'd been adopted by Mrs Chevan a year ago. She was a sweet older woman who had no idea that Poco had gotten at least five dogs in town pregnant over the last eighteen months. It wasn't until Ernest Potter showed up at her door, red in the face and holding an armful of puppies from his standard poodle, that she realized it was time for Poco's wild, and promiscuous, days to end.

'Have a good night,' they said, grabbing their backpacks and purses and heading out the door.

I threw the deadbolt and headed back to my office. I sank into the chair behind my desk and gave a cursory glance at the lab reports that held nothing concerning. A low ding sounded on my laptop, alerting me to a new email.

The sender's name sent a chill down my back. I hadn't seen or heard from Belladonna in two years. My finger hovered over the line to open it. What did she have to say after all this time? My guess: a request for money. It was usually the only reason she popped her head out of the dark hole she'd been hiding in.

The alarm buzzed on my phone, reminding me of the time. Not wanting to think about Belladonna for another minute, I shut down the computer and rushed toward the stairs at the back of the clinic.

Flora panted happily beside me as we climbed the stairs to my apartment. When I bought the building, I had my contractor gut the entire floor, and build out two bedrooms, two bathrooms, a nice galley kitchen with a breakfast bar, and a seating area that could accommodate a tiny bistro table, a large couch and a coffee table.

'You ready to stretch those legs, girl?' She gave a sweet bark and followed me into my room. My outfit from last night was still strewn across the floor, and it forced me to think about Bryce. I gathered up the clothes and hated how the scent of him on the material filled all my senses. No matter how good he looked, or smelled, he was off limits.

As I dumped the clothes into the laundry basket, I pushed away Aster's prediction about him. Years ago I'd accepted that I'd spend my life alone, and Bryce showing up, no matter what color Ast saw in him, or what he could do with that spectacular mouth, was not going to change that.

# Chapter Nine

## *Outside My Comfort Zone*

The email from Belladonna weighed on my mind as I walked to the trailhead. Why was she reaching out now of all times, especially when things felt like they were going sideways here?

If I'd believed in bad omens, I'd be searching the trail for a four-leaf clover, because I could use any kind of luck right now. Instead, I checked my watch. Twenty minutes until sunset. I'd have to hustle, but I could get to Wildwood Point just in time.

Flora tugged on her leash, and I let her guide me up the steep, rocky path. The sun's rays stretched out across the sky. A wide embrace of a subtle golden yellow that melted into a deep orange. I needed this. The peace and quiet. The chance to get out of my head for a little while.

A cool breeze caressed my cheeks while we worked our way up the mountain. Flora stayed by my side as I headed off the main trail to an alternate path I'd learned about from Lia. It was a tougher hike with a series of switchbacks that the SAR team used for training. I began to pant as I tackled the steep, narrow inclines that required you to use your balance.

For ten minutes I went all out, moving without stopping until the blood raced in my veins, and the pine-scented air filled my lungs. I dug my boots into the dirt, concentrating on the muscles contracting in my legs.

Bunnies scampered out of low-lying bushes. A family of robins inched to the edge of a branch on a nearby aspen. The crackle of dry brush deeper in the forest alerted me to a family of deer peeking out of a dense copse of trees.

The appearance of animals usually brought a calming stillness, but today all that raced through my body was fear and anger, and a lingering worry that Clo would know about the email from Belladonna, and guilt me into responding.

The more I stretched my legs, ascended higher up the trail, the more I had to focus on my breathing, sucking in more oxygen as I climbed.

It was just a few more yards to the top of the ridge. It was my secret spot. A place to hide away from my worries – like Lia's refusal to share what had been bothering her these last months. How Aster wrapped herself up in other people's relationships so she could avoid her own lack of a love life. And, of course, Bryce's damn article.

Since I was old enough to form memories, I had the drive to protect my sisters. As the oldest, I didn't have any other choice. Belladonna flitted in and out of our lives like a destructive summer storm. Showing up unexpectedly, flipping over everything in sight, and then disappearing just as quickly. Sure, Clo housed and fed us, but my sisters needed comfort, reassurance, and they looked to me for that steadiness. And if anyone taunted or threatened them? A fighter buried deep in my soul rose out of the ashes. She was less Xena: Warrior Princess and more of a velociraptor, keen on using her razor-sharp talons to destroy anything that might threaten her family.

Belladonna's email flickered through my mind again. The last time she was home, she'd promised she'd stay in Harvest Moon. Even offered to help Aster in her shop. Then, like she always did, she disappeared one rainy night without a word. Aster pretended she wasn't hurt, but it was clear by the wobble of her lower lip every time I saw her for the next few days that Belladonna had, once again, broken her heart.

Flora's short bark wrenched me out of the memory. She darted forward and dragged me up the narrow dirt path. Along its edges, trees bent into a natural arch, shadowing the path from the fading afternoon sun.

'Slow down, girl. We'll get there soon.'

She continued to strain against the leash. It only took a few more steps to understand her agitation. Bryce stood against a flat wall of rock that overlooked the valley. Indy panted at his feet.

'Hey! Wasn't expecting to see you here.' He scrubbed a hand over his head; a slight sheen of sweat coated his toned forearms. A bright blue athletic shirt made his hair look like rich copper. The smile that spread across his lips unlocked something wild and angry in my chest.

'What the hell are you doing here with Indy?' I bent down and petted the dog's head, trying to sense any lingering signs of poisoning.

'He was bouncing off the walls in the cabin. Today he drank several bowls of water and ate a good meal. I know you don't think much of me, but I do care about my dog. I'd never put him at risk.'

The indignation in his voice made me pause. Made me wonder how much of my frustration over my own family, my own problems, made him an easy target for my anger.

'Fine but keep an eye on him just in case.'

'You know I will.'

I stepped to the edge of the ridge and pulled in a lungful of air. 'How did you get up here? This trail… it's not for tourists.'

He let out a short, barking laugh. 'I'm a tourist now?'

'You're not exactly a local.'

'You'd be surprised what people share when you put them at ease.'

Yeah, he was full of it. I'm sure all he had to do was flash that confident smile, make that gentle tilt of his head like he was really listening, and the locals would spill their guts – which was my fear.

What would it take for someone to feed him a story about Lia's unique connection to the land? Or Aster's ability to predict a person's perfect love match, all just to convince him there was some kind of magic here?

Those aching knots in my shoulders returned, and I focused on the vast emerald forest spread out before me.

He took a few steps until he was beside me. 'I can go. You may not believe this, but the last thing I want to do is make you uncomfortable.'

He kicked at a loose rock near his feet. Chuckled as my gaze narrowed on those stupid expensive boots. 'They're starting to break in.' He patted at the pockets of his brown cargo shorts. 'Brought these just in case.' He held out the mound of Band-Aids I'd handed him the other day. 'I promise I'm learning, Dani.'

He was too damn charming. And the way he said my name so softly, like it was something precious, was almost indecent. He took another step forward, and I swore for no more than a flicker I saw that orange glow.

I shook away the image. No more. I was done getting caught up in the 'true love' fantasy. The belief that there was one person on the planet who was truly meant for me. It was the one thing Belladonna and I agreed on – love was nothing but a rush of chemicals in our brain. An entertainment industry ploy to convince us that everyone got a happily-ever-after. It's what made people buy books. Watch endless romantic movies.

'Who told you about this trail?'

'I was at the tavern—'

'Mo needs to stop talking. This path is supposed to be off limits to everyone except search and rescue.'

'Yet, the last time I looked, you're not a first responder.'

'But my sister Lia is.'

'She's quite the personality. If there'd been a sharp knife near her at the coffee shop, I think she would have hurled it in my direction.'

'Lia would never be that overt. She's more of a poison-you-in-silence kind of woman.'

A warm throaty chuckle spilled from his lips. 'Poisoning aside, I'm glad you're here. It gives me more time to grovel.'

'There's not enough groveling in the world that'll make me forget how you conveniently hid who you were.'

He tucked his muscled arms across his chest and arched a single brow that on most men might look ridiculous, but on him was too damn sexy. 'Not so sure about that. Groveling is sort of my specialty.'

'Oh, please, do tell.'

'I suck at dating. My job has always been the number one focus in my life,' he admitted. 'I can start something, but it always ends in flames because I'm traveling, and I'm terrible at phone calls and texts. If I could do my job without my phone, I'd chuck it straight into the forest right now.'

At least there was one thing we could agree on. Back when I started the clinic, Aster convinced me I needed to start a social media account. Post pictures of the cute dogs and other animals I treated to drum up business. But once word started to spread about me, weird comments about magic began to pop up. I threatened to delete the account until Bree agreed to take over posting, keeping me from getting anxious anytime I saw a new comment.

'Why write an article about Harvest Moon? You usually do more serious pieces, like ferreting out corruption in small governments, or calling out politicians who are cagey about where they get their election donations.'

A slow grin spread across his face. 'You've been reading up on me, huh?'

'It's more like "keep your enemies closer" and all that.'

'Enemies.' He inched closer. 'Is that what we are?'

'Well, no, I mean, yes,' I stuttered. 'For now, I reserve judgement on exactly what we are.'

His gaze never moved from my face, wandering the lines of my nose, over my cheeks, halting at my mouth. 'That's fair,' he said on a ragged breath. 'I promise you I'll only write the truth about what I find here.'

His words were like jumping into an icy lake. I couldn't flirt with him. He was here to write some idiotic piece about the town, and my job was to protect my sisters. To knock down whatever ridiculous tales the locals spun to get people to spend precious dollars on oversized cowboy hats, and T-shirts that said mind-numbing things like *There's always magic to be found in Harvest Moon.*

Sensing my unease, Flora tugged on her leash, pulling me toward the rest of the trail.

Indy started to turn in circles, yanking Bryce sideways.

'See, look, I did listen to you. A leash.' He bent down to nuzzle Indy's head, a silver glimmer swaying below his neck. 'And tags.'

'That's good,' I mumbled as Flora tugged again. 'I should go. I want to finish my hike before it gets too dark.'

'Can I join you if I promise to stay quiet? Not ask any questions?'

'Do you have that kind of restraint?'

He set his chin. 'Absolutely.'

I should have said no. Being alone with him was a mistake, but before I could make up an excuse to leave, Flora leaped toward the winding trail leading deeper into the woods.

We walked side by side, the dogs happily trotting along. Another breath of soft wind twisted through the trees, cooling off my warm skin. That scent of juniper Clo loved did a small dance around my head, filling my nose.

Bryce pulled in a full, cleansing breath, like he was smelling air for the first time. 'I can't believe I fought coming here.'

'Fought it? Why?'

'Having to deal with my uncle's house, the land, it's outside my comfort zone. I thought it'd be best to hand the job over to a law firm and let them handle the details.'

'What made you change your mind?'

His full lips pinched together. I knew that look. It was the same face Lia made when you were bordering on an uncomfortable topic.

'I needed a break.' Another flash of vulnerability, maybe regret, streaked across his face. 'Plus,' he said, changing his tone to be breezier, 'I wanted to let Indy run around a bit. He doesn't have many places to roam in Studio City. Out here he can go wild.' He quickly followed it with 'On a leash, of course.'

'You *are* learning.' The rise of the path grew steeper as we neared the top of the ridge. 'Do you like living in Los Angeles?'

'It has its perks. There's always live music going on at the clubs in West Hollywood. Farmers' markets on the weekends at the Rose Bowl. The beach is only a short drive away if there's little traffic. Which there hardly ever is, because driving in LA is like trying to cross a crowded parking lot. Don't get me started about the 5 South headed toward Orange County on a Friday afternoon.'

I had no idea what he was talking about, but I enjoyed the way his voice went lighter. How his eyes crinkled at the edges as he told me about his life.

'I've never wanted to live in a big city. My kind of traffic is when the two-lane road leading out of town stops because Randall Pelgrew is steering his cows to a new pasture.'

'Life is slower around here, that's for sure, but I do miss my mom. She only lives ten minutes from me.'

'And your dad?' I wasn't the nosy type, but that urgent pull toward him made me greedy for more details about his life.

'Never had one. I mean… well, I had one, obviously, but when my mom told him she was pregnant, he took off.'

'Sorry,' I said, tugging on Flora's leash when she got too far ahead. 'I know what it's like growing up without a dad.'

'But at least you have family. Sisters. I'm an only child.'

'Why does that not surprise me?'

He blinked for a second, his firm shoulders giving a little. 'Do I give off that vibe?'

'Determined. Ambitious. Self-sufficient. Doesn't shy away from difficult situations. Aren't those typical traits for an only child?'

'Careful. That almost sounded like a compliment.'

He gave me that quick flick of a grin. It wasn't so much arrogant as confident. Like he was comfortable in his own skin, knew what he wanted out of life, and I hated that it made the blood spark in my veins.

We continued to climb, and I loved the pull in my muscles. The rapid rise and fall of my breaths. How up this high everything looked cleaner. Shinier. Full of possibilities.

The afternoon sun was turning into its regular shade of orange creamsicle as it started its slow descent toward the horizon. In silence, we ascended the trail until we reached Wildwood Point. My favorite place in all of Harvest Moon.

Bryce stopped short and whispered a throaty 'Oh shit.'

A flourish of deep green trees furled out for miles. The clouds overhead resembled gooey marshmallows stretched out across the sky.

'This sure as shit beats the LA smog.'

He paced along the edge of the point, the rocky ground beginning to give way under his feet. I snaked my hand around his waist, dragging him back until we stood against another sheer wall of rock. The heat of him pulsed beneath my fingertips, and a calm settled over me. It wasn't so much peace, but a deep aching sense that he was a safe space. That for some reason he was meant to be a main character in my story, which made absolutely no sense considering I'd only been able to think of him as a villain now.

'Look at you taking care of me. Worried about my safety.' He playfully brushed a loose hair back from my cheek.

I quickly let go of him and inched away. 'As much as you annoy me, I don't feel like calling my sister and her team in for a rescue. And the cell signal out here is spotty at best.'

His eyes continued to trace the lines of my face. It wasn't one of those hungry stares from the clinic, but more of a soft caress. Like he wanted to study every freckle and line.

I was not kissing this man again, even though every inch of me screamed to reach out and stretch my hands down the length of his corded arms. Tug his hips forward so I could feel the heat of him.

Needing to do something with my hands, I pulled the collapsible bowl from my backpack and filled it with the extra water I'd brought along. Like they'd always been around each other, Indy and Flora took turns lapping up a drink.

Bryce turned to face the view. Put his hands on top of his head, his shirt rising up to reveal a swath of muscles rippling across his back. I pictured what it would feel like to slide my hands over his skin. How he'd taste if I pressed my mouth against the crease between his shoulder and neck, the subtle hint of salt lingering on my tongue.

I tugged on my ponytail, forcing myself back to reality. This was what happened when it'd been too long since you'd had sex. You started fantasizing about touching a stranger, who you weren't even sure you liked, much less trusted.

'A guy could get used to this. Maybe I'll just stay here and become a hermit.'

I forced my gaze away from him, leaning down to stroke Flora's head. 'But you just listed off all the things you like about LA.'

A twitch in his cheek said I'd hit a nerve. 'It's all right.'

He walked a few feet forward, making sure to stay away from the edge. 'I can see why my uncle loved it here. There's a sort of peace to it all.'

'This place is good for reflection. I come up here when I'm struggling with a problem, or when I need to clear my mind.'

'Does it help?' he asked with a sad dip in his voice.

I hesitated before answering. This spot was where I came to hide from Belladonna whenever she'd suddenly appear. To me, she was a wraith. Always bringing darkness to every place she went. She swirled into a room with rainbow-hued skirts and silky-thin blouses and charmed every male, no matter their age. Her hair was always dyed a deep midnight black and set in tight curls that hung all the way down her back. A pair of worn-in, brown Lucchese boots covered her feet whether it was nine or ninety degrees outside. She was colorful. Vibrant. Always showing up with gifts from the last city she visited. She thought she was a joy in our lives, when in truth she was nothing but a bad tornado crushing everything in its path.

Maybe if I ignored her email, like I did her, it'd eventually disappear too.

'I know I promised not to ask any questions,' he said, interrupting my thoughts. 'But I know a way I can prove to you that what I want to report will be honest.'

'I'm listening.'

'Help me with my research. Show me around town. Introduce me to people who will tell me the real story about Harvest Moon.'

What he was offering was a chance to have a front-row seat to what he'd be writing. What he'd be researching. A chance to protect my sisters and Clo if needed.

The wind picked up, making the fallen leaves dance around us in a circle. A crack of brush from skittering rabbits, the call and response in the trees from the robins, always happened when I climbed this trail. I was used to the animals tracking me, but I hoped Bryce wouldn't notice that we weren't alone.

His steady gaze stayed on me and I started to answer when my phone buzzed. Three dots danced on the screen, the signal doing its best to try and reach me. A second later, a quick succession of texts popped up.

'Problem?' he asked.

'I need to head down. There's an emergency coming to the clinic.'

'What kind of emergency?'

'Judge Greene's dog, Julius, got into a tussle.'

'With another dog?'

'No, a porcupine. He's got a face full of quills.'

His eyes widened. 'That sounds painful.'

'It is. We usually have to sedate the dog to get them all out.' I picked up the bowl and shoved it into my bag. With a quick whistle, Flora followed me down the trail. When we got to a lower part of the path where I could get a stronger signal, I started to call Bree until I realized she and Jessa were on the way to their concert.

'Dammit,' I muttered.

'What's wrong?'

'Both my employees are out of town. The last time this happened we had to remove over forty quills. It's a much faster job with two people. I'll have to call Lia.'

'I can help you. That is, if you're willing to put me to work.'

'No, it's okay. Lia can probably get someone to fill in for a short time during her shift.'

'Dani.' His determined voice made me look up from the screen. 'Don't bother your sister. I'm right here, and I owe you one.'

It would be easier to let him come along than to bother Lia, who would definitely drop everything to help me but grumble about it the entire time.

'Seeing a dog with a face full of quills can be hard. Sure you won't get squeamish?'

'Squeamish?' he said like he was offended.

'Thought for sure you were going to pass out with Indy at the clinic, and he wasn't even bleeding.'

'I've reported from war zones for fuck's sake.'

I gave him a knowing look.

'Helping another dog feels like paying it forward. I swear I'll be fine.'

'I'll agree, but only if you promise to warn me if you get light-headed. It can be hard to see a dog in so much pain.'

Indy trotted up beside him and nuzzled his leg.

'I can get through it. I promise.'

We headed back down the trail, and I tried not to think about what happened the last time the two of us were alone in the clinic.

# Chapter Ten

## *Easy Prey*

The minute Judge Greene walked through the clinic door with Julius, I tightened my grip on the edge of the reception desk. Dozens of bright white quills covered the dog's face and head.

'I swear to you, Dani, I've trained Julius better. The ol' boy caught the scent in the woods and took off before I could get to him. When I heard the growl, the yelp, I knew it was bad.' His lips pinched together like he didn't appreciate Bryce being a witness to his dog's predicament. 'Eric's in New Orleans working at a Broncos game. He's not gonna be happy with me when he finds out this happened. Again.'

Poor Julius cowered at the judge's feet. 'Buddy, this is the third time this year. Haven't you learned your lesson yet?'

Julius let out a whimper in response. His tail whipped around and hit me in the legs, and a zap of dizzying heat shot through my bones, the shock of it making me stumble. Bryce's hands flew out toward me, but I shook him off.

'You know the drill. I'll need to sedate Julius because this will be painful. Bring him back and we'll get started,' I said to the judge.

Once inside the main exam room, I turned to the cabinets above the sink and pulled out the supplies I needed for sedation, as well as drugs for pain management. I ordered the judge and Bryce to heft the dog onto the table. I shaved down the fur on Julius's front right paw and inserted the IV line.

Bryce's gaze stayed on me the whole time. Clocking me as I ran my hand over Julius's back to see if the porcupine had struck any other place on his body besides his muzzle.

As soon as Julius was out, I said, 'Judge, you helping? The more hands on deck, the quicker Julius will be pain-free.'

'I, uh, think I'll wait outside. Where's Flora? She's always a good companion.'

'She's up in my apartment with Bryce's dog.'

'Oh? What kind of dog do you have?'

'Chocolate Lab.'

'That's a great breed. Had one growing up as a kid.' For a moment the judge paused, his eyes going watery at the state of an unconscious Julius, before he shuffled out the door.

'He comes off as a gruff old guy, but he's a total softie, right?' Bryce said.

'Last time this happened, it was at one a.m. I forced the judge and his husband, Eric, to work beside me, because I didn't have the heart to wake up my vet tech. The judge had a hard time getting through it. He really loves Julius.'

'Even more of a reason to get this dog well. Where do we start?' he asked steadily.

'We need to wash our hands first, and then I'll show you what to do.'

After we finished at the sink, I set out a clean surgical towel along with a set of needle-nose pliers, a few hemostats and two surgical basins filled with water. Bryce took the sterile gloves I offered, and I put on my own.

'The tiny barbs on the shafts of the quills cause them to migrate inward and deeper into the tissues.' I pointed to one of the needle-like tips. 'You need to grip the quill close to the skin.' I demonstrated on one lodged next to Julius's nose. 'Pull with slow and steady pressure to avoid breaking it.'

Once I had the first quill out, I dropped it into one of the kidney-shaped basins. Bryce grabbed a pair of pliers and went to work. We pulled and tugged in silence for a few minutes until he let out a pained yelp.

'Son of a bitch.' He shook out his hand. 'Those damn things hurt.'

'Oh, I forgot to mention. Try not to touch them.'

He arched a brow like my late reminder was payback for his lying, which I had to admit was not my intention, but a good payoff.

'I didn't realize porcupines were so vicious.'

'They're not.' I handed him another glove. Motioned for him to swap it with his punctured one. 'This' – I waved at the array of quills in Julius's mouth – 'is how porcupines defend themselves. Imagine being a small animal. Easy prey. You're minding your own business when an interloper, who is all kinds of intimidating, enters your territory without any kind of warning. Your first reaction is to protect and defend yourself.'

He tugged out another quill. 'Why do I think we are not talking about porcupines anymore?'

I ignored his comment and flipped up Julius's tender lip. Five more quills were embedded in the soft tissue.

This dog. Hadn't he learned that trying to bite the damn thing only inflicted more pain?

I grabbed a hemostat and focused on the job at hand. Bryce paid attention to the area on Julius's cheeks. Every few minutes, his gaze slid in my direction. A twitch of a smile lifted the corner of his mouth like he was admiring my technique and wanted to impress me with his own progress. We went back to working in silence, the basins turning red as we added more bloody quills.

'Do you consider this work your life's purpose?' he asked, trying to pull out a particularly tough quill near Julius's right ear.

'That's an oddly intense question.'

He shrugged. 'I'm trying to make conversation without you thinking I'm pumping you for info about the town.'

I went back to nudging out the quills, cautiously probing Julius's mouth with my finger to make sure I didn't miss one. If all the quills weren't removed they could do a lot of damage. Migrate down through the throat, stomach, or intestinal tract, causing problems for the dog later on. Julius was part of the first litter of puppies I'd helped deliver. I'd be heartbroken if I hadn't been thorough, and he got sick later on.

'The animals in this community are considered family. It's an honor when a neighbor brings their pet to me and asks that I care for them.'

His gaze softened the same way it had before he slid his hand behind my neck and pulled me into that unforgettable kiss. The memory of his low moan lit up parts of my body that hadn't been touched in way too long.

'Do you only work on domestic animals?'

His question snapped me out of my thoughts. Reminded me what a bad idea that kiss had been.

'In a small, rural area like Harvest Moon, I'm the only vet for fifty square miles. That covers a lot of agricultural and farmland. I help with calving if a cow is having a birthing issue. Float horses' teeth. Even castrate bulls when needed.'

He casually crossed one leg over the other, and I bit back a laugh.

'Do you consider your job, your writing, to be *your* life's work?'

He grimaced as he coaxed out another quill. 'When I started working for small newspapers after college, I thought so. In the last couple of years, though, my commitment has wavered.'

'Why?'

He rubbed the top of his wrist over his mouth like he needed a moment to consider how to answer. 'I had two professors in college who wrote for several high-profile newspapers. One was embedded with a marine squad during the first Desert Storm. The other one worked for years out of the Washington, DC bureau, covering a variety of presidents. Much of their curriculum centered on ethics. What was considered the core of good reporting. How your own personal bias had to be left at the door when you're telling a story. I loved the idea of getting at the facts. Laying the truth out for readers and letting them decide how to feel.' His jaw went tight. 'Sadly, it's not like that anymore.'

Julius let out a small whine, and I worried the anesthesia may be wearing off. I moved to the counter, filled another syringe, and gave him a small top-off.

'How has it changed?' I said, going back to work on the rest of the quills embedded in Julius's muzzle.

'It's all about clicks and likes now. The more shocking the headline the better.' He plucked out another quill near Julius's right eye. 'There used to be a joke in newsrooms that "if it bleeds, it leads."'

He blew out an agitated breath. 'Facts don't matter anymore. Biases too often inform what is said, not only in print, but on air, too. Now if you're a hack on a cable news network, and you're looking to make a quick buck, you write a scathing tell-all about a beloved president,' he fumed. 'It's frustrating for those of us who are still dedicated to the ethics of journalism.'

He shifted his forceps higher up to pull more quills from poor Julius's forehead. 'And don't get me started on the billionaires buying up reputable media and then using it as their own moral and political platforms.'

'Tell me how you really feel, Bryce,' I said, trying to get him to take a breath.

The bitter laugh that slipped out of him was surprising. 'That was a lot. I'm sure the last thing you wanted was a lecture about the demise of modern journalism.'

'Honestly? I like hearing about what you do. What your beliefs are.'

Another smile curled up the corners of his lips. I didn't want this with him. The easy banter. How the conversation felt too real and raw. Too much like the exchanges I'd had with Max.

I stayed quiet while we worked for another few minutes, making good progress with Julius, whose poor face would be swollen for days.

'We've danced around the story you're writing about Harvest Moon.' I sighed. 'Should we talk about it? Because it feels like the elephant in the room.'

'Ask me anything you want.'

'You didn't answer my question up on the point. Why this town? It's not your usual kind of story.'

'So we're back to that, are we?'

'Like I said, enemies closer and all that.'

He pointed the pliers in my direction. 'That is something I'm going to change. Mark my words.'

'Stop tap-dancing. Why take an assignment about a sleepy Colorado town when you're used to reporting on war-torn countries? Places facing a hunger crisis?' I went back to pulling more quills as I added, 'Does this have anything to do with your article in the *LA Sentinel* last May?'

'Fucking Google,' he said under his breath.

'It is the first result that pops up for your name. Did that movie studio really sue you for ten million dollars?'

The veins in his neck pulled tight as he took a gulp. 'That story… it was complicated.'

'It's going to take at least another hour to get all these quills out. We have time.'

He hesitated, before saying, 'For years I've wanted to work on a big investigative feature, and the studio story sort of fell into my lap. It came in as a tip to my email. At first, I didn't believe it, until I started doing some digging. I mean, hours and hours of interviews and research. Basically, a year and a half of my life. The story turned into some of my best work. My best writing.' He set down the forceps, scrubbed his hand behind his neck, which I was quickly learning was his anxious tic.

'The break I needed came in an email eight months ago. An anonymous source sent me documents showing how the head of a big Hollywood studio was embezzling money. It was going to blow the story wide open. We're talking a possible Pulitzer, because the corruption went deep into the belly of the film business. When I went to my bosses, they were thrilled. Newspapers are a dying breed, and any kind of exclusive story you can bring in is huge.'

'Embezzling? Is nobody honest anymore?'

'In all my years of reporting, I've learned one big thing. People get desperate and panic. Make stupid choices. Hold back the truth because they think it might implicate them in some way.'

'What happened next?' I asked.

He set a hand on Julius's back, giving him a gentle pet. 'The piece appeared as a front-page exposé. At first, people said I *was* going to get the Pulitzer. But then two months ago, when I went into work, my publisher was waiting at my desk. He took me into his office. Said the studio was suing me and the paper for millions. That they'd discovered my source, and that person had recanted every word.' He pushed out a full, weary breath. 'As part of an out-of-court settlement to protect them and me, the paper agreed to print a front-page retraction. State I'd used unverified sources.' The stricken look in his eyes shook something inside of me. 'I pleaded for more time. Asked to reach out to more sources. Dig a little more so we could fight the lawsuit. Prove what I'd written was accurate. The publisher said the matter was done.'

He let out a defeated sigh. 'Just like that, in a matter of minutes, my career went up in flames. Ten years of experience. Of writing about topics that meant something to me, and then, like a nightmare, the phone stopped ringing.' The way he shook his head, like he still couldn't believe it, was hard to watch. 'So, to answer you, I'm here writing about Harvest Moon because it's the only job I could get.'

The internet results had not given much detail, and the cautious part of me wondered if he was spinning this tale now for my benefit. To loosen me up. Get me to trust him. My skepticism born out of years of dealing with Belladonna. But the way he kept petting Julius, how he looked embarrassed when he admitted he couldn't find a job, said he was being honest. That he had everything to lose by confessing the truth to me.

'I'm sorry, Bryce,' was all I could offer in the moment.

He gave a subtle shrug and went back to working on the last of the quills. Julius whined again as I plucked out the final barbs around his mouth. Once I examined his muzzle, I removed my gloves and did a final check of his body, running my hands along his neck until a sharp, biting pain shot through me.

'Shit!' A large white quill sat in the pad of my index finger. I pulled it out, and Bryce was beside me in a flash, tugging off his gloves, and yanking out the edge of his T-shirt to staunch the small bead of blood. The heat of him surrounded me. His warm breath spilled over my face. Those stunning eyes went molten, and his wet lips parted.

It would be easy to reach out, slide my hand around his neck and pull him in. Brush my mouth over his in a kiss I knew from past experience would be electric. He gave me a confident smile. Pressed his hips against mine like he wanted the same thing.

He leaned his forehead against mine. Breathed out my name in a low growl that made my core heat. He ran a knuckle down my cheek. Gently cupped my jaw. Warning signs flashed in my head, but my body was urging me to melt into him. To suck in his lower lip. To make him groan. I moved in an inch until there was a sharp knock at the door, and the judge barged in.

His gaze darted between us, a smirk drawing up the corners of his mouth. 'Excuse me. I only wanted to check on Julius.'

'He's all finished,' I said, putting space between me and Bryce. 'Fifty-four quills this time.'

'Oh! That's our highest count,' the judge replied.

I turned back to the counter, the burn of embarrassment heating my cheeks. 'We'll bring him out in a few minutes. He'll need pain and anti-inflammatory meds for five days. And if you notice unusual swelling or abscesses, bring him right back in.'

'Will do. Thanks again, Dani.' The judge shot out his hand in Bryce's direction. 'Appreciate you assisting the doc today.'

'Of course.' He shook his hand. 'Glad to help.'

'See you both outside in a minute.' The glee in the judge's voice was not hard to miss. 'Don't forget about the festival planning meeting next Friday, Dani.'

'I'll be there.'

As soon as he was gone, I pressed a towel to my fingertip until the flow of blood stopped.

'Hey.' Bryce stepped closer. His hands out like he had every intention of pulling me in again.

'Let's not do this.' I cut him off. 'You were kind to help, but there's nothing more between us.'

His eyes softened. 'I'm not going to press you, but I want to say one more thing.'

He walked to the cabinet where he clearly remembered I stored the first aid kit. Once he had the paper off a Band-Aid, he slid it over the top of my finger. 'This article. I have to write it,' he said with a low rasp. 'Like I said on the trail, I'd love to have your help with the research.'

Now that I knew his whole story, it was clear he wouldn't let this go. At this point, I had two choices: let him have free rein. Only report on what the local business owners told him, because they had a vested interest in the publicity. Or, I could help steer the direction of the article. Convince him the rumors about my sisters, the town lore about generations of magic, were only stories told to add an air of mystery to our sleepy little part of the world.

As much as I hated that this was my reality, the answer was clear. I had to protect my family. Protect this community I loved so much.

'Meet me at the library tomorrow at three o'clock. I'll introduce you to Ms Ruthie. She's the town's main librarian and the keeper of Harvest Moon's archives.'

'Thanks. That would be very helpful.' He hefted Julius into his muscled arms, strutting out the door like he thought he'd won. Little did he know I had a plan too. He could look through the archives all he wanted, but that didn't mean he'd find anything. The last time a reporter came to town, he'd turned our lives upside down. After that horror show, Ms Ruthie promised that a stranger would never get close to the important documents about this town again, and I was going to make sure she kept her word.

# Chapter Eleven

## *Standing at the Edge of a Cliff*

Instead of being located in some historic brick and ivy-covered building, the Harvest Moon Library was housed in a narrow, two-story, oatmeal-colored storefront at the edge of the main artery of downtown.

Ms Ruthie ran the place with an iron fist, hunting you down on the street, your place of business, or even in a restaurant, if you had an overdue book that had a long hold list. Judge Greene was notorious for being the biggest 'late fee' culprit.

It was amusing to watch tiny Ms Ruthie go toe to toe with the judge at the bakery. The poor man was only trying to eat his jelly donut, not get a lecture on good citizenship. It was no wonder she was best friends with Clo. While they had the smiles of elderly grandmas, they could intimidate you like a military general.

I pushed through the opaque glass door. Ms Ruthie sat at the information desk, observing the library like its tried-and-true guardian. Her silvery-white curls framed her full face. The edges of her mouth twitched when she saw me coming.

'What do I owe this surprise visit to?'

'Can't I come by and say hello to my favorite librarian?'

She pulled off her cat-eye glasses and gave me that look that often made misbehaving kids flee from story time. 'Dani, let's not play games. What do you need?'

'Can you pull the records from the town's early incorporation but leave out anything about the Perkins and McGuire families?'

Her right brow arched. 'What is going on? Why do you need that information?'

'That doesn't matter right now. Please, grab those materials and do not tell my grandmother I was ever asking for them.'

Her glasses slid down her nose. 'I don't hide anything from Clo.'

'You will, or I might let it slip about your recent Vespa excursions.'

She gasped. 'Dandelion McGuire, you wouldn't!'

'I would, Ruthie. Clo cannot know I'm looking into the archives.'

We stayed in a quiet stalemate until she gave in. 'It was only a few spins around the block,' she said in a wounded voice, like that might change my mind.

'I'm sorry, weren't you laid up in Silverton for a month last year with a broken arm, hip and pelvis because of your Vespa crash on the highway? And did you not swear to your life-long best friend that you had sold said Vespa?'

'Yes.' She rolled her deep brown eyes, not appreciating how I had her pinned in a corner. 'All right. This stays between you and me.' She stepped closer. Lowered her voice. 'But your grandmother, she can't know about my little spin…' She stopped mid-breath when the door to the library swung open, and Bryce took long strides toward us.

Her left eyebrow now joined the right high up on her forehead. Under her breath she murmured something about 'a young Robert Redford'.

God, not her too. Bryce was just a man. An athletic, smart, ridiculously attractive man. But still, just a man.

He stopped next to me and stuck out his hand. 'Hello there. I'm Bryce O'Dell.'

I shook my head as our tough-as-nails librarian melted like the spring snow.

'Ruth Ansleigh. Pleasure to meet you.'

'Librarians have always had a special place in my heart; I was a big reader as a kid. Still am.'

She actually giggled at him. 'I can always tell the readers.'

'Where do we get started?' I said, breaking up their lovefest.

'Oh.' Ruthie hesitated. 'He's helping you?'

'Yes, Bryce, as I'm sure you've heard around town, is writing an article about Harvest Moon.'

That anxious twitch returned to her mouth. 'Mo might have mentioned something about that to me at a recent bunco night.'

*Of course she did.*

'Why don't you have a seat at one of the tables.' Ruthie gave me a confident stare, now understanding my request. 'Give me a few minutes to grab the information you need.'

She took off, her little feet tapping against the hardwood floors as she raced for the staircase that led to the upper level where the town's archives were stored.

He glanced around me. 'No Flora today?'

'Ms Ruthie loves me, but even she has rules about animals in the library.'

He nodded and wandered off in the direction of the stacks. Towering floor-to-ceiling bookcases covered the entire back wall of the building. For a small town, we had a wide collection ranging from biographies to mysteries and romance books. I trailed Bryce as he strolled up and down the aisles.

You could learn a lot about a person when you followed them through a library. What spines or titles happened to catch their attention. How they stopped at certain sections. Pulled books off the shelves to read the summaries. Apparently, he was a military thrillers and space exploration kind of guy.

'Did you serve?' I asked, curious about his past beyond the small glimpses he'd already shared with me.

'You mean like in the military?'

'Yes, you seem to be drawn to that kind of book.'

'No, but my grandfather was in the navy. They lost his ship, the USS *Arizona*, in Pearl Harbor.'

'Were you two close?'

Like he needed a distraction, he pulled a book about Gothic architecture from one of the shelves. 'He lived with my mom and me for five years before he passed. The guy could be gruff at times, but he also taught me how to play gin rummy. Change a tire. Made sure I always pulled out a chair, held a door, for a lady.'

'Sounds like a good man.'

He took a thick gulp, nodded as if he couldn't conjure any more words about the person who had clearly made a difference in his life.

'Like I told you, my dad was never around. He died alone in Las Vegas when I was ten. My grandpa moved into our small bungalow in Toluca Lake a few months later. He'd had a heart attack, and my mom didn't want him living on his own anymore. It was weird at first, because it was always just the two of us, but I think my mom liked having another person to care for. She's a nurse and likes feeling needed.'

I followed behind him as he pulled more books off the shelves.

'What about you? Are you close with your mother? Is she in town too?'

'No. She's never stayed around long,' I said, trying not to sound bitter. 'My grandparents raised us, because my mother was always too busy trying to find herself in some other part of the country.' I didn't like the way his eyes clouded with sympathy. 'We were fine. My grandfather passed a long time ago and Clo, she's always been a rock for us.'

'From the few moments I spent with her, she seems...' He pressed his lips together as if choosing his next words carefully. 'Resolute.'

A small bubble of a laugh left my lips. 'Interesting word choice. Accurate but interesting.'

'Told you I like words. Certain phrases. My grandpa, his name was Emmett, he said you shouldn't open your mouth unless what you had to say had meaning. I think about that a lot when I work on a story. Consider every word I put on the page to ensure it has the most impact.'

A book with a red spine and gold foil letters at the end of the aisle caught my eye. I plucked it off the shelf and said, 'That must make writing a chore. Constantly stopping and thinking about every single word.'

'Not for me. It's a creative challenge. To search through the data bank in my brain and pluck out the exact right word.'

'Again, sounds daunting.'

The corner of his full lips edged up into a smile. 'I may also cheat a little.'

'What do you mean by cheat?'

He stepped in close, the scent of peppermint gum on his breath. 'WordHippo,' he said like it was the sexiest thing in the world.

Once again I couldn't control my laughter. 'No! Like the thesaurus site online?'

'Yep.' He gave me a wide grin that made my stomach flip. Dammit. There was that covert charm of his again.

We stood toe to toe for a few more seconds, his eyes lingering on the way my hair was twisted back from my face. His hand moved as if he wanted to touch me, but he shrank back when Ruthie appeared a few feet away.

'Dandelion.' Ms Ruthie crossed her arms over her chest, her eyes narrowing like she'd caught us in a compromising position – which this was not. 'The books and journals are sitting on a table in the study room.'

'Thank you. We'll head that way right now,' I said as she continued to give us a withering look.

When we reached the stairs leading to the second floor, Bryce let out a small laugh. 'Dani is short for Dandelion?'

I shot him a dark look. 'Not a word.'

He chuckled under his breath as Ruthie tracked our movement up the steps. 'Why do I feel like we've been busted like teenagers caught kissing in the bathroom?'

'That's just Ruthie's way,' I said, ignoring the way my brain wanted to replay, once again, that kiss we'd shared in the clinic.

*Yeah, I really need to get out more.*

When we reached the top of the stairs, he let out a sharp breath. 'Holy shit. This place is amazing!'

Looking at this non-descript building from the outside, you would never imagine that a space like this existed. The roof was vaulted at least thirty feet high. Rough-hewn beams made of dark wood sat in a cross-hatched pattern against the ceiling. Three six-foot mahogany tables were placed around the room with small Tiffany-style glass lamps settled on each end. A large stained-glass window depicting what looked like a tree of knowledge, books dangling at the end of the branches, took up one entire wall. On one of the tables sat the books I'd requested.

Bryce shifted around me, but I stayed planted in my spot, unable to take another step forward. This felt too much like standing at the edge of a cliff with my toes pointed over the edge. For years I'd ignored the rumors and whispers about my family. Pretended that the magical tales this town sold to gullible visitors was just part of the tourism shtick. It'd been safer to make those choices, because it protected me and Lia and Aster. But even though I'd agreed to do this, asked Ruthie to pull archives excluding material about my ancestors, I worried this was all heading into dangerous territory.

Bryce may have claimed that he didn't believe in the magic angle, but the stories around here could be convincing. The more people spun our 'gifts', the easier it would be to add it as a thread to make his article as sensational as possible, even if none of it was true.

'Hey.' Bryce's voice was like soft honey. 'You okay?'

I wanted to say no. Run from the room and never look back. I remained in my spot, though, because Lia and Aster needed me to do this. Needed me to prove to this man that who we were, what we meant to this town, was nothing more than three women using their skills, talents and intelligence to make Harvest Moon a special place. But that small part of my heart, the one that always wondered if Belladonna was hiding dark secrets from us, forced me to nod and head straight for the stack of books waiting for us.

# Chapter Twelve

## A Lot to Protect

Who knew color-coding could be such a damn turn-on?

Bryce pulled a set of rainbow-hued notepads from his messenger bag and wrote out the years in neat, simple script on each one. 1873. 1875. 1876. 1887. 1904.

I don't know how he did it, but he even made the number four look sexy.

Without sparing a glance at me, he set a note at the top of the table and then laid out each book based on the date embossed on its rich brown leather spine. He repeated the move until at least five books were crowded under their labeled year. I cleared my throat, and he looked over at me, his eyes stricken.

'Shit. Sorry. I get into work mode and lose track of everything around me.'

'No.' I flailed my hand toward the neat stacks. 'You're making the job easier.'

'Okay, good.' He smirked. 'Let's start at the furthest date back and work our way forward.'

I laid a hand on a time-worn tome, whose yellowed pages and cracked cover said it'd been sitting in a dark and dusty place for much too long.

'Who said anything about *you* leading?' I said, a little heavy on the snark.

'That's fine by me. I like it when a woman takes control.'

I bit the inside of my cheek, reminding myself we were here to work, not flirt, even though the raw grittiness of his voice made several parts of my body tingle.

*Stop it. No matter what Aster says, this guy is not THE ONE.*

She'd been wrong once. She was wrong now.

The wafer-thin pages scratched against my fingertips. Most of the early archives covered the basics of the town's incorporation. Requirements for getting government funding for things like a post office and a bank.

'Dandelion, huh?'

I knew he wasn't going to leave it alone.

'My mother, Belladonna, is obsessed with a book called *The Fellowship of Flowers*. She swears by it. Says that personalities can be determined by asking someone what their favorite bloom is. When I was born, she named me Dandelion because they're considered a symbol of resilience.'

He paused. Gave me an assessing and amused gaze. 'Yep, it fits you.'

I swiped at his shoulder, but he caught my hand and threaded his fingers through mine. Like so many times before, there was a blast of heat between us followed by a small tug toward him. He gave me a satisfied grin like he felt it too, and I pushed the thought away because I was being damn ridiculous.

'And Aster means?' he said in a low voice.

'Wisdom and patience.'

He bit into his full lower lip, and all I wanted was to trace the mark with my fingers. 'What about Lia?'

'It's Camellia,' I said roughly. 'This one I have to hand to Belladonna. It represents passion, and my sister loves to passionately argue.'

That got a laugh.

'And what does your father think of all these floral names?'

My body stiffened, and I pulled away.

'Forgive me. That's none of my business.'

'We all have different fathers. None of us have ever met them, and Belladonna has never offered up their names.'

'Like I told you, my dad wasn't really around, either. But my mom is pretty great.'

I wished I could have said the same thing about Belladonna, but I couldn't. She'd always put herself first. A fact that had stung for most of my life.

He cleared his throat and said, 'Should we get back to it?'

'Yes,' I managed to choke out.

We went back to studying the archives, passing several books back and forth. With each one we set aside, the knot in my chest loosened. All of this was going to be a fool's errand. Prove that there was nothing here that would lend itself to the tales of magic.

'Have you heard how Julius is doing?' He reached for another large tome, brushing my shoulder, and my pulse kicked up again.

'I called the judge at lunchtime. He was still a little panicked about the whole thing. Worried about how swollen Julian was. He and Eric love that dog more than anything.'

He gave an understanding nod. 'I can sympathize, but last night he seemed smart. Like he was a level-headed guy.'

'Smart. Yes. Level-headed, not so much.'

'What do you mean? He *is* a judge, right? Isn't being level-headed a requirement of the job?'

'In the courtroom, he's fair and impartial. Outside, he does everything in his power to defend this town. That means he can get a bit assertive.'

'I've only been here a few weeks, but I can understand why he'd be that way. There's a lot to protect here.'

He gave me that weighted stare as he sat back, stretched his arms over his head, revealing a strip of tan skin, and a peek at the top of his black boxer briefs. I hated the way my throat went bone dry. How my fingers ached to touch him.

The pull toward him made zero sense. I'd always been cautious. The one who asked questions. Probed people's intentions and motivations. But for some reason, every single time I was around Bryce, I was drawn to him. Like he was the strength of the tide pulling me out to sea. The flame that drew a moth closer.

I forced my attention back on the archives in front of us. 'Have you always been comfortable interviewing people? I'd guess that requires a special kind of patience and skill set.'

He tented his hands on the table. 'I suppose. The key is to put the person at ease. When I speak to an informant, witness or even a victim, I explain what I'm trying to do with my piece. How offering up information can be difficult, but it can lead to greater change.'

He was committed, resolute, and I needed to know more. 'Give me an example.'

He settled his weight in the chair as if readying for a long story. 'My first real reporting job was for a small newspaper in Orange County. A secretary at a local high school was accused of embezzling money from their parent-teacher organization. She refused to talk to me because her lawyer told her to stay quiet, but there was something about the situation that was off. She lived in a shoebox-sized apartment. Drove a twelve-year-old car that desperately needed a new transmission. Didn't wear fancy clothes or jewelry. If she had stolen the ten thousand dollars that was missing, where was it? Because she wasn't spending it on herself.'

'Offshore bank account? Hidden underneath her mattress?' I joked, but his face stayed sober.

'Through a little more sleuthing, I found out she was overdrawn at her bank too.' A flicker of shame rippled across his face. 'I'm not proud of what I did next. For a few days, I followed her, eventually approaching her outside the local grocery store with what I'd learned. I promised I'd be fair if she trusted me. Talked to me. Told the truth.' The bracketed lines around his mouth tightened. 'We sat down the next day at a coffee shop she chose. I asked about her life, her family, her dreams. They were all honest and simple answers. Not the responses of an embezzler.'

The edges of his brows dipped together like the memory of that time still twisted something dark inside him.

'You can't leave it at that. What happened to her?'

'She confessed that she'd been having an affair with the school's principal. It was a rebound after his divorce. He took the money to pay off his debts but got scared. Made it look like she'd stolen it.'

'What a shithead,' I seethed.

'It's worse. She said she loved him. Believed covering for him was proof of her commitment. I told her I'd hold the story for forty-eight hours so she could tell her attorney and set things right.'

'Did she?'

'Yes. She ended up giving the guy up and getting her heart broken in the process.'

'But you kept her out of jail.'

He gave a sad nod, a reddish-gold lock of hair falling onto his forehead. 'But I also blew apart what she believed was real.'

He went silent, rubbing the edges of the worn paper between his strong fingers. 'That's enough of a downer for today. Have you found anything?'

There was a hitch to his shoulders. A sharp cadence to his breath. He was holding something back, but I'd learned from Lia that when you pushed people for answers they weren't ready to give, they shut down. 'No. Nothing yet.'

He grabbed another book and went back to studying the pages.

I forced my attention back to my own reading about the town in 1873. It provided a few interesting details about Harvest Moon. How it was first incorporated by Norton Rothwell, a pioneer who wanted to settle the land for himself and his family. Other pioneers quickly followed, believing the area was lucrative for mining. Eventually Rothwell became a leader, being elected the town's first mayor. From what I'd gleaned from Grandpa Beau before he'd passed, the McGuires came to town ten years later, escaping a challenging life in the Scottish Highlands.

Over the next years, the town swelled as silver was discovered in places like Leadville, Silverton and Aspen.

As we read, the stairs to the second floor creaked. Ruthie's scrutinizing stare appeared at the top of the landing like she was expecting Bryce to have me spread out on the table naked. The thought alone had me fanning myself.

'Are you warm?' He started to move from window to window. 'I can crack one of these open if you need it.'

'Bryce, I'm fine.'

I waved him back to the table, as Ruthie disappeared back down the stairs. He picked up another book, and I focused back on the one in front of me dated 1875. I flipped page after page. When I reached the last entry, I closed the back cover. An odd swell in the center of the leather had me flipping to the inside back page again.

Bryce's phone rang and he glanced at the screen. 'It's my mom. I have to take this.'

I shooed him away like it was fine, and he moved to a quiet back corner of the room. As soon as he was distracted, I ran my hand over the back page. Along the edges, there was an odd, faded yellow stitching. I worked a fingernail under the threads until I had most of it loosened. Sliding my hand into the open pocket, my fingers skidded over rough material. I gently tugged, and a cracked leather journal no bigger than my hand came out.

With Bryce still talking to his mother, I opened the front cover. The scrawled script inside the first page noted the journal had belonged to Roy Naylor, the town's sheriff. The writing was muted with age but still legible. Most of the entries covered the town's day-to-day activities.

I continued to skim the pages, until my gaze snagged on an entry that mentioned a small fire at the town's new mercantile. It was a basic story, but what caught my attention was the name of the owner, Jeremiah Bristow, who had a fiancée named Ambrosia Perkins. I closed my eyes, picturing the sepia-toned photo in Clo's house. The young woman standing in front of the apothecary. A solid set to her shoulders, and a determined fire in her eyes.

The entry stated that the back half of the building caught fire, and that, luckily, the volunteer fire brigade, along with a horse-drawn water pump, had managed to extinguish the blaze. It was a simple statement of facts until the final line.

> *When questioned, Mr Bristow swore the stove in the backroom had never been lit. That the last person in the building was his fiancée, Miss Ambrosia Perkins.*

My gaze flew to the next part of the entry.

> *Miss Perkins is the daughter of Sylvia and the late Francis Perkins, known to have been one of the wealthiest miners in town until his passing, leaving several businesses, including the apothecary, to his wife and daughter.*

I flipped forward several pages looking for any other mention of Ambrosia, but there was nothing recorded until seven months later.

> *Mr Jeremiah Bristow spent a night in jail after several witnesses claimed he struck a barmaid at the Harvest Moon saloon. Mr Bristow was released the following day into the care of his wife, Ambrosia, who is carrying their first child.*

The following pages outlined more of the town's history. The continued influx of miners. How a local hotel opened up Harvest Moon's first restaurant. I continued to leaf through the journal until another entry, dated March 2, 1876, made me grip the pages.

> *Mr Jeremiah Bristow, aged thirty-three, and owner of the local mercantile, perished in a house fire. The blaze ignited in a bedroom, but no source could be found. I questioned his wife, Ambrosia, who could not explain how the fire broke out. I must indicate his death as an accident, even as people in town state there are other, darker, more sinister, forces at work in the home. That Ambrosia and her mother, Sylvia, were connected to the fire in some way. I questioned both women several times due to the scrutiny and fear running rampant about the town. The two women answered my questions without any hint of emotion, which I found suspicious. Though she tried to hide it with her clothing, bruises were apparent on the young widow's wrists and neck. The owners of the mines and several local business owners insisted I arrest Ambrosia. Declared that she was the only one with a motive to kill him. The town was eager for blood, convinced Ambrosia and her mother used devilish powers that caused Mr Bristow's demise, but I've found no proof of such a claim and have closed the matter.*

I shut the journal as the blood quickened in my veins. Bryce said his goodbyes to his mother, and I scrambled to tuck the journal under my right leg.

'Find anything?' He slid onto the seat next to me, my heart thudding so loudly I was convinced he could hear it.

'No,' I lied. 'Just more general details about the town right after its incorporation. How a saloon was built. A mercantile. A few other buildings, including an opera house that was meant to add culture to a town overflowing with dance halls, saloons and gambling dens.'

I yanked another book off the pile, forcing several other archives to crash onto the floor. Bryce scrambled around the table to pick them up. I feigned surprise and bent to my knees, swiping the journal into my bag, before setting a few of the books back on the table.

'Maybe you shouldn't stack them so high next time,' I said as Bryce adjusted the books into smaller piles.

'You're right.' He gave me a smile so genuine that it made guilt twist in my gut for hiding the journal.

He went back to his seat, and I pretended to immerse myself in the next text. Even as I studied the pages, I couldn't get the images of Ambrosia and her mother out of my head. When I was a child, my grandparents often squabbled behind closed doors about bloodlines and family history. I always thought it was because of Belladonna's rebellious behavior, but now I wondered if there might be more to it.

The more I tried to act calm, the quicker my breaths came. An image flared in my mind. A quiet summer evening outside the house, the smell of rain fading from the air. Aster begging for s'mores. Grandpa Beau complaining about the wet kindling in the firepit. I remembered Grandmother Clo sent us into the house with Grandpa for more marshmallows, even though we had a full bag. The way I hesitated at the door. Turned my head back to see my grandmother snap her fingers. Bright red flames igniting in the firepit.

Too many jumbled thoughts swirled through my head making me dizzy. I'd always written off the memory as a trick of the eye. Convinced myself that Clo had lit a match without me seeing. But after reading about Ambrosia, I was beginning to question every truth in my life.

# *Chapter Thirteen*

## *Knocked Sideways*

After four consecutive yawns, Bryce convinced me it was time to stop for the day. He hinted at dinner, but after hours of research, and what I'd discovered in the journal, I wanted to head home, take a long shower, and figure out how I was going to handle this new revelation.

Bryce hid his disappointment well, saying he'd call me tomorrow so we could discuss when we'd meet up again.

When I pulled into the driveway of my clinic, a familiar white sedan was waiting.

Aster.

Of course she was here. I'd been avoiding her calls. I wasn't mad exactly. More like knocked sideways by her revelations about Max *and* Bryce. How it reframed what I'd believed about my life for the last seven years.

The day Max left, he sat me at the table in our kitchen and held my hands lovingly. I was sure he was going to propose. Say we could move back to Harvest Moon and start a practice together. Instead, he delivered a blow that knocked my entire world off its axis. He admitted he'd been having doubts about us for a while. That he wanted to see what else the world had to offer. He really meant *who else* the world had to offer, but at least he had the decency not to say those words.

I'm not sure how long I disassociated after that. Hours? Days? All I knew was that the person who was supposed to be my forever left me. What did that say about me as a human? Sure, I could be closed off sometimes. Belladonna had made me that way. But I still had a tender heart. What I thought was a lot of love to give. At the time it made me doubt my entire life, and now, well, I didn't know what the hell to believe anymore.

Aster hopped out of her car, took determined steps toward me and threw her arms around my waist. 'I wouldn't blame you if you never spoke to me again, but I had to repeat how truly sorry I am. After what Mother put you through all those years, I wanted to be the one to make you happy, but I should have been one hundred percent sure before I said a word.'

*Mother.*

Aster was the only one of us girls who called Belladonna that. She'd seen her in a way Lia and I never could. Both of us believed Belladonna should have stayed put in Harvest Moon. Been a real parent to us. Aster thought Belladonna was a free spirit who'd lose her 'effervescence' if we tied her to our small town, even though Ast cried every time she took off.

I loved Aster, so I never argued about the responsibility that came with being a parent. How even though Clo tried to be a rock for us, what we really needed was the stability of our mother in our lives.

'I get why you did it, but you have to give me time to process. What you told me about Max being my one true love. The way I believed it heart and soul. How it crushed me when he left. It messed with my head, and now...' I let out a low breath, the weight of it all taking hold. 'I have to figure out what to do with your newest revelation.'

Her twin dimples made an appearance. 'You mean with the hot journalist?'

'Yeah, I'm not having that conversation with you, especially right now.'

All right, he was too damn handsome for words, but half of me wondered if my attraction to him wasn't just the fact that it'd been way too long since I'd been with a man.

I turned on my heel and unlocked the door to the clinic, refusing to let my mind wander to the cute way Bryce worried his full bottom lip when he narrowed in on a specific passage in a book. The rhythmic beat of his pencil against the page like he was singing a song only he could hear. How when he stretched, the edges of his T-shirt pulled up, revealing a line of hair that dipped into his waistband.

Aster, of course, wouldn't let it go. 'What does that mean? I know you were with him at the library today. Did you find something in the archives?'

'How the hell do you know that?'

She gave a coy shrug. 'You know this town. People talk.'

Before I could press her for more details, she had her phone out, her fingers flying across the keyboard.

'Who are you texting?'

'Lia. When you look like that' – she swirled her fingers in front of my face – 'it means you've discovered some kind of info that you're going to try your damnedest to hide from us.'

I reached for her phone, but she turned her back and kept typing.

When she was done, she gave me a satisfied grin. 'Her shift is over and she's on her way.'

'Why can I not get a moment's peace in this freaking town?'

She followed me down the hall and up the back stairs to my place. After I threw open the door, I spun around to face her. 'I'm jumping in the shower. Take Flora out and wait for Lia. You can grill me after I've had at least ten minutes' peace standing under nearly scalding water.'

She huffed out a petulant 'fine,' and Flora scrambled out of my bedroom with her tail wagging quicker than a flag flapping in a summer storm.

'Let's go, girl,' Aster called.

Once they were gone, I hurried down the hallway to my bedroom, stripped out of my clothes and jumped into the shower. As the water relaxed the tension in my shoulders, I planned what I would tell my sisters. There was no way in hell I could explain what I'd seen Clo do that night by the fire, but I could tell them about our family history. Even make a joke about how Ambrosia wasn't afraid to 'burn it all down'.

Literally.

My thoughts returned to the archives. How I'd hidden the journal from Bryce. It didn't prove anything. It was gossip. Rumor. But still, I could see all the ways he could spin it. His story today about the secretary proved when he got a hold of the smallest detail, had any kind of intuition, he was willing to go to great lengths to find the truth.

I'd done my best today, not letting him see me spiral. More than once he'd leaned in closer to me at the table. That soft cedar scent of his lingering between us as he made notes about one-off pieces from personal blogs about the town's supposed magical lore. I quickly reminded him those angles were used to draw in tourists, making my point by referring to the local business names.

There were even a few mentions about how we hosted an annual trick-or-treating event on the weekend before Halloween. The way our Veggie Fest at the end of summer drew people to town from as far away as Switzerland and Brazil.

When my skin started to go pruney, I left the shower, dried off, and put on a pair of sweats and a T-shirt. Before I opened my bedroom door, I pulled in a full breath, preparing for the interrogation squad, AKA my sisters.

A fire crackled in the hearth, warding off the early evening chill. Flora was already snoozing next to Aster on the couch. Lia sat beside her scrolling through her phone. My sisters were my twin hearts. The two people I was sure I'd never be able to live without. I mothered them. Scolded them. Cried when they hurt. Laughed with joy when they soared. The years I'd been away from them in Fort Collins had been almost unbearable. I tried now not to let worry color my face.

'You're out of beer,' Lia barked.

'Hello, sunshine. Good to see you too.'

I ignored the way she glowered and pulled down a bottle of red wine from a kitchen cabinet, grabbed three glasses and joined them on the couch.

Once I had the screw-top cap off, I poured each of us a generous glass.

We sat in silence, the snap and pop of the dry wood filling the air.

Shockingly, Lia was the first one to speak. 'Stop stalling and tell us how bad it is.'

I kicked my feet out onto the live-edge coffee table I'd bought from a carpenter in Ouray.

'It's going to be fine. The archives don't really say much.'

Lia pressed her lips thin like she didn't believe me. Out of all of us, she was the least trusting. That may have had something to do with the fact that Belladonna lost her during a camping trip she insisted they take when Lia was eight. Thank goodness even back then, Lia was in tune with the woods. She was able to follow her old footprints all the way out to the main road leading into town. When the sheriff brought her back to Clo's, I was sure our grandmother's head was going to explode.

Belladonna didn't show up for hours. When she did, she claimed she knew where Lia was the whole time. That she was testing her outdoor survival skills. In that moment, I was sure my head might pop too.

After that incident, Lia refused to acknowledge Belladonna on any of her visits. To this day, she couldn't look at our mother without a hint of disgust.

'How far did you go back?' Aster asked.

'To the town's incorporation.'

'And…' Lia prodded.

'One of the earliest residents was a man named Jeremiah. He had a fiancée, Ambrosia. Clo's great-great-grandmother.'

Aster's eyes lit up. 'The one in the picture from the house? What was she like?'

I took a big drink before pushing out my rehearsed story. 'From the little written about her, she seemed determined. Smart. That photo of her and her mother, in front of their apothecary was probably from the late 1800s.'

'Interesting,' Lia said, like her interest was piqued. 'Any weird incidents or stories?'

'Not anything that alluded to magic outright.'

I wasn't lying. I was protecting them.

'I suppose if there had been, they would've burned her at the closest stake,' Lia muttered.

'Hanged,' Aster said quietly into her glass.

Lia gave her the side-eye. 'What are you saying?'

'They never burned witches at the stake in the US. They hanged them instead.'

'Well, hell, that's comforting.'

Aster went on, ignoring Lia. 'The last recorded hanging was in 1692. Ambrosia lived almost two hundred years later.'

'The point is that all Bryce found today was meandering facts about how Harvest Moon came to be. How the town grew because of the mining and farming opportunities.'

The look of relief in my sisters' eyes was enough to tell me I'd chosen the right thing to do. They already had enough on their plates, and I was okay with shouldering all the worry for them. It was my job as their big sister.

'I've read a few of Bryce's articles,' Aster said in between sips of wine. 'The guy is thorough. Determined. Not sure he's going to write some puff piece about Harvest Moon just because he didn't find anything in the archives.'

'It'll be all right, you'll see,' I said.

'Really, Dani?' Lia said with a snip. 'I'm already getting questions from guys at the station, and Aster's having more issues too.'

'Lee Lee!' Aster snapped. 'You promised you wouldn't say a word.'

I sat up quickly. 'Are you having more weirdos come into the shop? We can get the sheriff on it, you know.'

Aster waved off my concern. 'I'm just getting more calls about matchmaking than flower orders. But, as usual, Lia is overreacting.'

'Overreacting? When your business starts to turn into a sideshow, when losers crowd the shop, pushing out real customers, you might change your mind.'

Aster set her wine glass down with a thud. 'What would you know about running a business? You practically live at the fire station, and when you're not there you're off hiding on the trails.'

Their furious, unyielding stares warned things could go apocalyptic at any moment. Guilt twisted in my stomach. How could I be upset with them keeping stuff from me, when I was hiding things, too?

'Stop,' I said in the voice I only used when I was tired of listening to them bicker. 'This is what Bryce wants. To set us all off so we make a mistake, do or say something wrong so he can twist it into content. We have to stick together, which means letting me handle this. Proving to him there's absolutely nothing supernatural here.'

'You think you can convince him, even with people like Mo and the rest of the shop owners whispering in his ear?' Lia snickered. 'They want this, Dani. To convince readers this town is mysterious, filled with magic, so they'll come and visit.'

'You let me handle Mo and the rest of the town,' I said.

Lia crossed her arms over her chest. Aster stared straight at the fire. Her sweet face was now taut with tension.

We'd been here before. Cornered. Worried about the next thing that might try and split us apart.

The summer I was sixteen, Lia was thirteen and Aster was ten, Clo fell on the stairs, breaking her hip. The accident required surgery and a two-week stay in a rehab facility. Our grandfather passed the year before, and no one could find Belladonna, because the last cell number she'd given Clo didn't work.

Colorado Child and Family Services got involved. Talked about putting us in foster care. I went to Judge Greene and begged him to let me take care of my sisters until Clo was released from the hospital. I was already making their lunches, picking them up from school, reading them stories at night before bed.

The judge wasn't swayed by my arguments, telling me I was too young to care for the girls full time. He gently ushered me out of his office at the courthouse. I sat on the faded yellow linoleum floor for hours, refusing when his staff offered both food and water. When the judge found me at the end of the day, he agreed he and Eric would move into the house. Act as our temporary guardians until Clo was ready to come home.

'You've both built good lives here.' I put an arm around Lia's shoulder. Smiled at Aster. 'This man coming to town will not change a thing. I'll make sure of it.'

It was a promise I'd made repeatedly to them, but this time I was terrified I wouldn't be able to shield my sisters from what came next. In the library today, Bryce had shown me he was a determined and committed journalist, and I worried it wouldn't matter what, or who, he'd have to sacrifice to get a story that would put him back in the game.

# *Chapter Fourteen*

## *Good Entertainment*

Judge Greene was in a foul mood. He paced back and forth across the stage area at the bottom of the town's outdoor amphitheater, his sharp steps reminding me of an army general about to lead his men into battle. Eric, who was an ex-NFL wide receiver, scrambled behind him, encouraging him to take deep, full breaths. To not get his blood pressure up.

Most of the town sat in the first three sections of the audience, shifting their bodies on tiered concrete benches that faced the stage. The amphitheater only sat about a hundred people but was the main gathering spot for any town event, whether it was a local dance academy's recital, or the community theater's attempt at doing their own version of Shakespeare in the Park. Today it was the scene of the final planning session for the town's annual Veggie Fest. A downtown event dedicated to growing some of the largest vegetables in the state. It brought in a good portion of the town's tourism dollars and was named one of the US's most memorable summer festivals by several major news outlets. A point of pride for many businesses and locals, including the judge.

I sat on a bench in the center tier about ten rows from the stage with Flora dozing at my feet. The copse of parched aspen trees surrounding the venue swayed in a slight breath of a breeze. Small bits of grass and bright green weeds popped up from the dry soil. The late afternoon sun warmed the top of my head, and I pulled the black band from my wrist and began to braid my hair to help with the blast of early September heat cooking my skin.

Clo and Ms Ruthie were perched in the row in front of me, swapping quiet whispers about the real reason we were all gathered here. The town's Veggie Fest was in peril due to a recent downpour that had flooded many of the town's dry fields, wreaking havoc on some of the monster-sized vegetables the locals grew for the summertime festival that happened in two weeks. The event had to be a success as it brought in almost twenty percent of the town's tourism revenue for the year.

Lia took the empty spot beside me, her muddy boots leaving a trail of brownish-red footprints in her wake. 'Where's Ast?' She used her bandana to wipe the sweat from her forehead. She had to be boiling in those khaki pants and steel-toed boots.

'Preparing for the Desiray wedding. Apparently, they sent Stargazer lilies instead of white for the table arrangements. When Marley's mother found out, her head practically spun around like that kid in *The Exorcist*.'

Lia gave me an amused look.

'Aster's words, not mine.'

Marley Desiray was a big deal in Harvest Moon. She'd done a lot of local theater and had a small part in a critically acclaimed independent film, which practically made her a celebrity in this two-stoplight town. Marley happened to be in Aster's high school graduating class, so she felt pressure to make sure the wedding flowers were extra special. It was also the first time in a while she hadn't made the match. She'd confided in me that it was a relief to be able to focus on her one job for this wedding: making the bouquets and table settings perfect.

Ms Ruthie patted Flora on the head before giving a friendly wave to Lia. 'How are the trails looking today?'

'Messy. We've had mudslides on at least four of them. When we have drought conditions, and then get a bunch of rain, things get dicey real quick. Chief Malbrough decided to rope off a few paths leading up to the ridge because I told him we were going to get more storms in the next few days. Not good when we have so many tourists here, many of whom ignore the closed trail signs.'

Elena hustled down the steps of the amphitheater toward us. I scooched across the cement bench to make room for her.

'Sorry I'm late. The milk frother is clogged on the espresso machine again. What did I miss?'

'Not much, except for Eric and Judge Greene running around like their asses are on fire,' Lia offered.

Elena pulled in a heavy breath, and I slung an arm around her shoulder. 'You okay?'

'Yeah, a little tired is all. I forget how chaotic the summer months can be. The tourists always wring me out. Every year they throw some new odd coffee order at me, and I have to scour the internet to figure out what the hell they're talking about.'

'What is it this year? Can't be any worse than that cold brew concoction with coconut mango whip,' I said.

She rolled her eyes over last summer's regular request. 'It's worse this time. They're all asking for a lavender peppercorn latte.'

Lia made a gagging sound, and I patted Elena's hand. 'Only a few more weeks. Once that first cold snap hits us, they'll hightail it back to their big cities.'

Elena and I continued to whisper about work when Ms Ruthie's inquisitive gaze found me. She leaned in and whispered, 'Did you take something from the archives? You know that's against the rules.'

I froze in my spot, praying Clo did not hear the question. Unfortunately, my grandmother had hearing like she was part bat.

'You were in the archives?'

The heat in Clo's voice made Flora whine. 'I, uh… had to do some research.' I shot Ms Ruthie a scalding look.

'Research on what?' Clo pressed.

'She was with that young man.'

Ms Ruthie was not helping. I made the move like I was holding handlebars, reminding her of the Vespa conversation, and her mouth snapped shut.

Clo narrowed her gaze. 'What young man?'

'Yeah, Dani. *What young man?*' Lia was still stewing over my helping Bryce.

'It was the guy who showed up the night of Aster's birthday. The one with the sick dog. He's here to write an article about the town, which I'm sure you've heard about.'

Clo's lips thinned into an unhappy line.

'I decided it was better for me to be involved. Steer the direction of the article in a certain way,' I said. 'Make it more about the town and its history rather than the crap about magic.'

Lia rolled her eyes. 'And you think this seasoned journalist with numerous writing accolades is going to let you lead him around by the nose?'

Guess she'd done her research after we'd talked the other night.

Clo's hesitant gaze darted between me and Lia. 'Did he find anything?'

'Only what I wanted him to,' I said.

Elena arched a brow. 'Look at you being all sneaky and devious. Didn't know you had it in you, but I love it.'

Clo was not as impressed. Neither was Lia by the dark looks she was tossing at me.

'I have it under control.'

Lia started to say more but stopped when Judge Greene called for the crowd to be quiet. He began with asking a few of the farmers about the state of their entries, making sure we hadn't lost too many of the veggies in the recent storms. When he'd learned almost everyone had saved their prized vegetables, he moved on to general business. First he asked about traffic control during the festival and volunteers needed for the pie-eating contest. The crowd murmured when he explained the new rules for the knives at the vegetable-carving competition, considering last year we'd had more than one over-eager participant who required stitches at the local emergency room.

Movement flickered in the corner of the amphitheater. Bryce took a seat on a stone bench on the lower left side of the venue. An old-fashioned reporter's notepad sat in his right hand. A pen in his left hovered over the page. In the fading afternoon light his hair was the color of warm copper. That floating feeling spread across my chest and I pushed it away.

I had to see him as the enemy. As the person who could make my life, the life of my family, miserable. But still, I couldn't shake the memory of his mouth against mine that night in the clinic. The throaty gasp he made as I parted the seam of his lips with my tongue. How hot he looked in the library with a pencil tucked behind his ear, those colored Post-its spread out across his research notebook.

'You're staring,' Elena whispered in a giddy voice.

'Not true. I'm only amused that he thinks he's going to learn anything here for his precious article.'

'Sure,' she said with a taunting laugh.

It was, well, partially true, because these meetings consisted of exactly three things: Judge Greene thinking this was his courtroom, barking out for quiet. Mo complaining about not getting a steep enough discount from the local brewers for the event, and Clo telling everyone to shut their traps and get on with it. It was good entertainment but not very informative.

The judge went on talking, asking for feedback on how the booths should be set up this year. Explaining how we were not doing the outdoor s'mores station due to the high fire risk, which caused more than a few unhappy grumbles in the crowd.

When he started strategizing about how the vegetables were going to be loaded in for the judging, Ernie Brewer raised his hand and asked about using a wheelbarrow to deliver his oversized eggplant. Elena let out a sharp laugh. Things only got worse when Jacob Newman insisted his cucumber was larger than Ernie's eggplant. This time, a loud snort escaped Lia's lips. Not to be outdone, Miriam Solarum raised her hand to ask about where to put her giant peach, and a roaring laugh flew out of my own mouth.

The judge tossed an angry look in our direction and Lia, Elena and I huddled together, trying to stop our laughter.

Clo leaned back and said, 'Whenever you girls are ready to grow up and ignore the not-so-subtle references to how the internet has turned vegetable emojis into sexual body parts, we can move on.'

I slapped a hand over my mouth when Ms Ruthie inquired what the peach emoji meant.

When we finally calmed down, the judge started asking about parking and security, and ten hands went up with questions. Elena groaned and plopped her head on my shoulder, her eyes shuttering closed. 'Wake me when they make some, well, *any* decisions.'

Lia snapped her wrist to look at her watch. 'That'll be in like three hours.'

My attention floated back to Bryce, who was now staring in my direction. He gave a quick wave and Lia let out another disapproving huff.

'Lee, trust me,' I pleaded quietly.

Her irritated stare stayed firmly in place as she bent to give Flora a scrub behind her ears.

Bryce went back to focusing on the meeting, and I thought about the journal I'd slid into my bag. The rumors about Ambrosia and the fire. Clo leaned over to whisper to Ms Ruthie, her hands settled in her lap. They were small. Browned from working in her garden. Normal. *Not tinged with magic.*

I pictured that scene around the stone circle again. The jarring snap of her fingers echoing through the cool night air. The smoke and flicker of orange flame coming to life in the pit. I was a child then. I was imaginative. Made up stories for my sisters at bedtime. Maybe I'd conjured up that memory of Clo too.

'And Dr McGuire will handle the children's area…'

That pulled me right out of my thoughts. Made my hand shoot straight up. 'I'm sorry, Judge. What was that?'

'The children's area. The face painting. Balloon-animal station. Strawberry-dipping booth. Lia said you'd take it over.'

Dread curled in my stomach. The children's area was an exercise in chaos every year. Kids sobbing when their balloon animals popped because they hugged them too tightly. Hands, faces, even hair, sometimes drenched in the melted white and milk chocolate used for strawberry dipping.

Last year, the pharmacist and his wife, Nora, took on the job, and by the end of the festival they resembled battle-scarred warriors, if warriors were covered in multiple layers of chocolate.

'Did she now?'

Lia gave me a smartass smirk. Oh, she wasn't getting away with this.

'Of course I'll do it, and Lia will help me.'

The taunting grin on Lia's face slid away, and before she could object, Clo pressed a hand to her knee, stopping whatever sharp reply was coming.

'No problem, Judge. *All three* of the McGuire girls are up to the task,' Clo stated.

He gave a nod and moved on to tent construction and garbage duty.

A smirk pulled at the corner of Bryce's mouth and his pen flew over the pages.

Good. This was what he needed to write about. The zaniness of this town. How people were always reluctant to volunteer until they were reminded of how some of the money raised allowed us to support important local causes like meals for seniors on a fixed budget and after school programs for kids.

Once the meeting adjourned an hour later, Elena fled back to the coffee shop and Lia headed to the fire station to talk to the chief about when the trails would be opened again. I raced to my truck with Flora at my side. I had less than half an hour before a scheduled puppy vaccination at the clinic. Before I could get away, Clo called my name, strode toward me with a determined look pinching the corner of her eyes.

When she reached me she said in that disappointed voice I hated, 'How long were you going to keep your plans with the journalist a secret?'

'It's not a secret. I hadn't gotten around to telling you yet is all.'

She gave me one of her patented *that is bullshit* looks. 'Honey, what are you doing? I know how you feel about this magic nonsense. And the last time an article was written…' She shook her head. 'I've heard this fella knows his stuff. You may not be able to distract him as easily as you think.'

*Is it nonsense to her?*

'Yes, I've got it handled. The only archives he saw were about the town's incorporation. The years of the silver rush frenzy. How the population slowly grew as more people visited and found that Harvest Moon was a good and quiet place to raise children.'

A part of me wanted to bring up her ancestor Ambrosia. See her reaction. But I held back. The center of town wasn't exactly the place to have that kind of conversation.

'All Bryce will have to write about is our basic history,' I said. 'The antics of this town, like that ridiculous meeting, and how Eric is very proud that he can grow a green pepper the size of a large man's head.'

The tight lines around her mouth didn't move. I gave another glance at her hands. In the light of day, those fuzzy memories of that night felt even more ridiculous. I'd been around Clo all my life. If she'd had any kind of magical power, I'd know about it.

'There's one other issue we need to discuss.' The way she spit out the word *issue*, it wasn't hard to guess what was coming next. 'Your mother called me. Apparently she sent you an email and you have not replied.'

'I have a lot happening right now. The last thing I need is more of Belladonna's crap.'

'Dandelion,' she said with a sad sigh. 'I know better than anyone how she's hurt you and your sisters, but in the end she is your mother. Take five minutes and answer her. Please.'

My first reaction was to say no, but Clo didn't ask for much. I was about to relent when Bryce appeared at the corner and jogged in our direction. Well, shit. Now I'd have to formally introduce him to Clo because they hadn't really spoken the night of Indy's sickness. I braced myself, because in a situation like this my grandmother could be a wild card.

'Hello, Dani,' Bryce said with a way-too-relaxed smile. He bent down and scrubbed under Flora's neck, murmuring something about Indy missing her. When he was finished turning my dog into a wet noodle, he stood at his full height and held out his hand to Clo.

'We didn't get a chance to properly meet when I was at your place with my sick dog. I'm Bryce O'Dell.'

'I know who you are, young man. Nothing happens...' She tossed me an irritated look. 'Well, *almost nothing* happens in this town without me knowing about it.'

'Yes, ma'am, I've heard that. In fact, I was hoping you'd be open to talking to me about the piece I'm writing about Harvest Moon. Everyone I've spoken to so far has said you're the lady in the know around here. That your input on the article would be critical to me portraying the town in the most accurate light.' There was that charming smile again. Little did he know my grandmother was anything but a pushover.

'Fine. Come to dinner tomorrow night. Be at the house at seven o'clock sharp and bring your appetite.'

I double-blinked. She was inviting him to dinner?

Bryce hesitated for a few seconds before replying, 'Thank you. I'll be there.'

This was a bad idea. The last thing I wanted was Bryce in my childhood home. Getting too close to the things I held most dear.

Before I could say a word, Bryce pointed a hopeful gaze in my direction. 'You'll be joining us, right?'

'I'll be there. You never say no to my grandmother.'

Clo gave me a knowing smirk and I said, 'Bryce, will you excuse us for a minute?'

He graciously stepped aside to check his phone.

'What are you up to?' I growled.

Her bony shoulders lifted in a casual shrug. 'I can do my part too. We need to understand what that man knows. Loosening him up with some wine and a good meal can't hurt.'

I couldn't help but laugh. The absolute wrong person to underestimate in this town was my grandmother, and Bryce was about to learn that fact very quickly.

My phone buzzed and I pulled it out of my back pocket. My shoulders tightened as I read the message.

'What's wrong?' Clo said.

'George Spellner's been worried about his pregnant cow, and now it looks like she's having issues. I'd better call Jessa and let her know I have to cancel the rest of today's appointments.'

'Why don't you let me take Flora to the clinic? I can tell Jessa when I get there,' Clo offered like she was trying to get back into my good graces.

'Thank you. That'd be helpful. I don't know how long I'll be there.'

Clo whistled, called Flora's name, and the two of them walked back toward the amphitheater.

'Did I hear something about a pregnant cow?' Bryce said.

'Do you ever stop eavesdropping?' I huffed.

He gave a shy shrug like that'd make me forgive his irritating ways.

'Yes. I have to head to the Spellners' farm.'

'Do you need help?'

'I've got this.'

'How about another pair of hands? Maybe someone to carry your equipment? Put me to work. I think I did pretty good with Julius.'

'Something tells me that even if I say no, you'll still figure out a way to get there.'

'True. So why not give in now and let me come along?'

There was that charming smirk again. How did he keep figuring out ways to break down my defenses?

'I guess you did prove with Julius that you could go a while without being squeamish.'

'You don't need to worry about me.'

'Oh, just you wait. Plucking a few quills is much different than a difficult live birth.'

He straightened his shoulders. 'I'm up for the task.'

I held back a laugh, because he had no idea what he was volunteering for. If he wanted me to put him to work, he was about to get a brutal lesson in rural veterinary medicine.

# *Chapter Fifteen*

## *A Gift Many People Don't Get to See*

Daisy Sue was corralled inside the century-old, wood-sided barn. She paced around the twelve-by-twelve calving pen, vocalizing every few seconds, which were all indications of active labor.

George stalked around the edges of the pen, his muddy boots crunching through fresh straw. Every few minutes he muttered under his breath like an expectant father. He was a fourth-generation farmer with a soft spot for his small herd of dairy cows.

I loaded Bryce up with equipment from my truck and ordered him toward the barn like he was my own personal pack mule.

'How's she doing, George?' I asked, stopping next to the pen and stepping into my coveralls.

He stalked toward the gate and quickly opened and closed it behind him. 'She's been like this for several hours. That's why I couldn't come to the town meeting. Too worried about her.' He slid the black cowboy hat off his head and rubbed it across his chest. 'You remember how difficult a time she had last year. This, well, it seems worse.'

Bryce huffed behind us like the weight of the gear was too much.

'Is there a reason he's here?' George bristled.

'He's like a horse fly. Can't get rid of him.'

That got a chuckle out of George.

'Set the bags down next to the gate, and wait out here,' I said to Bryce. 'Cows can be unpredictable, especially when they're in labor. The last thing I need is for you to get kicked by a twelve-hundred-pound animal.'

Bryce did as he was told, and even though his watchful stare was annoying, it was good to have backup in case we needed help with a calf in distress.

George's three border collies raced into the barn. They beelined straight for me and before they could crash into my legs, George made a loud whistle, stopping them in their tracks.

'Sorry,' George said, holding the dogs back. 'Thought they were locked in the house. Must have figured a way out of the dog door.'

Bryce gave me that same quizzical look from that day in town when the dogs surrounded me.

'It's all right, you can let them go,' I said.

'Hooks, Walker, Steinem, release,' George said. The dogs trotted toward me, and I gave them each a warm scrub behind the ears without a single flash of dizziness.

Bryce admired the dogs, who sat still at my feet. 'Interesting names.'

'I might be a farmer, but I went to a liberal arts college on the east coast. Took a feminist literature class, because a girl I liked was in it. She never gave me a glance, but the books we read made a lifelong impression.'

'Ever read Isabel Cañas?' Bryce said.

George scrubbed at his salt-and-pepper beard. 'No. Should I?'

'Absolutely. Start with *Vampires of El Norte*. You won't be disappointed.'

I hid my smile while Bryce continued to give George a long list of feminist must-reads. Damn. He was full of surprises.

Daisy's pacing inside the pen grew frantic, and I slid one of my equipment bags over my shoulder and entered through the gate.

'She's gonna be ornery,' George called out. 'Took me a half hour to get her into the pen.'

I set down my bag on the straw and took small, cautious steps, approaching Daisy from behind the tip of the shoulder so I wouldn't spook her.

'George,' I said, keeping my voice low and steady, 'grab some clean towels and leave them by the gate. Not sure what condition this calf is going to be in once it's out.'

He moved to a crate in the far back of the barn and loaded up his arms.

I inched in closer to Daisy. 'Hello, sweet thing.' I reached out, bracing for the shock of what I'd feel when I touched her. I started easy, rubbing a hand over her back. Thankfully everything was normal. No dizziness or zap of pain.

'Dani, you okay?' The latch on the gate shook like Bryce was trying to come in, but the sharp tone to George's voice stopped him.

'She's the best vet I've ever seen, and I've lived in this county for sixty years. Seen many come and go. Give her a minute.'

'I want to help.' Bryce's voice went firm.

George dropped the load of towels next to the gate. 'You *can* help by letting her do her job. Just watch and learn, city boy.'

I walked back to my bag and took out an OB glove, stretching it up my arm all the way to the shoulder. Bryce's eyebrows rose to his hairline as I slathered the sleeve with a mix of soapy water and lubricant. I swallowed a laugh, because I was positive he had no clue what he'd signed up for by coming here.

'Is Daisy struggling?' George asked.

'Let me do a quick exam to see how things are progressing.'

I followed Daisy around the pen at a safe distance. Her strides were slow from the stress of labor and weight of the calf. Bryce climbed up using the metal slats on the gate and leaned his elbows across the top.

When Daisy stopped moving, I safely approached her again. Once she clocked me, I took a few steps toward her backside, still using a calm voice. As I checked her, it only took a minute to figure out that the calf was alive, and in an anterior presentation.

'It all looks good, George. She can do this on her own.'

George tugged down on his Stetson and let out a full breath. 'Thank goodness.'

'You're doing good, mama.' I patted the cow's back and stepped away. Daisy walked around the pen again, her low mooing wafting all the way up to the barn's twenty-foot-high rafters.

I removed my glove and headed back to the gate, which Bryce quickly opened for me. The look of wonder in his eyes was almost too much. 'George is right. You really are the best.'

'You're too easily impressed. That's all normal work for a vet.'

'No. You didn't see what we did, Dani. The minute you got close, that cow relaxed. It's as if she sensed you were there to help her. That you could be trusted. It's not a good comparison, but when I first got Indy from the rescue, he wouldn't come near me. Wouldn't let me pet him. It took weeks of working with a trainer and a lot of patience to build what we have now. But you.' He shook his head. 'You've got a gift.'

There was that lilt to his voice again. Like he believed there was something supernatural happening. I ignored it and climbed up onto the gate beside him.

'What happens now?' Bryce asked.

'We let nature take its course,' I said.

Daisy moved around the pen again. The volume of her moos rose and her behavior grew more agitated. George stayed still but clocked the cow's every movement. She continued to pant and pace for another hour until she lay down on her side at the far edge of the pen. A few minutes later, the calf's head appeared. After a few more pushes, the full body slid out and landed on top of the thick bedding of straw.

Bryce's eyes widened. 'Holy shit! Did that just happen?'

I gripped the edge of the gate, waiting for any movement from the calf. If it looked like it was in trouble, we'd have to go in and help. We collectively held our breaths until the calf started to shift on the straw. Daisy began licking at it. A few minutes later, the calf lifted its head, and George let out a cheer.

Bryce's fingers threaded through mine, and that familiar connection between us made my nerve endings flare. For the first time in so long I didn't feel the hollow ache of loneliness.

Daisy cared for her baby like a good mama. The calf shifted on the straw and rose forward in a wobbly kind of balance. Daisy nudged the little creature until it finally stood on its own.

George let out a rough 'Atta girl.'

The calf turned to the side so I could get a good look at her. 'Yep, that's right.'

George let out a relieved breath. 'More milk for the farm. That's a good thing.'

Bryce beamed like the early morning sun as he watched Daisy connect with her newborn calf. 'Does Daisy need any kind of care now? Because that seemed like a lot of work for her.'

'No, but I'll stay for a bit. Make sure the calf latches on all right. Babies need that important colostrum from the mother's milk right after birth,' I said.

George added more straw to the pen for warmth. After another hour, the calf began to nurse. Bryce stayed glued to the gate, enamored with the new addition to George's herd.

'I'll be back in a few days to check on them, but if anything comes up before then give me a call,' I said, stepping out of the coveralls and sliding them into my dirty laundry bag. 'For now, please keep them together in the pen. The calf needs to stay warm, and space from the herd would be good for a little while.'

'Of course and thank you for coming out so quickly.'

'Happy to help,' I said.

George reached out and gripped my hand. 'There's no doubt in my mind you are one of the best things that's ever happened to Harvest Moon. I know it hasn't been easy, but I'm real appreciative of the fact that you came home to practice, even when a lot of folks here gave you plenty of reasons not to return.'

Bryce's head tipped to the side, surprise coloring the lines in his face.

'This is my home, George. Always has been. Always will be.'

'Your grandfather would have been proud of you.'

Those few words shook me. It was in moments like this that the loss of him felt the most painful. 'Thank you. That means a lot,' I said, blinking away tears.

He gave a sharp nod and moved back to the pen, watching the newest addition to his farm with a careful eye.

I slid the strap of my equipment bag over my shoulder, and Bryce picked up the rest of my gear. We walked in silence but it was hard to ignore his intense gaze as we ambled back toward my truck.

'You need to stop staring that way. It's beginning to freak me out.'

'I just...' He bit into his full lower lip. Studied the darkening sky like somehow he'd find the words he was looking for in the deep gray clouds. 'Is it weird to say that what just happened was magical?'

'While I wouldn't mind taking credit for *that kind* of magic, it's purely nature,' I said as I secured my gear in the tailgate of the truck. 'Farms are teeming with the cycle of life. Older animals come to their natural end, while new creatures begin their journey. As a vet, you get the privilege of being part of that circle frequently. It's a gift many people don't get to see.'

I held out a jug of water, and together we washed our hands and arms. Once I was toweled off, I pulled on my brown canvas jacket. The clinic's name was stitched across the front right pocket in bright yellow thread. Jessa and Bree had been so proud when they'd given it to me on the clinic's fifth anniversary.

I climbed into the truck and he joined me in the cab. A slow rain tapped against the windshield. We headed down the rural farm road back in the direction of Harvest Moon.

The potholes and rough patches bounced us around, and Bryce had to reach for the handle above the door to stay steady.

'Now I understand the need for four-wheel drive out here.' His voice rattled along with the truck. 'I'd bet it'd be easy to get stuck, especially when it's snowing.'

'Snow is bad but rain is a thousand times worse, because this road can become a muddy bog pretty quickly.'

Bryce clung to the door as we bounced and shifted in the cab again. 'What did George mean by the town giving you reasons not to return?'

I gave the truck more gas. The windshield wipers moved at a frantic clip, doing little to help with the rain that was morphing into blinding sheets. 'You're a smart guy who's researched the town; you can probably figure out the answer.'

'The whispers about magic?'

It was a lot more than just whispers, but that was not information I was about to give him.

'It's something like that.'

'There's more to the story but you're not going to tell me, right?'

*Damn straight.*

'How does it feel now that you've seen your first live animal birth?'

He smirked at my not-so-smooth change of subject. 'Is it weird that all I want to do is call and tell my mom about it?'

'No. Didn't you say she was a nurse?'

'Yeah. She works in pediatrics, but she started in labor and delivery. When I was a kid, she'd come home glowing. Tell me about all the babies that were born that day. How the mothers she took care of were brave and strong.'

A dull ache knocked against my chest at the affection in his voice. What I wouldn't give to speak about my mother that proudly.

We were only a hundred yards from the gate between the farm and the main artery that led into town when the road grew rougher, tossing us around like a bad carnival ride. The truck's frame shook and the display on the dash lit up with a bright red light.

'Crap,' I said, easing off the gas.

He leaned over to look at the dash, the heat of him pressing into my side.

God, he smelled good.

'The pressure reading for the back passenger tire is dropping quickly,' I said.

'Did we run over something sharp?' Instead of sliding back to his spot, he stayed close to my side like he knew it was sending small zaps of warmth through me. We inched toward the gate with the tire pressure plummeting faster than the rain overhead.

'Back tire is definitely punctured,' I said.

The storm continued to rage, and I pulled over.

'We should wait it ou...'

Before he could finish his sentence, I had the door open. I yanked my jacket over my head and raced to the rear of the truck.

If the stinging rain hadn't doused the heat in my veins, the flattened tire seeping into the mud most certainly would have.

'Do you have a spare?' He held his hands over his head as if that could keep him dry.

'No. The front right tire blew a year ago, and I used the spare then. The autobody shop returned it, but I never put it back on the truck.'

The rain blew sideways, soaking us to the bone.

'What about AAA?'

I pushed sopping wet hair from my forehead. 'This is rural Colorado; what do you think?'

He shoved his hands into his pockets, water dripping off his chiseled chin. 'Let's get back in the truck. No use in standing in this while we figure things out.'

We raced back to the doors and hopped inside. Thunder rolled overhead, followed by a white streak flashing across the darkening sky. 'Shit. That's not good,' I said.

His wet brows pinched together. 'Isn't this area in a drought? I'd think you'd be grateful for the rain.'

'Rain is good. Lightning is not. With all the dry timber in the forest, a wildfire could spark very quickly. And a lot of rain at once can cause flooding and mudslides. They've already had to close a few trails because of recent storms.'

Fat drops thudded against the roof, and I pulled out my phone and called Aster. It rang a few times before going to voicemail. I left a message and then did the same with Lia and my grandmother. Hopefully, someone would get back to us or at least send a tow truck.

'We might be here for a while,' I said.

'I don't mind. Any time spent with you is good.'

His light blue shirt clung to the planes of his chest. Water dripped from the hem of his jeans. Every inch of him was soaked, but he still gave me a genuine smile, and I tried not to get lost in the way he looked at me like I was something to be treasured.

'You need to stop doing that.' I grabbed my phone, glancing at the screen for any kind of reply from my family.

'Doing what?'

'Pretending you like me so you can get more information for your story.'

'I am not pretending,' he said firmly. 'Anytime I'm around you…' He closed his mouth. Shot a hand through his wet hair, tugging at the ends.

'Might as well finish, not that I'm inclined to believe anything that comes out of your mouth.'

'When I'm around you I feel light. Like a two-ton boulder has been lifted off my chest,' he admitted. 'Never in my life have I felt that way around another person. Quite honestly, I prefer to be alone. Guess that's why I'm a writer, because it's a solitary endeavor.'

There was something in the way he held my gaze. It wasn't so much honesty as vulnerability. Like he knew he was taking a risk but didn't care about putting his heart on the line. In all the years I'd spent with Max, he'd never been so open. His love came with walls. There were certain topics, issues, he never wanted to discuss. His family, his childhood, were complicated. Too many divorces and parents who'd let him down. Maybe that's why we felt safe in each other's arms, because we'd experienced the same pain and disappointment. But he also refused to show any kind of willingness to share his true feelings. As if speaking them into existence would make him less of a man. That somehow I would view him as smaller.

The thunder rolled on, and Bryce reached for my hand. 'Do you feel it?' he said in a whisper.

'Feel what?'

'The tug in the center of your chest? An ache that swells whenever we're together?'

It would be easy to lie to him. Pretend that he was alone in his feelings. But I'd spent my whole life being brave.

Pretending that my mother constantly leaving, people staring at me oddly, whispering under their breaths, was all okay. But I was tired of bearing that heavy weight. Of holding everyone in my world, besides my family, at arm's length.

He took my hesitation as an opportunity to inch back across the bench seat. Slide a chilly hand over my cheek that made me shiver.

'Shit, sorry. My hands must be cold.'

He began to move away, and I placed my hand over his. Like that night in the clinic, we didn't pull back but stayed mere inches apart. This time Bryce was the bold one, leaning in and kissing the corners of my lips. He whispered my name as his mouth glided over my cheek and slid to my ear. He murmured how soft my skin was. That my hair smelled like fresh straw and spring orange blossoms.

I shivered again, but this was not about the cold and wind seeping in the windows. It was about the wild need in his eyes. The eagerness in his grip as he reached out and pulled me onto his lap. How he adjusted me until I felt the delicious scrape of where he was already hard for me.

Taking his time, he kissed a path across my chin and down my neck to the hollow of my throat, where my veins pulsed out how much I wanted him. My fingers found the hair at the nape of his neck and I tugged him closer. He groaned against my skin. Tugged the canvas jacket off my shoulders and placed his hands beneath the hem of my T-shirt, tugging it over my head.

'Beautiful,' he murmured, leaning in to place a kiss over the lace bralette I was wearing.

The heat of his mouth made me arch, and he palmed my back, holding me steady. One by one, he nudged the straps off my shoulders and worked his tongue over my nipples, his warm breath turning them into stiff peaks.

'I've been dreaming about this since that night in the clinic. How I wanted to stretch you out, see every inch of you, watch as you writhed beneath me.'

'Too much talking.' I pressed my mouth to the corner of his chin, gripping his shirt and begging him to take it off. He responded to my command, and I sucked in a breath at the curves of his biceps, the sharp edges to his chest and abdomen.

Teasing him, I ground down, and he released a low moan into the edge of my shoulder. His mouth carved a slow, sinful path down my body. He stopped and looked up at me with hooded eyes. 'I want to touch you so bad.'

'What's stopping you?' I said.

That wicked gleam in his eyes returned as he flipped open the button of my jeans and slid a hand inside my underwear. 'Fuck. I love that you're already wet for me.'

He teased me gently with his fingers, and the moan that spilled from my lips knocked around the inside of the truck. The lights on the dash lit up. I went still, afraid I'd hit something as I moved under his touch. His thumb stroked a rough path over my clit, and my breaths came hard and fast. I rocked against his hand, desperate for release. With a firm grip, he lifted me off his lap and laid me across the bench seat. He scooted back until he was flush against the door and pulled down my jeans. His hand teased the outside of my panties, and I bucked beneath him whispering out a low 'please'.

'Please what?' he teased.

'Your mouth. I need it.'

'Where?'

'On me. In me,' I panted out. His fingers slid under the sides of my underwear and tugged them down.

'All you had to do was ask.'

That devilish grin was back. He placed a searing kiss against my lips before using his tongue to lick a path from below my belly button all the way to my center. His mouth sucked and swirled until he used his finger to part me and slid his tongue inside. I gripped the sides of the seat and hitched my hips up, needing him deeper. Like he could read my thoughts, he placed his hand beneath my back and edged me in closer.

The sight of him between my legs, reddish-blond hair wet from the storm, was so hot I spread my legs wider, and he grunted his approval. A building warmth filled my belly as he reached down with one hand and began to touch himself, the rhythm mirroring the soft stroke of his tongue. Rain fell harder against the roof, and the dash lit up again under the power of the storm.

That link between us bloomed like the sun inching above the horizon, and although this was wild, me relinquishing every rational thought, doing this on the side of the road where anyone could find us, I gave in to my ravenous hunger.

I began to quake beneath him, and like he knew I needed that extra nudge, his hand returned to my center, and along with his tongue and fingers I gasped and slid right over the edge into beautiful oblivion.

He held me close as the orgasm vaulted through me, whispering 'Unbelievable' against my body as if he could etch it into my skin.

When my soul returned to earth, he tenderly redressed me and lifted my body back onto his lap. Wrapping his hands around my waist, he tucked me in close. He was still hard beneath me, and I reached for him. 'No,' he whispered. 'I just want to hold you. Breathe you in for a moment if that's all right.'

Once again, he'd stunned me into silence. Max had been kind in bed. Sweet, but never emotional. The way that Bryce held me now, as if I was meant to be cherished, nearly broke me. I swallowed back the sob in my throat and buried my head deeper into his shoulder.

We stayed quiet as our breathing synced. His hands stroked the back of my head, and I eased into him, that buzzy tether between us tightening like nothing could sever what was growing between us.

'I sort of think the universe wanted this to happen,' he said quietly.

'What makes you say that?'

'A sudden storm. A flat tire. Feels like the fates wanted us to be together in this moment.'

I huffed out a laugh. 'Be careful. You're beginning to sound like a local.'

'Is that so bad?'

I pulled back. There was no way this cynical journalist believed any of what he was saying. Words of protest started to form on my lips when my phone buzzed on the dash. I grabbed it and glanced at the screen. 'Lia's on her way with a spare tire.'

'Too bad,' he said, placing a soft kiss on my forehead. His gentleness sent another shiver through me. What we'd just done was incredible, and I didn't regret it for a second, but I had to fix my clothes, school my face, before my sister arrived.

'I'm looking forward to dinner tomorrow night,' he said, tugging his shirt back over his head.

Shit. I'd forgotten about dinner with Clo. I was already hiding so much from my family, and now I had to pretend Bryce meant nothing to me. Which was going to be nearly impossible, considering my emotional connection to my sisters, and the fact that they'd be watching us like damn hawks the entire time.

# *Chapter Sixteen*

## *Stick to the Plan*

Clo was roasting a damn turkey.

I couldn't believe it.

Even at Thanksgiving, she complained about how long it took to cook a fifteen-pound bird. How all the time required to season and baste it was a pain in the ass. But here she was, shuffling around the kitchen, her snow-white hair curling up around her ears while she made a feast fit for a king.

Aster scurried around the table setting out the good china. Lia sat like a lump in our grandfather's favorite armchair, watching the entire spectacle with a grim expression. Flora's gentle doggy snore sounded from the corner. Her legs twitched like she was chasing rabbits in her sleep. At least someone was calm and relaxed.

Last night I tossed and turned, unable to banish the image of Bryce's tender gaze as he laid me across the seat. Worked me to a delicious high with his mouth. How I'd bolted away from him the second the lights from Lia's Jeepster flashed across the windshield. The excuses I'd made about how I needed to get back to the clinic, nearly pushing him out of the truck as I dropped him back in town.

I couldn't shake the worry that tonight was going to be a disaster. My sisters could easily read my feelings, and I wasn't sure how I was going to get through this dinner without spiraling out.

'Clo, why are you doing this? I don't think Bryce is expecting this kind of meal,' I said, frantically stirring the gravy bubbling in the saucepan.

'Don't you know anything about *The Art of War*?' She moved around frantically, stacking dishes and wiping off the butcher block island. This kitchen was her pride and joy. Grandpa Beau thought of every detail when he'd designed it. A wide farmhouse sink was perfect for washing the plentiful crops from her garden. He'd torn out the old and weathered tile countertops and put in a soft white granite. Replaced the ancient double oven and stovetop with state-of-the art appliances. I often caught her in quiet moments, running her hand over the counters like she could still feel his presence here.

'Knowing yourself *and* your enemy is the key to winning,' she said, scrubbing several knives and setting them in the sink.

'And you think part of Sun Tzu's master plan was to fill an enemy to the gills with turkey, mashed potatoes and homemade peach cobbler?' I said, batting away the thought that what we'd done in my truck was the absolute opposite of war.

'Of course! Once Bryce is good and stuffed, he'll be less on his guard. The tryptophan from the turkey will mellow him out. Lull his senses.'

'So you want him to pass out?' Aster leaned a hip against the counter, her gaze narrowing on me like she could hear the racing of my heart. Shit. This was going to be bad.

'No, silly girl!' Clo shot back. 'I want him comfortable. It's easier to extract information that way.'

'Were you a covert CIA agent at one time? Because the way you're talking it seems like it,' Lia called from across the room.

'I'm not being covert. I'm being protective. This man wants to write about our town. Our personal history. We need to be on guard, cautious about what we say to him, but we also need to find out his plan for the story. How he might try to twist facts as journalists tend to do.'

I shook my head and went back to stirring. In the short time I'd known Bryce, I'd figured out that he was good at reading people and situations. I had no doubt he knew exactly what he was walking into tonight.

The brown gravy with hints of rosemary bubbled in the pot. The dining area was filled with Aster's sweet hum as she straightened out the white linen tablecloth until Lia stiffened in the chair. 'His car is coming up the driveway. He's five minutes early.'

'That's fine, because we're ready,' Clo said, wiping her hands on the edges of her starched cream apron. 'Lia, start filling the water glasses. Aster, you open the wine.' She pointed to a bottle sitting near the edge of the counter.

My sisters did as they were told, and I continued to monitor the gravy. Once I was sure it was the right consistency, I turned off the burner. A few seconds later there was a sharp knock at the door.

Lia glared at me. 'Someone has to move and answer it.'

'Fine, but you get over here and stir,' I ordered.

I jogged to the stairs and Flora was quickly beside me. Once we were at the bottom, I hesitated in front of the door. Smoothed down the light curls that hung past my shoulders. Pressed at the collar of my soft blue T-shirt dress. I pulled in a breath and ran my hand over my lips. The sticky hint of deep pink gloss covered two of my fingers.

Did I look like I'd dressed up for him? Thinking it was too much, I dragged the back of my wrist across my mouth, blotting out the color.

Another knock made me jump. I straightened my shoulders and yanked open the door. Bryce stood in the threshold, and I had to swallow my damn tongue. His hair was neatly combed back from his face. A cornflower-blue polo brought out the color of his eyes. Pink dahlias surrounded by a handful of lavender and baby's breath sat in a short square glass vase in his hand. That buzzy feeling warmed my chest again. I let myself relax into it until Flora barked out her own greeting.

He gave Flora's head a gentle pat as his gaze slowly raked up my body. 'Hello, Dani.'

It was criminal the way his low voice lit up my insides. I must have stared at him too long because he said, 'Are you rethinking your grandmother's invite?'

'No.' I clumsily waved him forward, and he stepped in close, pressing a gentle kiss to my cheek.

'I can't stop thinking about yesterday.'

He was a damn menace. If he kept staring like he wanted to undress me, we were never going to make it through this meal.

I set my hands on his shoulders and gave him a gentle push back. 'None of that. You need to be on your best behavior. My family is up there, and they're like freaking emotional barometers. If you give me even the gentlest look, they'll know something is up.'

He grinned, made an animated cross over his heart. 'I promise to be a perfect gentleman, at least while other people are around.'

'Be good,' I hissed and pointed to the stairs leading up to the kitchen and main living area. That cedar scent of his hung in the air, and I tried not to look like an idiot as I breathed it in.

When Bryce reached the top of the landing, he walked straight toward Clo, who was washing her hands at the sink.

'Your youngest granddaughter said these were your favorite,' he said, handing her the arrangement.

Lia and I swung our heads in Aster's direction.

'What? He came into the shop and asked. It wasn't like I was gonna turn away his money.' She plucked the vase from Clo's hands. 'They're looking parched. I'll add more water.'

Once the tap was running, she tilted her head to look at Bryce. A small twitch at the corner of her mouth mimicked the one in the coffee shop. Could she see his color now? Was it still that same shade of persimmon that matched mine? Even worse, could she sense the heat between us? My heart stuttered, and I shoved the idea out of my head. This was not a moment to think about anything but getting him to reveal what he planned to write in that article.

'Can I get you a drink? Maybe something with arsenic?' Lia said in a quiet mumble.

'Lia!' Grandmother Clo chided.

'It's fine,' Bryce chuckled. 'It's clear that I'm walking into the lion's den here.'

'Pour him a glass of wine and be nice,' Clo ordered.

Lia spun around and did as she was told, filling a glass with a rich red blend and shoving it across the counter toward him.

'Please sit down. Dinner is almost ready,' Clo said.

'It smells great.' He walked across the open space past the dining table and seating area. For a minute he scanned the photos hung on the walls. My breath hitched when he narrowed his focus on the sepia-toned image of Ambrosia and Sylvia. Thankfully, Flora trotted toward him. He stopped to pet her as she sniffed at his jeans and shirt.

'Sorry, girl. Indy's at home tonight.'

Like she didn't like his response, she spun away and nudged her way out onto the deck. Bryce followed her, stopping at the back wall of windows. The setting sun painted the sky a rich shade of orange, reminding me once more of Aster's revelation about him.

'This is a beautiful view,' he said.

'My late husband, Beau, built the house in this spot so we could watch the colors rise and fall over the lake in the course of a day.'

'I'm sorry for your loss,' Bryce murmured before he took a sip of wine.

'It's been a long time, and I have all this to remember him by,' Clo replied.

Bryce gave an understanding nod and sauntered back to the living area. He moved his way around the couch and sank into Grandpa Beau's armchair.

Lia cursed under her breath, and I pressed a hand against her arm. 'Remember why he's here. We need to stick to Clo's plan.'

She went back to stirring the gravy, which stayed at a brisk bubble even though the burner was off.

Aster plopped the vase in the center of the dining table and went to sit on the chestnut-colored couch across from Bryce. 'Tell us a bit about yourself,' she said in her sweet and disarming voice. Bryce eased back into the chair. It was hard not to relax around my kind little sister.

'Born and raised in Los Angeles. Went to college in the San Francisco Bay Area.'

'Any brothers or sisters?' Aster said.

'Only child.'

'And your parents?' she pressed as Clo and Lia pretended they weren't listening to every word.

'It's just me and my mom,' he said with a short clip.

'But you have relatives here?' Aster said.

'Did,' he replied grimly.

'I knew Richard.' Clo placed a lapis-blue serving dish on the counter and began scooping mashed potatoes into it. 'He was a good man.'

'I wouldn't know,' Bryce said sharply and then took a deep, steadying breath. 'What I mean is I should have taken the time to know him. I regret that I didn't.'

His gaze slid over the framed photos sitting on the wood mantel above the stone fireplace and then glided to the McGuire and Perkins family pictures strewn about the rest of the room.

There was a sorrow I recognized in his eyes. It was the realization that a time had passed you'd never get back but wished you could. It was how I thought about Grandpa Beau's passing.

We lost him the summer I went to a special equine camp in Fort Collins. On a muggy June day, Clo found him in the garden under a tree. She thought he'd fallen asleep, but when she couldn't wake him, she knew he was gone for good.

I'd rushed home after that to console her and my sisters. Of course, Belladonna was nowhere to be found. It was just one of the many reasons why I wasn't quick to reply to her emails. Whenever you let her in, even if it was for a second, she managed to break your heart.

The timer dinged over the stove, and Clo waved us all to the table. Instead of waiting for me to point him to a chair, Bryce jumped up. He set his wine glass on the table and strode into the kitchen, swiping a pair of oven mitts off the counter. 'Please, let me,' he said once she had the oven door open.

Oh, he was good.

Clo gave him a smirk and stepped back. In one smooth move, he had the large roasting pan out and resting on the cooling rack set to the right of the sink.

'Dani, will you please do the honors,' Clo said, waving me away from the stove.

'I can carve—' Bryce started.

'Do you have surgical training like my Dandelion?' Clo snipped.

He shot me an impish grin. 'No, ma'am, I do not.'

Clo grabbed the oven mitts from him and slid them on. She reached into the pan and hefted out the rack holding the turkey, setting it on a thick cutting board with a border well to collect all the juices.

'It's been resting in the oven for thirty minutes so it should be ready.' She pointed to the row of tools (kitchen shears, boning, chef and carving knives) she'd set out next to the cutting board. 'It's all ready to go for you.'

'This is ridiculous,' I said. 'If you want it done right, you should ask Lia. She's a pro at gutting fish.'

'Nope. It's all you, *Dandelion*,' Lia said with an annoying smirk.

Aster tugged on the corner of Bryce's shirt, pointing for him to sit at the end of the table where Grandpa Beau once sat. Yet another thing that would probably set Lia off tonight.

'Grab the wine bottle,' Aster ordered. 'This often becomes a long and drawn-out battle over the proper way to carve a turkey.'

'There's a wrong way?' He set down the bottle in the center of the table and waved a halting hand at Aster so he could pull out her chair. Clo flashed an approving grin at him.

What was happening? Where were her *Art of War* plans?

Once she was finished giving him her dazzling smile, Clo pointed to the trussing twine and barked, 'Cut there first.'

I arched a brow at her. 'Now you're going to supervise?'

We had a five-second stare-down until she trained her gaze on Bryce and said, 'I'll take a glass of wine.'

Before Bryce could reach for the bottle, Lia was swiping it away. 'I've got this.' She filled Clo's glass at the head of the table and sank down next to Aster.

Yeah, Lia was not going to make this easy for Bryce.

With Aster peppering him with more questions, and Lia giving him multiple withering gazes, I went to work cutting away the twine and then removing the legs and thighs with the boning knife. As I worked, the weight of Bryce's stare made me glance up more than once. When our eyes locked, he gave me that same awestruck look from yesterday.

Aster clocked the rising flush on my cheeks. I dropped my head, focusing back on the bird while Bryce tried to engage Lia. He asked about her work, and the training needed to be on a search and rescue team. Unfortunately, he mentioned one of the trails they'd just closed, and Lia fisted the corner of the white tablecloth.

'Please tell me you're not one of those people who ignores trail signs. Because if you get caught, it's a five-hundred-dollar fine.'

'I would never do that,' he said quickly.

'You'd better not.' Lia wasn't giving him an inch. 'I've spent too many days rescuing people like you who don't know their skill level before they set off on a hike.'

'Camellia, modulate your tone please,' Clo said.

The chandelier above the table flickered once as my grandmother approached the table. Bryce was out of his seat and pulling out her chair.

'Thank you.' That warm smile was back. 'And just so you know, my granddaughter is usually on better behavior, but the dry conditions and lack of rain have put Harvest Moon at a very high risk-level for a wildfire. It's put everyone on edge lately.'

The gravy popped and spurted behind me. Maybe I'd looked at the wrong knob. I stepped back and removed the pan, held my hand a few inches above the burner but there wasn't any heat. What the hell? After Bryce was gone, I had to insist Clo have it serviced.

'I respect what you and your team do, Lia. In fact, I saw you all in action on the bluffs last week,' Bryce said.

'That was a fairly straightforward job.' She said the words casually, but her shoulders went tight.

'What happened, Lee Lee? I didn't hear about this in town,' Aster said.

'A thirteen-year-old kid was hiking with his family visiting from Denver. He was messing around behind them, looking at his phone, not paying attention to where he was going. His family got pretty far ahead and he lost track of them. When he realized it, he started to sprint into the woods, caught his foot on a rock and broke his ankle.'

'Your team was there quickly. Assessed him and he was on a stretcher and down the trail in no time.'

Bryce's compliment earned a rare smile from Lia. 'It's why we put in a lot of training hours.'

'Did you have to apply first aid, honey?' Clo asked after a sip of wine.

'Just a quick splint to stabilize the ankle.'

I slid a large pile of meat onto a white porcelain serving platter and approached the table. Bryce was up again, taking it from my hands and setting it in the center.

'Is he okay now?' I said as Bryce pulled out my chair, giving me an easy smile that shot goosebumps across my skin.

'Yeah, we found his parents a few minutes later. They took him to the hospital once we got him loaded into their car,' Lia said.

Bryce settled down into his own seat, his eyes never leaving Lia as she went on. 'The family called the fire station the next day to let us know it was a clean break. That the kid was feeling all right but would be in a cast for six weeks.'

Bryce pulled a notepad from his pocket and we all froze.

'I wanted to take a few notes about the rescue if that's all right. It'd be great to include in the article about the town.' He pressed a pen against the spot on his finger that was ink-stained. 'A few of the guys on your crew said the kid fell and was hidden in some brush. That he would have stayed camouflaged if you hadn't found him. They mentioned something about your acute hearing and sense of smell. How you have an oddly strong connection with the land. Can you tell me more?'

Lia went back to clenching the edge of the table. Aster dug her fingers into the side of her chair. Despite having plenty of water, the lavender in the vase drooped and withered.

We'd allowed ourselves to be dazzled by Bryce's charm for too long tonight. Forgotten the real reason Clo had invited him here. The real reason we should be on guard, even in the place all three of us still considered home. But his questions, his curiosity about Lia, were a good reminder that even though he flashed us smiles, acted like a gentleman, he was still our common enemy.

# *Chapter Seventeen*

## *A Woman Can Be a Terrifying Creature*

Lia's jaw was pure steel. She looked at Bryce like he was the devil, and to his credit he didn't flinch.

'Like I said, it was a straightforward job.'

'But they said you have *unique* skills.' Bryce let his meaning hang in the air. Aster watched the two of them with wide eyes, gulping down her entire glass of wine.

Lia didn't take the bait. 'I've been doing this since I was nineteen. You want a scoop? Here it is.'

Bryce leaned in, pen hovering over the page.

'Tourists come and visit. They want to be in the great outdoors because they've watched some nature documentary on TV, but they overestimate their hiking capabilities. Don't pay attention to the terrain, or the heat gets to them because they don't bring enough water. People forget it can get warm in Colorado, even in the mountains.'

Bryce's pen scratched across the pad. 'What about more complicated cases? Lost hikers reported missing?'

'What about them?' Lia shot back.

'How do you know where to start? Do you get GPS coordinates? Use your senses? Your skills on the trail?'

'It's called training,' Lia said through gritted teeth. 'On most calls it's a friend or family member reporting a loved one missing. We try to track their phone to find their last known coordinates. The team of volunteers gets a text or a call, grabs their gear and reports to the location. The incident commander or team leader tells us the scenario, what channels to put our radios on, what equipment needs to go with us, and then we hike to the last known location. Sometimes it's a rescue.' Her voice quivered. 'Other times it's a body recovery. There's nothing supernatural to it. It's damn hard work, and I love every second of it.'

Bryce went still. Aster and Clo held their breaths. How had I allowed this to happen? Let him get so close?

The serving fork slid out of my hand and made a loud clank against the platter. Everyone jumped, and I gave a tense smile as I grabbed the fork again and slid turkey onto my plate.

'More wine?' Aster squeaked, filling her own glass to the brim.

I stayed still, praying Clo had a plan to turn this disaster around.

Like he understood his mistake, Bryce slid the notepad back into his pocket. He reached for the mashed potatoes and put a large dollop on his plate before handing the bowl to Clo.

'Ast, are you getting those lilies you need for the wedding next weekend?' I said, scrambling to ease the tension.

She nodded and swallowed her mouthful of turkey. 'They're coming Friday, but, of course, now that Mrs Desiray has seen, and smelled, the Stargazers, she wants them in the table arrangements for the reception.'

Her breathing sped up. Aster always grew nervous before a big wedding, but this was added pressure due to her relationship with Marley, and the current spotlight on her semi-famous friend.

Lia leaned into her and whispered something that made Aster press her napkin to her mouth and stifle a giggle. She could be brusque at times, but Lia also had the ability to say the right thing in an important moment. It was why Chief Malbrough often put her in charge of high-intensity calls. The harder the task, the more my little sister shone.

Bryce watched the two of them with a keen eye. I hoped he saw what I did. Two sisters teasing each other. Swapping small jabs and laughing at inside jokes. That there was no magical charm in this house, or secret mystery about the McGuire women that he needed to document.

As my sisters continued to whisper, there was a sudden ease to his shoulders, a special lilt to his smile you wouldn't notice if you weren't paying attention. And, unfortunately, I was always paying attention to him.

We went back to quietly eating until my sisters got more wine in them. With the liquid courage making them brave, they turned the tables on Bryce. Interrogated him about his dangerous assignments in war-torn countries. Clo asked if those assignments made his mother worry, which he admitted they did.

'She was not happy when I told her about being embedded with an army unit while they took heavy gunfire. But observing that group of brave men and women, seeing their tactics, their determination, how they worked as a cohesive group, was fascinating.'

'I read about that,' Clo said. 'If I understand correctly, you were nominated for quite a few awards for that story.'

The way the tips of his ears pinked up was too damn charming. 'Yes, ma'am, that's right. But I got an earful from my mother after that. She begged that I work on more domestic stories. The terror in her voice has kept me stateside ever since.'

Clo made an understanding hum. 'I've been lucky to have my girls close by for most of their lives. When Dani went to school a few hours away, I panicked a little.'

The look she gave me was filled with so much love I had to swallow down the growing knot in my throat. Bryce's gaze moved to me. That warmth from the truck was back, and it made me feel understood in a way that was beyond explanation. Max and I had lived together for years, but he'd never pinned me with a stare that was filled with such immeasurable tenderness. I focused back on my plate, too afraid Lia and Aster would clock the heated connection between Bryce and me.

'I understood she needed to leave,' Clo went on. 'But it's hard to let go of the things you cherish, even when it's necessary. Your mother, I'm sure, felt the same way.'

Clo's voice shook as she focused on a photo of a young Belladonna on a nearby table. Whenever my mother swirled back into our lives, she brought chaos. I'd never considered how Clo felt when her child returned home, only for her to leave again on a whim with no idea of when she'd return.

Sensing the sadness in the room, Aster started a story about a little terrier who was the ringbearer at a recent wedding. How the dog went rogue on its cue, taking off into the nearby woods and burying the rings.

'It took over an hour for the entire wedding party to dig through the dirt until the small mesh bag was finally discovered. The groomsmen were dirty. Mud was caked under the bridesmaids' fingernails, but after it was over, everyone laughed. They even asked the photographer to document the mess.'

The tales continued as Lia talked about the mishaps of her new recruits. How they didn't apply enough sunscreen. Got easily winded on their fifteen-mile hikes through the rough Colorado terrain.

It didn't take long for Clo to start sharing stories about our feral childhood. Bryce especially loved the berry-hunting tale where all three of us girls ended up in a giant mud puddle.

'We squished our way back to the house, and Clo did her best to rinse us off,' Aster said in between giggles. 'When she couldn't get rid of the sludge in our ears, between our toes and caked in our long hair, Grandpa Beau got involved. One by one he tossed us straight into the lake. Warned we couldn't come out until we were good and clean. We squealed in protest but agreed it was one of the most memorable days of our childhood.'

The tales rolled on for another half hour. Bryce stayed still in his chair, witnessing the way we could finish each other's sentences and stories. Once or twice a flicker of sadness crossed his face. It made me wonder if it was hard to be an only child. To not know the love and affection of a sibling who offered you unconditional love, even on days when you were at your most unlovable.

When plates were empty and the wine was gone, Clo spread out the napkin in her lap and turned to Bryce. 'How much have you learned about our little town? Maybe I can enlighten you on a few things.'

He sat up straighter, rolled back his shoulders. 'I told Dani I wasn't here to write about the supposed magic in this town, but I keep hearing stories about you and your late husband's family lines. Can you tell me how and why those rumors started?' He dropped his chin. Shook his head like he couldn't believe he was having this conversation. 'Is there a thin line of truth in the stories? Like people believed they saw something, and over the years that spun out of control?'

Aster went still. Lia gripped the tablecloth again. I held my breath as Clo gave him a measured stare. 'Settle in, Mr O'Dell. You're about to get a story you'll never forget.'

Bryce set his elbows on the table, leaned in and waited for Clo. Her lips thinned as her gaze wandered to the family photos scattered about the room. The chandelier blinked again. One bulb in the center shimmered, clearly needing to be replaced.

'What is magic?' Clo started. 'There are fairy tales written about it. TV shows and movies that glorify its mythical appeal. But, in truth, magic is about control.'

'Control? How so?' Bryce asked.

'Claims of magic were used as a weapon. Wielded to frighten those who would not stay in line, especially women who dared to speak their minds, know their worth, and were murdered because of it.'

She toyed with the lip of her glass, resolve steadying her voice. 'You could claim that the rise of the sun in the morning, its dipping dramatically toward the horizon in the evening, is a kind of sorcery. The same holds true of how we plant seeds in the earth, and with a bit of sunlight, water, it becomes a beautiful field of flowers weeks later. Magic itself is all in the interpretation.' She set her chin. 'In Harvest Moon it's nothing but a vehicle for tourism. It just so happens that the brilliance and skills of my granddaughters, and long-whispered rumors about my ancestors, and my husband's family, started over a century ago, offer a perfect opportunity for this town to make a little money.'

Bryce's eyes went intense. 'Tell me more about those rumors. I've heard your great-great-grandmother Ambrosia was said to start fires with nothing but a snap of her fingers. That her mother had the ability to divine water. You're saying those stories were lies?'

*A snap of her fingers.*

Heat made a slow creep up my neck. How the hell did he know about Ambrosia and Sylvia? That journal was tucked deep below T-shirts and tank tops in a drawer at home. It could only be Mo, who kept running her mouth in spite of my pleas.

Not a single emotion moved over Clo's face. She set her napkin next to her plate and released a brittle laugh. 'Oh, Bryce, you may have years of being an investigative journalist, spent time in war zones, unearthed all kinds of political scandals, but you will never know what it's like to be a woman.'

His brows rose as her tone turned harder.

'A woman can be a terrifying creature if she has the strength to speak her truth. Fight for what she knows she deserves. Back in the times of Ambrosia, and her mother, Sylvia, women were taught from birth that they were to be weak and subservient to the men in their lives. First to their fathers, their brothers, and then, eventually, to the men they would wed. Any woman who could voice her opinions, her desires, became a being who was different than the mold. That difference was seen as a sign of darkness. Of rot. It only made sense that men would turn that power and strength into something they could villainize and destroy. Sylvia had money, a rare commodity in those days. With it, she could steer her own future. The future of her daughter. I'd guess the men who sought to woo the two attractive widows did not like it when their advances were turned down.'

The chastened look in his eyes said he knew Clo was right. It was a brilliant tactic. Remind him that years of violence against women who were deemed 'different' was rooted in men's own weakness. That their power was somehow being threatened. How the stories about Harvest Moon's magic were essentially that – stories that allowed men to keep their power.

'I understand that being able to uncover some dark secret about this town would help revive your career.' Her pitying look made him shift in his seat. 'But I also know from reading many of your articles that you value truth. Go ahead and talk to people in town. Continue to dig. Do as much research as you want about our history. I'll even tell Ruthie to give you access to whatever else you need from the archives.' Her gaze flicked to me and then back to Bryce. 'You'll see that we are nothing but a small Colorado town trying to survive on business and the goodness in the community. Nothing more. Nothing less.'

I was sure Clo's sermon had won him over until the twitch in his cheek said he understood her speech was overly polished. Rehearsed. Like her slickness was trying to gloss over a real truth.

He was good at his job, and even though Clo and I both were trying to wave him off, lead him in the wrong direction, he was too intuitive, too seasoned, to take our words at face value. Essentially, we were screwed. This dinner was nothing but a charade with an unhappy ending.

Aster cleared her throat and picked up the empty platter. 'You have to have some of Clo's homemade cobbler, Bryce. It's won her many blue ribbons.'

He rubbed at his belly. 'I'm not sure I could eat another bite.'

Clo arched a brow at him.

'But since I'm here, might as well give it a try.'

Lia helped Aster clear the table. The two of them chatted about the upcoming weddings she had on the calendar. How with fall approaching, Aster was eager to order lisianthuses, delphiniums and strawflowers for the shop.

Clo distracted Bryce again with more questions about his writing, but he kept turning the conversation back to the town.

I moved away from the table, helping with the cleanup and ignoring the heat of Lia's blistering stare. She wasn't dumb. She had eyes and witnessed the way Bryce's attention fixated on me. The way I averted my own gaze away from him. How most of my meal went uneaten because I was too busy trying to keep my emotions in check. Pretend I didn't have a rapidly growing attraction to this man who'd take off the second after his story was written.

Clo continued with her chatter, but there was an uneasiness to her voice. Like she understood Bryce had dug in. Was committed to learning all he could about us and our connection to Harvest Moon.

We could study and try to apply Sun Tzu's lessons, but Bryce had shown us he was also adept at battle tactics. I wasn't giving up, though. Tonight had taught me that when the McGuire women were together, we could hold the line, and, with strength and ingenuity, eventually win the war.

# Chapter Eighteen

## *Put on a Brave Face*

Gravel crunched beneath my tennis shoes as I walked Bryce to his car. Clouds moved across the night sky, revealing a waxing gibbous moon. A whisper of wind shook the branches in the towering ponderosa trees surrounding the house.

There wouldn't be many more warm, quiet nights like this one. Once fall descended, and the first snow arrived, all the beauty of nature would head into hibernation. It wouldn't be until many months later that a warm spring sun would coax the gems of the forest back to life.

'Again with this sky.' He tilted his head to the deep indigo blanket covered in too many twinkling stars to count.

'There's very little light pollution here. It makes it easier to see the constellations. Count them out one by one.'

'That'd take some time.' He smirked. 'But I'd like to try.'

His gaze stayed focused on the sky, and I waited for him to move. Say something about the way my family had grilled him for the last two hours. To explain how he knew about Ambrosia and Sylvia.

'I'd better head inside. Lia gets surly if I don't help with the dishes.'

'Stay for a minute.' The slow drag of his voice was hypnotic, and I stepped closer, feeling that tether tightening between us.

'Any hints at what you learned tonight? Might use in your article?'

That grin was back. 'I feel like I got pretty good insight into how the McGuire women work together. Fight together.' His smile faltered. 'Love and support each other.'

He scrubbed a hand over the stubble on his chin, and I had to resist the temptation to reach out and drag my thumb over the reddish whiskers. Ignore the memory of how they'd brushed against my bare thighs in the truck.

Like he could read my mind, see where my stare was focused, that smile widened. He slid a hand around my waist and nudged me into the hard lines of his body.

'It did make me wish for a sibling until—'

I chuckled not expecting that response. 'Lia can get a little salty sometimes.'

His face sobered. 'That's not what I was going to say.'

'Go on then. I'm curious about what's whirling around inside that brain of yours.'

He leaned in so those whiskers brushed against my cheeks. 'That cobbler.' The low rumble of his voice sent warmth through my core. 'If I had siblings, I'd never want to share.'

A full belly laugh burst from my lips this time. 'That's true. We often fight over the last bite.'

'See.' Now both of his hands were around my waist. 'I get complicated family dynamics.'

This time his attention didn't return to the sky. Instead, he brushed his hand gently over the planes of my cheeks. 'I do have one question for you, though.'

I should have moved, worried that my sisters would know what was happening out here under the moonlight, but that subtle tug between us was stronger than ever.

'Were you ever going to tell me about Ambrosia and Sylvia, or were you going to hide the journal forever?' The corners of his mouth twitched. 'I have to hand it to you, knocking those books off the table was a good diversion.'

I didn't move. Give any hint that I knew what he was talking about.

'It's all right.' His voice brushed over the cuff of my ear. 'I can wait until you're ready to share it. But it doesn't mean I won't find out what's inside anyway.'

Like that link between us was sliced straight in half, I stumbled away from him. 'You must be imagining things, because I don't have any journal. Maybe the high altitude is rattling your brain.'

'I know what I saw. What I've been told. I can be patient, *Dandelion*, but I have no plans to give up.'

My feet stayed frozen to the ground. If I looked at him, I was sure he'd see the truth written across the lines of my face.

The low melody of a Fleetwood Mac song floated out of the windows. Lia must have lost a bet. She never let Aster pick the music that filled the house while they did the dishes.

I appreciated the distraction, because it reminded me where my allegiance needed to be. That there could no longer be a flirtation between Bryce and me. No more heated moments where we ended up half-dressed with our mouths slick from the taste of each other. No… This all had to stop.

'Goodnight, Bryce.'

Like he heard the resolve in my voice, he took a slow stroll to his car.

I stayed in the driveway for a few more minutes, pulling in a lungful of clean mountain air, hoping the sudden knots stretching against my shoulders would loosen with each and every breath.

This wasn't hiding from my family. Avoiding the inevitable interrogation that was coming. It was calming the furious pound of my heart, because I'd have to admit how drawn I was to Bryce. That he knew about the journal and my poor attempt to hide it, which only made him more curious about what was written inside.

As the music grew louder, I headed for the front door. When I reached the top of the stairs, Aster was dancing around, swinging a dish towel above her head, and crooning about being taken by the sky. I cleared my throat, and Lia ran to her phone to close her music app.

Clo stood at the wall of windows facing the dark lake. The tension in the air was thicker than the late fall fog that hung like a ghost over the water.

'He likes you.' Clo broke the silence. 'And that terrifies the hell out of you.'

'Shouldn't it?' I said.

'Yes, it should,' Lia spat out from her spot at the sink. 'You know as well as I do what happened the last time a reporter wrote a story about this town. And now' – she flapped her arms out to the cleared table – 'you and Clo are inviting a journalist, whose magazine has half a million copies in circulation, into our home like some fucking honored guest! It's dumb and dangerous.'

'Lee Lee,' Aster said quietly. 'It's not that bad. He seemed nice.'

'Nice?' Lia closed her eyes as if gathering all her patience. 'I love you, Ast, but you don't remember what happened the last time a reporter was here. The chaos it caused.' She pulled in another wobbly breath. 'For our grandmother *and* Dani.'

Aster's eyes were pained. 'Tell me then so I can understand.'

A stream of memories rushed back to me like the world was tilting beneath my feet. I'd pushed that episode to the far back of my brain. Locked it away so it couldn't hurt me anymore. I'd spent most of my life trying to protect Aster, but she was a grown woman now. She needed to know what we'd endured the last time an article was written about this town and its history of magic. How with no more than six paragraphs, a single journalist turned most of the town against us.

I walked to the corner of Grandpa Beau's favorite chair and put my hand against it, needing to steady myself. Feel his strength.

'The year I entered middle school, a reporter from Denver came to town. He started asking all sorts of weird questions about witchcraft. Most of the locals blew him off until he started showing pictures around town of salt circles he'd found in the woods not more than five hundred yards from this house. Pools of what looked like blood in the dirt.'

Aster's mouth hung open.

'This town has always leaned into its supposed magical history, but it's been more subtle, unspoken, not something straight out of a horror film.'

Aster nodded along.

'The town, and the tourists, panicked, especially since the article mentioned the Perkins line and the rumors about Ambrosia and her mother. I got bullied for weeks at school because of it.'

I looked at Clo, whose face gave nothing away. 'People left hideous messages in our mailbox. Whispered behind our backs in town. The panic went on for nearly a month until the sheriff discovered the reporter had staged the blood pools and salt circles just to get a national story. Even with that truth, it took years for people to stop whispering "witch" under their breaths whenever Clo or I walked by.'

'Holy crap,' Aster said with a sigh. 'Why did you never tell me any of this?'

'Because you were young. There was no need to scare you,' I said.

'And because Dani is doing what she always does. Protecting us from the bad shit she thinks we can't handle,' Lia added.

'That's not true,' I protested.

'It is,' Lia shot back. 'Our entire lives, you've shielded us from any kind of worry. When Belladonna shows up, you become this wall that tries to insulate us from her callous actions. But guess what, Dani? You can't protect us from the realities of life. And this Bryce guy, he can act all charming at the table. Shoot a thousand flirty looks and smiles at you.' The pointed stare she gave me warned we'd sucked at hiding our feelings. 'But he's determined to write an article about this town and our history, and I have a feeling it's going to be a thousand times worse than what the reporter from Denver did to us.'

'Lia.' Clo used her gentle voice. 'You can't know that.'

'I can't? Bad shit happens all the time in this world. We may think we can stop it, but we can't. And the three of you pretending like you can keep this guy from writing about us, making up facts to get clicks and likes, is delusional.' She swiped her phone off the counter, grabbed her coat from the peg near the stairs and left without a goodbye.

Clo stayed frozen in place. A low buzz filled the air, and Aster pulled her phone out of her pocket. For a moment there was hope in her eyes, like she expected it to be Lia apologizing, saying she was coming back inside, but her shoulders slumped. 'Dalton's almost here. We're supposed to go to a movie, but I think I should stay so we can talk this out more.'

'No. Go have fun with your friend. Dani and I can clean up the rest,' Clo insisted.

She hesitated and I said, 'Ast, go on. We've got this.'

She stepped back from the counter, her jaw going hard. 'One day this family is going to treat me like a full-grown damn adult, but I guess today is *not* that day.'

Just like Lia, she grabbed her coat and took off down the stairs, the door slamming loudly behind her.

Clo's stare remained on the dark lake, and I moved to stand beside her.

'Do you agree with Lia? Are we in trouble?'

She waited a minute before speaking. 'It's moments like this that I miss your grandfather. He always had a special bond with her.'

'Clo,' I pressed. 'Is this as bad as I think?'

'I don't know. Lia was right. He certainly charmed us tonight.'

'Why help him then? Tell him to go back to the archives?'

'Because I've already asked Ruthie to limit the materials he sees this time.'

Her clipped voice warned she still wasn't happy about me keeping our first trip to the library a secret.

'Even if that happens, he'll still keep digging,' I insisted.

'Yes, because he has a lot at stake too.'

'How do you know that?'

'I looked up more than just his journalistic accolades.'

She went quiet again. Tugged her cardigan tighter around her shoulders. 'You must feel worried and conflicted too.'

Panic crawled through my bones. Had she figured out that I'd crossed the line with Bryce? Or maybe she knew about the journal. Had Ruthie given me away? I should have told her, but the truth stayed jammed in my throat.

'It's all right, sweetheart. Aster told me about Bryce's color.'

That panic stayed coiled within me for an entirely different reason now.

'She and I had a long talk about it.' A sad sigh left her lips. 'I made Aster understand that what she does, sees, can come at a price. Telling you what she did about Max, well, she was still trying to figure out her gift back then. It was a hard lesson for her to learn.'

'Just wish my complicated life wasn't part of that lesson.'

Her attention went back to the lake. 'The idea of soulmates can be tricky. Did you know your grandpa Beau was not the first man who caught my eye?'

'He wasn't?'

'No. There was a boy I knew in high school. Felix Cornell. He was the class clown. Always creating mischief. Hiding the teachers' answer keys for tests. Switching the classical symphony music with Elvis Presley during the daily announcements. He was my first kiss. My first real date.'

'What happened to him?'

'All while we were dating, people whispered behind our backs. Told him that I was descended from dangerous witches. That if he ever tried to break up with me, I'd curse him. Shrink his balls until they were smaller than grapes.'

'What?' I let out a roar of a laugh. 'That's awful.'

I quickly sobered when sadness crept across the lines in her face. 'People can be cruel when they want. Magic was a way they thought they could bully me, which you also know too well.'

My thoughts flashed to the bubbling gravy. The way the flowers wilted when our conversations grew heated. Even the weird flicker of the chandelier. I shook my head. All this talk of magic was making me see things that weren't there.

'The curse thing may have come in handy in Max's case,' I said, trying to make things light.

She patted my hand. 'Even I know you're too tender-hearted for that.'

'Yeah, that may be the problem.'

She arched a white brow. 'That needs some explanation.'

The connection I felt with Bryce was on the tip of my tongue, but instead I said, 'Lia spoke the truth tonight. I do shield her and Aster from a lot. When it comes to my own feelings, though, I tend to swallow everything down. Put on a brave face. Guess I have Belladonna to thank for that.'

She let out a resigned murmur.

'Did the rumors scare Felix off?' I said.

'No. He was too good for that. We were together until graduation. His family did not have money for college so he joined the navy. Got stationed in Hawaii and never came back.'

'That must have made you sad.'

'It did for a while, but the longer he was gone, the less it hurt. With time, I realized we would have never worked. We wanted different things.'

I took an uncomfortable gulp because her words were too much like the excuses Max had used when he'd left me. 'What other things did he want?'

'He had an adventurous spirit. Wanted to travel the world. I was happy here. Never saw my life anywhere else but in Harvest Moon.'

'And Grandpa Beau?'

A wide smile spread across her lips. 'We met while I was taking a pottery class at the community college. He was awful at it, but he kept trying.' She sighed. 'It was what drew me to him. He'd lope into the class, all long legs and skinny arms. Set his bum down on a stool in front of a wheel, slap out a chunk of clay and set his hands right to it. At first he could make a decently round vessel, but then it was like he got too much into his head and the entire thing would collapse.'

Her words reminded me of how much Grandpa Beau and I were alike. How we overthought every little scenario until things spun out of control.

I swallowed down the ache in my throat before asking, 'Had you known him before at school?'

'I'd heard his name here and there but never met him. There was a tradition in his family that the boys attend boarding school on the East Coast starting when they were ten. He didn't come back to live in Harvest Moon until he was eighteen.' She shook her head. 'He was a gorgeous man but such a clumsy oaf. One day he asked to carry my books, but once he had them in his hands he tripped over his own feet, and they went flying. Never seen a man go that shade of red before. Not even when he saw me naked for the first time.'

'Clo!' I yelped. 'Now I'm going to need to bleach that thought right out of my brain.'

She giggled. Clasped my hands. 'Sweetheart, I know you've had a complicated life. That you had to grow up much too fast, but you can't be afraid of love. Not like...' She pressed her lips together.

'Belladonna?' I finished.

'Your mother has always been her own person. From the time she was young, she was independent. Like Lia, she'd wander off into the woods. Make bouquets out of wildflowers that would make Aster proud.' She bumped her hip against mine. 'She loved animals too back then.' A brittle huff left her lips. 'But she was never interested in outward signs of affection. Never wanted anyone to touch her.'

The pain of regret in her eyes was palpable. I couldn't imagine accepting that you could never have a child, and then, when one finally arrived, they weren't interested in being close to you. I hoped that Lia, Aster and I had given her what she'd missed all those years with Belladonna.

'As your mother grew older, she began to see men as a means to an end. The first time she left Harvest Moon it was on the back of a motorcycle with some guy she'd met near the pharmacy. She was barely eighteen. A few months later, she landed in Denver, living with another man. In every situation, she'd worked things to her advantage. Once she got what she needed, she'd escape. Find someone new.' She held my hands tighter. 'You're different, my sweet Dandelion. Kindness radiates out of you. You love with your entire heart. Have such a gentle way with people. It's why you're such a good veterinarian. Why animals seek you out for comfort and care. A being like you is meant to be loved. To share your life with someone who will cherish every single part of who you are.'

'But that can't be Bryce, no matter what Aster says.'

'When you have enough life experience, you tend to see situations a lot clearer. Sense people's intentions. Aster may say Bryce's color matches yours, but I can't say if that's true or not. Only you can decide if he is your soulmate, but that also comes with complications.' Her eyes twinkled. 'My instincts say you're already beginning to understand that fact.'

I couldn't deny that from the moment I met Bryce on the trail, a part of me sensed a connection with him. That tether only grew stronger when he kissed me later that night. And when he touched me in the truck yesterday, eased that ache, it was like all the atoms in my body sparked to life. But tonight, we were back to doing that same cagey dance. Not trusting one another. Not letting our guards down. And that was the issue. We both had clear missions, which were diametrically opposed.

'Nothing can happen between us. He's here to write something so sensational that he can revive his career, and I'm pretty sure that sensational thing he needs is going to be us.' I couldn't help but deflate at my admission. 'Once he's gotten what he needs, he'll head back to Los Angeles and not give Harvest Moon another thought.'

'Perhaps,' she said. 'But people can surprise us too.'

She gave me a hopeful smile before heading into the kitchen. I waited a minute, taking another look at the inverted reflection of the moon on the lake. When we were kids, I'd often find Lia sitting in the dark on the night of a full moon. How she was mesmerized by the way the light glinted off the water. It was a reminder of how this house, this land, was a part of her. How she'd fight for it with her entire soul.

It made sense why she was so angry tonight. She considered Bryce's presence a threat to what she held dear. But there was something else there. Something that had been eating at her since before Bryce showed up. If I called her on it, she'd deny it, but I wasn't going to allow it to simmer too long.

Clo rattled around in the kitchen and I turned to watch her. What she'd said about not being afraid of love shook me. Aster may have claimed that Bryce was meant to be something special in my life, but that didn't matter. My job was to protect this family in spite of whatever I felt for him, and, after tonight, I was convinced I needed to do everything in my power to ensure he never got a shot at hurting a single one of us.

## *Chapter Nineteen*

### *Snow White Come to Life*

Bright yellow caution tape and *Street Closed* signs covered all the roads leading into the center of Harvest Moon. In two hours most of the town would be utter chaos thanks to Veggie Fest. Parking lots would be at capacity. Tourists and townspeople alike would jockey for position inside the dozens of white tents set up on the streets, looking for the sweetest homemade treats and examining the flowers, herbs and vegetables the locals grew with loving hands.

Even though she grumbled about it, Lia was taking her job in the children's area seriously this morning. When I delivered her coffee fresh from Drip! Drip! Hooray!, she grunted a 'thank you', took a few sips, and went back to focusing on the vegetables in front of her.

Before the crush of children appeared, we needed to cut apart mounds of carrots, peppers and celery, as well as set up water-soluble paint stations so kids could make their own vegetable-print paintings.

'So do you want to talk about what happened at Clo's dinner?' I said, leaning against one of the folding tables and blowing the steam off my own coffee.

'Nope.'

'Lee, come on. You've been avoiding it and me. It's not good for you to hold on to things so tightly.'

'I'm fine, and you need to stop doing that.'

'Doing what?'

'Managing me.'

This dialogue had been happening between us for years. Since she was ten, she'd been pushing back on the attempts I made to discuss anything that came close to serious. She was a vat of boiling, unspoken rage that I was terrified was going to explode at the wrong place and wrong time, hurting no one but herself.

'Do you blame me? Since last March, you've become more secretive. Every time I try and talk to you, I get the sense there's a fury you're barely containing. Does it have something to do with Belladonna? Has she contacted you too?'

'She knows better than to reach out to me after what she did to Aster the last time she was here.' Her focus went back to chopping vegetables with a little too much force. 'Why the hell is she calling you?'

'It was an email.'

'Did you respond?'

'No.'

'Well, that's one good thing I've heard today.'

'Lee,' I pleaded. 'Talk to me.'

'Where's the chocolate? Shouldn't it be here by now?' She focused on slicing up more red and green peppers and putting them in paper bowls around the six-foot folding table.

I'd learned not to push her when she wasn't ready to talk, but I wasn't giving up. She was holding on to some kind of pain too tightly, and I wouldn't let her crash and burn.

'Mo is supposed to be delivering it any minute,' I said.

She tipped her chin to two large wood crates in the corner of the tent. 'Randall Pelgrew picked those from his farm this morning. Brought them by a half hour ago. He said to text him if we need more.'

I walked to the crates and cracked open one of the slatted lids. The sweet scent of Honeycrisp apples wafted through the air.

'Should I start slicing them up?' I said.

Just as she was about to answer, Julius shot into the tent, barreling right for me. The Great Dane's massive body slammed into the folding table, and Lia jumped up to catch it before it toppled.

'What the hell?' she huffed as Julius trotted toward me and bowed his head for a pat.

I smoothed the fur on top of his head. Bent down to get a look at his healing muzzle. As I touched his lips, ran my hands down his neck, I waited for that familiar cramping in my bones. The dizziness and tinge of metal on my tongue. When nothing shocked me, I looked into Julius's big brown eyes. 'You staying away from those porcupines?'

He let out a small whimper like I'd reminded him of his pain.

'Dani,' Lia huffed. 'You have to get him out of here.'

I grabbed the dog's collar and moved outside, waving down the judge and Eric, who were scurrying around the tent across the street readying it for the pie-eating contest.

'Missing something?' I called to them.

Both their heads snapped up. Eric gave the judge a withering look before coming to collect Julius.

'Sorry, Dani.' Eric was dressed in jeans and a white Denver Broncos polo that he often wore when he worked the sidelines during home games. He'd taken the job as a commentator when his days as a player ended with a bad break to his right tibia. 'We brought his bed into the tent, and he was content a minute ago when I checked on him.'

'It's all right. Gave me a chance to look him over after the recent quill incident.'

Eric's lips went firm. 'I keep telling Gerald to not let him stray too far in the woods, but I swear Julius knows where those porcupines are hiding every time.'

'Leash him up for his walks,' I said, feeling like that was a refrain I kept mentioning to all my clients.

'Will do. I promise.' He gave me a wide smile, bunching up his warm brown cheeks, before he tugged Julius away.

Once I returned to the children's tent, Lia gave me a pointed look.

'What?'

'I swear you're freaking Snow White come to life. We can't go anywhere without some critter wanting to get close.'

'It's the kind and sweet vibe I give off,' I said with a tease.

'Good thing that reporter wasn't here. God knows how he'd twist it.'

'You know his name. And one dog coming to greet me is proof of nothing.'

'Okay, *Snow*,' she muttered before going back to her vegetables.

I slid the lid back onto the crate, but not before grabbing one tempting apple, rubbing it against my T-shirt, and giving it a good bite. 'Where's Aster?' I said as juice dribbled down my chin.

'She texted me five minutes ago. Said she had one errand to run, and then she'd be here.'

'Please tell me she did not book any events for today. We're going to need her once the kids show up,' I said.

'All she said was that it was something important we needed for today.'

I walked back to the table in the center of the tent and grabbed a few paper bowls. 'Might as well start cutting up the apples while we wait for her.'

Lia's mouth puckered.

'What now?'

'They get brown when you cut them up.'

'That won't matter if the kids are covering them in chocolate.'

She shrugged. Went back to her own work.

'We are not doing this all day. Say what's on your mind before I go all big sister on you.'

'People are talking. Ever since that dinner at Clo's, Bryce has been turning over every stone in Harvest Moon. Asking probing questions about the town's history, and about our family lines. Elena even told me that he had coffee the other day with the chief. What the hell does the chief know? He's only lived here a few years.' She stopped, the lines hardening around her mouth. 'And Aster—'

'What about her?'

'He's been talking to her matched couples. Asking them about their original interactions with her. How she brought them together.'

A chill raced through my veins. I was supposed to be protecting my sisters, not letting Bryce dig through their lives with a machete.

'I've spoken to Bryce a couple of times in the last few days, and he's given no indication that he's discovered anything earth-shattering. If he had, he'd definitely show up at my door to interrogate me.'

'So you *are* talking to him regularly. What else are you two doing?' she said with too much bitterness.

'I'm staying on top of this, Lee. That's all you need to know.'

She muttered something about who was on top of who and I ignored her. Went back to inspecting the apples. The tension rose until she finally murmured, 'Do you really think he'd say a word to you if he found something?'

That knowing look he gave me as he asked about the journal and Ambrosia flashed through my head. Yeah, I was not sharing that piece of information.

'Have you ever known anyone in this town to stay quiet when it comes to gossip?'

She shook her head.

'As long as nothing weird happens, all he'll have is the basics found in the archives. What people have told him. A lot of that is myth and can't be proven. And if I know anything about Bryce, it's that he's serious about his sources and his facts.'

'Yeah, right, nothing weird.' Her gaze lingered on the table Julius almost knocked over before she went back to her vegetable art.

After plucking a handful of apples from the crate, I grabbed a cutting board and went to work. The sounds and smells of late summer filtered toward us. A few tents away, a vendor from Leadville made kettle corn, the scent of sugar and cinnamon coating the air. The judge and Eric had set up a wireless speaker, and songs from old country favorites like Johnny Cash and Merle Haggard had me humming along.

I continued to slice up the apples, putting them in sealed plastic containers, and setting them inside a nearby cooler to keep them cold. As I was getting into a good rhythm, Lia's shoulders tensed. Her head whipped left and right, and she said a very guarded 'Fuck.'

Before I could ask what she'd sensed outside, the tent ruffled and Bryce appeared looking like a too-hot lumberjack. A deep blue Henley clung to his broad shoulders. Jeans that fit his ass so well it should have been illegal. And he was still wearing those boots, which had to be broken in by now.

'What are you doing here?' Lia grumbled.

'I heard this is the best and busiest tent in the festival. Thought I'd offer my services.'

Lia arched a brow. 'Services? What are you planning to do? Interrogate the children until they cry?'

'Lee,' I chided her.

'No, it's a fair question. I was hoping you'd give me a job, Lia. The one nobody in this tent wants to do,' Bryce said.

You had to hand it to him, even though Lia looked like she wanted to dropkick him to the county line, he was still trying to win her over.

She paused for a few seconds before a devious look spread across her face. 'The apple-dipping station is all yours.'

'Lee,' I said with caution. We'd both heard the stories about how it took the pharmacist and his wife three days to get the chocolate out of their hair last year. 'Pick another job for him.'

'No.' Bryce stood his ground. 'Give me directions, and I'll do it.'

Lia ignored my searing look and walked him over to the table where we'd set up the dipping station. Not more than ten minutes later, Mo showed up with vats of melted chocolate and set them out near the table. The veins in

Bryce's neck pulsed like he knew he was in way over his head. It was the opening I needed to get him and his prying eyes out of here.

'Hey. We've got this. Why don't you walk around the festival? Go to the main tent and see the enormous vegetables the locals grow.'

'Nope. I'm here to do a job and' – he inched closer – 'I like watching you work.'

He stared at me with those stunning blue eyes, and I lost all damn thought until Lia cleared her throat. 'I need more peppers.'

'Right. I'll grab them,' I said.

Bryce walked over to the dipping station, and my gaze veered back to how well those jeans fit him.

'Dani,' Lia barked, knowing all too well where I was staring. 'Peppers.'

Dammit. How did that keep happening? I ignored the heat in my cheeks and tossed a few in her direction.

The music outside changed to an upbeat song, and we all bobbed our heads as we made the final preparations for the kids. I was back to slicing apples when Aster bounded into the tent. Her hair was back to its silvery blond, the edges dipped in a vibrant magenta shade. A canvas bag was tucked into her side.

'Where've you been?' I asked.

A wide smile blossomed on her face, and she whipped a handful of cotton out of her bag. I tried not to snort at the horror in Lia's eyes. 'What the hell have you done, Ast?'

With an impish grin, she unfurled the material to reveal three cotton-candy-pink coveralls. Each of our names were embroidered in baby-blue thread on the left pocket.

'Aren't they cute?' she squealed. 'And look at the back!'

*Makin' Magic with the McGuires* spread across the material in a swirly cursive script.

Lia let out a pained groan. Bryce smiled but did a good job of not reacting.

'Wow, Ast! That's something!' I said, unable to contain my laughter.

Lia's jaw tightened. 'Absolutely not!' She lowered her voice. 'You know how I feel about… pink.'

Aster pushed out her bottom lip. Gave Lia that little frown she hated. 'Do it for me, Lee Lee. I don't ask you for a lot. And these are practical. This way we won't get fruit and vegetable juice and chocolate all over our clothes.'

She turned to Bryce. 'Sorry, you're on your own. And stop being an asshole and talking to the couples I've matched. It's starting to piss me off.' She blew him a kiss that morphed into the middle finger.

This time he laughed even as Lia shook her head. Aster dug her feet in. 'Wear it or I'll tell Clo you're not cooperating.'

For the last few weeks, Lia had complained to Clo that she was too busy to help at a booth during the festival. That she needed to help man the SAR tent. Answer questions for potential volunteers. Clo informed Lia she *would* help without reservation or face our grandmother's wrath for a good long time. Lia could stand up to most people in town, but she always withered when it came to Clo.

Lia held out her hand. 'Fine but remember payback's a bitch.'

Aster slapped it onto her palm and then handed over mine. Together the three of us slid the pink coveralls over our clothes. Bryce grinned at the entire spectacle.

Yep. We were definitely giving him fodder for the article.

'Selfie time!' Aster said with way too much glee.

Bryce held out his hand. 'Here, let me take it.'

Aster handed over her phone, tugging us both in before saying in a rare sharp voice, 'Lia, you'd better smile.'

After snapping at least a dozen photos, Bryce handed Aster back her phone. Lia, still grumbling, pointed Aster to a square card table near the tent's entrance. 'Start setting up for the balloon maker. She left laminated pictures of what she can make. According to her, having a limited number of choices helps the kids make their selection quickly.'

She set her bag down and flounced to the corner. An hour later, the sound of a steel triangle being rung signaled the opening of the festival. Lia pulled in an uneasy breath, and I patted her shoulder. 'Come on, this will be fun.' She gave me a half-smile and I wanted to shake her. Insist that she tell me what was making her act like a grumpy bridge troll, but before I could push again, a swarm of eager children flooded our tent.

Over the next two hours, the McGuire girls and Bryce did an odd sort of dance, skirting around each other as we helped with art projects, chocolate dipping and swallowing back laughter as the sweet older woman making the balloons sang funny songs as she worked, many of which were inappropriate for kids. Think sea shanties laced with a ton of salty language. At one point, Bryce started singing along in a deep baritone, which the children loved.

Our lunch replacements arrived at noon. I explained the general rules about the stations to the teenagers. Told them the best place for their phones was in their pockets, because they were about to be covered in chocolate and a variety of fruit and vegetable juices.

When we left the tent, I had to squint as the bright summer sun hit us. Aster dashed off to check on the staff at her store, while Lia insisted she needed to talk to her friends at the SAR tent.

I stretched my arms and tilted my head left and right. It'd only been two hours. How was I already exhausted? I saw at least thirty animals in a full day at the clinic, but kids hopped up on sugar and late-summer fun were something else.

I closed my eyes, pulled in a deep breath, until the sound of rattling ice caught my attention. Bryce handed me a large cup. 'Iced tea. After that' – he flailed his hands at the tent – 'I thought you could use it.'

Once I'd drained the glass, he cocked his head to the teeming streets. 'Want to walk around? I could use a personal guide for the event.'

I glanced back at the tent. Those kids were going to eat the high schoolers alive.

'If you want to make sure I write an honest article, it's your job to show me the festival. Unless you'd rather have me talk some more to the shop owners. Get their take on the town's history. I think Mo said she had a few more details for me.'

Oh, he was evil, because he knew the last person I wanted him talking to again was Mo.

# Chapter Twenty

## *Deeply Connected*

I didn't answer right away. He crossed his toned arms over his chest. Tapped those damn boots against the asphalt. Streaks of chocolate covered his cheeks, the top of his hands, and spread across his jeans like a bad Jackson Pollock painting.

He didn't have to step up and help us in the tent. He could have continued his interviews. Taken notes about the town and the tourists. How they reacted to the festival. Instead, he'd chosen to volunteer with us, and I hated that meant something to me when I should be trying to box him out. Keep him from our lives.

'Fine. I'll go with you as long as you agree that your journalist hat is off for the day. No questions for me. No grilling the locals.'

His grin widened and he stuck out his hand. 'Deal.'

I shook it and hated the way that bungee between us stretched and writhed. Like he felt it too, he rubbed his thumb against my palm and I quickly pulled my hand away.

'Where do you want to start?' I asked.

'The SAR tent.'

'That's odd. Why?'

'I have to see what Lia's crew thinks of her pink jump-suit.'

His full-chested laughter was too much, and I groaned and took off through the growing crowd.

'This isn't the way toward the tent.'

'We are not going there. If Lia knew what you were up to, well, have you ever witnessed a bull see red?'

Another boisterous laugh filled the air as I moved in the direction of where the local growers showed off their collection of unique wildflowers: calypso orchids, elephant's head, silvery lupine. We wandered in and out of the next several tents. In one, local artists showcased their interpretations of a Colorado sunset, lavishing canvases in crimson, tangerine and mulberry hues. Some artists painted the bluffs, dotted in wild bluebells and lilacs during the summertime. Others captured the quiet peace of the mountaintops after a heavy snow. Several steps away, sculptors displayed pieces fashioned out of clay and steel, many of them depicting the birds native to Colorado like the American robin, the Cooper's hawk and the great horned owl.

We darted in and out of several more tents, and I pretended not to notice the parade of local dogs and feral cats following us. How every time we stopped and observed some handmade treasure, a new animal joined the pack. If Bryce noticed, he thankfully did not say a word.

The streets were packed tighter than the slopes on the first day of ski season. We elbowed our way around strollers, large hordes of families and tourists who'd spent way too much money on oversized cowboy hats in the Western-wear store.

At the end of the block, Bryce stopped short in front of the food stalls. 'What is a deep-fried Oreo?'

'Oh, come on. It's traditional fair food.'

'Never had one. Think I should try?'

'The answer is yes.' I nudged him toward the stall.

As I stood on the corner, more dogs made their way to me. I petted heads, and scrubbed ears, happy that all I felt was warm fur and a bit of slobber.

Bryce inched closer to ordering as the pharmacist, Fred Ellery, and his wife, Nora, clocked me from a few yards away.

'Looks like you came prepared for the children's tent.' Nora scanned me from head to toe, her thin lips pursing. 'We should have thought of coveralls, Fred. It would have made our lives easier.'

The poor man's gray eyebrows pinched together as he stared at the chaotic splashes of chocolate across my arms and legs like he still had trauma from his assignment last year. 'That's true, dear. Glad I'm only committed to winning the pie-eating contest for the sixth year in a row!' He rubbed his belly in anticipation.

'The coveralls were Aster's idea. She's always thinking ahead.'

Nora leaned in, her short black curls bouncing against her cheeks. 'Have you seen that journalist around here?'

I tipped my chin to where Bryce stood.

A stricken look crossed her face. 'I think you should be aware that he's been asking us a lot of particular questions.'

'What do you mean by particular?' I said, trying to keep my voice level.

'He's interested in the pharmacy because it once belonged to your ancestors. Wanted to know if we had any old files or historical records about the place,' Fred said.

Shit. He was still chasing details about Ambrosia and Sylvia. I was glad he'd agreed not to talk about the town today, because I still hadn't figured out a way to explain away the journal if he pressed me on it again.

'We didn't tell him a thing, because, well, when we bought the place all the business records began in the mid-1950s. Apparently, the earlier documents were lost in some kind of fire,' Nora said.

Fire. I swallowed down the bile climbing up my throat.

Bryce handed over his money and turned back in our direction. Nora gave me a hesitant smile, tugged on Fred's arm. 'Take care of yourself, Dani.' Her words were more of a warning than a kindness.

Bryce made his way back with his concoction in a red-and-white-checked paper bowl. 'This looks really good.'

'I need to go,' I said haltingly.

He paused with the cookie halfway to his mouth. 'No. Please stay.'

When I didn't reply he looked in the direction Fred and Nora had gone.

'They're nice people,' he said, setting his treat back into the paper bowl.

'Is there anyone in this town you haven't interrogated?'

'Dani,' he sighed. 'Let's not do this.'

'You're right. Let's not.'

I started to walk away, but he caught my hand. 'Please,' he said with a weary breath. 'We agreed to not talk about this. Today, I only want to experience the festival. Spend time with you. Can we do that?'

He was back to rubbing that delicate circle against my palm. Spending time with him was a bad idea. He was getting too nosy. Too close to things I didn't want him to know.

He let go of me and gingerly picked up the treat, taking a careful bite. His eyes closed, and he made a low moan that was too much like our time in the truck. 'Holy crap. That may be the best thing I've ever tasted.' He smiled with a wicked little spark. 'Well, one of the best things.'

Heat flared in my cheeks and he held out the fried cookie. 'Want to try?'

His gaze flicked to my mouth and his eyes lit with anticipation.

How did I keep walking this sensuous line with him when I was supposed to be keeping my distance?

He waited, and I finally pressed my mouth around the edge. The quick breath he sucked in made me think he was reliving our time in the truck too. Using his thumb, he swiped a loose crumb from the corner of my mouth. It was the most basic touch, but it lit up every single one of my nerve endings like I'd touched a live wire.

'I really want to kiss you right now,' he said in a tight whisper. His hand moved to cradle my cheek. We were standing in the middle of the street, festivalgoers streaming around us, and all I could think was how I wanted his mouth on mine again. It was dumb. Reckless, especially after what Nora had just revealed, but that yank in my chest was too hard to ignore.

I began to lean in until my phone beeped, reminding me that this was nothing but a bad idea waiting to happen.

'If you want to see the rest of the festival, we should go. I need to head back to the children's tent soon.'

Disappointment flashed across his face, but he said, 'Lead the way.'

Only a few steps from Mo's tavern sat a white tent that was as long as the local high school's football field. When we walked inside, Bryce came to a sudden stop, his mouth hanging open.

Ten feet in front of us on an elevated pedestal sat a squash that was nearly the size of a washing machine. On the next pedestal was a red radish as big as a baseball. He tore his phone out of his pocket and took at least a dozen photos.

'Wait.' I pointed in the direction of the granddaddy of them all: a pumpkin that was close to the size of a golf cart.

'You've got to be kidding me! When you all talked about this at the meeting a few weeks ago, I thought the vegetables would be big, but not this big. How did the festival get started?'

This was a part of the town's history I was happy to share. 'In the early 1950s, we had a city councilman with a brother who lived in Alaska. He went to visit him one year, and his brother took him to the state fair. Part of the exhibits were these giant vegetables. Apparently, a decade before, the owner of one of the railroads offered a twenty-five-dollar prize to the farmer who could grow the largest vegetable. The councilman loved the idea. How it brought the community together. He pitched it to town leaders when he returned home, and in 1955 Harvest Moon had their first Veggie Fest.'

'How is it even possible to grow a pumpkin that large?'

That earned Bryce a few dark stares from the locals who were still primping and preening their giant veggies before judging.

'What did I say wrong?'

'The growers keep their techniques to themselves, but I overheard Randall running his mouth after one too many beers at the tavern a couple of years ago.'

He arched a reddish brow. 'Okay, you have to tell me.'

Mrs Poppel, who runs the local berry stand, caught my eye. Shook her head.

'Can't tell you. Closely guarded town secret.'

He rolled his eyes and walked toward the massive pedestal where Eric's volleyball-sized green pepper sat. 'You're very lucky. This kind of community event is rare these days. People are usually too caught up in their own lives to want to give back. Or in this case' – he cocked his head to the watermelon that was the size of a large dog – 'share their creations.'

'They don't do this kind of thing in Los Angeles? Not even in some of the small suburbs?'

'Not that I know of. But now that I've seen it here, it makes me wish they did.' He turned back to the watermelon, going suddenly quiet. 'I envy you. The peace that comes with living in this quiet place.'

'It has its perks. I like seeing people I've known since childhood. Treating their pets or their children's or grandchildren's pets.'

'That's what I mean. There's history here. A solid tether of family.'

'Your uncle didn't have any kids?'

'Nope. I'm the only one left to carry on both the Richardson and O'Dell lines.'

'Family comes in all shapes and sizes, Bryce. I bet you have friends, people you work with, who you consider family.'

'Of course, but since I've been here, I've been struck by how much people knew and liked my uncle. That day when I first met the judge here on the street, that wasn't the first time someone made me aware of how much they'd miss my uncle Rich. How he'd made such a major impression on people over the years.'

'It's what happens in a small town like Harvest Moon. People care, but they definitely get into your business too.'

I glanced at Mrs Poppel, who eyeballed us with equal parts intrigue and suspicion.

'You're lucky to have your sisters. Your grandmother,' he went on. 'To be so deeply connected to one place.'

'I've never thought of it that way. This has always just been home.'

'Treasure that. It's a real gift.' He kicked at a rock with the toe of his boot. 'When I was eight I was obsessed with the movie *The Goonies.* Have you seen it?'

'That's the one with the kids who find the pirate ship, right?'

'One-Eyed Willy's ship,' he said, like he was pleased I could follow along. 'Part of the reason I liked it so much is that all those kids were fighting to stay in the one place where they'd grown up. The small town where they felt safe. They were willing to risk life and limb to stay together.'

There was an unexpected sadness to his voice. He'd traveled the world. Been to exotic places. Reported on important world events. It was odd to have him speak about community and home like they meant something to him. I'd always seen him as this focused and committed journalist, but I was beginning to notice cracks in that sleek, professional façade he presented to everyone in town.

'What else is there to see at this festival?' he asked roughly like he hadn't been expecting to share something so intimate.

'I have to head back to the children's area, but there's a pie-eating contest soon. And the speed-woodchopping competition is always a crowd pleaser.'

He pressed his palm against mine, and the heat of him sent another shock through me. I should have pulled away, but his touch felt too right.

'Sure I can't convince you to hang out with me a little longer?'

His touch made my mind fuzzy. Was sharing something so vulnerable about himself all part of his ploy to get me to let down my guard? Or was it possible that he wanted to know me beyond what was whispered about my family in town? That he also felt that tether growing between us?

I let myself consider that possibility until Aster sprinted into the tent. She stopped in front of me, huffing and puffing like she'd just run a mile.

'What's wrong?' I said, her sudden entrance drawing more than a few stares.

'I've been looking for you everywhere.' She dragged in another gulp of air. 'Lia needs you. Right now.'

'Why?'

'Mara Johnson's gone.'

'What do you mean she's gone?' I said.

'I mean the deputy mayor's daughter is missing.'

# *Chapter Twenty-One*

## *Eerily Silent and Still*

Aster continued to pull in gulps of air as she tried to catch her breath. 'Banjo's gone too. Darren thinks they may have taken off into the woods behind the amphitheater. He got distracted with his duties as deputy mayor and lost track of her. They've asked that you come and help.'

She tapped her hand against her elbow three times. A decades-old sign us girls had made to communicate as kids. It said we needed privacy from our grandparents, or from Belladonna whenever she showed up unexpectedly, which always made us unsettled.

'Let's go.' I clasped her arm, leading her out of the tent.

'Wait.' Bryce chased after us. 'Let me help. What can I do?'

'Go away and stop bothering my clients,' Aster huffed.

Yeah, she wasn't letting that go.

He stayed in step with us. 'You'll need more people if there's a search party.'

'Is there any way we can stop you?' I said, swapping a weighted glance with Aster.

'Nope,' he said firmly.

-

We raced through the streets, dodging in between tourists and local families. Clo waited for us on the corner near the tavern. She wrung her hands together. Swayed nervously like she was about to jump out of her skin. She'd become good friends with Darren and Mara over the years, even inviting Mara over to help in her garden.

Once she caught sight of us, she asked Aster to help her round up some more locals for the search. While they headed back into the throng of the festival, Bryce and I made for the entrance to the amphitheater.

Lia stood in a circle with a few men and women from the fire station and some SAR volunteers. She'd changed out of her pink jumpsuit and was back to her regular uniform of cargo pants and traffic-cone-orange SAR shirt. The group talked for a few minutes, putting together a plan. A tall, muscular guy with a shock of white-blond hair stood a few feet away speaking to Mara's father, Darren, who looked like he might crumble at any moment.

'How old is this girl?' Bryce asked.

'She's eleven.'

'Does this happen a lot? Kids getting lost? There are a lot of woods around here.'

'Most of the kids know not to wander off, but if they want to get away from their parents, hang out with their friends, the forest is the best place to go.'

'Sounds like you're speaking from experience.'

'There were times when the quiet of the forest helped me think, but I also knew not to wander so far away that I couldn't find my way back.'

'What will they do first?'

'Divide into teams. One crew will go on foot. Some on four-wheelers. Others on horseback. A basic grid search. They'll need to work quickly, though.'

'Why?'

'It'll be dark in a couple of hours. As soon as the sun goes down it gets cold, especially the higher you get up into the forest.'

Bryce stayed quiet, but his narrow focus said he was mentally taking notes on the scene. Putting every movement, every snippet of sound, into his memory for the article.

For the first time this thought did not make me nauseous. Lia and her team were extraordinary, and if Bryce could document that for the world it was a good thing.

As we waited for Lia to finish her meeting, Jessa and Bree jogged in our direction.

'What can we do to help?' Bree asked, her stare narrowing on Bryce.

'We're waiting on Lia for instructions,' I said.

'I'm Bree. This is Jessa. We work with Dr McGuire. Who are you?'

'Bryce O'Dell. I'm a… friend.'

Jessa's brows shot up.

'You're that reporter? The one with the dog who got into the weed?' Bree's tone was venomous, but Bryce didn't wither.

'That's right.'

'Why are you here? This is a town matter,' Bree snapped.

'I want to help. The more hands the better, right?'

Jessa bobbed her head. 'We need to find Mara and Banjo quickly. That dog is nearly thirteen. The terrain farther into the forest will be tough for him to navigate.'

Bree continued to stare daggers at Bryce until the rescue team broke, and Lia stalked toward us. Her attention flicked once to the blond guy, and the line of her shoulders quickly tightened.

'What do you need?' I said as soon as she stopped at the edge of our circle.

'Why is he here?' Lia gave Bryce a tense stare.

'I just asked the same question,' Bree said.

The tension was already neck high and none of this would help us find Mara.

'You need another set of eyes. I can be helpful if you'll let me.' Bryce spoke up before I could.

Lia scrubbed a hand through her poof of curls. Huffed out an irritated breath. 'Go join the crew over in that small huddle near the entrance. They're going to do another sweep of the festival and the shops. Make sure we didn't miss Mara somewhere. Jessa and Bree, please go with him. Check the library and that spot behind the candy store with the picnic tables the kids like.'

'Does she have a phone you can track?' Bryce asked.

'No. Darren, her dad, hasn't allowed her to have one yet, and he's kind of beating himself up over that right now.' Lia's stare darted to where the poor man was pacing and yanking on the ends of his dark hair. 'He thinks that's the reason she took off. Her friends have been teasing her about it.'

'Okay. I'll go with the group,' Bryce said. 'Hopefully, we'll find her.'

'Stay with Bree and Jessa. Don't wander off. I don't need to send out another search party.'

He gave Lia a mock salute and jogged off.

Darren stayed huddled with the blond guy.

'Is that a new volunteer?' I said.

She let out an irritated breath. 'Nope.'

'You want to talk about it?'

'Again, no. What I do want to discuss is how far you need to go into the forest before Banjo can sense you.'

'Lee, I have no idea. I've never put that to the test. Animals, they just find me.'

Without another word, she turned for the trail. I followed quickly, keeping up with her steady pace. More than once she stopped and tugged me to the side of the path. Her expert hearing tracked the movement of the four-wheelers before I could see them coming our way.

Once they passed us, we continued to climb up the steep terrain. 'Never thought I'd say this, but it's a good thing Aster bought us those stupid coveralls, because it'll be easy to spot you on the trail.'

'Don't ever say that to her or she'll start buying us matching clothes for holidays too.'

She flashed me a brief smile but it faded as soon as the blond guy jogged down the trail toward us. A few days' worth of scruff covered most of his chin, and his arms rivaled the size of some of the local tree trunks.

'I've asked Darren to stay here like you instructed. To keep his phone on in case we have to contact him. I'm on radio channel four if you need to call for EMS.'

'Thank you, hopefully it will not come to that.' She said the words so stiffly I thought her jaw might crack in two.

The big guy shot out his hand toward me. 'I'm Aiden Pelphrey.'

Lia tensed as I shook his hand. 'Dani McGuire.'

His eyes sparked. 'Your sister, Lee? The vet?'

*Lee? Well, that's interesting.*

'Yep, that's right,' I said when Lia did not bother to respond.

'It's a pleasure. I've heard a lot of good things about you.'

Lia fisted her hands at her sides. Oh, there was definitely history between them.

'Really? Are you from around here?' I pushed, which made Lia grit her teeth harder.

'I grew up in Ouray. Went to CU Boulder for undergrad. Been working in Wyoming for a while.'

'How long have you been volunteering with search and rescue?' I said.

'Ten years.'

Huh. Same amount of time as my little sister.

'I work with a different county. I'm in town because, uh, well, I know a few guys... people.' He gave a shy glance to Lia, who I swore was doing her best to hide the blush on her cheeks. 'I mean I know some folks here.'

Lia pointed at the crew heading farther up the north trail. 'Enough with the twenty questions. Let's go,' she said, tugging me forward.

'Nice meeting you,' Aiden said.

'You too,' I called over my shoulder.

Lia moved up the path like a soldier on a mission, and I chased after her.

'Lee, he's cute. Why haven't you—'

'Not another word, Dani. I swear.'

Her fists clenched again, and I bit my tongue. I definitely wanted more details about Aiden, but for now we had to focus on our one job: finding Mara and Banjo.

-

There was no need to speak as we ascended the trail. Lia and I both knew our roles. She dropped her shoulders, tipped up her chin to scent the wind. Her gaze focused on the ground, picking out small changes in the terrain, broken branches, overturned soil, anything to determine if Mara came this way. Every few paces she'd stop, turn her head left and right as if she could hear the woods speaking to her. 'Wind is picking up from the east at twenty-one knots. It's going to get worse as the sun sets.'

Her steps continued at a brisk pace, and I tried to keep up. The muscles in my legs stretched and pulled. I used my peripheral vision to track the animals in the brush for odd behavior, but nothing was unusual. A few squirrels raced to the end of the branches on the high trees. Deer edged closer to the trail's edge and clocked my movement. If Banjo was close, these animals were not aware of it.

'Lee, anything?'

'No, and it's starting to piss me off.'

We were only fifteen minutes into our search when footsteps echoed through the forest. Aster took long strides to keep up with Bryce as they ascended the trail toward us.

'I told you to help Bree and Jessa,' Lia sniped at him.

'There were too many people. I found Aster, and she thought you might come this way so I followed.'

'The terrain is going to get rough. You need to go back to town.' Lia looked at me for help.

'Bryce, we can't slow down. We have to locate Mara quickly. Go and find my grandmother and Ms Ruthie. They'll find some other task for you.'

I had faith that the three of us together could find Mara, but that couldn't happen if Bryce was tailing, and studying, us while we searched.

Since we were children, we could sense each other's feelings and intuitions. It was like we operated on the same low frequency. A buzzing, like static electricity, coursing through our heads and fingertips, allowing us to keep track of each other.

On long summer days, we'd disappear into the woods for hours, making flower chains, climbing trees and being our feral little selves. Clo never worried about us, because she understood the unseen cord that bonded us. Allowed us to navigate the woods as one. Lia was our compass, Aster our discerning eyes, and me, I was watching, tracking, the movements of the animals. During those long days, we hardly spoke to each other, our heightened connection more vital than actual words.

'I've been in combat zones,' Bryce argued. 'Had to hunker down with troops in some pretty uncomfortable spots in the desert. I can keep up. And if what you say is true about needing to find her as soon as possible, you need another set of eyes.'

Lia made that triple tap on her arm, but I didn't have any other suggestions on how to keep him away.

'We have a lot of ground to cover,' Lia said, relenting. 'Don't make me regret letting you come along.'

He gave my sister a nod, and the four of us spread out. Every few minutes one of the crew or Lia would call out for Mara, but the forest remained eerily silent and still.

As we hiked up the trail deeper into the woods, I grounded myself in the soil, that low buzzing spreading over my body like warm bathwater. With a few deep breaths, I opened myself to feel any hint of Banjo. Aster took small steps, using her attachment to people's color, and sense of emotion, to try and tap into Mara's path.

The tense set of her jaw warned she wasn't having any luck.

Lia's head was on a constant swivel, scenting the air, going still every few minutes to see if she could hear or sense any movement. More than once, she warned of unsteady boulders and fallen branches ahead before we reached them.

The tension between us was palpable. A dull ache throbbed beneath my breastbone. Like they felt it too, both girls massaged a hand against their chest.

Bryce stayed a few paces behind us, the heat of his stare burning into my back. When I turned to meet his gaze, he was back to watching Lia. Keeping track of Aster's movements. I pretended like I didn't see them, but rabbits, marmots and chipmunks peeked their way out of the bushes. Hovered at the edge of the path like they were waiting for me to pass.

Having Bryce here was dangerous, but it was too late now.

We spent another forty minutes on the trail until we reached the first open ridge. Lia passed around a water canteen. Once we'd wet our lips, taken a few gulps, we continued along the narrow, rocky path. A swath of aspens spilled out in front of us. The churn of the Arkansas River thirty feet below made the air cooler.

Lia's crew walked fifty yards ahead, continuing to call out for Mara. We stayed in a single-file line and were almost to the next ridge, which led farther into the forest. I tugged my sisters to the side of the trail while Bryce hung back.

'Do you think she even came this way?' I said.

'I get a brief scent and then lose it on the growing wind. And I'm hearing nothing but the whoosh of the river below,' Lia said.

'Ast?' I prompted.

'No sense of any kind of heightened emotion, which you'd expect from a young girl lost out here.'

'What about up ahead?' I said. 'Sometimes you can see much farther than either of us.'

Her chin tipped down and she shook her head.

'We have to keep moving. I worry about what will happen once it gets dark,' Lia said, taking off on the trail again. Aster and Bryce followed, but I remained a few steps back, trying to catch my breath and not give in to the fear that we were searching in the wrong place.

The group disappeared at the arc of trees that led away from the ridge and into the forest. That buzzing remained at a fever pitch, causing a blinding throb in the back of my skull. As I took a moment, a dozen pika hopped out of the dense brush. The small, furry creatures resembled rabbits but with no tail. They raced to the edge of the path in a frenzied mass and stopped as if glancing over the trail's edge. I inched closer. The wind skirting through the trees, gentle sway of branches, were all the normal kinds of forest music I was used to. I waited. Stayed still, anticipating the small creatures' movement back into the brush, but they remained frozen in place.

A pull in my gut urged me forward. My chest ached and that throb in my head moved to my temples. Banjo was close.

I slid down onto my belly a few feet away, my pink coveralls skidding across the dirt. Inch by inch, I crawled to the edge of the ridge, my movement sending the pika fleeing back into the safety of the forest.

At least fifteen feet below was a ledge covered in a clump of trees. A flash of something silver, a dog collar, made me jump to my feet, but as soon as I was upright, I calculated my mistake. Loose gravel and dirt slid out from under me as a portion of the ground gave way, taking me straight down with it.

# *Chapter Twenty-Two*

## *Your Sister is a Badass*

Sharp rocks and pieces of old branches clawed into my back. I careened down the side of the ridge, digging my fingers into the dirt but couldn't stop my forward momentum. The farther I slid, the deeper the branches cut into the coveralls, tearing straight through to the skin on my arms and back. The slick bottoms of my tennis shoes made me sail down faster. My only saving grace was that I was headed straight for the ledge and a small copse of trees that would break my fall.

After a few more bumps, and the unsettling tearing of cloth, I landed with a painful thud against a tree. Stars swam across my vision, but I was safe. Alive. My breaths came in rapid bursts until the sound of a tiny steel jingle made me sit up.

I moved to my hands and knees and crawled around the side of a tree. Mara sat with her back against the trunk, eyes closed, her breathing even like she was asleep. An angry red cut sliced across her forehead, and she held a hand against her right shoulder. Her beagle, Banjo, lay across her lap. When he saw me, he limped in my direction. The moment his right front paw touched my hand, a familiar shock vibrated through me. Both of them were in rough shape, and I had to steady my breathing before I spoke.

The last thing I wanted to do was scare an already terrified child.

'Mara, I'm here to help,' I said in a soft voice.

Her eyes slid open and tears immediately spilled down her dirty cheeks. 'Dr McGuire? How did you find me? Is my dad here?'

Her dark hair swung across her shoulders as she tried to inch forward. The slight movement made her let out a heartbreaking cry.

'Try not to move, sweetheart.'

'My shoulder. It really hurts.' More tears wet her cheeks while she watched me gingerly examine Banjo's body. He whined under my touch but remained still. From the way he was favoring his right paw, I was convinced he'd broken a bone or two.

'Is he hurt?' Mara whimpered.

'Maybe his paw, but I won't know until I can get an X-ray.'

She started to sob again, and I squeezed her hand. 'I'm going to call for help. Hang on.'

Thankfully my phone was still lodged deep in my pocket. I held it up for a signal, but nothing registered. My sisters and Bryce had to realize I wasn't behind them, but that link between us was fading.

I shouted at the top of my lungs for my sisters. For Bryce.

'It won't work,' Mara said quietly. 'The river below is too loud.'

*Think, Dani.*

I inched farther out on the ledge and held my phone up again.

'Your phone won't work either?' Mara said with a tremble. 'How will anyone find us?'

I cursed under my breath. The thing was basically a useless brick down here.

I took a moment. Listened to the wind sing through the trees until an idea hit me. I pressed the button for my music app. Last week, Jessa had downloaded a few of my favorite playlists to use in the office so I didn't need a Wi-Fi signal.

After a few taps, and raising the volume up as high as possible, Van Morrison's 'Brown-Eyed Girl' echoed across the forest. I scooted closer to Mara and held her hand. Halfway into the second chorus, the shouts came. First Bryce's low voice, followed by Aster's strangled call of my name.

I silenced my phone and crawled my way to the back of the tree. Above me, Bryce, Lia and Aster teetered at the edge of the ridge.

'Are you hurt?' A painful hitch colored Lia's voice.

'I'm okay. Mara's with me and she needs medical attention.'

'Is that Lia?' Mara said.

I crept back to her. 'Yes. There are a lot of us out here looking for you and Banjo.'

'Your sister is a badass.' Her cheeks pinked up. 'Don't tell my dad I said that. I'm not supposed to curse.'

I gave her a smile. 'It's our secret, and I agree. Lia *is* a badass.'

'Can Mara climb up on her own or does she need the rescue litter?' Lia called.

'Send the litter,' I shouted back.

'I'm going to call it in. Hold on,' Lia said.

Mara closed her eyes. Pulled in another painful breath. 'I'm sorry. This was such a stupid idea.'

'Wanna tell me what happened?'

She turned into my side, making herself smaller. 'I was at the festival with my friends at that spot everyone likes behind the candy store. They were all talking and making jokes about a sleepover they had last night.' Her eyes filled with tears again. 'Without me.'

'That must have been hard.'

Her chin trembled. 'I got mad and took off. My dad and I come up here on Sundays. We read. Talk to my mom. It's a special place.' Another tear tumbled down her cheek. 'My friends said they didn't invite me because I don't have a phone. They were texting funny memes, and then the idea for the sleepover came up.' She gave Banjo a loving pat on the back. 'They forgot about me. Like I wasn't part of the group anymore.'

My heart ached for Mara. She'd lost her mother two years ago in a car accident. Darren was a good father, but growing up without a mom was hard. I understood her all too well. The only difference between us was that I had my sisters and Elena, who would never leave me out of a special moment.

'How mad do you think my dad is?'

'I can't answer that, but I'm sure he's going to be happy to see you. Hug you again.'

She laid a hand across Banjo's head. 'I was running and hit a patch of rocks and gravel. Shot off the ridge and slid straight down, landing a few feet away from here. It was painful, but I managed to crawl under the shade of this tree.' Her thumb rubbed against one of his silky ears. 'Banjo, he came after me. Never stopped.'

'He's a good dog.'

She gave me a sad smile. 'He's the best.'

I asked her more questions about school and her favorite subjects, trying to distract her while we waited for help.

'The rest of my team are two minutes out, Dani.' The sound of Lia's voice made us both turn. Her helmet was the same shade of orange as her T-shirt. Once she found solid ground, she clipped off the rappelling line and took measured steps toward us.

Mara's look of awe and wonder as she watched Lia made me proud. 'Badass' was the perfect term for my little sister.

Lia moved in and I whispered, 'Possible broken collarbone.'

She took another few steps and bent down to examine Mara. Her touch was gentle. Her voice low and kind. This was a side to Lia most people never saw. She may be a grump with adults, but when there was a child involved in an emergency call, the chief always sent her. She had a remarkable way of soothing even the youngest soul. Making them feel protected and safe. I was damn proud of her, and I didn't tell her that enough.

'I need you to listen closely, Mara,' Lia said. 'The search and rescue team is going to lower down what we call a rescue litter. It's a big, long steel basket. I'm going to help you climb into it. Once you're lying flat on your back, I'll strap you in, and then, with me tethered beneath the basket, I'm going to use our rope system to pull us back up to the top of the ridge. That sound okay to you?'

'Can Banjo come with me?'

'No. It's not safe,' Lia answered.

She tugged her dog close. Shook her head.

'Banjo should go with me,' I said. 'Lia will give me her backpack.'

She grimaced. 'I will?'

'Yes, I'll put Banjo inside it and climb back up with him.'

Lia frowned but didn't offer up a better suggestion.

'I need you to be my partner on this one, Mara,' Lia said. 'Be fully focused, so we can get you into the basket and make sure you're secure. Can you do that for me?'

Mara's eyes widened, stunned that Lia would trust her with such an important job. 'Yes, of course.'

After a few conversations about logistics over the radio, the SAR team lowered the rescue litter. The steel basket bumped against the side of the ridge, the attached ropes sliding it down an inch at a time.

I helped Mara stand, cautioning her not to make any jarring movements to protect her collarbone. Once she was upright, I took Banjo from her and that jolt of pain and heat flooded my veins. The taste of steel and copper sat heavy on my tongue. He definitely had a few broken bones.

Lia stepped closer. A white helmet with a goalie-type mask dangled from her fingers.

Mara shrank back. 'What's that for?'

'I need you to wear it. The helmet protects your head inside the litter, and the goalie shield will make sure falling rocks or dirt don't hit your face. But that won't be a problem, because I'm a total pro.'

Lia winked at Mara, who gave her a confident smile back. 'I believe you.'

Once the helmet was on Mara, the snap secured beneath her chin, Lia helped her lie down inside the litter.

'It's like being in an open coffin.'

I hated that Mara even knew that image.

'Consider it more of an open-air swing, with the rest of us just giving you gentle pushes upward.' Lia gave a firm nod to reassure her.

Mara tucked her chin and closed her eyes. 'Okay, I'll picture that and not me swaying thirty feet above the river.'

'Smart girl,' Lia murmured as she strapped her in with what she called webbing before cinching four thick black bands over Mara's chest, torso, thighs and ankles.

'You're in good hands with Lee,' I said, gently patting Mara's hand.

'Thank you, Dr McGuire, for finding me. I'll never forget it.'

Lia gave me a dark look before she clipped a rope to her chest harness. She radioed back to the team that she was ascending. With a quick yank on the ropes, Lia's body slid beneath the basket as if she was cradling it in her lap. Inch by inch, she pulleyed her way back up the ridge with Mara.

I waited for a half hour until Lia rappelled back down with extra ropes and a harness for me.

'What the fuck, Dani?' she said as soon as her feet hit the ground. 'Did you slide down here on purpose? I was halfway into the forest, and it was like a rubber band snapped in my chest. Ast felt it too. We panicked when we couldn't find you.'

'I stopped on the trail because I sensed movement, and there were these pika all lined up at the edge of the ridge like they were telling me she was here.'

Her angry resolve crumbled, and she swiped at her watery eyes. 'Mara must have been terrified. Why didn't Ast sense her fear? Better yet, why couldn't I scent her? See where she fell?'

'Up this high, the wind and the mist from the river below could have interfered with your skills. She also said she shot off the side of the ridge while running. With all the gravel around here, and the traffic from the hikers, it'd be easy to miss.'

She didn't like my answer and crossed her arms over her chest. 'What about Ast?'

'When I found Mara, she was asleep. Poor kid was exhausted. That's why Ast couldn't sense her panic.'

Her rigid shoulders gave way as she scanned my torn coveralls. 'I don't know what I'd do if I ever lost you.' Her voice broke. 'These past months have been hard, and I'm sorry if I've been grumpier than usual.' She pulled me into a tight hug with Banjo nestled between us. 'You are my rock, you know that, right?'

'Yep. Just like you're mine,' I said wincing slightly.

She pulled back and blinked away tears, surveying the cuts on my arms. 'You're sure you are okay?'

'Yes, I'm lucky I only have a few scrapes.'

'Isn't that the damn truth.' Her jaw went hard. 'Give me a quick explanation of how you ended up all the way in the hell down here.'

After I explained about the glimmer of silver on Banjo's collar, and my idiotic mistake on the ledge, she grabbed my hands. 'Don't you ever scare me like that again.'

'I promise, no more careening off ledges.'

She grimaced before reaching down to grab the climbing gear she'd brought. 'Can you do this on your own, or should the guys send the litter back down for you?' she said with way too much snark.

'Shut up and help me get back up the ridge.'

As soon as I had the climbing harness on, she put Banjo into the backpack and slid it onto her own shoulders. 'I'll take the dog. You need to focus on getting back to the top of the ridge. Take your time. Go slow, like I taught you when we were kids.'

'Who's managing who now?'

She let out an irritated chuckle and delivered a half dozen more orders about keeping the rope tight. With the wind tugging its way through my hair, we began the climb side by side. While I wouldn't admit it to Lia, I ran every single thing she'd ever taught me about climbing through my head as we went. It took a slow but steady twenty minutes before I reached the top of the ridge.

Five members of the SAR team, and a few of Lia's crew from the station, were waiting. Aiden approached with long strides and clipped me off the line and then went to help Lia. Fire Chief Malbrough's thick white mustache twitched as he gave me the once-over. 'You all right, Dr McGuire?'

'A little scraped up, but other than that I'm fine.'

Darren stood two steps behind him. 'Dani,' he heaved out, glancing over his shoulder to where two EMTs had Mara propped up against the base of a tree. 'I have no words, except thank you for finding my girl.'

'You're welcome. She's a pretty tough kid.'

Aiden pulled Banjo out of the backpack, and as soon as he was on the ground he limped toward Mara.

Darren's face crumpled. 'What's wrong with Banjo?'

'I think he may have injured his paw. Can I take him to the clinic for an exam? I'll bring him back to your place as soon as I check him over.'

'Of course. If you ever need anything, you let me know. I am in your debt.'

'That's not necessary. Go and be with your daughter. She needs you.'

That tension in his mouth went slack before he jogged over to her.

Once the crowd dispersed, Bryce was in front of me, yanking me into a tight hug. I let out a low hiss and he stepped back, his eyes blazing. 'You *are* hurt. I'm calling over one of the EMTs.'

'No,' I argued. 'They're just a few cuts. They need to focus on Mara right now.'

He started to protest until Aster nudged him out of the way and wrapped me in her own embrace. This time I was smart enough to bite back the pain, because I did not need the two of them ganging up on me.

'What were you thinking? You scared the hell out of us, him the most I think,' she whispered into my ear.

I gave her elbow that triple tap, and she sank into me, reading my worry that Bryce was still watching us.

'You sure you're good?' she said. When I nodded she stepped away to check on Lia.

Bryce approached me hesitantly, scanning my body for any sign of injury. The panic and raw fear in his gaze shook me. I stepped closer to reassure him, and he gently pressed his hands to my cheeks. I couldn't sense emotion like Aster, but the heaviness in his touch, the threadiness to his breath, had me stroking the tops of his hands. I'd questioned earlier if he was toying with me, offering up small glimmers into his own life to get me to let down my guard. But with him holding me now like he never wanted to let go, I understood this wasn't a game to him.

We stood quietly, locked in our own world, until Aiden approached us. 'Sorry to interrupt, but I need to get Dani out of that gear.'

Bryce slowly let me go, and I held my hands out to my sides while Aiden loosened the line from my waist. Unhooked the harness and the clips.

Aster stood a few feet away. There was a cock to her head. A thin press of her pink lips as she watched him move. She saw his color. Knew his match. I wondered who it was. If she'd even tell me.

Bryce watched her too like he recognized her far-off gaze.

Crap. That was gonna be another topic of conversation too, I expected.

When I was free of the gear, Aiden walked to Lia. 'McGuire, let me help.' Much to my shock and surprise, Lia let him work the ropes off her harness.

Aster smiled at me. Mouthed 'McGuire' with a twinkle in her eyes. She wasn't letting that one go with Lia.

Bryce slid his fingers through mine and pulled me off the path into a set of trees ten steps away. His hands were at my shoulders, in my hair and slowly running down my arms.

'You're bleeding.' He pointed to the top of my right arm, the sharp, torn edges of the coveralls stained a deep crimson.

'Like I said, I'm fine.'

He shook his head. 'Aster was talking a mile a minute, and Lia was too far ahead.' The hard line of his shoulders deflated. 'I should have been clocking you behind me.'

'You didn't do anything wrong. I grew up in these woods. On these trails. For years, Lia has been telling Aster and me not to get too close to the edges of these ridges. Hell, I even told you that when we were hiking a couple of weeks ago.'

He continued to stare at me like if he blinked I might disappear before his eyes.

'What happened today was my fault. I know better. Please do not blame yourself.'

The grip of his warm hands on my shoulders remained. 'Watching the three of you today. How you can almost read each other's thoughts. Play to each other's strengths. It's really extraordinary.'

'Except for when one of us veers from the plan,' I said, trying to shake this conversation.

His beautiful mouth remained firm. 'Don't do that. Don't make light of what just happened.'

'Bryce, I. Am. Okay. Let it go now.'

There was a lingering question in his eyes that I did not want to address. This was not about magic. It was about understanding this terrain. Each of us confident in our own special skills. Our connection to each other. But no matter how much I insisted on that truth, I'm not sure he would believe me.

'They're sending the four-wheelers this way to take us down. Are you two ready to go?' There was a tease in Aster's voice like maybe we wanted to be left here alone.

Bryce slid his hands down my arms, and I couldn't hold back another wince as my raw skin protested his touch. He leaned in and brushed his mouth over the shell of my ear. 'You're coming home with me. Tonight, let me take care of you.'

The insistence in his voice made heat curl in my stomach. 'I have to take Banjo to the clinic.'

'After you're done, then.' He threaded his fingers through mine. 'Please, don't say no.'

I should have drawn a line in the sand. Held my ground. What we'd done in the truck felt like leaning too close to an open flame, but being alone with him in his home? That was walking straight into the fire.

He held my gaze and that cord between us wound tighter.

I was tired of being brave. Putting up a front. Tonight, I wanted to take whatever he offered, no matter the consequences.

# Chapter Twenty-Three

## *You'd Be a Fool Not to Listen*

Indy waited by the door. He did a little prance the moment he saw Flora beside me. I walked inside Bryce's cabin and gave Indy's head a gentle pat. Not a single tremor coursed through my body.

'Hope you don't mind that I brought Flora. She was wound up from all the chaos at the clinic with Banjo, and I couldn't leave her behind.'

'No, I'm glad she's here. By the looks of it, Indy is too,' Bryce said.

The two dogs chased each other in a circle before speeding out of the room.

'Kind of a bummer way to end the festival, but I'm glad Mara is safe.' Bryce slid the satchel off my shoulder and set it on an old antique table by the door.

'Bree came by the clinic to help me. She said none of the tourists knew what was happening. And according to Judge Greene, we were way over our regular attendance numbers.'

'Is Banjo okay?'

'Unfortunately, he has two toe fractures in his right paw. He'll have to wear a splint for several weeks.'

'And Mara? Is there any update?'

I loved the way he'd become so invested in Darren and his daughter. How his eyes crinkled with worry when he'd asked about Banjo.

'Her collarbone is fractured, but Darren said she's home and doing well. Her friends have been coming over to check on her, which has helped extinguish a lot of her fears.'

'You forget how hard it is to be a kid sometimes until you witness it first-hand. The way she climbed out of that rescue litter, though, with her chin up, eyes filled with determination even though she was in pain, was amazing. She's a tough girl.'

'I think a lot of that was for Lia's benefit, because Mara's a big fan of my sister.'

'Shit, after watching her today, I'm a member of the Lia McGuire fan club too.'

Indy raced back into the room, lay down and rolled over. I gave his tummy a thorough rub and his right leg jerked out in joy.

Bryce gave his dog an amused look. 'Careful, he'll lie there for hours if you let him.'

After a few more belly scratches, Flora trotted back into the room, and she and Indy were off again. Bryce took my hand and led me forward. The cabin was rustic with basic furniture and a small kitchen. A large brown leather sofa, matching recliner and an old oak table were the only items in the living room. A massive stone fireplace took up the rest of the space. There were no knickknacks, picture frames or anything that showed Rich's personality. I'm pretty sure if you looked up the definition of 'bachelor pad' in the dictionary, an image of this cabin would be front and center.

'My uncle Rich wasn't big into collecting things. As my mom often told me, he was into living a basic life. She did try to spruce up the place a bit when she came to visit, but he always waved her off. Told her he didn't need much to be happy.'

He pointed to a sliding glass door at the back of the space and I followed. As soon as I stepped out onto the massive redwood deck, I understood why his uncle didn't want for much. Acres of dense forest spilled out all the way to where the trees met the mountains. Carving out a path between the trees was the wildly churning river.

He pointed to a hand-carved Adirondack chair on the deck, and I sank into its steady structure. Flora trotted over and lay down beside me. I closed my eyes, trying not to wince at the press of my raw skin against the chair. Once I was comfortable, I allowed the sounds of nature to calm me. Let the scent of dry bark, pine needles and crisp wind, melt all the tension from my body.

'I get now why your uncle was thin on the decorating. With a place like this, the stunning silence, breathtaking views, I doubt he'd need much more.'

The wind tugged at my hair, the warmth of the setting sun melting my bones into the firm feel of the chair. I'd been going a hundred miles an hour since we'd found Mara. Now that I had time to think back on today, my muscles clenched and my jaw ached. Lying down on my stomach at the edge of the ridge, not being smart about where I placed my feet, was beyond stupid. I pulled in an unsteady breath, trying not to think how differently today could have gone.

'Dani.' Bryce's stilted voice made me open my eyes. Around my chair sat a ring of birds. Nuthatch. Goldfinch. Robin.

The birds hopped closer. Didn't attempt to fly away, even when I shifted in the chair.

'Why is it that every time I'm around you, animals seek you out?'

'I give off the vet vibe,' I said casually.

'It's more than that. They sense a gentleness, a kindness that's rare.' His eyes went warm. 'At least that's what I get from you.' That searching look crossed his face again. 'I need you to know that I'd never do anything to hurt you. And today... when I couldn't find you... I thought my heart was going to burst out of my chest.'

The sincerity in his gaze was not an act. Neither was the way his hand trembled when he reached out to lovingly stroke a knuckle over my cheek. Even as I stared into those deep blue eyes, Lia's voice rang in my head. Warning me he was here to make life a nightmare for us. That he was butting into our lives where he didn't belong. But the more time I spent with him, the less I saw that cunning reporter.

'Gentle? Really?' I forced my tone to be light. 'As I recall, the first time we met I wasn't all that gentle.'

He pressed his lips thin. 'I deserved it, because I acted like an ass.'

'*Indy doesn't do leashes*,' I said in a haughty impression of him.

He scrubbed a hand over the red scruff on his chin 'That's exactly what an ass would say to a beautiful woman who'd just called him out for being an idiot.'

Heat flooded my cheeks, and I turned my attention back to the birds, who continued to hop around my chair, ignoring Flora entirely. 'If it's any consolation, I did think you cared about Indy. That was pretty clear in the way you stumbled out of the woods. Took a header straight onto the dirt.'

He let out a low, sexy chuckle. 'Not my finest moment.'

'You've improved since then.'

He kicked out his foot and dragged my chair closer. 'Care to elaborate?'

'You listened to George at the farm when he told you to hold back. To trust me. And you didn't hesitate when Lia gave you orders today. Stayed with Aster when she came back to the trail to look for us.'

'I've only been in Harvest Moon a short time, but I've learned that when a McGuire woman gives you an order, you'd be a fool not to listen.'

'Huh,' I said with a taunt. 'So you like being told what to do?'

He leaned forward and set his hands on my thighs, the heat of his touch searing through my coveralls. 'Is this okay? I can't seem to keep my hands off you.' His right eyebrow hitched. 'It's like you've bewitched me.'

I let out a caustic laugh. 'Sure, and I drove here on my broom.'

'I'm serious. Never in my life have I believed in magic, but this hunger to be close to you, to touch you.' His voice dropped into a gravel-like tone that sent my heart racing. 'It's like I'm absolutely one hundred percent under your spell. The spell of this town.'

'You do know magic isn't real, right?' I joked, even though some small part of me wondered if that was true.

'Yes, of course, but there's something chemical happening between us that defies logic.' He bit into his lower lip. Blew out an unsteady breath. 'Please tell me you feel it too.'

He was supposed to be the enemy. The one I needed to distract, throw off the scent of any story about my family, but he was right, that pull I felt toward him grew stronger each day.

I'd be lying if I said I didn't want to touch him. Ask for a repeat performance of what we'd done in the truck. I'd tried every single day, but I couldn't wipe Aster's claim about him being my soulmate from my mind. Even if she was right this time, that didn't mean I was beholden to him. This could easily be nothing more than a passing attraction. A quick way to take the edge off whatever was sparking between us. Maybe if we lit that flame and let it burn out, we could both be sated and move on.

'It's been a long and slightly painful day.' I leaned in close enough to brush my lips over his. 'Any thoughts on how you can distract me for the night?'

That wicked grin I'd come to recognize as trouble slid across his face. He scooped me up from the chair and carried me back inside. I laid my head against his chest, loving the rapid beat of his heart against my ear.

We passed through the living room and turned down a short hall. He kicked out his foot and the first door on the left swung open, revealing a bathroom with a massive glass enclosed shower. He set me gently on the counter and closed the door.

'The bathroom?' I said with a tease.

'I said I wanted to take care of you, so sit back and let me keep my promise.' He stepped in between my legs so I could feel the heat of him through his jeans. 'Is this a good enough distraction?'

'I like where this is going, but I still have on too many clothes.'

His eyes flared as he tugged me off the counter. He inched the zipper down to where it stopped at my navel. His hands went to my shoulders, sliding the pink material off. He bent down, tugging at the cotton until it pooled at my feet. With gentle hands, he removed my tennis shoes and then lifted one foot at a time until the coveralls were in a neat pile on the ground.

'What's next?' His heated gaze raked up and down my body, and any doubt I had about this was gone. I wanted his hands on me. His mouth against my skin.

'These jeans are a little tight.'

His fingers inched up over my calves, taking their time moving to my thighs; he hovered near the zipper. I had to suck in a quick breath as he dragged a finger over my center. He stopped for a minute. Closed his eyes. Licked his lips, like he could feel my wetness beneath his fingers. I placed my hand over his and he made a slight hum under his breath, whispered, 'Not yet,' before his fingers were on the button of my jeans. He slid them down my legs, and like the coveralls, he removed them one at a time.

His hungry gaze swept over my lacy, pink underwear before he slid his hands up my torso and eased my T-shirt off. I waited for him to touch me, but he stepped back and dragged the Henley over his head. Like the sun had given his skin a dozen tiny kisses, freckles dotted the top part of his pecs and eased over the curve of his shoulders. My mouth watered as he reached for the snap on his jeans and tugged them off.

His breaths came out in ragged bursts as I stepped closer and slid my hand inside his boxer briefs. He was hot and hard as I began to stroke the length of him. His eyes shuttered closed, and he leaned into the slow way I ran my hand up and down his shaft, teasing the end of his cock, which was already dripping wet.

His hand palmed the side of my neck and he pulled me in for a kiss. It was hot and hungry, and I wanted more. I ran my hand across the muscles defining his abdomen. Over the line of fine reddish hair that cascaded down his chest.

The day we'd first met on the path, I'd ignored that feeling of butterfly wings fluttering against my ribs. How even though he'd talked like an idiot, the way he looked at, and cared for, his dog said he was a gentle and good man. The tension of that line growing between us grew tauter with each passing day. In this moment with him looking like he wanted to devour me, that tether between us became a jarring snap, yanking me in, sucking all the oxygen from my lungs. Like on the ridge today I was in freefall, but this time I was hurtling straight for a destination I'd known I'd wanted since the moment he'd showed up at Clo's, all gasping questions and desperate pleas that I save one of the most precious beings in his life.

'While I'd love to fall to my knees and devour you right here, I want to take care of you first. Make sure we clean up your cuts. Is that okay?' he asked breathlessly.

Tears burned the corners of my eyes at his tenderness, and all I could manage was a weak nod.

He dropped his underwear and opened the glass shower door, turning on the water. Steam quickly filled the room. He took my hands and walked carefully backwards until we were both under the spray. I started to protest, pointing to my now wet underwear, until he sank down and eased them off. My hands stroked his soaking wet hair, and I tugged back his head to look at his face. He smiled and stood slowly. The hard heat of him pushed against me.

I wanted to reach for him, but he held me still as he unhooked my bra and tossed it over the shower door.

He set his mouth against my neck, his hands tracing the line of my shoulders and moving to the top of my back, which made me wince.

'Hey, I've got you,' he whispered.

'Sorry. My back must look awful.'

He snaked a hand around my waist, tucking me against him. 'You are a fucking vision, Dani.' He brushed aside my hair. Pressed another searing kiss to the slopes of my breasts. I wound my hands around his neck, tugging him closer, but as soon as he touched the skin on my back I winced again.

He inched away, grabbed the soap and rubbed it between his hands. His touch was light, careful, as he worked the suds down my back, over the gashes on my forearms, and across the deep cuts on my palms.

He pointed the spray in my direction, suds disappearing down the drain. A second later, the scent of cedar and mint filled the air. With slow circles, he worked the shampoo into my hair. I sucked in another low breath and his hands stilled.

'Does that hurt?'

'Guess I didn't realize I scraped up my scalp too.'

He leaned in and pressed his mouth to the back of my ear. 'I'll be careful, I promise.'

When I didn't respond, he turned me to face him. He held me in that tender gaze, and all the words I wanted to say, *Is this real? Is my sister right about us?* stayed locked in the base of my throat.

'You're spiraling. I can see it in your eyes.' His palm went back to the side of my neck, and I loved the way it made me feel steady. 'This is about you and me, Dani. In this moment I do not give a shit about any article. All I want is you. Are we clear?'

He feathered his thumb over my cheek. Pulled me closer until I was flush with his slick, wet body. 'Tell me what you want now.'

I slid my fingers against his and brought them to my breasts. He ran his hands over the taut, achy nubs. Massaged them as I arched back for more. His mouth pressed into my collarbone.

A moan slid from my lips while his hands traveled down over my stomach and stopped at my hot center. He started with a slow rhythm of circles before he slid one finger inside, and I let out a small whimper of relief.

'More?' he growled.

'Yes,' I gasped.

He slid in another finger and I rode his hand. The heat of the spray, the sound of his hitched breaths, the coiling of the muscles in my stomach, unleashed a delicious need. I bucked and arched, loving the steady thrusts, how he knew how to curl his fingers to hit all the right spots. The tense coils loosened inside me until he slid in one more finger, filling me up, making me come undone. He pressed more kisses to my neck and into my hair as my body shook and quivered.

When my breathing smoothed out, he said, 'We should get you toweled off and into some clean clothes.'

He reached to turn the shower off and I stopped his hand. 'We're not done here.'

He arched a brow. 'What did you have in mind, Dr McGuire?'

'How about I show you?'

I nudged him back against the white tile. He made a low hum as I stroked him. I loved the satisfied murmurs that spilled from his throat. The way he whispered my name like if he said it enough it would be permanently etched in his mind. When he moaned like he was on the edge, I slid in closer. He wrapped a hand around my waist and his eyes opened, pinning me in place.

'I haven't been with anyone in a long time, and my last tests were clean,' he said.

'Me too, and I have an IUD.'

The hint of desperation in his gaze was so uninhibited, so greedy. He walked me backward until I was flush against the wall. His hands wrapped around my waist and he lifted me up and I sank right down, taking him as deep as possible.

'Oh fuck,' he groaned as he held me tight. 'Wait a minute,' he gasped. 'This is goddamn bliss. I want to savor it.'

I could have listened, but those tight bands of need built in me again. Like he understood what I wanted, he began to move, slowly sliding in and out, the head of him teasing and taunting the outside of me. The moan that spilled from my mouth had him gripping my hips tighter. His movements came in focused thrusts as he held me in place, took me deeper, unlocking all those aching muscles inside me. For a second, the lights in the bathroom flickered.

'Distracted enough now?' he said hotly against my neck and I let out a laugh.

'Keep telling me what to do,' he growled. 'Where I should touch you, lick you. How you want to be fucked. I want to please you in every way possible.'

Every word he spoke sparked a fire inside me. Unleashed a hunger I'd been burying for too long. 'I want more. To be completely filled.'

I panted into his neck as his hand moved to my sensitive center. His thrusts became more insistent, and I used his shoulders to gain leverage until he was so deep that the need inside me built until I could barely hold on.

I said his name like a prayer and he gasped, 'Wait for me. I'm nearly there.'

The lights shuddered again as if the whole room was vibrating. In an agonizing tease, he pulled out of me, swirled his hips, the head of his cock slick as I pleaded for him, and he slid into me again. With panting breaths, he urged me to let go. That beautiful heat rose up in my core. A cry spilled from my mouth as he pushed me over the edge into a delicious and euphoric high.

The lights in the bathroom blared an intense white. As Bryce found his own release, one bulb and then another exploded with a jarring crack. I yelped as the room was engulfed in shadows and the heavy cloak of evening.

Still holding me with a vice-like grip, Bryce let out a full-throated laugh. 'There is so much about this old place that needs to be fixed.' He pressed another open-mouthed kiss against my shoulder. 'Or it could be what we just did was so hot, we short-circuited the damn place.'

A small, tight chuckle spilled from my lips even as a knot of dread bloomed in my chest. While I wanted to believe that what just happened was about the age of this place, a worry buried deep in the back of my mind warned that the sudden pulse of electricity had nothing to do with hot sex. I pushed away the thought and let Bryce quickly towel me off before he took my hand and led me down the hall to his bedroom.

# Chapter Twenty-Four

## *Reckless*

Bands of white morning light broke through the blinds as I woke next to Bryce's naked body. It was hard not to snuggle up next to him. Caress his back. Bury my head in his neck and get lost in his warmth again. I'd thought all we'd needed was one sleepless night to get it out of our systems. Burn bright for a few hours and then the candle would burn out.

I was so wrong. That ache in my chest to be near him only bloomed wilder as the lull of sleep softened the lines around his eyes and mouth.

When I'd driven to the cabin last night, I'd known what I was doing. That the hunger and ache in his eyes mirrored mine. It was crossing that final line. Making a choice I could never take back. But after yesterday, the way he held me tightly after I'd made it back onto solid ground, tenderly touched me when he removed the dirt and gravel from my hair, said what was happening between us was much more than a game of cat-and-mouse… I'd never expected this. Expected *him.* For so long I'd believed I'd always be alone, but now there was this undeniable want. A thing I was too afraid to say out loud, to imagine for too long: hope.

My stomach gurgled. We'd talked several times about dinner last night, but every time we tried to make it out of the bedroom, one of us would pull the other back, and we ended up burying ourselves back in the shelter of each other's arms and the mounds of blankets on the bed.

I stretched and the scrapes on my arms and back protested. What I'd done yesterday on the ridge was stupid. Reckless. But I wouldn't change anything, because this morning Mara and Banjo were waking up safe in their own home.

Bryce let out a contented sigh. For a moment I thought about climbing back in next to him. Shutting out the world for a few more blissful minutes, but my mind never worked that way. As soon as I was conscious, my brain began dissecting last night, not just the amazing sex, but the way we had to carefully navigate our way out of the bathroom to keep from stepping on the shards of glass from the broken light bulbs.

Bryce insisted it was the old cabin. That his mother had warned him the wiring and plumbing were ancient, but the way the electricity flared as blood raced in my veins last night, I couldn't help but worry that it was much more than that.

All my life I'd sworn none of the McGuire women had magic, but I was beginning to question those beliefs. I needed to see the lights again. Examine the way they'd exploded. I convinced myself that if I could understand their breaking point, it would assure me that the reason they blasted apart had nothing to do with the supernatural.

After picking up my jeans and shirt off a nearby chair, I inched out the door. Flora snoozed next to Indy a few feet away. I tiptoed down the hall, sliding on my clothes and trying not to groan at the material scratching across my raw skin.

Across the hall from the bathroom was a small den, and curiosity had me peeking inside. The walls were covered in black-and-white photos. Some were landscapes. Others were candid shots of the ski mountain over the years. Children gripped old rope tows. A couple snuggled on a metal chair lift, their old wooden skis dangling in the air.

I moved in closer to the small rounded-edge desk in the center of the room. The screen on Bryce's laptop showed an aerial photo of Los Angeles at twilight. The compact streets and serpentine swirl of homes and businesses reflected below. A small leather notebook sat open next to the laptop. Every instinct inside me screamed I should walk out of the room, but I had to remember my vow to my sisters. To Clo. To make sure that the article wouldn't tear our lives apart like last time. I leaned in and scanned his cramped handwriting.

> *I followed the women up the switchback paths. There was an unmistakable link between them. An unspoken language that relied on their connection. Lia could read the path. Her elite sense of hearing guided them forward. The youngest sister, Aster, has a unique level of sight, clocking the shifting trees, broken branches. And then there's Dani. Animals sensed her presence. Rabbits scampered out of burrows, colorful birds hopped across tree branches, deer inched out of deep green blinds to be near her. As the rest of the team continued to look for the young girl, Dani understood how to find her. She hid it from me, the*

*rest of the crew, but she'd sensed Banjo's presence the same way she'd sensed Indy's illness. There is much more here than the three women claim. On that trail today, I felt it: the vibration of an unseen force, the strength of an unyielding power. I will not give up until I get to the truth about this town and what the McGuire women are hiding. More research needs to be done on Ambrosia Perkins and the earlier ancestors.*

A raw dryness coated my throat as I turned the page. Boxes and connecting lines filled the entire paper. A genealogical chart connected my family line, starting with Sylvia and Ambrosia and leading all the way to me, Lia and Aster. Under some of the names were small scribbles indicating fire, water, earth, animals, sight. Each notation attached to only the females in the family line.

*Continues on the next page*

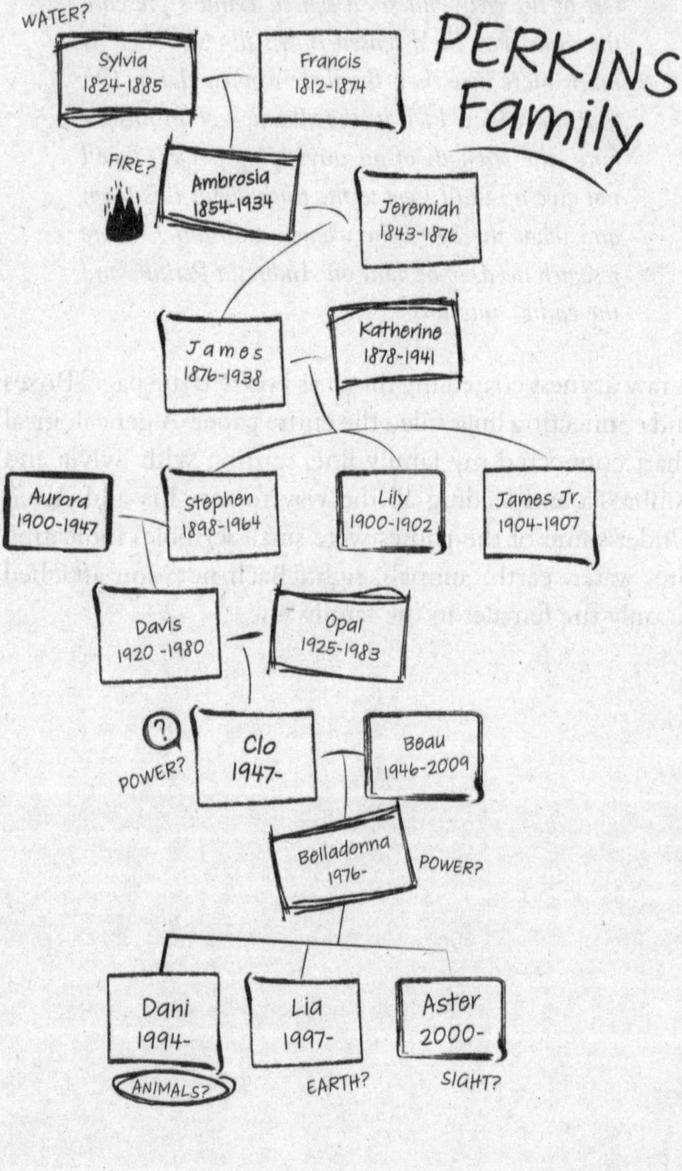
PERKINS Family
WATER?
Sylvia 1824-1885
Francis 1812-1874
FIRE?
Ambrosia 1854-1934
Jeremiah 1843-1876
James 1876-1938
Katherine 1878-1941
Aurora 1900-1947
Stephen 1898-1964
Lily 1900-1902
James Jr. 1904-1907
Davis 1920-1980
Opal 1925-1983
?
POWER?
Clo 1947-
Beau 1946-2009
Belladonna 1976-
POWER?
Dani 1994-
Lia 1997-
Aster 2000-
ANIMALS?
EARTH?
SIGHT?

A tidal wave of dread crashed over me. Threatened to pull me under. Had he written this yesterday when he came home? Or even last night, while I was asleep? Right after he'd whispered all those promises and then taken me to bed?

Underneath the notebook was a file folder. I flipped it open and my world tilted. At least a dozen photos spilled out across the desk. Candid shots taken with what appeared to be a telephoto lens. The first image nearly stopped my heart: me on the street near the pharmacy. The next two photos made bile rise in my throat. Lia in front of the firehouse. Aster talking to a customer inside her shop.

What the hell? Was he stalking us?

I'd made a huge mistake allowing him on the search yesterday. Letting him into our lives at all. He was desperate for a story, and exposing what he believed about my family was the only way to make that happen.

I fled the room and grabbed the rest of my clothes. Tugged on my shoes and picked up my bag. With a low command, I called for Flora and she followed me out the door. I put my truck in neutral and rolled backward. At the edge of the driveway, I turned on the engine and drove away. My thoughts muddied as I navigated my truck down the mountain. A sob jammed its way into my throat. Had the kiss – the sex – been a means to an end for him?

It was too much like Max. How I'd been so sure he'd cared about me, until he walked straight out the door. Bryce wasn't any different. He'd get what he needed by any means necessary and then leave.

Maybe all this time Belladonna had been right. No man could be trusted.

I steered the truck in a familiar direction. My grandmother was the only one who would know how to clean up the mess I'd made.

-

Clo sat in the rocking chair Grandpa Beau had made especially for her. It was all smooth lines and rounded arms. The height and width were a perfect fit for her tiny body.

I should not have been surprised to find her out on the deck. Waiting. Like she knew I was coming. I pulled open the front door and ascended the stairs with Flora close behind. As soon as I was out the deck's screen door, she had me wrapped in her arms. My tears fell in a flood and she didn't say a word.

She was not a 'touchy-feely' kind of grandmother, but she knew when the weight of the world was too much for each of us girls to bear.

When my shoulders stopped heaving, and the waterworks slowed to a trickle, she stepped back and held me at arm's length. 'I think you might have kept your enemy a bit too close.'

'You think?' I said with a rough laugh.

'Sit down and tell me about it.'

I sank into the wooden chair beside her. Another one of Grandpa Beau's creations that reminded me of a Stickley. Flora wandered to a shady spot on the deck and lay down. 'I've screwed everything up. Badly.'

She tugged her long white braid over her shoulder, fiddling with the tie at the end. 'What makes you say that?'

'I thought I was distracting Bryce. That I could stay on top of this. Prevent him from writing anything wild about us.'

'And now?'

'He's been watching us for what looks like a while. Taking notes. Photos. When we were in the archives, I took a journal that had notes about Ambrosia and hid it, because it claimed she had magic.' I scrubbed a hand through my hair. 'Real. Fucking. Magic.'

She pressed her hands against her lap, her shoulders tightening up around her ears. 'What else? When your cheeks go blotchy it means you're hiding more.'

The flash and pop of the lights in the bathroom played on repeat in my head.

'Did you hear how we found Mara?'

Her lips puckered. 'Yes, Lia and Aster were here last night. They told me *you* weren't exactly thinking straight when you went after her.'

She gave me that weighted look I often got when I acted before I thought something through. 'Seems to be a repeated theme this past month.' Her gaze flicked to the bandages covering the scrapes on my arms. 'I'll give that man credit. At least it appears that he looked after you.'

I pushed to my feet and walked to the railing. The early morning sun inched above the tree line, creating a mirror image against the pale blue water in the lake. Its shores slapped with a heavy current even though there was hardly any breeze.

'Tell me what's really bothering you. It's about more than Bryce and his story.'

I paused, unsure how to ask the woman I'd loved and trusted my entire life if she possessed magical abilities.

'You'd tell me…' I hesitated because once I cracked open this can of worms, there'd be no turning back. 'If… what that journal said was true… if we really did have magic, right?'

She tilted her head. Paused for a minute too long. 'What makes you ask that question?'

'One time I thought I saw…' I shook my head, too embarrassed to admit I'd been spying on her. 'When I was about twelve we used to make s'mores by the campfire all the time.'

'I remember. It was your grandfather's favorite part of the summer.'

'One night, I thought I saw you light the fire with nothing but a snap of your fingers. And then I read about Ambrosia. That the locals believed she'd used magic to burn down her house with her abusive husband inside.'

She didn't answer. Instead, she rose and disappeared into the house. A minute later she was back, her right hand clutched into a fist. Her fingers unfurled, showing me a basic red-tipped match. 'Your great-grandfather, Davis, used to take me out into the woods on long weekends. He was a survivalist and insisted I learn how to take care of myself in case I ever got lost.' With a quick flick of her thumb across the top of the match, she brought it to a blaze.

'Holy shit,' I murmured.

'It's a good party trick, but it's not magic, Dandelion.' She blew out the flame. 'What I said the other night to Bryce was true. What men don't understand, they villainize. After her husband died, Ambrosia sold the mercantile. She and her mother, Sylvia, ran the apothecary, and it did well.' She reached out and held my hands. 'The men did not like their autonomy. Called them witches to try and strip their power away. These days they've changed the word from "witch" to "bitch", but it's still meant to steal women's agency.'

'But even if it's not real, Bryce can claim it is. That could be a lot of clicks and likes for him. It would bring more people to town. Make the tourists act even stranger than they already do. And after the last article…' All I could do was deflate back into the chair next to her.

'Would that change how you go about your life? How you care for the animals at your clinic? What about Lia? Would she stop her important work? Would Aster keep quiet about what she felt and saw?'

'No. We'd push on like we always do.'

'When Bryce first arrived, I was afraid too. But now that I've had time to think about it, I'm not. People here have watched you girls grow up and become an important part of this community. We got through the scandal with the Denver reporter. This will pass too.'

I didn't believe her. During those darker days, I'd been a witness to the way the shop owners flinched when she'd entered their businesses. Treated her like she was some kind of demonic entity. She'd tried to hide it from me, but on those long rides home she'd gripped the steering wheel in either anger or fear, her steely resolve never revealing which.

She reached out and squeezed my hand. 'The McGuire women have been through a lot harder things than one article in a national magazine.'

I owed this woman so much. She looked after me and my sisters in a quiet and resilient way, which gave us wings. Allowed us to carve our own path in spite of Belladonna's whirlwind interferences. I could say 'thank you' a million times to her, and it would never be enough. She may have not agreed, but I needed to protect her now, the way she'd always looked out for me.

'While you're here, we should probably talk about another matter.' She shifted uncomfortably in the chair as the screen door squeaked open. Just when I thought things couldn't get any worse, the world proved me wrong.

'Hello, my precious Dandelion. How come you haven't been answering my emails?'

Streaks of gray threaded through Belladonna's dyed black hair. A cavern of lines cut into the areas around her eyes and mouth. That signature deep brown lipstick she always wore bled around the outline of her thin lips.

Clo withered at my pained gaze. 'She arrived late last night. I couldn't turn her away.'

My first thought wasn't about how my mother had once again showed up unannounced. Or how she had crappy timing. My immediate concern was Lia and Aster. What kind of trouble our mother's presence would cause them.

'I'm not in the mood for pleasantries this morning. Why are you here, and how soon can I get you to leave?'

## *Chapter Twenty-Five*

### *Full of Empty Promises*

'Is that any way to greet your mother? Especially since I've come to stay a while.'

'You'll have to elaborate on that one. For you, "a while" can mean anywhere between two hours and two months.' The scrapes on my back protested as my skin pressed against the hard edges of the chair.

She nervously glanced at Clo. 'I sensed I was needed here and came home. And from what I heard inside, it sounds like I arrived just in time.'

'In time to do what? Make things worse?'

She crossed her arms over the thin black lace top she was wearing. 'That's not fair.'

'Let me refresh your memory. The last time you were here, you promised Aster you'd help her in the store. That she could take on more weddings because you'd be around to handle the day-to-day. But as soon as she loaded up her calendar, you disappeared quicker than the sun on a January day.'

'There was a last-minute opening at a retreat in Santa Fe,' she sputtered. 'They needed a seasoned yogi to lead some advanced Ashtanga classes.'

'Oh.' I flapped my hands out to my sides. 'Then you're totally forgiven, because some retreat a state away is much more important than the promise you made to your youngest daughter.'

She shook her head like I was some petulant child. 'You know I do not enjoy it when you raise your voice.'

'Really?' I jumped to my feet. 'Well, I do not enjoy it when you show up out of nowhere, flip our lives upside down and then fucking take off again.'

I bent to kiss Clo on the cheek. 'Call me when she's gone. Flora, come on.'

I fled the deck, took the stairs two at a time and slammed out the front door. The lake rolled and shifted again. The current surged higher up on the dirt shore, startling some of the herons in their nests. I pushed Flora up into the truck and peeled out of the driveway.

Whenever Belladonna showed up, things went to hell quickly. A gnawing throb began in the back of my head and inched its way toward the raw spot on my scalp. It only took me ten minutes to get to the clinic, but when I pulled in, a small SUV was parked in front of the entrance.

Crap. Could this day get any worse?

I stopped the truck, slammed the door and strode past Bryce, who was sitting on the top step. He looked too good in his faded jeans and a plain white T-shirt.

'I woke up and you were gone. Why didn't you say anything? I would have made you breakfast.'

'Go away, Bryce. I've had a crap morning, and all I want to do is go inside, crawl into bed and go back to sleep for the rest of this Sunday.'

He stood and reached for my hand, but I stepped back. 'I don't want you here.'

He bowed his chin and shoved his hands into his pockets. 'Did I do something wrong? I thought last night was important until I woke up to an empty bed.'

Anger, fear and frustration became a tsunami in my head, and I swallowed down the tremble in my throat. 'This isn't going to work. I need to focus on my job. You have to write your story,' I said, unable to keep the venom from my tone. 'Let's agree that last night was a one-time thing that *will not* be repeated.'

He stepped closer, his deep blue gaze desperately searching my face for answers. 'Talk to me, Dani. If I screwed up, then I need to know how I can make it up to you.' He planted his feet like he had no intention of leaving.

'Exactly how long have you been stalking me and my family?'

'Stalking?' he choked out.

'I saw the photos on your desk. The ones of me on the street. And my sisters just quietly going about their lives.' Rage built in my chest. 'You've been lying this whole time, and I'm an idiot for believing a single word that has come out of your mouth.'

He scratched a hand through his already tousled bed head. 'This story was originally supposed to be written by my friend Hank. He came here six months ago and took those shots. Another job overseas came to him, and he knew I was struggling to get work. It took a while, but he eventually talked me into writing this piece because I had a connection here.'

'That doesn't explain your lies. Why on the trail, and later that night, you pretended like you didn't know who I was, but you really did. You should get a damn Oscar for those performances.'

He was already shaking his head. 'Hank sent those pictures to me a couple of weeks ago, but he got the zip code wrong. They didn't show up until last week. I'll show you the envelope as proof.'

'And the line you fed me? "*This isn't about the article. It's about you and me.*"' I spat his own words back at him.

'That was the truth.'

'Bullshit. Were you waiting for the minute I finally fell asleep last night so you could sneak into your office and write all the sordid details about Mara's search? How long have you been building my family tree, Bryce? Because that looked like it took a long fucking time.'

Sensing my anger, Flora growled and took a step in front of me.

Bryce paled and let out a thready breath. 'When I don't understand things, I write, Dani. What you read was private. It was me puzzling out what I saw yesterday. Trying to make sense of the connection I witnessed between you and your sisters. There are things at work in this town that aren't normal. How animals react to you. The way you can feel their aches and pains. How Lia can hear the woods. Connect with the land. I've talked to at least six couples in town who swear what Aster can do borders on the supernatural. And last night…' He laid his hands on the top of his head and walked in a tight circle. 'The lights shattering. I thought it was the electricity, but I checked the fuse panel this morning, and it looks like Rich replaced it a few years ago.'

'We've been over this,' I flung back. 'Each of us girls does have a gift, but it's not magic. We understand animals, people, the land. As for the lights, the bulbs could have been defective.'

His shoulders crumpled. 'I noticed the other night at dinner that when Clo got worked up, the chandelier above the table flickered.'

'Now you're reaching. Making things fit the narrative you need to tell.'

'No. I'm trying to get to the truth.' He sank down onto the step. 'This last year has been a mess for me. It's like if I can't write, I can't breathe. It's the only thing that makes sense in my life.' He tugged on his hair again. 'I'm trying to figure out a way to do this where I can tell the story without hurting you or your family. Please, just give me time to figure it out.'

'And what does that look like exactly?'

'I'm trying to balance things. Write an article that will get me back to work but will also tell a real story about this town. You, your family, are a part of that tale. I've seen it in the way the town treats you and your sisters. Clo. You're respected. Admired. That won't change once the article comes out.'

It was exactly what my grandmother said, but they were both wrong. People in town didn't think I noticed, but I caught the odd lingering gazes tossed in my direction at the clinic, the market, the pharmacy. The slight tilt of the head, puckering of lips, the fixed stare, as if they were questioning if my magic simmered just below the surface of my skin.

That old article had stripped my ability to relax. To believe people could see me just for me. The salt circle thing had been a hoax, but that journalist's words had carved a small dark hole into my heart. I couldn't let Bryce make that wound any deeper. Not for me. Not for my family.

Flora leaned in close as if sensing my heartache. 'You should leave now,' I said as firmly as I could.

'Please, let me come inside. Explain more of my thoughts about the story. How I'm desperate to make this work with us.'

He was so earnest. It'd be easy to let him in. Allow him to spin some story to placate me. But when I looked at him now, all I saw was Max. A man full of empty promises and lame excuses. And Aster's gift be damned. Believing in a man who was only going to betray me was not a trap I was walking into again.

'No, I've seen enough to understand where this is going.'

His eyes went sad as he stood. 'My article isn't due for another few weeks. I'm here if you change your mind. Want to talk.' He turned and made for his car and then stopped. With his back still turned, he said, 'Mo told me about Max. How he hurt you. Some people wait a lifetime for what's happening between us. Don't throw it away because you're scared.'

Flora let out a low whine, and I urged her through the front door, unable to watch him drive away. Once we were inside, I slid down and let the tears come again. Flora lay across my lap to comfort me. Another aching sob filled my chest as I considered if Bryce was right. Was I scared to let him in? To trust him?

Flashes of the day Max left, suitcases in hand, filled my mind. It was just another reminder that I was a failure, because I couldn't protect my family, or my own damn heart.

# *Chapter Twenty-Six*

## *Always Two Steps Ahead*

'You are *not* hiding in this clinic for one more minute.'

Bree leaned against the door leading into the main exam room. Her bright pink scrubs were covered in dog hair and surgical scrub solution. 'Jessa and I are going to play pool at the tavern, and you're coming with us.'

'Not tonight.' I placed more gauze squares and cotton swabs into the cabinets above the sink. 'The other rooms have to be restocked. There's also a ton of charts that need updated notes, and Flora desperately needs a bath.'

It sounded like an excuse, but it was true. Every morning for the last week I was up at dawn and out on the trail with Flora. I tried to convince myself it was because I wasn't sleeping, but it was more about the fact that I did not want to run into Bryce.

Jessa appeared in the doorway, and the two of them stood in warrior stances. 'We're not letting up until you agree,' Bree pressed. 'This is your town, and you can't let some outsider dictate your movements.'

In a fit of frustration yesterday, I let it slip about my fight with Bryce. How the plans for his article were about to blow up my entire family's life. Bree suggested intimidation in the form of a few local loggers. Jessa asked if we could booby-trap his cabin. After I talked them both off the ledge, they watched me silently. Quietly pushed treats in my direction. Fielded any problems or complaints I didn't need to know about.

'Come on, Dani. One beer. One slice of Mo's terrible pizza that comes straight out of the box and right into the microwave. A couple of games of pool. It'll be a good distraction,' Jessa begged.

They stood as a united front, and I'd hear about it for weeks if I didn't give in.

'Fine.' I pointed a stern finger at them. 'But when I'm ready to go home, no guilt trips.'

'We promise,' they said together.

The jarring sound of the front door creaking open had Jessa rushing back to the reception desk. Bree stayed in the doorway. 'Offer still stands to send over Tobias and a few of his logging friends to scare him a little.'

'That's not necessary. Bryce would just figure out a way to use it as color for the article.'

She let out a reluctant huff. 'All right, but my boyfriend and his pals can be intimidating when they want to be.'

I bit back a smile. Tobias was massive, but he also played Santa Claus every year for the town's tree-lighting ceremony, so it was hard to picture him threatening Bryce.

'Pokey is here for his nail trim,' Jessa called down the hall.

Bree rolled her eyes and I laughed. 'That dog is ferocious and you know it.'

'He's an eight-pound chihuahua, Bree.'

'Yes, and he uses every bit of that weight to snap at me. Good thing we have that new grooming hammock that keeps him from taking chunks of skin out of my fingers.'

I had to admit Pokey was a tough case. He was deathly afraid of the nail clippers, but Bree exuded enough alpha behavior to get the dog to cooperate.

She took a slow walk down the hall. When she opened the door to Exam Room Three, she was greeted with a snarl. I pressed a hand to my mouth to keep from laughing and went back to work, dreading that in a few hours I'd actually have to pretend to be sociable.

-

The scent of burnt pepperoni, old beer and drugstore cologne smacked me in the face when I walked into the tavern. All the town regulars sat on the cheap vinyl stools at the bar. The judge and Eric gave me a wave. A few of the local farmers, including a smiling George, tipped their hats in my direction as I passed.

Bree and Jessa had already staked out a spot at the center pool table in the far back room. Two full mugs of pale ale sat on a nearby high-top table.

The girls spotted me across the room, and Jessa waved her arms, making more than a few gazes veer in my direction. When I reached the table, Jessa was still flailing about until Bree reached for her arms and said, 'We are not flagging in a 747.'

Jessa let out a giggle.

'How many beers has she had?' I said.

'One.' Bree smirked. 'She's a total lightweight.'

A thick glass with a dark-brown stout and a creamy foam top landed on the table. Mo stood a few steps away with one hand propped on her hip.

'I haven't been to the bar yet,' I deadpanned.

'After what you did for Mara and Banjo, drinks and food are on me tonight.'

'I don't want to owe you anything, Mo, especially since you keep spilling secrets that aren't yours.' I was still angry that she'd said anything to Bryce about Max. I pulled my wallet out of my canvas bag, but she took a step back.

'Not taking your money tonight, Dani.'

I started to object again until Bree interrupted. 'We'll take a large pepperoni pizza and breadsticks.'

'Ooh, can we get some of those fried pickles too?' Jessa squealed.

'Dani?' Mo said like she needed my permission.

'If it's on the house, add in another round too.'

'Done.' She strode away without another word.

'That woman owes you a hell of a lot more than pizza and beer, but it's a start,' Jessa said with a hiccup. 'The way she runs her mouth about your family. She swears it's the key to bringing business into town but that's such a crock of shit.' She reached for her beer and took another big gulp.

Bree chuckled and helped her lower the glass to the table. 'Slow down there, J. We have all night.'

Jessa wiped a hand over her mouth and giggled again. It took her two tries to heave her wobbly little body up onto the tall chair at the high-top.

'Who's up?' I tipped my chin to the table.

'We flipped a coin. I'm playing you first. Eight-ball okay?' Bree said.

'Rack 'em up.'

I moved to the wall where the pool cues hung like thin wooden soldiers in a neat row. After plucking one off the squeaky hinges, I chalked the tip. A familiar voice made me look up. Lia sat in a corner booth with the fire chief. Their heads pressed together in a tense conversation. I pulled in a full breath and strode in their direction.

'Evening, Chief.'

'Dani. Good to see you,' he said like he was relieved to have a break. 'Lia and I were just talking about the incident with Mara and Banjo.'

'How is Mara doing?' I asked.

'According to Darren, she's on the mend,' the chief answered.

'That's good to hear.'

'Lia and I were going over the rescue,' he said uncomfortably. 'Seems she has a few suggestions for how we can do it better next time.'

'Lee did a good job. In fact, Mara called her a badass.'

A reluctant smirk lifted Lia's lips. 'She did?'

'Yep. You've got a fan there.'

'See. You need to ease up a bit,' the chief said.

She reached for her glass, downed the beer in a single gulp and pushed to the edge of the booth. 'See you tomorrow,' she grumbled before stalking to the exit.

'Should I ask?' I said.

He smoothed his hand over his mustache. 'Your sister is very good at her job, but she doesn't always play well with others.'

'Tell me something I don't know.'

The corners of his eyes pinched in sadness. 'I'm serious, Dani. Seth Cambridge is leaving his captain's position to move to Bozeman in three months. Lia could take the test. Easily slide into his job, but—'

'She doesn't play well with others,' I parroted back.

'Talk to her. Get her to think about what it means to be in a leadership role. If she can't ease up' – he shook his head – 'there are others who want to move in and take that job.'

Lia could be immovable when she thought she was right. That kind of attitude would never earn her friends or the respect of her peers.

'I promise we will have a conversation about it.'

He grabbed his baseball hat from the booth and plopped it on his head. 'We're one of the best fire stations in Colorado because of your sister's organization and ingenuity, but she needs to get out of her head.'

'I hear you, Chief.'

'I'll say goodnight then.'

Lia's job was her world. Aster and I talked about that fact a lot. But she also needed another focus or purpose. When we broached the subject with her, she waved us off. Told us to mind our own business. There was such a thing as being too caught up in your own job, which I was reminded of as an annoyed Bree pointed at the pool table.

I chalked the end of my stick again, a flutter of blue dust filling the air.

'Lia all right? When she walked out of here she looked like she wanted to kick someone's ass,' Bree said.

'It's Lia being Lia.' I shrugged.

'Flip a coin to break?' she asked.

'No, you go ahead.'

She leaned her arms down onto the green felt, setting the white cue ball behind the head string. After she let out a smooth breath, the pool cue slid between her fingers and she launched the ball in a straight line toward the neat triangle.

The pack broke apart, shooting multi-colored balls out in several directions. She deflated when the cue ball careened into a side pocket. 'Well, that was awful.'

I grabbed the cue ball and moved around the edges of the table, scanning the lines to figure out the best shot. The solid orange five-ball hovered on the edge of the right corner pocket. I leaned over, and with a gentle tap of my cue, it dropped into the hole.

'Woohoo,' Jessa called out.

'Hey, whose side are you on?' Bree grumbled.

'I'm team McGuire Clinic,' Jessa replied, taking another long pull on her beer.

'You may have to call Stewey later, to come and take her home,' I said as I passed Bree, sizing up my next shot.

'Already way ahead of you. Texted him on my way here. Told him to be ready.'

'Why am I not surprised?'

'Because I was your best hire ever, and I'm always two steps ahead of you.'

'That's true. It's why I pay you the big bucks,' I said.

That finally got her to smile. I bent close to the table and banked the solid green six-ball against a bumper before it slid into a side pocket.

'So you're good at pool too, huh? Why am I not surprised?' said a deep, honeyed voice.

Bryce stood a few feet away, his own pool cue gripped between his fingers. Faded, well-worn jeans hung across his hips. A dark blue Denver Broncos hat sat low on his head.

'I have many talents,' I flung back, too pissed that even after everything that'd happened, I still felt that tug toward him.

'Yeah, I know that.' He gave me that too-sexy grin that he thought would soften me up. He was wrong.

'Funny hat for someone who's from LA,' I said.

'Eric gave it to me. Said he has a ton of leftover gear from his playing days.'

'Of course he did,' I fumed. Why did it seem like everyone in this town was clearly charmed by this guy?

He set a handful of quarters on the green felt. 'Next game?'

'It's girls' night.' Bree stalked around the table, sizing up her next shot.

'Yep,' Jessa hiccupped. 'Go away, troublemaker.'

Bryce arched a brow.

'Nothing is a secret in this town,' I said, ignoring the way he tried to get closer. 'Now, if you'll excuse me, Bree is about to miss this shot.'

'Am not!' She tried to bank in the nine-ball and missed the pocket by an inch.

'How about a little wager?' Bryce pressed.

'You have nothing I want.' I moved to the far end of the table. 'Four-ball top corner pocket.' I took the shot, banking the solid purple ball against one side of the table before it careened straight into the pocket.

'Impressive.' Bryce leaned against the cue, his forearms flexing.

Screw Aster's statement about his color. I needed this guy out of my life.

'You play one game with me.' He sank his teeth into his full lower lip, and I forced myself to ignore the memory of the way that mouth had been all over my body only a week ago. Brought me to a dizzying bliss that would take decades to forget. 'If you win, I'll sit down and show you everything in my files and on my laptop.'

That got my attention.

'But if I'm victorious, you go on one date with me, and we don't discuss anything about the article. Just you and me, a five-star meal and a great bottle of wine.'

Bree let out a brittle laugh. 'Yeah, you'd have to drive to Breckenridge, which is like an hour drive away, to make that happen.'

Bryce's stare turned soft. 'Exactly.'

Jessa let out a squeal behind me. Bree leaned on her cue. The mischief in her eyes urged me to take the deal, because she knew I'd been playing pool for years and could easily crush Bryce. At lunch one day right after she'd started at the clinic, we'd swapped stories about our families, and I told her about the special bond I had with Grandpa Beau. How we'd come to this tavern every Sunday to have the fried chicken special and play pool. I didn't realize it at the time, but it was his own sneaky way of teaching me math and physics. As he sauntered around the table, he'd explained how playing pool was all about simple geometry. Lining up your shots with the right angles. How striking the ball with a measured force made all the difference.

Beating Bryce would be easy, but I still hesitated. I'd let my guard down with him once, and it bit me in the behind. There was no saying it wouldn't happen again if I opened the door for him.

'You don't trust me to keep my word.'

I set my hip against the table. Gave him a fiery stare. 'You've lied to me how many times now?'

The room grew hushed. It would be great if I didn't live in a place where my life felt like a constant spectacle.

'Hey!' Bree shouted at the patrons. 'Mind your business. Go back to your drinks and your meals.'

Jessa wobbled off her stool and went to the jukebox. An old Bon Jovi song filtered through the speakers, and the town was distracted again.

'How about this, I'll also throw in final review of the article before it goes to my editor. You can make any changes or deletions you want.'

I narrowed my eyes, sensing a trap. 'Why would you do that?'

'Because *I* have nothing to hide from *you*.'

His meaning was clear. I was the one who still had the journal. Who was still keeping secrets.

When I stayed quiet, he added, 'Your friends can be a witness to the offer. Make sure that I don't go back on my word.'

Bree shrugged. 'Your choice, but it sounds like a decent deal to me.'

'I agree,' Jessa shouted a little too loudly from the table.

This ridiculous scene was one of the many reasons why I liked my quiet life. 'One game. Winner takes all,' I conceded.

That gorgeous smile of his lit up the damn room. 'Let's go.'

Even as the warning bells went off in my head, I pointed at the table and said, 'We need to finish this game first.'

With 'You Give Love a Bad Name' blasting through the room, it took me less than five minutes to sink the rest of my balls. The crowd let out an appreciative shout as I walked back to the table and took a long pull on my beer.

Bree swung out her mug in Bryce's direction, taunting him. 'Good luck. You're gonna need it.'

# *Chapter Twenty-Seven*

## *You Better Grovel*

By the grave look on his face, Bryce realized his miscalculation. To his credit, he stepped forward, pulled all the balls out of the pockets and racked them.

'You break,' he said like he was being generous.

'No, you go first. It might be the last shot you get.'

The regulars left their stools and hovered nearby. Mo delivered our drinks and food and never left. She must have loved that we were giving her patrons free entertainment.

Ignoring the growing murmurs, Bryce pulled back his pool cue and in one smooth movement shot the cue ball straight at the tidy triangle. The balls spit out across the table in a colorful explosion. A few banked off the sides before the orange-striped thirteen-ball teetered once before dropping into the right side pocket. Chin tilted back, shoulders loose, he ambled around the table.

A few people in the crowd whispered advice. Judge Greene was the loudest. 'Number twelve ball in the upper right corner.'

*Traitor.*

Bryce took the guidance. A single gentle tap made the ball roll into the pocket. The song on the jukebox changed to 'Foolin' by Def Leppard. The gold-and-green billiards light over the table flickered like the fates were laughing at me.

The crowd's whispers grew. Bryce took his time lining up his pool cue with the nine-ball. 'Top left corner.' The trajectory was off, hitting the side of the felt table and bouncing away from the pocket.

Grandpa Beau's one piece of coveted advice about pool was that you had to stop and survey the table. Envision each shot so the balls tumbled in one after the other. My heart ached at the thought of him. How he always had confidence that I'd choose the right thing. If he was here now, he'd lean in and whisper, 'Trust your instincts and kick his butt.'

The glass light fixture flickered again. The heat of Bryce's stare singed into my back, but I refused to look at him. If he wanted to walk close to the fire, he was going to get burned.

My first shot sent the solid purple four-ball into the right center pocket. Each and every ball I sank after that caused the crowd to cheer. It didn't take more than three minutes to clear the table. The crowd let out another roar, Bree and Jessa shouting the loudest. Mo proclaimed the show over and ordered the crowd back to their seats. It was the first decent overture she'd made in a long time.

Bree walked in my direction and slid the cue from my hand. 'Twenty bucks says he knew he was going to get his ass handed to him in public. It's a poor attempt at an apology, but maybe you should talk to him. It might make you feel better.'

The light above the table flared once more. I ignored it and pointed at Bryce. 'Outside. Now!'

Bree took the cue from him. 'You better grovel. A lot.' She walked to the high-top, encouraging Jessa to eat a handful of fried pickles.

Without looking back, I headed for the front door. A few lingering tourists darted into the last open shops before they closed for the night.

'Didn't know I was about to get hustled,' Bryce said.

In the fading evening light, his hair was a dark russet. The slight stubble on his chin made him look rugged, and I hated that those coils in my stomach tightened.

'I think you did. It was your idiotic way of apologizing again.'

His grin went wide. 'Did it work?'

'What the hell do you want from me, Bryce? With all the research you have, you can write your article. Tell the whole world about the town and the supposed "witches" who lurk among the ordinary people. Mo will love you for it. Hell, every business owner will probably want to make you an honorary citizen. Give you a damn key to the city.'

'That's not what I want, and you know it.'

'What I do know is that if you write what you think is true about the McGuire women, I won't be able to stay. Neither will Lia and Aster.'

'You're giving me too much power,' he argued.

'I'm not. Do you have any idea what it's like to have people come into my clinic and look at me like I'm some kind of freak while I treat their pets? That there are people who make appointments just to come inside and search for some kind of magical clues. Like I might be hiding a pentagram, or a spell book in a secret spot.'

I tore my hands through my hair, hating the fact that they were trembling. 'Lia goes out on a call, and her crew watches her as if she's some kind of odd homing beacon who can magically point to where a fire has started. More than once, it's made her question her place here too. And Aster.' My voice wavered. 'There are men who come into her shop and act creepy. Demand that she help them find their soulmate. One time…' I broke off, trying not to picture that man cornering my baby sister. How awful it would be if people swarmed her shop, demanding she find them their match. 'It's hard enough to live a normal life here. Your article will only bring more attention to our already scrutinized existence. Don't you see that?'

'The last thing I want to do is hurt your sisters or you.'

'But that is exactly what you'll be doing.'

'You can't know that.'

'I do,' I shouted, drawing a few leery gazes from the tourists walking past the tavern.

'Explain it to me, then.' The plea in his voice was too much.

'Twenty years ago, a reporter was here. He wrote a bunch of bullshit about my family. Falsified proof that we were witches. Things with the town went bad very quickly. Clo was nearly broken by it.'

'And you? You were, what, thirteen then?'

'Twelve. They say middle school is hard but try throwing in murmurs about being a witch to a voracious pack of teen girls. Every day was like walking through a minefield. People put voodoo dolls in my locker. Slid ugly, vile notes into my backpack.' I pulled in a shaky breath, the memories too painful.

'You said "falsified"?'

'Yes, the guy made it all up because he wanted the story to go national. Make a big name for himself.'

'That must have made people around here apologize. Feel bad for believing the lies.'

My laugh was rough. 'Nope. It played into what they already believed. They want the business magic brings, just not the people who supposedly wield it.' I glanced at the ground, toed at a loose rock with the tip of my shoe. 'To this day, when I go into the Harvest Moon Market, the owner, Marylee, makes the sign of the cross when she sees me. Like I'm some devil she needs to cast out. Do you know how much it sucks that the people who live in the place I consider home think I'm evil without a damn shred of real evidence?'

'Wait. The thing George said at the farm about coming home in spite of people. Is this what he was referring to?'

'Yes.' I hated the pitying look in his eyes. 'My point is that your words will have weight. If there's even a whisper alluding to my family line, people around here will run with it. Use it as a way to make trouble for us again.'

He scrubbed a hand behind his neck. Let out an achy breath. 'I don't know what to do. Writing is in my blood. In my soul. I can't live without it, Dani. One captivating article about this town. Its mysterious history.' He shook his head. 'It could get me back on the map. But I also know from past investigations, like the one with the school secretary, that a story can cause ripples that change a person's life.'

'You're good at your job, Bryce. I've read what you've written for the *Post* and the *Times*. Please, find another way to get back to your life. I'm begging you.'

'Give me some time to think of a plan.' He tried to sound convincing, but his voice was bleak, like he was hurting too but couldn't figure a way out.

'God, I am such a fool. Once again, I let Aster convince me she was right, and now I'm paying the price.'

His head snapped up. 'Aster? What do you mean?'

'Nothing,' I bit out, cursing the fact that I'd let that slip. 'Goodnight, Bryce.'

I started for my car when he called out, 'Wait. You won the bet. I'm a man of my word. Come to the cabin tomorrow, and I'll show you every bit of research I have. We can talk more about a way to make this right.'

His voice broke on the last words. After everything that had happened between us, how could I trust him? I was keeping things from him too, and that combination of lies made it impossible to have a real relationship. To build anything when the foundation could crumble at any moment.

'It doesn't matter anymore, Bryce. You're going to do what you need to do and so am I.'

He called out for me once more. Asked me to wait, but I jumped inside the truck and peeled away from town. Tears streamed down my cheeks as I drove to the clinic. I'd failed my grandmother. My sisters. My life was about to shatter again, and I had no way of stopping it.

# *Chapter Twenty-Eight*

## *Midnight Mojitos*

Flora greeted me when I walked in the door. I bent down to pet her, and she nuzzled into my chest, sensing that I needed comfort. I let a few more tears fall and then pushed out a full breath.

I was done crying over the situation. Over Bryce. For now, I had to focus on what I could control. My work. My future. Although I had no idea what that would look like once Bryce told the world about the 'magic' he believed the McGuire women possessed.

My bones were heavy and my mind was numb. In the bathroom I turned on the faucet, wiping away the trails of mascara streaks on my cheeks. All I wanted was to crawl under the covers and hide from the world. I walked into my bedroom with Flora close behind when the sound of my doorbell filled the room.

Shit. I could not handle an emergency tonight.

'Flora, stay.'

I hustled down the stairs and through the door that separated my living space from the clinic. Several knocks followed another ring of the doorbell. Whoever was on the other side was about to get an earful.

'I'm coming,' I shouted. Once the deadbolt was thrown, I yanked open the door. Elena stood on the porch. Her hair was in a messy bun, and she was wearing her favorite Denver Nuggets sweatshirt she'd found at a thrift shop in Ouray a few years ago. Behind her, Aster bounced on her toes. The purple hoodie she wore nearly drowned her small body. Lia stood a few feet away wearing a black sweatsuit and a somber look.

Crap. Bree must have called them when I fled the tavern.

'I'm not in the mood for company.'

'Sorry, but we're still coming in.' Elena walked past me.

Aster pulled me into a hug. 'There's been this awful ache in my heart all day, but the shop's been crazy. I'm sorry I didn't call you.'

She dipped her chin, and I bent until she looked me in the eyes. 'You are not responsible for my happiness or sadness. We've talked about this.'

'I know, but it's hard when you're hurting.' She pulled a folded mailing envelope from the back pocket of her jeans. 'This was near the front door.'

I took it as Lia hovered a few steps away. A pitcher filled with green liquid was gripped in her hand. 'We're drinking mojitos until you forget about that asshole.'

'While I love and appreciate you all, this can't happen tonight. I'm exhausted,' I pushed back.

'Too bad.' Aster slapped her hands onto her hips. 'I already called Dalton. He's making an extra-large margherita pizza and a dozen blazing hot wings for us. Said he'll personally deliver them in twenty minutes.'

The three of them proceeded down the hall toward my apartment. Even though I wanted to go to sleep, forget this night ever happened, a part of me was relieved they were here. That I didn't have to wallow in my misery alone.

At the top of the stairs, Flora greeted them with a sweet bark. Elena sank to the floor beside my couch, and Flora made herself at home in her lap. Aster plopped onto a stool at the breakfast bar, and Lia went to work in the kitchen, pulling down glasses from the cabinet above the sink.

I set the envelope on the counter and fell into a wooden chair at my small round dining table. 'Might as well tell me what Bree said when she called you.'

Aster's brows shot up. 'Bree?'

'Yeah, I assumed she called you after I left the tavern.'

The three of them went suspiciously quiet.

'Was it Jessa?' I said.

Elena focused on giving Flora a quick rub behind the ears. 'Bryce called me, and then I reached out to your sisters.'

'What? How does he even have your number?' I said.

'He's been in for coffee a couple of times, looking for info about the history of the buildings in town. Asked if he could have my number in case he had any more questions.'

'And you just gave him your digits?' I grumbled.

'He made it sound like it was a tourism article, and I saw it as another way to get people into town. To stop into Drip! Drip! Hooray! and get a cup of coffee.'

My heart twinged. In all my rantings about what the story would do to my family, I'd forgotten that an article bringing tourists to town would be a boon for my best friend's business.

'What exactly did Bryce say to you during this call?' I said.

Elena went back to petting Flora's head. 'That you were upset. How you shouldn't be alone. That he wanted you to be surrounded by people who loved you.'

Aster pulled in a little gasp.

Lia stilled in the middle of the kitchen. 'He said that?'

'Yes.' Elena sighed. 'You probably don't want to hear this, Dan, but that man cares about you.'

'If he cared, he'd walk away from this. It all feels especially awful now after…' I bit my lip, and Flora hopped off Elena's lap and sank down next to my chair.

'How close have you two become?' Aster hedged like she already knew the answer.

I choked out a brittle laugh. 'He has a crescent-shaped scar right where the deep V to his hips begins, if that tells you anything.'

Lia handed me a full glass. 'Think you need this.'

I downed the mojito in one gulp, the sharp sting of rum burning the back of my throat. She took the empty glass from my hand and walked back to the kitchen to fill it again.

'Okay, so you slept with him.' Aster righted her shoulders. 'That's a good thing.'

'How is that good?' Lia said sharply as she pushed a drink across the counter to Aster before stalking over to Elena and handing her a glass too.

Aster took a big gulp and licked her lips. 'Not enough mint.'

'Fine. You make them next time,' Lia said with a smirk. She loved it when our quiet little sister found her voice.

'I will,' Aster pushed back before returning her attention to me. 'It's been too long since Dani had any affection. And…' She took another sip. 'When you two are together his color gets brighter. More intense.' She hesitated again.

'Finish that thought,' Lia said, setting another full glass down next to me.

'The bond between Dani and Bryce is different from my other matches. It's like the more time you spend together, the stronger it grows. It's almost unbreakable.'

'That means what for Dani?' Elena took a drink and shivered. She was more of a micro-brew girl.

'He strikes me as the kind of guy who when he wants something, he's not about to let it go,' Aster said.

'We don't know any of that to be true,' I countered. 'What's clear to me is that his article, saving his career, means more to him than anything that's building between us.'

I didn't feel the need to sugarcoat the truth for them. For too long I'd hidden issues with Belladonna from my sisters, and eventually keeping those secrets came back to bite me in the ass. I started to confess that our mother was back in town until Elena jumped to her feet.

'Enough about men tonight. We are here to drink, eat pizza and dance.'

Lia and I groaned at the exact same time. Dance had been Elena's minor in college. When she brought up music, it was immediately followed by the need to teach us some wild routine she'd seen on the internet.

She pulled her phone out of her pocket and synced it to my wireless speakers. A second later, a boppy tune from the 1990s blared through the room. Knowing she was always a willing partner, she reached for Aster's hand. They started to do some intricate moves that required complicated footwork and at least two spins.

Lia nursed her drink in the kitchen, trying to blend in with the cabinets. Elena pranced over and yanked her out from her hiding spot. Lia gave me the evil eye. This was her living nightmare, and if she had to participate, I did too. I drained my glass and attempted to follow the routine Elena insisted was easy.

The mojitos blurred the edges of my raw nerves. I jumped and bounced around to the beat. Lia laughed when Aster tried to spin her in a circle. Flora barked and wobbled back and forth on her feet like she wanted to be part of the party. Elena sang along with the pop diva at the top of her lungs.

I hated that Bryce knew this was what I needed. That I'd simply turn into myself if left to my own devices. He was a pain in the ass. A problem that could not be solved, but I had to give him credit. My best friend and my sisters were a surefire cure for sadness.

One song blended into another, and we ended up in a conga line moving around the room. Lia hopped out of her spot more than once to refill our glasses. When the pitcher was empty, we turned to red wine. We laughed and danced until the doorbell rang.

Aster grabbed my hand and boogied to the stairs. When we were on the ground floor, she did a series of spins that made me dizzy, or was that the alcohol?

She threw open the door and sang 'Hello' to Dalton, who looked at her with amusement. He filled most of the doorway with his tall lanky body. His dark curly hair was pushed back off his forehead.

'Uh-oh.' He chuckled. 'Are you having another dance party with cocktails?'

'Maaaaybeee,' Aster said with a giggle.

He forced his face to be serious. 'As your best friend, I should tell you I'm offended I was not included in this revelry.'

Aster poked a wobbly finger against his chest. 'This is a no-boys-allowed event!'

He glanced at me over her head and mouthed, 'How many has she had?'

'Enough,' I said back.

He shook his head and handed me the pizza and box of wings. My stomach grumbled. I'd been so mad at the tavern I'd forgotten to eat. 'How much do I owe you?'

'It's on the house.'

His mouth pinched at the corners. Aster could never keep a single thing from him, even when it came to my sad love life.

He reached gently for Aster, who danced in a wobbly circle. 'When you're done here, call me. I'll drive you home.'

'Not necessary.' She stood on tiptoe and booped his nose. 'This is a sleepover.'

I bit back a laugh. That was news to me.

'Drink some water. Take a couple of ibuprofen before bed. You know how you feel after a night of rum.'

'Pinky swear.' She gripped his small finger before taking the food from me and dancing back to the stairs.

His longing gaze followed her the entire way. Poor Dalton. He'd been crushing on Aster for years, and she was completely oblivious to it.

'For what it's worth,' he said, focusing his attention back on me, 'I think Bryce is a good guy who's only trying to do his job.'

'Yeah, I heard that he's got you charmed too.'

'He's been into the shop several times. We've chatted about what makes Harvest Moon special. That's all.'

'Has he pumped you for info on Aster?'

Suddenly he found the mat in front of my door very interesting. 'I haven't said anything he didn't already know about her synesthesia and matchmaking talent.'

In high school, Aster didn't have many friends. It was too easy for them to ask about who liked them, and when Aster did not give them the answer they wanted, friendship quickly turned to bullying and isolation. Luckily, she had Dalton. He shielded her from most of the gossip and was a safe place for her to land when the staring and whispers became too much.

'Doesn't it worry you that if more people come here, it could make matters worse for Ast?' I said. 'You've been in her shop. Watched customers be weird, especially with that recent incident.'

'Yeah, that was freaky, but I wouldn't underestimate how much this town cares about all of the McGuires. If one outsider steps a toe out of line, the people here will circle the wagons so quickly that person's head will snap.'

The set of his jaw warned he'd fight any force not only for Aster, but for all of us. He really was a good guy. I hoped Aster would recognize that one day.

'But what if that call is coming from inside the house?' I pressed.

His brow furrowed. 'Meaning?'

'Come on. You've been in council meetings. You're part of the small business coalition. Mo would do anything to get more bodies into the tavern, no matter what it costs or who it hurts. There's no telling what kind of BS she's already fed Bryce.'

'There's more to it than tourism and the bottom line for Mo.'

'Like what?'

He took an uneasy breath. 'That's not my story to tell.' His phone beeped with a text. 'Gotta go.'

'Another delivery?'

'Yeah,' he said in a clipped voice.

'Let me guess. Bryce?'

He bit into his lip. 'He asks about you. A lot.'

I waved his comment away. 'All he wants is dirt on my family.'

A flicker of conflict crossed his face. 'I gotta go. Please remind Aster to hydrate.'

'I will.'

The sounds of another 90s pop tune floated out of my apartment. Tonight I wanted to forget about Bryce and that stupid article. Spend time with the most important women in my life. But tomorrow, I'd have to drop the bomb to my sisters that Belladonna had once again found her way home.

# *Chapter Twenty-Nine*

## *Fighting the Whispers*

Rum was not my friend.

One mojito turned into a blur of several mojitos last night as we laughed, danced and demolished the pizza and wings. Aster was splayed out next to me in bed. How was it possible that a person so small could snore that loud?

I wandered to the bathroom and brushed my teeth for a good five minutes, hoping it would remove the feeling of ten little sweaters piled on top of my tongue.

The clank of pots and pans pulled me toward the kitchen. Lia stood at the stove, pushing around a massive batch of eggs in a frying pan. The waffle pattern from the blanket on my couch was imprinted on her right cheek.

Yeah, she'd also had a few too many. The last thing I remembered was her digging through my cabinets looking for a bottle opener, insisting she needed another glass of wine.

'Morning,' I said with a voice that sounded like I'd swallowed sandpaper.

'Hey,' she growled back.

'Where's Elena?'

'She took off at four. Said she needed to get ready to open the coffee shop.'

I wobbled my way to the breakfast bar, the room still spinning. 'Was she okay to drive?'

'Yes. She stopped drinking after we drained the pitcher of mojitos.'

I climbed onto a stool, the smell of the eggs twisting my stomach.

'You want to talk about what's bothering you?' She pointed the spatula at me. 'And don't say the article, because it's more than that.'

'What? You're sensing my emotions now too?' I was way too tired and hungover for this. I laid my hands on the cool marble, leaned in to press my cheek against it.

'No, it's just that you suck at hiding your emotions,' she said, going back to stirring the eggs.

I was glad she was focusing on the pan. It was probably better that I didn't look her in the eyes when I delivered the news.

'The morning after I was with Bryce, I discovered something in his office.' She stayed quiet, letting me finish what I needed to say. 'There were photos of us in a folder next to his desk. Like he'd been surveilling us for a while.'

She continued to scrape at the pan. 'He was basically stalking us? Is that what you're saying?'

'Yeah, I confronted him about it. He claimed a friend of his was originally assigned to the story and started looking into the town, into us, first. That the guy got a better assignment and gave the job to Bryce. Sent the photos along to help him. Bryce claims they got lost in the mail and only showed up last week.'

She tipped her chin to the folded envelope I'd placed on the counter last night. 'Maybe you should look at that.'

I peeled my body off the stool, grabbed the worn yellow paper and unfolded it. Bryce's name was scrawled across the front in thick black pen. The return address was a red stamp from Metropolitan Lifestyle Network. Written above the ink was the name Hank Jorgenson. The metered postage said July 18, followed by a succession of stamps after. July 29. August 12. August 29. Like it'd been ping-ponged through several post offices. I forced my eyes back to the address again. The zip code was off by two digits.

With shaky hands, I set the envelope on the edge of the counter. Lia scanned it, the corner of her mouth twitching. She grabbed a plate from the cabinet and slid a batch of eggs onto it. 'Eat. You're greener than the leaves on Clo's precious watermelons.'

My stomach protested, but I said, 'Hand me a fork.'

She yanked open a drawer next to the sink and handed me one. 'As much as I hate to say it, I don't think there's much we can do now but let him write the article.'

'What?' I mumbled through a mouthful of eggs. 'You've been the one fighting this the entire time!'

'After my talk with the chief last night, I've been thinking. Aren't you tired of fighting the whispers about us?' The catch in her voice chilled me. 'I'm exhausted, Dan, and I'm…' She shook her head. 'I've decided to put in my notice on Monday. I'm going to talk to Seth Cambridge about joining his team in Bozeman.'

Now I was sure the eggs were not going to stay in my stomach. 'Lee, no.'

'Maybe if we aren't all in the same place the talk will die down.'

'We're stronger when we are together. You know that.'

She focused on the pan again. 'When we were looking for Mara, Bryce watched our every move. How the three of us can be in sync. Read each other. There's no doubt that he's going to write about that moment.'

The words in his journal flashed across my mind, and I hated that she might be right.

She placed a trivet onto the counter and set the pan on top of it. After grabbing her own fork, she proceeded to eat straight from the pan.

'There's more to it than just the search,' I confessed. 'Weird things have been happening when Bryce and I are together.'

'What kinds of weird things?' she said with her mouth half-full.

'Flaring lights when...' I closed my eyes. 'Let's just say when things got intimate between us, the light fixtures in his bathroom exploded.'

Her brown eyes widened. 'Holy shit! Really?'

The sound of footsteps kept me from saying more. The conversation about her leaving was not over, though.

Aster came around the corner. Brown mascara made shadows beneath her eyes, and her hair sat in a tangled mess around her shoulders. She slowly mounted a stool and whispered, 'Coffee.'

Lia popped a pod into the machine. The deep nutty scent of espresso wafted toward us. Once it was done, Lia pushed a mug across the counter. Aster took a slow sip and smiled. 'Coffee truly is the best morning gift.' After another gulp, she said, 'I heard you guys talking about some kinda explosion?'

Lia went back to gobbling eggs out of the pan. Aster let out a disgusted huff.

'You want some?' Lia said with a full mouth.

'Gross, no. And stop being a heathen. Eat off a plate like a normal person.'

I focused back on my own food until Aster said, 'We're not doing this. I hate it when I come into the room and you both quit talking. Stop protecting me. I am not ten anymore!'

Her chin became granite. The edges of her fingertips turned pink as she gripped the countertop.

'When Bryce and I were together the other night… there may have been a power surge that blew out the bathroom lights.'

She pressed a hand to her mouth. 'Um, okay. Is the electricity faulty in his cabin?'

I stayed quiet while Lia snickered.

Aster's gaze swung between us. 'Oh shit. You don't think…' She broke off like she was too afraid to say the words.

'I don't know,' I finally confessed. 'Some stuff's been off between us.'

Aster filled her coffee all the way to the lip with creamer. 'What do you mean by "off"?'

'When I first met Bryce on the trail, I can't explain it, there was an instant pull toward him. Like I was hooked on a line and being slowly reeled in toward him.'

Aster nodded. 'That's your connection I was talking about last night.'

'There's something else going on. On the ridge that day with Mara, it was more than the animals acting odd. I sensed Banjo. That he was hurt, all without touching him.' I took an unsteady breath. 'It's like the moment Bryce arrived, everything got amplified. Has anything like that been happening to either of you?'

They shook their heads.

I kept my mouth shut about the suddenly bubbling gravy. The wilting lavender. What I'd just revealed freaked them out enough.

Lia finished the rest of the eggs while Aster sipped her coffee. Every part of me wanted to be quiet about Belladonna. She hadn't left Clo's in a week, but she would soon, and I needed them to know she was here before they got confronted with it in town.

'There's one other thing.'

They both went still.

'Belladonna is back. She's staying at Clo's.'

The color seeped out of Aster's cheeks. Those familiar hard lines formed around Lia's mouth. 'Why is she here?'

'I didn't stay around long enough to ask.'

'What did Grandmother Clo say?' I hated hearing the heartbreak in Aster's voice.

'She acted like she was caught off guard. But you know she'd never turn Belladonna away.'

'Clo is giving her shelter even after the shit she pulled with Ast last time?' Lia fumed.

'She is her daughter, Lee,' I said.

'Maybe she's here to apologize. Make things right,' Aster said with too much hope.

Lia opened her mouth and I gave her a firm look, warning that her next words had better be kind. She pressed her lips together and rounded the counter until she was in front of Aster. 'Hey,' she said in a soft tone she reserved for our little sister. 'You could be right, but let's stay on our guard this time. At least until we know why she's here. What she's up to.'

'Okay,' Aster whispered.

Lia held out her arms and Aster sank into them.

I hated that the reappearance of our mother did this to them. Belladonna could be charming. Wave away her past indiscretions like nothing and expect our forgiveness. But I wasn't opening the door to let her hurt us this time. I'd do everything in my power to make sure my sisters were protected, even if it meant going against everything Clo wanted, because this time Belladonna was going to stay out of our lives for good.

# Chapter Thirty

## *Question Your Instincts*

With birdsong filling the trees, and a handful of rabbits hopping around Clo's garden, I walked up the driveway toward the house. Ever since I'd confessed the truth to my sisters about Belladonna a week ago, I'd been thinking about all the ways I could get our mother to leave Harvest Moon. I'd offer her money, or whatever else she wanted, to get her out of town because, at this point I was willing to do anything to make Aster stop moping and smile again.

Flora loped happily beside me, her fur and paws caked with red dirt from our hike. She was going to need a bath again, but I didn't mind. Her sweet demeanor, the way she stayed close to me today, was the only thing keeping me calm.

Clo was back in her spot on the second-floor porch, resting in the rocking chair. Her far-off gaze fixed on the lake and the two herons who had made a nest in a little outcropping on the north bank. The thick layer of clouds, faint scent of burning wood, the whip of the wind yanking the rust-colored leaves from the trees, were all signs that fall was creeping closer.

I pulled open the front door and made my way up the stairs, Flora on my heels. The house was quiet. Usually when Belladonna was around, the place was in absolute chaos. Dirty dishes filled the sink. Books on yoga and naturopathy sat piled on the countertops, and some kind of sitar music dripped out of the family-room speakers.

Before I could push out the screen door, Clo said, 'There's fresh sun tea in the fridge.'

'I'm good,' I said, sinking into the chair beside her. The roof's overhang provided just enough shade to protect us from the late afternoon sun.

'Did you light the fireplace recently?' I asked.

'No. Why?'

'Thought I smelled burning wood in the air.'

She glanced back inside. 'I suppose Bella could have lit one last night.'

I bristled at the mention of my mother and focused on the herons circling the lake.

'Heard about the pool game,' she said, breaking the silence.

'Let me guess, you got a call from the judge, who by the way was trying to help Bryce win.'

She turned to me with an arched brow. 'No, it was Mo. I think she's having second thoughts about the article.'

'Yeah, right,' I said, still bitter she'd told Bryce about Max.

'Dani,' she said in a gently chastening tone. 'I understand you're hurt. That you're working overtime to protect me and the girls, but sometimes…' Her shoulders gave a little.

'Sometimes what?' I pressed.

'All I'm saying is that if you give people a chance, they can surprise you. Do the right thing.'

'I'm sorry,' I bit out roughly. 'Were you not sitting at the same table as me when Bryce accused us of having magic? And I learned after the pool incident, that he's desperate. He needs the article to be sensational so he can draw interest. Reanimate his dead career.'

She took my hands and pressed them between her fingers. 'He hurt you deeply, didn't he?'

'Bryce? Well, of course! He wasn't honest about who he was when we first met. And over the last few weeks, he's basically interrogated everyone in town about us.' I left out how he'd made me feel cherished, even loved, the night we found Mara. The deep brutal ache that coursed through my bones when I'd discovered what he'd written in his journal about us. There were some details of my life my grandmother did not need to know.

'I wasn't talking about Bryce,' she said.

The next breath stuck in my throat and I couldn't speak.

'Max was the first man you ever loved. The first person you trusted who was not a member of this family. I'd imagine that when he walked away from you, it made you question your instincts.' She glanced to where one of Belladonna's gauzy scarves lay across the back of the couch. 'Made you feel abandoned again.'

'This is *not* about Max.'

'Isn't it? Bryce may have not been truthful at first, but I had a front-row seat to the way he watched you at the table. That man is dedicated to his work, but he senses there is an important connection between you two. That's why he's trying so hard to figure out a balance between how to save his career and still have you.'

'He did say he'd show me the final article before it went to his editor. That I could delete whatever made me feel uncomfortable. Promised he'd figure this out.'

'That's quite an offer.'

'I still don't trust him. How can I after... well, everything.'

'That may be my fault.' Belladonna stepped out onto the porch. Now I remembered where Aster got her stealthy approach. I had not heard a single footstep before she appeared.

To my shock, she wasn't dressed in a frilly patchwork skirt and sheer blouse, but in a simple gray jumpsuit instead. Her face was void of her signature spidery eyelashes and thick black kohl. It was a shock to see her without a full face of makeup, and it made her look much younger than fifty.

Belladonna walked past me and that scent of hers, amber and patchouli, clung to the dry air. 'Mother has told me about Bryce. About the article and your fears. And...' She actually looked stricken. 'Aster's prediction about him.'

'This has nothing to do with you.' It was hard not to lash out at the lazy way she made herself at home in a place she could never bother to stay in for more than a few weeks.

'It has everything to do with me.' Her gaze darted to Clo like they were sharing some secret knowledge, which only made the rage in my veins bubble hotter. 'From a very young age, I made you take on too much responsibility. In my deluded way of thinking, I considered you an old soul. Made it easier to take off on my own selfish wanderings, because I'd convinced myself you could take care of Camellia and Aster.'

Clo tried to reach out and take my hands again, but I shook her off. This was all bullshit. Belladonna had never admitted she was wrong about any of her choices.

'Your mother has been going to therapy,' Clo said quietly.

'It's been hard, but I've begun to accept that I did many unforgivable things to you and your sisters. To my own mother.' Her lower lip trembled. 'And to my sweet and patient father.'

Her face may have been clean. The clothes on her body different. But those were all façades. It didn't mean at her core she'd changed who she really was.

'You can deliver as many apologies as you want, but they don't change the years of pain you've caused Aster or Lia or Clo.'

'Or you,' Belladonna added.

'Keep me out of this,' I seethed.

'That's not possible. From what Clo has shared, that man from vet school, Max, he hurt you. You pretend to be strong. Act like it doesn't matter, but it does. You've managed to build this impenetrable wall around you, because you've spent your entire life battling me, and the horrible things I've done to you. That is a regret I will have the rest of my life. I can't change it, but you can choose to be different from me. To open your heart in a way I never could.'

Her words were too much like what Bryce said to me about being scared.

'And why is that?' I lashed out. 'Why couldn't you stay with my father or Lia's father or Aster's? None of us even know their damn names.'

Belladonna walked forward and laid a shaky hand against the worn railing. That faint scent of burning wood filled the air again. The once quiet lake now swirled with a choppy current.

'Dandelion, honey. Take a breath. Listen to what she has to say,' Clo said in that soothing tone.

'No. This conversation has been brewing for years. Every time I try to have it with her, she runs away. That's not happening this time.'

I waited for my mother to make an excuse. To turn and run. Instead, she planted her feet, set her shoulders, like she was ready to take whatever hard truth I was about to deliver.

'Did you not care enough about us to tell us who those men were? Think we didn't deserve to know them? Have them in our lives? You stand there and claim you don't want me to be like you, that you want me to open my heart, but how can I do that when I never had a real male role model? Sure, I had Grandpa Beau but he was *not* my father.'

'I promise if you give me some time, I'll tell you everything you want to know.' She cast another weighted look at Clo that made me uneasy. 'I owe the truth to you and your sisters.'

'Bella, maybe now is not—'

Clo's words were cut off by a jarring alarm blasting out of my phone. The screen filled quickly with a flood of texts from Lia that made my blood run cold.

The thick gray clouds. Faint scent of charred wood in the air. I should have recognized it. A fire was burning in a dry patch of land only fifteen miles away.

'What's wrong?' Clo pulled the phone from my hand, her eyes darkening. 'Bella, call Judge Greene and Eric. Tell them to bring their largest ladders. I also need them to tow over the portable water rig they have and all their hoses.'

Belladonna gave me a wide-eyed stare. 'Wildfire?'

'Yes. There's not an evacuation order yet, but we need to be ready.'

Belladonna nodded and rushed inside to use the landline.

While we had a minute alone, I stepped closer to Clo. 'What are the two of you hiding? It's the reason she's back, right?'

'We can't do this now.'

'Clo,' I pressed. 'I won't let her hurt Aster and Lia again. Neither of them can handle it.'

This time she clasped my wrist before I could step away. 'You may not like it, but your mother is correct about one thing. It's time you stopped pushing things away that are right for you. Every single minute of your life you do not need to act like the eldest daughter. Feeling like you're responsible for everyone. That you have to control all the variables around you in order to ensure things go right. The way you've always acted older than your years. How you keep all your feelings bottled up.' She glanced back to the house. 'I know Bella has hurt you, but this time I need you to listen.'

I was about to protest, tell her that Belladonna had nothing I wanted to hear, when the groan and squeal of Lia's Jeepster cut through the air. Behind it was the grind of another engine. I moved to the far end of the deck. In a swirl of dust, Lia's truck vaulted up onto the top of the driveway with Aster holding on from the passenger seat. A familiar black SUV was behind them. What the hell was Bryce doing here?

I moved through the house and went down the stairs, meeting them in the driveway. Clo followed me out the door.

'You get my texts?' Lia grunted, tugging at the red bandana around her neck. Aster stayed behind her, her gaze fixed on the churning orange sky. I wasn't the one that could sense emotion, but by the tremble in Aster's jaw, the steel in Lia's voice, it was clear the wildfire was burning out of control.

'Yes.' Before I could say any more, Belladonna walked outside and Lia's face became an unemotional mask.

'Mother, I've called for the water rig like you asked.' She smiled at Lia and Aster. 'Hello, my girls, I've missed you.'

Lia ignored her and pointed to the garage. 'Ast, help me pull out all the hoses. We need to hook them to the faucets on the north and south sides of the house. Start soaking all the dry brush as far as you can get the lines to reach.'

Aster stayed frozen, her gaze fixed on Belladonna. The pain etched into the lines of my little sister's face was heartbreaking.

I gripped her arm, pulling her a few feet away. 'Are you all right?'

She gave me a reluctant nod, her small body trembling. I needed to distract her. 'Do you know why Bryce is here?'

'He got the alarms too. Lia said he came to the station to ask questions, probably for his article. Insisted he follow us here so he could help.' Her voice was barely a whisper.

'If it's too hard to be here with Belladonna, I can get Bryce to drive you back to the Blossom.'

'No, I'm staying,' she said roughly. 'I'll go help Lia with the hoses.'

Belladonna walked toward Aster, and I blocked her path. 'Not now.'

She shrank back at the acid in my tone. I started to tell her to go inside when Bryce stepped toward us tentatively.

'Dani, what can I do?'

'You can go home,' I said.

Bella raised an eyebrow and shot out her hand. 'You must be Bryce.'

He glanced at me, waiting for an introduction.

'This is Belladonna,' I said flatly.

His gaze moved to my face, and I hated how his first reaction was to check in with me. Try to clock how I was feeling about my mother's presence. My heart twinged but I pushed the feeling away. There were bigger issues to deal with right now.

'Nice to meet you.' Bryce gave her hand a quick shake. 'Wish it could be under better circumstances.'

My mother gave him a look that was part curiosity, part suspicion. It was a little too late for her to pretend to care now.

'Go inside, Belladonna. Take Clo with you. We've got things organized out here.'

Like she understood the grit in my tone, she went to Clo and coaxed her back inside.

'How long has your mother been here?' Bryce asked with a careful voice.

'You need to leave,' I said, no longer interested in answering any of his questions. My anger must have carried across the yard, because Lia stomped toward us.

'Now is not the time for the bullshit that's happening between the two of you.' She tipped her chin to the black smoke rising in the distance. 'That is heading this way quickly.' She closed her eyes, pulled in a full breath. 'Those winds are going to gust up to forty miles an hour. We need bodies to keep the house and the surrounding property wet.' Her eyes opened and turned hard. 'Forget your drama and start helping.'

In years past when a wildfire had threatened the area near the cabin, the three of us girls had been able to keep it safe, but the rare look of fear in Lia's eyes had me swallowing down my protests about Bryce. Any fire this time of year was bad, but with our current drought conditions, despite the small bits of rain we'd had, the blaze could easily eat up dozens of acres within an hour.

'I'll go help with the hoses,' I said.

Bryce was right beside me. The heat of his stare said he wanted me to look at him, talk to him. Instead, I focused on working with my sisters to unspool the yards of green coils twisted together in the garage. Our arguments would have to wait for another time, because right now all that mattered was saving the only place I'd ever called home.

# *Chapter Thirty-One*

## *Tinderbox*

Bryce straddled his way over the second-floor railing and set his foot on the rung of the ladder set against the house.

'You got it steady?' I called to Lia as she waited below.

She gave me a thumbs-up.

'Bryce, she's anchored the ladder below. Go ahead and climb.'

He hesitated like he was measuring the drop to the ground.

'Second thoughts? You don't have to do this.'

'It's not that. There are so many things I want to say to you.' The hitch in his voice was too raw.

'Lia's right. This isn't the time. We need to get the roof sprayed down. When this is over, when Clo's house is safe, we'll talk.'

He bit into his lower lip, tucked the spout of the hose under his arm and began to climb, stopping at the roof's apex. Once he was set, I leaned over the railing and called out, 'Ready for the water.'

A screech of air passed through the tubing and a wide stream shot out of the spout. Bryce steadied himself on a rung and sprayed the hose back and forth, soaking every wood shingle.

I wanted to stay angry with him, but he'd sent my best friend and sisters to be with me after the ridiculous show we'd put on inside the tavern. He'd left that envelope by my door to prove he was telling the truth, at least about the pictures. And now, he was here, balanced precariously on a roof, helping us try and save my grandmother's house.

'Dani!' Lia shouted. 'Get your ass down here and start covering the dry brush.'

I rushed into the house and Belladonna followed me to the top of the stairs.

'What can I do?'

'Stay out of the way.'

Clo let out an irritated huff from where she stood in the kitchen.

'Fine. Keep Clo company until the judge and Eric get here with the water rig.'

I raced down the stairs, out the door and around the side of the house. Bryce was flanked in shadow. The wide arc of his spray conjured a colorful spectrum. He took short, measured footsteps across the roof, dousing every shingle. Panic expanded like a balloon in my chest. One wrong move and he could pitch right off the side, which was at least a fifteen-foot drop. I wasn't mad enough to want to see him in traction.

I pushed the thought from my head as the sky filled with a deep gray haze. Waves suddenly spiked in the lake, sending water crashing against the dirt shores. The tang of burnt wood and dry brush filled my nose. The fire was eating up ground faster than expected.

At the side of the house I untangled the hose, stretching it out as far as possible. Once I had the knob turned, a warm blast of water hit the dry grass and weeds.

For the next half hour, I soaked every inch of ground around the north side of the house, including Clo's garden, which now resembled a mud bog. A few lost carrots, heads of romaine, were better than a charred house.

The judge and Eric ripped up the driveway in their truck, did a quick three-point turn, and backed in the mobile water tank. Another truck and SUV were right behind them. Mo jumped out of the truck with Elena climbing out of her passenger seat. Dalton scrambled out of his own car.

Belladonna rushed out the front door. There was no time for pleasantries as the judge, Eric and Mo started connecting the hosing lines to the tank and handed them off.

Elena and Dalton raced up to me.

'Give us a job,' Elena pleaded.

'Go help Belladonna on the other side of the house. Dalton, can you climb up onto the roof with another line and help Bryce spray it down?'

They quickly took off in the direction of their assignments.

Belladonna and Elena took turns working the area around the south side of the house, doing their best to wet down the trees, but even I knew that with one shift of the wind, a single spark, the area would flame up like a tinderbox. It wouldn't take long after that for the entire house to go.

Time was not on our side. The sun was dipping toward the horizon, and it wouldn't be safe for Bryce and Dalton to stay on the roof much longer.

I called to Belladonna, and she met me on the side of the house where I was working. 'Keep soaking. I need to get Bryce off the roof.'

'I like how he showed up and went right to work helping.'

'Don't start.' I turned away and rushed to where the ladder was propped on the front of the house.

Clo walked out the front door. She clutched two cardboard boxes spilling over with family pictures and small mementos like Grandpa Beau's whittling knives and his favorite Zane Grey novels.

'What are you doing? Why do you have Grandpa Beau's things?' I said.

Clo clutched the boxes tighter to her chest like they were precious. 'I'm getting the car ready to go.'

'Why?'

Her shoulders trembled as Lia rushed out the front door.

'What the hell is going on?' I said.

Elena raced around the side of the house. She always came running when she heard my panicked voice.

'Fire has turned, thanks to the winds. It's headed this way,' Lia said.

'We're not ready. Eric and the judge haven't been able to drive closer to where the brush is thicker near the lake,' I said.

'There's no time,' Lia shot back. 'The chief called and told me we have to evacuate Clo. We need to get her out of here in five minutes. Go inside and help her with the rest of the boxes.'

'No, someone needs to get to the brush surrounding the lake,' I insisted.

'I'll do it,' Elena jumped in.

'Grab Mo. She can help too,' Lia said.

Elena took off and Lia gave me a heavy look.

'Aster can take Clo. I am not leaving.'

She pushed out a heavy breath. 'Get Belladonna. Let her know the situation. She can go with Clo. The less people in the way of the crew when they get here, the better.'

'I'll tell her.'

The sky had turned the color of a badly bruised peach. A thick wall of smoke blocked us in on all sides. Wind shook the trees like an angry phantom. I rounded the house and found the hose on the ground making a gigantic puddle.

'Are you freaking kidding me,' I cursed. Why couldn't Belladonna handle the simplest task?

I stalked in the direction of her footprints leading away from the house and into the woods. The trail led to a downhill slope and into a wide sweep of forest. Flashes of red and yellow flames danced between the trees.

It was too close. I jogged my way down the slope, but there was no sign of my mother. The wind picked up again, and I had to shield my eyes from the dust and dry leaves spiraling through the air. I turned in a circle, finally finding her footprints moving into a dense patch of forest.

The farther I walked, the heavier the heat licked across my skin. In the distance the roar of flame, cracking of branches, was deafening. She was close. I could sense her somehow. Like there was a force pushing me deeper into the trees.

Rabbits, deer and elk scattered. Ahead Belladonna's footprints were still visible. Why was she heading into the fire? Did she have a death wish?

I should have turned around, followed the animals out, but I had to know what the hell my mother was doing.

A few feet ahead, the forest parted into a wide circle void of trees. A flash from my childhood hit me. Grandpa Beau striding out here with a chainsaw, while we three girls chased after him. He'd shooed us back to the house. Told us we deserved a special spot in the forest to play. To have campouts. To learn about the beauty of nature. None of us had been here in years. Not since the incident with Clo in the hospital when we thought the county might split us up. The day all three of us lost our childhoods.

The smoke turned the air into a gray, suffocating blanket that clawed at my lungs. Cracks and moans came from the trees. Heat filled the air, and I called for Belladonna.

No answer.

She was probably running again. Too scared to face what was happening to her mother. To her own children. I hated what she'd done to us, but I kept searching because I didn't want her to get hurt out here.

'Belladonna!' My voice echoed like a boomerang, scattering into the wind and then whirring its way straight back at me.

I hurried past the circle and strode farther into the woods. If Lia was here she'd be cursing me out, warning me to go back to the house, but I had to find my mother.

About one hundred steps ahead, the flickers of red and gold grew brighter. Branches tumbled from trees. Birds squawked as they departed their nests. Mice, squirrels and chipmunks raced to higher ground.

Ten feet ahead, Belladonna stood among the chaos, her image flickering in and out of the haze of smoke. I called her name again, but she didn't move. Was she sick? It made no sense why she wasn't responding.

I inched closer until a monstrous wet hiss filled the air. The smoke crowding the woods went from charred black to a pale gray in an instant. My gaze darted skyward. The chief must have called in water tankers. But there was no drone of engines or loud churn of propellers.

That hiss and spewing sound filled the air again. The smoke parted and Belladonna stood like a scarecrow propped up in a cornfield – eyes closed, hands stretched straight out from her body. Water bubbled up from the ground like a hidden spring, rising inch by inch, dousing the white-hot embers once they struck the ground.

The smoke grew murky, stinging my eyes. I rubbed at them, not sure what I was seeing. Ten paces away another stream of water rushed across the dry soil, this time spilling out in a gush and soaking my tennis shoes.

Bryce's words from our dinner with Clo throbbed inside my skull.

*Documents state her mother had the ability to divine water.*

No. It couldn't be. My mother often spoke of magic, but she couldn't *do* magic.

'What the hell, Belladonna?'

My mother snapped out of her trance, spun toward me and her mouth opened in a silent scream. The crack behind me rattled in my ears. A massive branch broke away from a hundred-year-old ponderosa tree above me. I should have moved, dived out of the way, but the shock of the sight held me in place. Belladonna's blood-curdling cry filled the air, and then I was airborne, my body thrown sideways like a rag doll. I rolled three times until my shoulder crashed against the base of another tree. My head knocked against the bark as the falling branch missed me by mere inches. My bones ached. Smoke filled my lungs. My mother's cries vibrated through the forest.

'Dani, are you all right? Can you hear me?' Bryce cradled me in his arms. Ash and wet leaves were tangled in his hair. Blood trickled from his freckled nose. I tried to speak. Ask about my mother, but stars swam across my vision until the world sank into a hazy swirl of black.

# Chapter Thirty-Two

## *Like a Millstone Around My Neck*

The panicked voices came first, followed by the jarring shift of my body. Strong arms cradled me against a steady chest. That familiar woody scent filled my nose. Flickers of blurred images. Onyx-black smoke. The sizzle of heat. Sheets of unexpected moisture. A jarring crack from a tree played in my head like a bad movie.

'What the hell happened? Why are you carrying Dani?' Lia shrieked.

Bryce kept walking until Clo, using a low and measured voice, ordered him to bring me inside. The jarring clomp up the stairs made my head ache.

'I need to know what is wrong with my fucking sister!' Lia demanded.

'Stop yelling,' I managed to say as her cursing rang in my ears.

'Set her down on the couch,' Clo said.

A second later my back was against a firm cushion. There were a dozen hammers beating against my skull, but I forced my eyes open.

'Dani.' Aster sank down beside me. 'Where are you hurt?'

I started to sit up, but Bryce's warm hand pressed me back into the cushion. 'You have a cut on your head. Clo's gone to get the first aid kit.'

'Does she have a concussion?' Belladonna's voice wasn't too far off.

Flashes of her in the forest. Water seeping up from the ground. Flooding its way toward the trees. The images were hazy and the smoke was dark. Was I imagining things?

'Can someone please tell me how Dani got like this?' Lia's voice was too thick. Too scared.

Bryce slid his hand over my palm and gripped my fingers. 'A rogue spark flew into a tree. The branches caught flame. One snapped loose, dropping down close to where she was standing.'

'He pushed Dandelion out of the way. Kept it from falling right on top of her.'

Was that a sob in Belladonna's voice? I'd never seen her show any emotion, much less shed a tear.

Clo hustled out of the bathroom with a basket full of supplies. She stopped in front of me, her hair a fuzzy cloud around her face. 'Can you sit up?'

'Of course.'

'Take it easy,' Bryce whispered as I moved.

'She hit her head against a tree.' Belladonna paced in front of the wall of windows. Her dark hair fell in tangles around her face.

Clo looked to where Lia leaned against the kitchen counter. 'Should we check for a concussion?'

Lia pushed her way forward until she was crouched in front of me.

'Her pupils look equal.' She cupped her hand over my right eye and then pulled it away, repeating the same motion with the left. 'Good reactions.' Her gaze moved to the cut in the center of my forehead. 'Do you have a headache? Are you dizzy? Any blurry vision?'

'No. I'm fine, Lee.'

'She did pass out for a second,' Bryce offered.

'It was all the smoke. I'm okay now,' I insisted.

'Let's get you patched up. That scratch is superficial, but it needs to be cleaned,' Lia said.

Clo held onto the basket, shoving around the items like she was unsure what to do next.

'Hand me an alcohol swab and one of the small gauze bandages with adhesive,' Lia said in between bursts of static and muffled voices squawking out of her walkie-talkie.

'We have to get back to soaking the roof. The fire, it was coming for the clearing Grandpa Beau made for us as kids.' I tried to stand but Bryce nudged me back onto the couch.

'The wind has shifted. Fire is moving to the west. They've already got it forty percent contained,' Lia said, dabbing an alcohol pad against my head.

'But it was coming down the mountain.' I winced at the sting. 'I saw it until...' That image of rising water filled my vision again. Belladonna and I locked eyes. I searched for an answer in her face, but before I could get any kind of read on her, she turned and headed into the kitchen.

Lia gently pressed the bandage against my head. 'Until what?'

'There was all this kindling. Dry brush and leaves. It was a powder keg waiting to go up and then...'

Aster leaned in. Bryce's mouth twitched, and I swallowed my words. None of them could know about the water. How Belladonna forced it to douse everything in the fire's path. It wasn't real. It couldn't be.

'Dani. Take a few deep breaths.' Bryce gripped my hands. He'd been only a few feet away. Had he seen the water too? Been a witness to whatever I thought I saw in those woods?

'Let's stand up,' Bryce said in a gentle voice. 'I want to take you to the hospital. Have them look you over.'

I tried to ground myself to the floor. Stop my world from spinning out of control.

Clo hadn't flinched when I'd asked her about the firepit. Claimed what I'd seen wasn't real. Even though I wanted to believe what happened today was some trick of the eye, the smoke obscuring my vision, there was no arguing what Belladonna had done. I'd stood ten feet away from it. Watched as the water was pulled from the ground like my mother was some kind of human pump.

'No, I'm fine. I only need to rest for a bit.' I made a wobbly push to my feet. 'Thank you for keeping me from getting crushed. For keeping the house safe.' I forced a smile to my lips. 'I'll talk to you later, okay?'

He held on to me, our hands perfectly entwined. That bond we shared tightening with each and every breath. He'd risked his life for me. Helped save the only home I'd ever known. Been honest about how he was struggling between what was right for his own future and what he felt for me. But after what had just happened, what I'd seen Belladonna do, there was no way things could work between us, in spite of Aster's prediction. I knew the truth now, and maybe Bryce did too. There was no other choice but to push him away. Protect the people I loved, even if it meant destroying my own happiness.

'Let me walk you there,' he offered.

My pleading gaze shot to Lia and she didn't hesitate. 'I've got her, Bryce.'

She latched her arm around my waist and guided me a few steps away to where Aster stood. They linked arms with me and led me to my old bedroom. I was grateful for their support, because even though my back stayed erect, my chin hard as a rock, inside my heart was breaking.

-

'Sit,' Lia ordered.

I sank into the deep green comforter on my childhood bed, and Aster bent down to remove my soaked shoes. Lia leaned against the doorway until Belladonna and Clo made an appearance a few minutes later.

'Is he gone?' I asked.

Clo nodded while Belladonna remained quiet.

'Good, because I'm tired of secrets, and it's well past time you told us all the truth.'

Lia crossed her arms over her chest. 'What has Belladonna done now?'

Our mother flinched like someone had slapped her. Aster walked to her side and gave her arm a comforting pat, which only made Lia grumble louder.

'Dani, you're hurt. You need to rest. We can do this another time,' Clo said.

'No! The two of you are going to spill every truth about the McGuire women, starting with how Belladonna managed to flood the forest with water she pulled from the damn ground!'

Aster's eyes went wide and Lia cursed.

'Dandelion,' Belladonna said in a voice she was trying very hard to keep calm. 'You hit your head. The water you saw was from a previous tanker drop.'

'Stop lying!' The shout that tore from my throat made the world spin again. I fixed my gaze on Clo. 'You owe us this. Please, be honest.'

Belladonna paled. 'Mama, you can't.'

Clo wrung her hands together. Years of pain and heartache shone in her eyes. 'Your father went to his grave angry with me for keeping the truth from the girls. Since we buried him, I've held the weight of it like a millstone around my neck. It's time I stopped carrying that burden.' Belladonna shook her head as Clo set her jaw. 'Girls, we will give you a minute. Come out to the family room when you're ready.'

Aster stood frozen in place. 'Dani, what the hell went on in the woods?'

'Oh, Ast,' I said quietly. 'It's very complicated.'

Lia stood erect, one foot halfway out the door. 'Dani.' I hadn't heard that break in her voice since she'd crawled into my bed as a child, afraid of the thunderstorms raging outside. 'I can't stay. If I hear what I think is coming, it'll break me. I'm already carrying so much anger for Belladonna.' She scrubbed her hands over her tired eyes. 'And with what happened earlier this year... My mind can't take one more burden. Can you understand? Forgive me for being weak in this moment?'

'Oh, Lee Lee, nothing about you is weak,' I said. 'We all deal with our own pressures, fears, worries in our own way. Go ahead and leave. I understand.'

She tried to walk away, but I jumped up and wrapped her in a hug. 'We are here for you always, no matter what.'

Her arms tightened around me. 'I know,' she said in a small voice that reminded me too much of our complicated childhood.

Aster moved in and we held on to each other. Shockingly, Lia was the last one to let go. My beautiful sister, who was ferocious, smart and incredibly brave, gave me and Aster a sad smile before fleeing for the stairs.

Lia would eventually want to hear the truth, but she understood her own limits, and it was clear she was at her breaking point.

As much as I wanted to pretend that I hadn't been a witness to Belladonna's behavior in the forest today, in my heart I understood it was time for the darkness in our lives to recede. For the truth about who we were as sisters, mothers, daughters and granddaughters to finally be ushered into the light.

# *Chapter Thirty-Three*

## *Another Striking Blow*

Belladonna stood near the mantel. She'd tied her hair up in a messy bun, more of that gray poking out from her roots. She pressed her hand over the photo of Grandpa Beau standing near the edge of the lake. A bright smile lifted his lips as he showed off his latest catch.

Whenever she would reappear at the house, Grandpa would pick her up in a big bear hug and swirl her around in a circle. Belladonna would protest, especially if she was pregnant again. Grandpa would carefully set her on her feet. Crow about how happy he was to have her home.

It took longer for Clo to warm up. I think that had a lot to do with me. How I'd stare at this mysterious creature who claimed to be my mother but was rarely a part of our lives.

I took the open spot next to Aster on the couch, the room still tilting and shifting like a ship on a stormy sea.

'Lia get a call from the station?' Clo asked.

'No.' I gave her a firm look. 'She said she couldn't stay. I think you know why.'

In the fading light, Clo looked small and fragile sitting in Grandpa Beau's favorite chair. Her words about keeping the secret until his death stung. There'd been so many times I'd seen their heads close together, shoulders up around their ears, as they tried to mask their harsh words. I always assumed it was about the challenges of raising us three girls. How they'd thought they'd have a quiet retirement, not be parenting small children again. All these years Clo had continued to keep this secret, and I needed to know why.

'Clo, please help me understand what is happening. The reasons you kept the truth from me. From all of us,' I said.

'That's not her fault,' Belladonna said. 'She was honoring a request I'd made of her a long time ago.'

'What kind of request?' Aster said.

Belladonna focused on the line of pictures documenting our family's history. Her fingers trembled as she reached out to touch the old photo of Ambrosia and Sylvia. 'When I ran from Harvest Moon at eighteen, I felt free. Lighter. It was liberating not to have people constantly watching me like I was some kind of freak. I could wear what I wanted. Date whoever came along. I finally had control. Power over the things I hated about who I was.'

'I don't understand. What didn't you have control over?' Aster pressed.

'Give her a chance to talk, sweetheart,' Clo said.

'For a short time, I was lulled into a childish belief that I could steer the path of my life, and then I got pregnant with you, Dani.' She turned watery eyes on me. 'I was terrified, but you were this normal little cherubic being that filled a space in my heart I didn't know was empty. It gave me such hope and joy. Made me believe everything was okay. So I had Lia, and you, Aster. My sweet final baby.'

‘What changed? Why did you leave us with Clo and Grandpa Beau?’ I said, unable to keep the anger from my voice.

‘That was never my intention in the beginning. But then my world crashed down when animals started seeking you out, Dani. I understood you had a gift. At that time, Lia and Aster were still so small.’ She clasped her hands in front of her. ‘I’d convinced myself that because you all had different fathers I’d shifted the fates. But the Perkins blood is stronger than I gave it credit for.’

‘We know all this.’ Aster pressed her hands down firmer into the couch. ‘What is it that you wanted Clo to keep from us? That made you stay away all these years?’

Belladonna pressed a shaky hand to her mouth, and Clo gave her a reassuring nod. ‘The summer I turned thirteen, I was invited to a swimming party. It was a big deal, because most of the kids at school were mean to me. One of the girls made fun of my bathing suit because it was pink and orange and green, and she said it made me look like a watermelon. It was just a mean girl being cruel, but you’re so tender, vulnerable, at that age.’ Her breaths became more stuttered. ‘The kids all laughed, and it ignited a tornado of fury inside of me. The stronger my rage grew, the more the water in the pool shifted and swirled around the girl. The power of it tugged her under. A boy managed to rip her loose from the grip of it before she drowned. Her parents were angry. Told the family who owned the pool that their drain was dangerous. That it nearly killed their daughter, but I knew better.’

Belladonna moved to the wall of windows that faced the lake. The water thrashed and churned against the dirt shore, kicking up into tall spouts.

Aster's mouth fell open. I stayed frozen in place. All these years, none of us had ever noticed the way the lake reacted to her.

'I kept that day a secret from your grandmother.' Belladonna's breath warmed the glass. 'But as I got older, my power grew. By just looking at water, I could get it to wave up, splash onto the shore. In the winter, I could focus on the ice, make it shift. Crack. Up on the ski mountain one year, I got into a fight with a boyfriend and caused a small avalanche. Your grandmother heard about it. Confronted me when I got home.' Like all the fight had gone out of her, she whispered, 'You can tell the rest, Mama.'

'That night your mother told me everything. She was terrified. Wasn't sure what was happening to her. I told her about the history of the Perkins women. Their power over water.' She shot me a pained look before saying, 'And fire.'

The revelation was a stinging slap. I'd always counted on Clo to be honest. To not hide any hard truths from us. But with one sentence, she'd proven how naïve I'd been.

'Wait.' Aster's beautiful green eyes widened. 'Clo can control fire? And… out in the woods earlier? Mother used water to stop the flames from eating up the forest?'

'Yes,' Belladonna said shakily. 'And you…' She couldn't manage to say the rest.

'My synesthesia isn't a weird fluke? The way I can see color, sense emotion is…' Aster's small body shook. 'It's magic?' She took an uncomfortable gulp. 'And Dani with the animals? Lia with her connection to the woods? It's supernatural?'

'Perhaps, but I'm not entirely sure,' Belladonna offered quietly.

'What the hell does that mean?' It was rare to hear Aster snap at our mother.

'None of you exhibit the hallmarks of magic from the Perkins line,' Belladonna answered.

'We're freaks of some kind, then?' Aster's body continued to tremble, and I pressed my hand on top of hers.

'What Bella means is that you do have some kind of gifts, but it's unclear if they are related to magic.'

'What do you mean by "unclear", Clo?' I forced out.

'There are people in this world who can hear a beautiful song, and without any training can play it from memory on a piano. There are those who can read a passage from a book, a piece of poetry, and recite it right away because they have an eidetic memory. Is that magic or a blessing? We don't know, but we believe you girls do have gifts, we're just not sure if they're tied to magic.'

I flashed to the breaking bulbs in Bryce's bathroom. The wilting flowers and oddly bubbling gravy. That sure as hell felt like magic, but I couldn't think about that right now. I was too worried about what all of this was doing to my little sister.

'Bryce,' Aster stuttered. 'He was in the woods. If he saw the water, if he reports that Belladonna has magic, it's going to be like that reporter from Denver, right?' Her uneven breathing picked up again. 'I could lose my business. And Dalton. He's been so good to me through all the rumors and whispers, but what if this is all too much for him?'

I inched in closer to her on the sofa and tried to pull her in, but she was on her feet. 'How dare you!' she screeched at Belladonna. 'I defended you. Claimed you were eccentric, unique, but this whole time you were running from us so you wouldn't have to explain the truth about what you are. What *we* are?'

'No!' Belladonna protested. 'For years, I'd been able to keep my powers at bay. Then I lost my job. Was struggling with money and had three babies to feed.' Her voice broke. 'In a hotel room in Reno right after you were born, I tried to give you a bath, Aster. My mind started to swirl, panic. The water rose up over your face,' she said on a choked breath. 'I ripped you out of the tub, held you to my chest, and sobbed, knowing that you...' Her stare shifted in my direction. 'That none of my babies were safe with me anymore. Before I left you all here, I made your grandmother promise not to tell you about the magic.' She wiped the tears from her eyes. 'I wanted you to have normal lives. Not be haunted every single day by the legacy of this family.'

'You were wrong. That legacy has permeated every single part of our lives,' I said sharply.

'Oh, my Dandelion—'

'But you kept coming back,' Aster interrupted. 'And then you'd just leave us again.'

Belladonna gave a sad nod. 'Every year I return, hoping I can control it. And every year, as soon as I arrive, my power over it wavers. That time I promised to stay and help you in the shop, I was sure I was mastering it, but then your grandmother told me she was going to tell you all the truth. I got upset, and my focus slipped away again. The water in the lake started to flood the forest. Race toward this house.'

'If you can't control it, why the hell are you back now?' I said.

'As Clo told you, I'm going to therapy. I've found with some deep breathing and visualization I can push back the flow of magic. Today, I used it in the forest. Directing where the water went. How it flowed. It gives me hope that I can stay. That I can be close to you girls and my mother now with little risk.'

Every sentence, every confession was another striking blow. Aster sobbed next to me. I pulled her into my side, and she collapsed against my chest. 'This is all too much,' she cried. 'For years, you let us believe you didn't care. And then you swoop back in today and do this? If Bryce saw what you did, our lives will be ruined.'

The desperation, fear, in Aster's voice made me sit up straighter. More than ever she needed me to be strong. Protect her and Lia in the way I always had.

'I'm going to talk to Bryce. Find out what he saw.'

'And if he says...' Aster fixed an angry stare on Belladonna. 'That he knows about *her*?'

'I can convince him what happened in the woods was nothing but smoke and water from a tanker we couldn't see.'

'And you think he'll believe you?' Aster swiped tears from her cheeks.

'I don't know, but I have to try.'

I moved to stand and the ground was still wobbly beneath me.

'Please stay here, Dani. You can talk to Bryce in the morning.' Clo tried to reach for me, but I stumbled back.

'No. Your lies have made this mess. The only way to save what small threads of hope we have left is to talk to Bryce tonight.'

-

It took me less than twenty minutes to get to Bryce's cabin. The minute I pulled into the driveway, it was clear he was gone. The chairs on the outdoor deck were hidden beneath a large khaki tarp. All the lights inside were out, and the front door was locked. I sank onto the step in front of the house and my phone beeped with a text from him.

> My editor called and said she needed me in LA. They had to pull an article at the last minute from the spring issue, and they want my piece to fill the space. It's due by the end of the day tomorrow. I'm sorry to go back on our wager, but I can't miss this deadline. Don't know when I'll be back in Harvest Moon.

Three more dots appeared on the screen. I waited for an *I'll call you* or *Talk to you soon*. Any hint at when he might return, but after a moment the dots disappeared.

The ache in my chest was so raw that I had to suck in a breath. So much for my promise to Aster about convincing Bryce that what he saw was not real. Our fate was in his hands, and I had a bad feeling that our peace, the quiet life we'd once known, was truly gone the moment Bryce found Belladonna and me in the woods.

## *Chapter Thirty-Four*

### *More to the Story*

The hinges on the library's front door closed with a deafening squeal. Even though it was small, the journal I'd taken weighed like a brick in my pocket. I tried not to look at the aisles where I'd wandered with Bryce, the thought of him too painful.

Ms Ruthie sat regally on her chair at the information desk, a queen surveying the layout of her kingdom. She didn't bother to look at me before saying, 'I hope you're returning what you pilfered from my archives.'

'*Your archives?*'

Her glasses skidded down her nose. 'When you guard them the way I do, they often feel proprietary.'

I pulled the journal from my pocket and set it on the desk.

She pressed her lips thin. 'Heard anything from that reporter?'

'No,' I answered flatly. 'And you know his name is Bryce.'

She gave me a determined look and pointed to the staircase leading to the second floor. 'You and I should talk.'

Ruthie was a fierce friend to Clo, and it was pointless to argue, because she wouldn't let me leave until I heard her out. She grabbed the journal, and I followed her up to the study room. The late afternoon sun seeped through the stained-glass window, color spilling across the floor like a muted Monet painting.

Bryce had sat at our table near the window, all smiles and teasing only a few weeks ago. The heat and scent of him close enough to touch. He was long gone and yet that link, bond, between us felt as real as if he was only sitting inches away.

Ms Ruthie pulled out a chair at one of the mahogany tables. Sank down into the one next to me with a tired huff. 'I'm still a little miffed that Clo didn't call me when you were all scrambling around during that wildfire two weeks ago.'

'You were in Denver. What were you going to do? Speed back on your Vespa?'

Her left brow hitched up. 'When it comes to supporting your grandmother, do not underestimate me, Dandelion.' She laid her hands flat on the table, her shoulders inching up to her ears. 'Clo and I have been through a lot. When she lost Beau…' Her eyes went watery. 'That was a difficult period. You were old enough to remember that time, but you don't know the entire tale.'

Unease writhed like a snake in my chest. 'Enlighten me.'

'Clo's told me you are aware of certain things about Bella, and, in turn, her.'

When I stayed quiet, hands folded in my lap, she said, 'Like Beau, I was always encouraging her to be honest with you girls. But your grandmother is loyal to a fault sometimes. She'd given Bella her word, and she wouldn't be shaken from that promise.'

'And that made my grandpa unhappy. Clo already explained that to Aster and me.'

'That's true, but there's more to the story.'

There'd been so many family revelations lately, so much sadness, I wasn't sure I wanted to know more, but the set of Ms Ruthie's mouth said it was important.

'Go on,' I said in a muted voice.

'Beau understood Clo in a way no one else could. A lot of that was probably because of all the history and rumors swirling around their families. She could be at ease with him. Not hide any part of herself.'

'That makes sense.'

Her eyes went sad as she went on. 'But her ancestors, they'd been through a lot over the decades. Clo's mother, Opal, she married into the Perkins bloodline. When she discovered what Clo could do, it terrified her. That terror turned into cruelty.'

'But Clo was her child.'

'People fear what they don't understand and, sadly, Opal was very unkind. I think your grandmother was relieved when she learned she couldn't get pregnant. There was a part of her that thought without any children between her and Beau, the magic would be ended for good.'

'Well, that didn't happen, obviously, but it does explain Clo's reticence and worry once Belladonna was born.'

Her gaze moved to the blaze of warm yellow sun bursting through the window. 'When your grandmother discovered what Bella could do, she worried her child would end up being bullied in the same way she was. That fear seeped into their relationship, and it soured things between them. Clo will be the first one to admit that's why Belladonna took off right after she turned eighteen.

The pain she carried after that, Beau felt it all too, because he loved her so much. He didn't want her carrying that burden with you girls, too.'

'She kept the promise, and truth about the magic, from us because she was trying to make up for what happened before with Bella?'

'Partly. She also wanted to protect you girls, the way she believed she was protecting Bella,' she said with a sad sigh.

'Is this your way of telling me that we should ease up on Clo a bit?'

'As her best friend, that is my duty, but there's something else I think you should know about this.' She tapped at the cracked brown leather cover of the journal. 'It'll bring a lot of clarity about who the Perkins women are, and why you all feel such a strong tether to the line.'

I sat back in the chair. 'I'm listening.'

She opened the worn pages of the sheriff's journal to an entry I'd already read several times: the day Jeremiah died.

'This is the story from one man's point of view, and there are many facts left out.' She pressed her fingers against the time-worn ink. 'Clo's told me about this incident several times. It's old family lore by now. It piqued my interest that this was the only narrative, though.' Her eyes filled with determination. 'I did some digging, looking at other first-hand accounts from people who lived in Harvest Moon at the time. I even discovered a few records written by the deputy who was assisting the sheriff.'

I moved to the edge of the chair. 'What did you find?'

'As usual when it comes to history, especially in regard to women, only half the tale was told.' She flipped the journal back to the first mysterious fire at the mercantile. 'Jeremiah started out as a miner. He got lucky. Found some gold in northern California. Came here to try his luck with silver. When he wasn't successful, he started the mercantile. He was young and strong. The women in Harvest Moon took notice of him right away, but he set his sights on Ambrosia from the start.' Her throat worked uncomfortably. 'He hid his dangerous and abusive ways from her until after they were engaged. That slimy toad knew once he had Ambrosia in his grasp, society would frown upon her backing out.'

'Bastard,' I murmured but motioned for her to go on.

'After reading all the notes and records I could find, I suspected that the first fire was set by Ambrosia after he struck her in the mercantile. It was a warning to him, a warning he did not heed. They went on to marry, and the incident with the barmaid came months later. I believe that was the final straw for Ambrosia, especially since she was pregnant.'

She went quiet, her fingers toying with the edge of the journal. There was a tic in her cheek like she was holding back an important fact. Waiting for me to put it all together.

'You don't think Ambrosia set fire to the house,' I said quickly.

'Her husband was a real douchebag, but no.'

'Okay, so what makes you think she was innocent?'

'Jeremiah swindled numerous people in town. Was a gambler and a cheat. I found an account of that final night from the deputy. Jeremiah was thrown out of the saloon after it was discovered he'd hidden a few aces up his sleeve while playing poker. Not more than a half hour later, the house went up in flames.'

'And Ambrosia? Where was she?'

'There was a history of colic in the family. Word was that she'd been spending nights with Sylvia so she could help care for the young baby, James.'

'So she had an alibi? Why was that not written in the sheriff's account of the night?'

Her thin pink lips pursed. 'There were lot of other people in town who wanted Jeremiah dead, and who knew the rumors about Ambrosia. That's why they set the fire. They wanted her to take the blame.'

'But the sheriff, he never outwardly cleared her. He knew the truth but never told a soul?'

'Back then, the folks who ran the saloon and other nefarious businesses were powerful and persuasive people. The sheriff obviously did not want to dig too deep.'

'So he just let everyone think she was a murderer? That she'd killed her husband with magic?' My angry voice batted about the rafters. Ruthie's gaze flew back to the library, reminding me that even up here I needed to be quiet.

'Sadly, it was easier to let people believe what they wanted, rather than tell the truth.'

'That sheriff was a damn coward.'

'True,' she said with a sigh. 'The only decent thing Jeremiah did was leave the mercantile to Ambrosia. She sold it for a pretty penny, most likely to the men who killed her husband. For years after, the women struggled to keep the apothecary going because of the rumors. The one thing those men did not bet on was the will and bravery of Sylvia and Ambrosia. They were stronger than the ore mined in these mountains. They stood together, found strength in each other, until they eventually turned the apothecary into a profitable business.'

She closed the journal, and my mind churned with a handful of emotions. Relief that my four-times great-grandmother was not a killer. Anger that the sheriff did not have the courage to tell the truth. A thin vein of guilt weaved its way through my bones. My blood had stood their ground. Not run away when things got tough, even when those around them thought they were inhuman.

'You're quiet.' Ms Ruthie broke through my thoughts.

'I'm confused, mad and a little ashamed.'

'Oh, honey,' she said with a sad hitch in her voice. 'I didn't tell you this story so you'd feel bad. All I needed you to know is that your family, the women in your line, they've endured many horrors, but they've always stood together to face whatever hideous lies were thrown at them. I believe you and Lia and Aster can do the same, no matter what that journalist writes.'

She set her chin. 'I don't normally do this, but I think you should hold on to the journal for a while.' She pushed it in my direction. 'Read it over again. Gather strength from knowing Ambrosia and Sylvia stood firm, even in the face of all the accusations against them. I can't tell you what to do, but there are many people in this town who love and admire you and your sisters. It may be uncomfortable for a while, but time passes and people have short memories.' Her hand slid over the top of mine and squeezed. 'I hope you'll trust in the fact that you belong here. That you and Lia and Aster make this town a better place.'

Her phone buzzed with a text. 'I have to go. There's someone at the desk who needs help.' She gave me a sad smile. 'No matter what happens, both your grandmother and I will always be here for you.'

She disappeared down the stairs, and I tucked the journal against my chest. I was glad I knew the truth about Sylvia and Ambrosia. How brave they'd been at the most difficult moment of their lives. The question was, did I have that same strength to fight for what my sisters and I had built here?

## *Chapter Thirty-Five*

### *Shaky Ground*

Every time my inbox dinged with a new email, I scanned the subject line to see if it was a digital copy of Bryce's article. He'd been gone four long weeks. I'd tried to keep busy. Loaded up the clinic's schedule with extra hours, but he still inhabited every corner of my mind.

He'd sent two brief messages since leaving Harvest Moon. One that let me know he'd arrived in California safely. The second was a few cryptic lines that said he was thinking about me and had to work on some things before we could talk more. Every time I read it, which was too many times over the past month, my mind ran wild with all the things that had gone unsaid between us. How that might influence what he wrote in the article.

A steaming flat white slid onto the counter in front of me.

'With the first hint of frost, it's actually beginning to feel like November,' Elena said, pushing an almond croissant beside the white porcelain mug.

'You have to stop with the pastries.'

'"Drown your sorrows in wine and good sweets" has always been my motto,' she said. 'Or, you know, a good roll in the sheets with a hot mysterious man.'

'Really? I've known you for years, and I've never heard you say that. In fact, when was the last time *you* went on a date? Was it that loser from Boulder who kept insisting you needed to invest in Bitcoin?'

'Hey!' She pointed a finger at me. 'We're talking about your disastrous love life, not mine.'

The day after Bryce left, I showed her his text. Elena insisted he'd be back. Swore that a guy who stared at me like I was a rare pink sunset was not someone who'd simply walk away. I loved her optimism, but I was sure of two things. Bryce was never coming back and the article was absolutely going to blow apart my world.

'Did you hear about Mo?' she asked casually.

I tried to not let my eyes roll back in my head. 'What has she done now?'

'She's leaving. Her son-in-law is in some kind of financial trouble, and that's why she's been so stressed about her business. She sold the tavern to help. She's going to live near her daughter and their family in Santa Fe.'

I pressed a hand to my forehead. That explained her desperate need to fill the tavern with tourists. A part of me wondered why she hadn't been honest when I'd confronted her, but if anyone understood keeping secrets, and complicated family situations, it was me.

'Sold it to who?'

'Ask her.'

Like the little phantom she was, Aster slid onto the stool beside me. This week her hair was a shade of silvery blue. It'd been three different colors over the last month. She hadn't wanted to talk any more about what Clo and Belladonna had revealed, but her constant trips to the salon spoke volumes.

Elena already had a latte and a chocolate croissant ready for her. 'Tell your sister who bought the tavern.'

'Dalton agreed to take it over.'

'Isn't he busy with the pizza parlor?' I said.

'His lease is up at the end of this month,' she said with a mouth full of pastry.

'It doesn't make sense.' I pushed a napkin toward her. 'The tavern doesn't have a pizza oven.'

She took a quick sip of her drink. A cute white foam mustache covered the cupid's bow on her upper lip. 'He's gutting the tavern. Says the place has bad vibes. Needs a total facelift. He's putting in a massive new oven, updated furnishings and décor.' She gave me a big smile. 'He even promised a regular flower order for all the dining tables.'

'That's good news.'

I held back my next thought. If Bryce's article claimed what I thought it would, Dalton's new restaurant would be packed, but that also meant Aster's business and my practice would likely be flooded with a load of new weirdos.

Even knowing this, anticipating it, I'd decided that no matter what the article said, we had to stay. This was our home. Our life was here. My conversation with Ruthie had reminded me that my family tree had been shaken many times by accusations of magic but never been knocked down.

Magic. Even thinking the word gave me heartburn. I hadn't let myself accept the thought that the connection I had with animals could be supernatural. I understood them. They understood me. In the end, that was all that mattered.

Elena and Aster continued to chat about the new plans for Dalton's place. I swirled my spoon around in my drink. Images of the day Bryce first appeared here filled my mind.

He'd hidden who he was, but he'd also reminded me that what I did was important. That it had an impact on the community. I just hoped everyone in Harvest Moon would remember that once the article was published.

'Thinking about Bryce?' Aster asked in between nibbles of her croissant.

'Yeah,' I confessed.

She took another bite, a smudge of chocolate taking up residence on the upper lip next to the deflated foam. God, she was a mess, but I loved her so much.

'I stand by what I said. He is your match. Your soulmate.'

'He's not coming back, Ast, even if you're right this time. His life, his career, is in LA.'

'Whatever this is.' She lowered her voice. 'Intuition. Synesthesia. Magic.' She wrinkled her nose. 'The link between the two of you is strong. Mark my words, he's not done with Harvest Moon yet.'

There was so much faith in her eyes that I didn't want to argue. Too many other things were on shaky ground, and I wanted her to believe in this one concrete part of her life.

'Heard from Lia?' she asked.

'She went on a three-day hike. Said she needed to clear her head. Would call when she got back.'

I'd seen Lia for exactly ten minutes since the moment she'd left our grandmother's house the night of the fire. She still wouldn't reconsider leaving Harvest Moon and was serious about staying away from Belladonna and Clo. I'd decided to give her the space she needed, but she couldn't run from the truth forever.

Elena came back with new drinks for us, leaned her elbows on the counter and said, 'What's Lia told you about that hot blond guy who's been hanging around town?'

'You mean Aiden?' Aster said, her eyes quickly flashing with amusement before she sobered. She'd seen something about him the day of Mara's rescue but was keeping quiet about it.

'Yeah. I saw him and Lia talking, well, more like arguing, outside the station last week.'

'Arguing? About what?' I said.

Elena shrugged. 'Not sure, but it looked pretty intense.'

Crap. Lia didn't need another worry in her life.

Aster continued to wolf down the rest of her croissant and eyed mine.

'Here.' I pushed the plate in her direction.

Elena went back to wiping down the counter. She was mid-scrub when she stopped and narrowed her gaze. 'Uh, your sister's back.'

The thud of heavy boot stomps made their way toward us. Lia appeared a second later, a chaos of dust, dirt and tangled brown curls. What was tucked underneath her arm made my blood go cold. 'Is that what I think it is?'

Her eyes softened, and I hated how her chin trembled as she nodded at me.

She laid the glossy magazine on the counter. The four of us stared at it like it was a venomous insect we were all too afraid to touch.

'Did you read it yet?' I asked breathlessly.

'No. I wanted to do it with you two.' She deflated onto a stool next to Aster. 'I'm sorry I ran away the night of the fire. We've always tackled the difficulties of our life together, but this time I left you hanging.' Her lower lip trembled and Aster squeezed her hand. 'I hope you can forgive me and accept that I will never walk away from you guys again. That as long as you're in Harvest Moon, I will be too.'

Ruthie's words about the strength of Ambrosia and Sylvia played in my head. No matter what happened next, I was sure the three of us would be okay, because we had our bond, our love, our sisterhood, to see us through.

Elena dabbed at her eyes with the corner of her apron. 'Every time you guys make up after a fight, it makes me wish I had a sister.'

'You do.' Aster beamed at her. 'Well, I mean you have three.'

Elena blinked back more tears and swiped the magazine off the counter. 'Do you want me to read it and tell you the verdict?'

My sisters turned to me for an answer. I trusted my best friend. She'd warn us if the fallout was going to be bad.

'Go ahead,' I whispered.

Elena flipped the pages and then stopped at the center spread. Her gaze flew back and forth across the page, and I swear not one of the McGuire girls took a single breath for the next few minutes.

When she was finally done, she laid the magazine down and closed the cover.

'Well?' Lia prompted.

'Is it bad?' Aster heaved out.

With a gleam in her eye, Elena said, 'Who wants more coffee?'

She strutted away, and Lia grabbed the magazine. Her shoulders trembled as she began to read the article to us. The opening paragraphs were cinematic, describing the hiking trails, the town and the community. There were portions dedicated to Veggie Fest, and the hard work done by the firefighters and SAR team, especially during Mara's rescue.

I held on to each beautiful line, hearing the cadence of Bryce's voice in my head. How he managed to paint such a colorful and fascinating picture of the place I loved. Lia pulled in a steady breath and read out loud the portion about the town's history, and its strange ties to magical lore.

She was nearly to the end when she stopped abruptly, her eyes blinking like she was holding back a whirlwind of emotions.

No. It was bad.

Why hadn't Elena warned us?

'Did he talk about the fire? What he saw in the woods?' I asked.

A shockingly wide smile lit up Lia's face. She pushed the magazine across the counter until it sat in front of me. 'Read the last lines. I'm pretty sure they're a message for you.'

# *Chapter Thirty-Six*

## *Not the Kind of Magic That Turns Frogs into Princes*

Flora loped a few paces ahead of me on the trail. Her ears bounced against her head, and there was a sweet prance to her feet. All morning she'd been a bundle of energy. Nudging her wet nose against my cheek to wake me. Circling my legs in the kitchen while I packed our bag for a hike. It was like she could read my mind. Feel the anticipation and repeated stutter of my heart, which I was wondering now if she could.

Ever since I'd read Bryce's final lines in the article, it'd played on a constant loop in my head. The hidden message so discreet, he knew I was the only one who'd understand.

> *I wandered into Harvest Moon, Colorado a jaded and cynical man. The whispers about magic seeming like nothing more than a badly told joke. A ploy to draw in tourists. But when I hiked up to one of the ridges at sunrise, witnessed the dark blue sky being slowly painted with the colors of a new day, I was reminded that there are many kinds of magic. There's a hint of sorcery in the way the town's residents plant seedlings, resulting in monstrous vegetables the size of a small lawnmower. A spellbinding draw in the way the*

*mountain breeze becomes a siren song, pulling you higher into the clasp of nature's embrace. But the most stunning, most mythical, element to Harvest Moon is its people and how they love and care for one another. The way they cheer on their greatest feats like growing a pumpkin the size of a golf cart. Or circling up the community when one of their own is hurt or lost.*

*Yes, it is true. There is magic in Harvest Moon. It's just not the kind of magic that turns frogs into princes or mice into footmen. It's more enchanting than that, but you'll only know that truth if you visit this place, hike to its most secret ridge on a Saturday morning, the second week of November and discover what kind of spell it will put on you.*

A heady rush of anticipation spread through my veins as I recalled those final lines of his article. Now, he was only a few steps away. He'd be flesh and blood before me. Close enough to touch. To press my mouth to his. Hear that low rumble in his chest as I kissed a sensuous path down his neck.

My breathing picked up at the thought. Heat spread across my chest. Maybe I didn't need this heavy winter coat after all.

Flora pulled on her leash, urging me on. Birds chattered in the trees. Bunnies scampered among the low-lying brush. A few warm stares from deer in the deeper parts of the forest focused on me.

Was my connection to animals magical? I wasn't sure, but it didn't change how I felt about what I did. In fact, it made me more passionate. Made me appreciate what it brought to my life.

With prodding from Bree and Jessa, I'd agreed to hire more help for the practice. Open for a few more hours on Saturdays. Hold more vaccination and neuter-and-spay clinics in other counties. I even considered doing speaking engagements covering the positive aspects of running a small-town practice, and how it can not only help the locals but the outlying farm communities as well.

Did I still get the weird customers who came in and asked inappropriate questions? Sought out spellbooks and signs of hidden pentagrams in small corners of the clinic? Yes. But it was easier to swallow now that I'd accepted who I was, and what I wanted. For the first time in my life I felt content, and most importantly, whole.

Flora let out a sharp bark and took off at a sprint. I raced after her up the steep slope and around a corner to where a narrow outcrop looked out onto the forest. I couldn't hide my smile as she careened toward Indy. Chased him in a circle. The old pals reunited once again.

Bryce leaned back against the rock. A black ski jacket covered his broad shoulders. He'd cut his hair and let his stubble grow out to a healthy five o'clock shadow.

The minute his gaze landed on me, he stalked forward and wrapped me in a tight embrace, pulling me off my feet and spinning me in a circle. 'I take it you got my message?' His hot breath against my skin lit up my entire body.

'Yes, but you took your sweet time getting to the most important point.'

His chest rumbled with a laugh. I leaned in closer and he set his cheek on top of my head. 'I had a lot to say, but a part of me knew that if I wrote about this place, you'd understand exactly what I was trying to say.'

'Your instincts were right.' I snuggled into him, remembering the way my body responded to his, opening up like a desert wildflower getting its first taste of rain.

'God, I've missed touching you.' His fingers moved to my hair, gliding through the loose strands. 'Every day I was gone, I dreamed of this. Being here with you at sunrise. Your warm body pressed to mine.' His eyes went wicked. 'Stripping you down and tasting you again like that day in the truck.' He tugged my hips toward him, lining our bodies up perfectly. 'Is it wild to say that when I'm here with you, I feel complete? Like whatever this bond is between us I want more of it? Today. Tomorrow. For years to come?'

As if he was too afraid to hear my answer, he tipped his head and pressed a soft kiss to my forehead. I melted into his touch. Max had given me comfort and security, and I'd assumed that would be enough. But with Bryce holding me like I was a dream, I understood he was my safe space. My home.

'Nothing about what you just said is wrong.' I rose up on my toes and kissed him. I loved the low moan that rumbled in his throat as he palmed my neck, drew me in, his hands skimming down my coat. His kisses weren't hungry but filled with a mind-spinning tenderness that curled my toes. As he tightened his embrace, and stroked his tongue over mine, I let myself relax for the first time in weeks. Let myself accept the gentleness he was offering.

The tighter he held me, the more the journal nestled in my pocket jammed against my hip bone. If we were going to make this work, I couldn't hide anything from him. Clo and Belladonna had been doing that to us our whole lives, and it was going to take time to sort that out. Which would be possible now considering Belladonna had promised to stay in Harvest Moon for a while. Lia still refused to talk about what happened the night of the wildfire, but she was Lia. She always did things in her own time, and Aster and I had learned to be patient over the years.

'I want to talk about the day of the fire,' I said with more bravery than I felt.

His eyes narrowed on the journal I'd pulled out of my pocket. 'What about it?'

'Before the branch came down, you need to tell me what you saw.'

He scrubbed a hand behind his neck. Pressed his lips together. His hesitation was killing me.

'I was on the roof and watched you go into the woods. Lia came up the ladder and offered to spray for a while. I climbed down and went after you. The heat from the fire, the smoke, it turned thicker as I walked. The only way I knew where you were was because I heard you calling for Belladonna.'

His eyes pinched at the corners. 'The further I walked into the forest, the louder the roar and hiss of the fire grew. I kept going, even when the trees started to groan under the weight of the heat and flames. That wall of thick gray smoke pressed in around me, but I couldn't stop. I had to get to you.' He dropped his chin. Shook his head. 'It sounds ridiculous but there was this odd ache inside of me that warned you were in trouble. Only a few seconds later, I heard the crack in the trees. Watched as that branch fell straight toward you, and I sprinted to push you out of the way.'

I pressed my ear against his chest, the gentle thump of his heart beating out a sweet symphony. He'd risked everything to save me. I'd been so wrong not to trust him.

'And Belladonna?' I whispered.

'Once I had you in my arms, she was right behind us. The smoke cleared, and a wet heat closed in from all sides. It was like a cloudburst was following us until we reached higher ground.'

For a flicker, I swore I saw that persimmon color in the outline of his body. That tether between us knotted tighter, becoming a warm link that could never be severed. All fear and worry drained out of my being. This was the right thing to do.

I laid the journal on his palm. 'If you want to learn more about Ambrosia and Sylvia, you can read all about them.'

He ran his hand over the cracked brown leather. With the gentlest touch, he slid the journal back into my pocket. 'Here's all I need to know, Dandelion McGuire. Your kindness, your gentleness, is sensed by everyone around you, both humans and animals.' He glanced to where our dogs were snuggled together on the side of the path. 'There *is* something magical about you, but it's how you care for others. How you so bravely want to protect your family.'

A slow smile lifted his lips. 'How lucky I feel that you allow me into your orbit. How grateful I'll feel if you let me stay.'

That connection between us locked into place like a deadbolt sliding home. For the first time, I let myself believe that Aster was right. That this irritating yet bold and brilliant man was meant to be mine.

I laid my hands against his deliciously stubbled cheeks and leaned in for another kiss. His arms locked around my waist as he sucked in my lower lip. I settled into the feel of him, relishing the scratch of his whiskers against my neck.

While he was gone, I'd forced myself to consider that I may never touch him again, feel the heat of him pressed against my body, and it had devastated me.

'There was never a single doubt in my mind that I'd come back to you. Tell me you feel the same way.' He rubbed his thumb over my cheek. 'That you ache with the same greediness. That a wild kind of ravenous need courses through you too.'

I laid a kiss against the hollow of his throat, loving the way his frantic pulse thrummed beneath my lips. 'I do. I've felt it since the moment you stumbled out of the woods,' I whispered, sliding my hands beneath his jacket, aching to feel the warmth of his skin against my hands. 'It only grew as I watched you jump in to help Julius. Made those ridiculous color-coded notes in the archives.'

He let out a low chuckle. 'I may be a writer, but I don't have the words to express how I feel about you. The way my heart becomes hollow when you're not in my line of sight. How my hands feel useless if they aren't stroking your soft skin.' His arms tightened around my waist.

'It was hard having you gone,' I said, swallowing the sob filling my throat. 'Even though you explained why you left…' I turned away so I'd have the strength to push out my next confession. 'I wasn't sure you'd ever want to return to this place. You sent those few texts and then went silent. I thought you might be done with Harvest Moon… and me.'

He turned me to face him. 'I'll never be done with you, Dani.' There was such devotion in his eyes that I had to remember to breathe. 'I should have been better about staying in touch,' he admitted. 'But my focus was on getting back to LA and settling things with the magazine.'

'What do you mean by "settling things"?'

'They weren't thrilled with the first draft of the article.'

'Why?'

'Because they wanted it to have a more supernatural feel. Thought it'd add more flavor and intrigue. They even pitched me a ridiculous headline. "Be Mesmerized by Real Magic in Harvest Moon".'

I raised my brows.

'Yep, it's bad. You can say it.'

'It's very... hokey. Doesn't seem like the slick headlines they usually choose.'

'Luckily, I talked them into giving me free rein to write what I wanted. Once they saw the piece as it is now, the picturesque photos I included, they let me have my way.' He lovingly cupped my chin. 'It was true. Every word. There *is* magic here. Just not the kind everyone imagines.'

This time his kiss was slow and playful. He nipped at the edges of my mouth. Used his tongue to split the seam between us. I sank into him, loving the circle of his embrace. The way he panted out my name as I ran my hands down his chest.

The dogs began to bark, chasing each other in a playful circle.

'Looks like we aren't the only ones glad to see each other,' he said.

'I'm pretty sure Flora has been moping since the day you left.'

'Is that right?' He gave me another hungry kiss. 'Was she the only one moping?'

'Hmmm. I don't remember.'

'Liar.' He tucked me against his chest. The sun made its slow ascent, and I loved the way it warmed his cheeks.

'I meant what I wrote about this place. How it gets inside your bones and doesn't let go. When I got back to

LA, it was claustrophobic. Too cramped. Too suffocating. Even Indy felt it. He'd go out onto the small patch of grass near my condo and turn in circles. Whine like I was pulling some kind of prank on him.' He stroked a hand down my arm. 'I broke my lease. Thought this might be my home now.'

I tipped my head back to look at him. 'Are you serious?'

'The dozens of boxes in the cabin would say yes.'

'But your work?'

'See, Dr McGuire, there's this thing called the internet.' He chuckled. 'Plus, I want to take you on that date to Breckenridge to make up for the way I didn't live up to our wager.'

'True, but I liked the outcome.'

'My mother is thrilled with this turn of events, too. She's already planning to visit regularly. I will have to travel some for assignments with my full-time gig at Metropolitan, but I'll make it work.'

'Way to bury the lede!'

His gaze went devilish. 'Why is it so hot when you speak journalist?'

I pressed another kiss to his mouth.

'It also makes sense to be here, considering what Aster said about me. Always did like the color orange.'

I froze in place, my jaw dropping open. 'That day at Drip! Drip! Hooray!, you heard her?'

'Part of my job is to be a good listener.'

I stepped out of his arms quickly, stumbling back. 'She can be wrong. It's not exact. It doesn't mean you have to believe it.'

'I will admit I thought it was ridiculous at first—'

'You don't have to stay. I mean you're not obligated to me in any way.'

He closed the space I'd made between us and pressed his fingers against my hip bones. 'Your sister didn't need to say a word, because I already knew. When I came out of the woods the day we met, it wasn't my stupid boots that made me trip. It was seeing you. In that split second, my body started vibrating on another frequency. It was kismet.'

'Kismet? Did you get that from WordHippo?' I teased.

He let out a full-bellied laugh. 'Fate. Destiny. Whatever the hell you want to call it. Up until that day, I'd been swimming my entire life underwater, but the minute you came into view, I broke the surface.' He tipped up my chin. 'From that moment, I understood the person I'd been searching for my whole life was standing in front of me. She just happened to be glaring at me like I was the biggest asshole on the planet.'

His large hand slid to my neck, and he pulled me closer. 'All I need is for you to believe in us too, Dani. I know you've been hurt, but if you trust me with your heart, I swear it'll be safe with me. Always.'

Even though I'd denied it, when I first encountered him on the trail, felt that tug between us, I understood he was meant to fill the space in my heart too. I leaned in and gave him a kiss, making it clear that I wanted him to be mine forever.

Birds sang in the trees. Small animals rustled in the brush around us. Bryce turned me until my back was tucked against his chest. The rhythm of our breaths synced as the sun broke the horizon, bathing the forest in a delicate, golden light. I settled into the cradle of his arms, grateful we could experience another gorgeous, dare I say magical, day in sleepy little Harvest Moon.

# *A Letter from Amy*

Dear Reader,

When I first started writing this book, I was inspired by the magic in everyday things that we often take for granted. The pink bloom of a sunrise in the morning. The wash of purple across a sky at sunset. How wildflowers can pop up in an empty field. The subtle hint of orange blossoms in the air once spring finally arrives. All of this to me feels… magical. This idea led me to think about people's special skills and how those skills and, perhaps, intuition could almost be interpreted as supernatural.

With the Sisters of Harvest Moon, I wanted to lean into that thread of mystery. Play with the idea that magic could possibly be real, and what that revelation would mean to three sisters who are struggling with who they are and what they mean to their small community. How it would test their bond and their own ideas of the future.

It's been so much fun to start this series with *Clearly Charmed*. I hope you will stay for the ride as we learn more about Dani, Lia, and Aster, and how their stories bring real truth and beauty to the town of Harvest Moon.

Please note that this book does touch upon some subjects like parental abandonment and death of a family member. As the small-town vet, Dani also treats ill and injured animals on page. If any of these topics cause you discomfort, please read with care.

Happy reading!

Amy

## *Amy's Playlist*

'Sweet Disposition' – The Temper Trap
'Nice To Each Other' – Olivia Dean
'Superposition' – Young the Giant
'The Prophecy' – Taylor Swift
'come closer' – sombr
'Swoon' – Beach Weather
'Between Two Lungs' – Florence + The Machine
'Rhiannon' – Fleetwood Mac
'Falling' – Harry Styles
'I Dare You' – The xx
'Dancing With Your Ghost' – Sasha Alex Sloan
'You Give Love a Bad Name' – Bon Jovi
'Eldest Daughter' – Taylor Swift
'doomsday' – Lizzy McAlpine
'Somewhere Only We Know' – Keane

# *Acknowledgements*

I write about family. A lot. That's probably because they are who I hold most dear. Who I owe for being able to do this job day in and day out. I'm very thankful for David, Olivia, and Ryan, who nod and smile when I throw out weird story ideas or talk about the ups and downs of publishing. I feel blessed every day that you are all part of my world. To Jon and, especially, Camilla, who reads all my books and is such an enthusiastic cheerleader for my work. I love you very much!

Thank you to my editor, Jennie, who saw something in my wild pitch about three sisters and their ties to a town's magical lore. Your notes and insight continue to make me a better writer. Also, many thanks to the entire Hera team (editorial, art, publicity) for the work they do on my behalf.

To my agent, Jessica, who took me on when I needed help the most and is a great advocate for my work. I'm really looking forward to all the things we will accomplish together.

A big shout-out to the veterinarians who helped me get the details right in this book. Thank you for answering my weird questions about caring for both large and small animals. You were beyond patient and kind, and I'm eternally in your debt for taking the time to help me.

My writing crew has gotten me through some rough days. A big thank you to the Friday Write gals and the entire AZ writing crew. Your feedback and support is always golden. A mega big thank you also goes to my long-time critique partner, and the incredible designer of the Perkins family tree, Kelly deVos. Our Sunday meetups mean a lot to me, and I appreciate your spot-on feedback. A shout-out also to Ginger Scott, who literally lets me talk her ear off any time we meet for lunch. I value our friendship so much.

I continued to be inspired by the poetic lyrics of Taylor Swift. Thank you, Taylor, for writing 'The Prophecy,' which was the spark that ignited the idea for this series!

Last, but not least, to the readers. My heart is light every time I get to meet any of you in person. Thank you for loving my work and being kind to me over the years.